Unbecoming

Unbecoming

and other tales of horror

Mike O'Driscoll

ELASTIC PRESS

ISBN number: 0-9548812-7-3

Printed by MRT Response, Bristol, UK

Cover design by Mike Bohatch
Cover layout by Dean Harkness
Typeset by Andrew Hook

Published by:
Elastic Press
85 Gertrude Road
Norwich
UK

elasticpress@elasticpress.com

www.elasticpress.com

Thanks is a small word but it's due in big helpings to the following people for their support, advice and encouragement over the years: Chris Reed, Nicholas Royle, Ellen Datlow, Andy Cox, and all the good folk at Albedo One. A special thanks to Con Connolly, one of my earliest critics and without whose wise words I might not have persisted. Blame him.

For his patience, faith and sense of adventure, respect and thanks are due by the tonnage to my editor, Andrew Hook.

For Yvonne and Jessica and the late, great Eric –
you three are here.

Table of contents

We Will Not Be Here Yesterday

There is so much of myself in the work, it's impossible to quantify. I've always maintained that if the art is to have an integrity, then it demands my heart and soul. You might say that, in a literal sense, the work is me.

Jerome Dupin, interview with Matthew Greenberg, *Modern Art Review*, October 1997, p.23.

Visitors are warned that much of the material contained in the exhibition is likely to cause offence, for which the management can take no responsibility.

Notice at entrance to installation *Work in Regress*, Museum of Modern Art, New York, Summer 1999.

Cave paintings ... are now generally and understandably seen as art, indeed in many of their examples as major art. Yet they are commonly sited in dark and inaccessible places, and we really do not know how often, if at all, they were generally seen within the period and culture in which they were made.

Raymond Williams, 'Identifications', in *Culture*, London, Fontana Press, 1981, pp.119-47.

The question everyone seems to have ignored yet which demands to be asked is, why do we take them seriously? The furore surrounding their latest 'exhibition' at Galleria D'Annunzio perfectly illustrates my point. Consider *final frontier*, two blurred photographs, one depicting a young girl and boy hand in hand on a shore, the other showing the same scene but without the kids; how is one supposed to react to it other than with indifference? Or what to make of *What we gave in return*, a work consisting of six vials mounted on a plinth, each purporting to contain a different variety of human waste? If the purpose is to alert us to the moral degeneracy of the perpetrators of such crap, then they have succeeded. But if Dupin and Pandolf have some other intention in mind, if they are – in their own words – 'attempting to forge a new aesthetic', then they have failed utterly. Shit remains shit, no matter how much you dress it up.

Ashley Axnard, 'The Emperor Dresses Down', *Salon.com*, January 27, 1998.

My first impression was one of scepticism. A circular panel about four feet in diameter in an otherwise featureless wall. There's a button to the left of the panel, which when pressed, causes it to dilate like something out of a science fiction movie. The space inside is poorly lit and not particularly inviting, but curiosity overrides my anxiety and I climb inside. Crouching over, I grope along a dark passage for fifteen or twenty yards. Reaching an opening, I jump down into the first module. Here are four separate pieces, the connection between them not immediately apparent. On a white pedestal at the far side of the room stands a gramophone player with a 78rpm recording of Hank Williams' 'Long Gone Lonesome Blues'; to the right, between the third and fourth exits, laying on the floor is a handwritten version, in English, of Walter Benjamin's essay 'The Work of Art in the Age of Mechanical Reproduction'; directly opposite these unbound pages, there is some type of orchid – forgive my ignorance of botany – while in the centre of the room, on a small glass table, are what appear to be eight drops of blood. Approximately once every fifteen seconds, and for the duration of no more than two seconds, a message is projected onto the wall from which I've just emerged. It says 'I don't get it,' which, at the very least, brings a smile to my face.

Karl Fraction, 'No Way Out' in *Zone-Ex* iv, Fall, 1999, p.63.

Work in Regress occupies eight separate modules, interconnected by a series of tunnels. One can only view the work as it is intended to be seen by following the prescribed route. While curious patrons are free to deviate from this route, the artists are not liable for subsequent disorientation or loss of any description. The route is clearly marked and the modules numbered in sequence above each entrance. Please refrain from any discussion of the work until after you have emerged from its space. Force no doors. Ignore all unspecified instructions unless specified otherwise.

Artists' 'Instructions to the Scopophobe', from *Work in Regress, Exhibition Catalogue*, Kirk Varnedoe and Laura Mulvey, MOMA Publications, 1999, p.3.

I guess what I find most disconcerting about *Vacant Lot* is the lack of real substance. Somehow it dupes you into believing there's more to it than there really is. You can spend hours trying to unravel the mystery it suggests but ultimately it's a waste of time. There is no mystery, just sleight of hand. Call it magic if you want to, but it's not art.

Nicholas Sporlender, writing on *Time Stood Still*, in *Silver Web*, Winter, 1995.

MK: Much has been said about your working methods, with many critics questioning the – shall we call it 'balance of power'? – within the partnership. Without wishing to further muddy the waters, can you tell me a little about the collaborative process in practice?
JD: 'Balance of power' suggests a relationship based on detente, which, I'm afraid, is inaccurate. Max and I are always at loggerheads. I think for any creative partnership to be successful, there must be a certain amount of friction between the parties involved. If we were to agree on everything then I'm sure that would manifest itself in the work.
MK: In what form?
JD: A certain lifelessness, which, unfortunately, appears to me to be the defining characteristic of most modern art. What does Hirst, for instance, give us but dead things?
MK: So you're saying the partnership is based on equality and mutual respect?
JD: Of course. Take *Vacant Lot* – had it not been for Max's skill in prefabrication, then the work would not have the form it has today.
MK: It wouldn't exist?
JD: No. It would exist – of course it would exist – I created it after all.

Mike O'Driscoll

The point is that its material form would be different.

MK: Which would surely make it a different piece.

JD: I don't understand why this is so hard to grasp. In the creation of any work of art, be it *Vacant Lot* or *Guernica* or *La Gioconda*, the moment of creation precedes the act of construction. The creative act is the progenitor of the material realisation of the work. You see?

MK: Which implies a hierarchical relationship within the collaboration.

JD: Yes, of course.

MK: A fluid relationship?

JD: The truth is both Max and I understand our roles, the necessary dynamic, in the entity that is Dupin and Pandolf. Whatever income we derive from our work is divided equally, and that's as it should be. Of course, Max has been known to have the odd grumble about our financial arrangements but bear in mind his finely developed sense of irony.

MK: Irony?

JD: Max likes to have his sport with impressionable art critics.

Jerome Dupin interviewed by Melanie Krauss for *Art & Design*, no.13, April 1993, pp.57-58.

Visitors with a history of coronary illness are advised that they enter module 3 at their own risk.

Warning, in *Work in Regress, Exhibition Catalogue*, p.40.

"Who can say if it's real? I mean, that's not really the point. What matters is the effect it has on you. Speaking for myself, when my gaze moved from the print to the cast, from the video clip to the object itself, the cumulative effect, well, it just fucking blew me away."

Maurizio Cattelan, on module 2 of *Work in Regress* in *The Secret Life of Dupin and Pandolf*, documentary for Channel 4 Television, UK, Tony Kaye, producer, broadcast February 29, 2002.

The image of a lone foot suggests not motion, but caution, the taking of a single step. The gaze moves slowly around the room pausing in turn at each of the other three items that make up the installation. All are feet. More significantly, all four are representations of the same foot. Its shape and size suggest a male, though the evidence of a pedicure questions this assumption. Certainly, it is not the foot of a Pollock

4

raging across a horizontal canvas to disappear forever into the oblivion of *White Light*, nor the narcissistic despair of Picasso stepping over the threshold of his own *Le Charnier*. This foot is the antithesis of abandon. Occupying this space, it is at repose. Consider the monochrome image, a foot resting on some solid but indefinable surface, severed from its limb three or four inches above the ankle by the frame's edge. On the floor in the centre of the room, a life-size cast of the same foot, next to it a sock and a Nike sports shoe. Curiously, they belong to a right foot while this, like the others, represents a left. On the opposite wall, a film shows the lone foot in motion. What the foot is connected to we cannot see. Taken out of context, its motion seems inexplicable. Do these contortions represent the act of walking? Jumping? Maybe kicking. In the absence of any evidence to the contrary, one concludes that the foot moves of its own volition. Thus the sense of relief, of calm, evoked by the last item in module 2. Suspended eerily in formaldehyde, softly glowing in the muted light, the foot is somehow detached from the memory of material existence.

Kirk Varnedoe, *Work in Regress, Exhibition Catalogue*, p.66.

"Damien Hirst always admired their work. Look at the whole bisected animal thing – what was it other than an elaboration on what they'd been doing for years. He admitted as much to me and you can see it in the way his *Contemplation of the navel from the male perspective* seems to echo the mysterious internalisation of their *We Will Not Be Here Yesterday*. If you see the two works displayed alongside each other, as they were in the *Ripe* exhibition in Paris, you'll notice how they seem to engage in a secret dialogue. Having said that, Dupin was never slow to dismiss Hirst as little more than a charlatan."

Pierre Ozenfant, in conversation with Melvyn Bragg for unbroadcast documentary on Dupin and Pandolf, March 2000.

[This art] offers only a way down, to where the dislocation of forms drags thought down with it.

Georges Bataille, 'Le "Jeu lugubre"', in *Documents*, no.7, 1929, p.86.

"Jesus ... fucking ... wept."

Mike O'Driscoll

Unidentified voice, played back on a continuous loop, forming part
of the *Less is less* installation in module 6, *Work in Regress*.

I knew Max Pandolf back in the Village. He'd been in the city a couple
of weeks after graduating from some Buttfucksville college somewhere
out west. A quiet kid, never had much to say for himself. Good with his
hands though.

Jayne County, interviewed in *The Secret Life of Dupin and Pandolf.*

*Why do you think we employ a firm of accountants, if not to keep the IRS
off our backs? I've spoken to James and he assures me there is no
problem. I really do wish you'd talk to me, Max, before jumping to
conclusions and making all sorts of wild accusations. Nobody has been
inquiring about your finances, the IRS have made no demands. I suggest
you stop trying to second guess James. Instead, I think you should call
him and apologise, let him know that you have complete faith in his
ability to handle our affairs.*

*As for the other business, I'm almost certain that I didn't say what
Hitchens wrote but he'll never admit to having distorted anything.
Writers like Hitchens assume they have some sort of 'no bullshit'
reputation to protect. I would contact Vanity Fair and ask Graydon to
print an apology but I think that would only make the situation worse.
Better to ignore the whole thing and let the work speak for itself, as we
have always done.*

Excerpt from handwritten letter from Jerome Dupin to Max Pandolf,
date unknown.

If you're asking whether or not subsequent events influenced the impact
it had beyond the art world and its institutions, then the answer is yes.
Name me one other piece of visual art in the last fifty years that had a
comparable effect. Warhol never came close and people like Koons or
Emin with her shitty bed never had any fucking thing real to say.
Picasso maybe, but he was long dead. What people forget is that an
awareness of the work had permeated the wider community long before
the discovery of Pandolf's note in module 8. Fraction, in *Zone-Ex*, was
merely articulating what many of us felt when we experienced it for the
first time. For years artists had been saying their work was about getting

beyond something, whether that was consciousness, materiality, politics, religion or sex. What they missed, what *Work in Regress* showed is that once you've stripped away all the shit, what you're left with is nothing. There is no beyond beyond.

'X' spokesperson for the Con-Art Collective, San Francisco, quoted in 'O Gainsayer, where art thou now?', Charles Shaar Murray, in *Face*, February 2002.

"Oh please, not the eyes."
"It is necessary."
"Something else, I'm begging you."
"What else?"
"I – "

Unidentified voices, played back at one minute intervals, as part of the *Eye No* installation in module 7, *Work in Regress*.

The interior space is modelled on the late 16th century anatomy theatre in Padua, Italy, which – if you'll excuse the pun – was at the cutting edge of surgery back then. Projected onto the domed ceiling are the images of figures in contemporary costume, jostling with each other to get a view of what's happening down here. It comes as a shock to realise that they have usurped our scopophilic role and positioned us as the viewed object. This disorienting effect is amplified when your eyes take in the four paintings that hang from the walls. From left of the chamber's entrance and moving clockwise, are *The Anatomy Lesson of Dr Sebastiaen Egbertsz* by Aert Pietersz, Rembrandt's *The Anatomy Lesson of Dr Deijman*, Cornelis Troost's *The Anatomy Lesson of Dr Röell* and finally, François Sallé's *The Anatomy Lesson at the École des Beaux-Arts*. Spread over an operating table in the centre of the chamber, their pages splayed and held open by a sternal retractor, are a variety of books and journals whose subject – after careful scrutiny – appears to be the works of Dupin and Pandolf. Transparent tubes run from the books to a stainless steel cylinder and back again. Laying face up between the jaws of the spreader are the useless paddles of a defibrillator. The implication is clear and it's as uncomfortable for us as it must be for the artists. It forces us to question our own judgement, to re-examine our preconceived ideas about art. I stared at my fellow

Mike O'Driscoll

viewers and recognised the unease etched in their faces. We filed sheepishly into the next tunnel, wondering if it was possible that the wool had been pulled over our eyes?

    Karl Fraction, *Zone-Ex*, Fall, 1999, p.70.

Dupin told me that *What we gave in return* operates on two levels, the first of which subverts the audience's expectations about meaning, while the second is directed to the work's originators. I suspect he was being disingenuous because clearly the implication is that Pandolf's contribution to the piece is peripheral, perhaps limited to the contents of the vials themselves. Which begs the question, does he know Dupin is taking the piss? And if Pandolf missed the slight, small wonder that Ashley Axnard – as usual – misread the intentions of the piece.

    Christopher Hitchens, in *Vanity Fair*, February 1998.

"Sir, can I ask you about module three?"
"No _____ way."
"Why not?"
"You been in there?"
"I haven't had the opportunity yet."
"Yeah well, take my advice and stay the ___ out."
Reporter turns to young woman:
"What about you, miss – can you tell us what you saw in there?"
"No."
"You don't want to say?"
"I can't."
"Perhaps if you could just – "
Woman covers camera lens with left hand; voice heard offscreen:
"Just ___ off and leave us alone."

    Edited footage from news report filmed outside Museum of Modern Art, broadcast on CNN, July 4, 1999.

The content of dreams, however, does not consist entirely of situations, but also includes disconnected fragments of visual images, speeches and even bits of unmodified thoughts
[...]
Not even the speeches that occur in the dream-content are original

compositions; they turn out to be a hotchpotch of speeches made, heard or read, which have been revived in the dream-thoughts and whose wording is exactly reproduced, while their origin is entirely disregarded and their meaning is violently changed.

Sigmund Freud, from 'On Dreams', in *The Standard Edition of the Complete Psychological Works of Sigmund Freud*, J. Strachey (ed.), London, 1953-74.

Germaine Greer: I've never heard such bullshit. I mean, we've been here so many times before I'm amazed we're even talking about this. What it does tell us is that the art establishment haven't yet cottoned on to the reality that Dupin and Pandolf were one trick ponies.
Mark Lawson: But surely the fact that we're discussing it says something about the way it's imposed itself on our consciousness?
GG: Oh come off it – we're talking about it because the BBC have asked us to.
ML: A rather cynical view there from Germaine Greer. Tom Paulin, surely there's more to it than that. Now that *Work in Regress* has finally come to London, what do you think it says to us?
Tom Paulin: Nothing – it says absolutely nothing.

The Late Review, presented by Mark Lawson, with guests Germaine Greer and Tom Paulin, broadcast on BBC Television, January 18, 2002.

If less really is less, as the aesthetics of sound and silence, light and shadow in module 6 suggests, then how does one approach the mystery of module 7, *Eye No*? The artists offer no clues to interpretation. One is set adrift, abandoned on an ocean of doubt.

Laura Mulvey, *Work in Regress, Exhibition Catalogue*, p.125.

"I'm saying hunger is desire and if art is anything, then it's a manifestation of desire, right? So yeah, it's obvious I'd be interested in what they did. I knew these guys in the early days. They useta hang out at my place and when I started working at Vincente's they ate there all the time. They knew food – very discriminating palates. Later on, when I opened my first restaurant in SoHo, I let 'em stage their first exhibition there. It was fucking wild, lemme tell you. I think somebody hadda call the cops 'cos things were getting way out of hand. But that was Dupin for you, he had this unique take on life, useta say to me, 'Vicki, life is for exploiting.' We had some times.

"So I went to the show and like anyone who understood what they were about, I expected to be surprised. Tony Bourdain had told me they'd called the fifth module *Insatiate*, and he'd warned me not to eat before I went in there. If it's Bourdain telling you that, you heed what he says. So I get through the first four and it's pretty fucking out there, as you'd expect. I mean, I'd seen a lot of their work, but this *Work in Regress*, well, in module 3, that's the first time I ever saw a guy puke at an art show. And he wasn't the only one. The stench was awful. After that, for me number four was a breeze. But by the time I got to *Insatiate* – and that was a horrible journey – I just wanted to sit quietly for a coupla moments and collect my thoughts. No fucking hope of that.

"It hits you as soon as you enter the room – the noise. I've worked in restaurants all my life and I've learned that no two people eat the same way. You watch and you pick up on the different nuances, the way one woman will pause with her fork about an inch or two from her mouth, then bring her head forward like a bird. Another broad will bring it all the way to her lips and then hold it there, carrying on yakking till finally she returns it to the plate. You see guys who shovel it down and fellas who'll pick and prod. You can always tell a guy who's been in the joint by the way he eats – he'll have an arm curled around his plate like he's afraid some fuck is gonna try stealing a mouthful of that slop. So, I know about watching people eat, but here's the thing – how many of us ever actually listen to the sound of eating? That's what grabs you when you enter module 5. The noise just slams into you like a wall of sound. Grinding, crunching, slurping and gulping noises, people belching, farting, slobbering, sucking and I don't know what else. And with this cacophony of consumption going on, you're not aware at first of the screams. It builds up slowly, until you ask yourself, what is that? Initially, I thought it was a pig, like, squealing, but as it grew, I knew it was human. Not the kind of sissy pants shit you hear in horror movies. This was real, coming from somewhere deep down, full-throated and I'll tell you, whatever was causing it, I didn't want to know about.

"And the sculpture? Well, we've all heard the jokes but at the time there was a lot of people didn't know what they were looking at. I did. Food is my business and digestion is part of that, so I had some inside knowledge. It's modelled in some kind of plastic, which was a material

Pandolf liked to use, and the fucking thing glowed. Green, like those straps kids wear round their necks at Halloween. It was suspended from the ceiling, this fat, wormy tube rising vertically before turning at right angles and across for maybe eight inches, then that kink where it would be tucked up behind the stomach. From there it drops vertically, then slants inwards and down to those last couple kinks. You had to imagine what would be around it, the organs, the intestines, skin and bone, but once you figured out what it was, all you could think of was what was inside it. And what do you find in a colon except shit? Which I guess was the point, right?"

Victor D'Annunzio, speaking to Julian Schnabel, in *The Legacy of Dupin and Pandolf*, Discovery Arts Channel, March 2002.

In contemporary modern painting, the object must become the *leading character* and dethrone the subject. Then, in turn, if the person, the face, and the human body become objects, the modern artist will be offered considerable freedom.

Fernand Léger, 'The Human Body Considered as an Object,' in *Functions of Painting*, New York, 1973, p.132.

He's a tall, imposing man with dark, lustrous hair and intense, blue eyes. There's something almost intimidating about him which, perhaps unconsciously, makes you a little wary. But after spending the best part of ten hours in the company of Jerome Dupin, a very different picture begins to emerge, that of a man whose charm and self-deprecation are at odds with the guarded, even curt figure he presents in public. Take the question of his relationship with Pandolf, a subject I was initially – given the rumours of a growing rift – hesitant to broach. After spending the morning together, we lunched at *Odelay's* on Broadway and I guess he could tell that I had something on my mind.

"You haven't mentioned Max at all, my dear," he said, apropos nothing.

My face must have been a picture. I gulped my Shiraz and tried to pretend that it was an oversight.

"Don't be afraid to ask the right questions."

If Dupin was telling me to go ahead and ask, who was I to ignore him? So I gave it to him straight. "Is there a rift between you and Max Pandolf?"

"No." He smiled, his voice was calm. "Sure we have disagreements, but you have to expect them in any kind of professional partnership."

"What about the reports suggesting that Pandolf is refusing to work with you in future?"

"I've seen those, yes. Curious how they're never sourced. The truth is Max is tired, he needs a vacation. You know, neither of us has taken a break in ten years. He'll come back fitter and stronger, ready for the fray."

"So you will work together again?"

"Put money on it. I've already started planning the next work. On his return, Max will take my concept and give it form."

"Can you tell me about it."

"As a rule, I don't speak about works in progress, but in your case I'll make an exception. Here's a clue – it will be a new direction."

Which, given that each of their previous works seemed to chart new territory, doesn't exactly constitute a clue. "What's Pandolf's view of your concept?"

Dupin gazed at the wine glass he twirled in his hand. "He doesn't know yet what it is. That's how things work with us. Max is, if you like, an anti-conceptualist, and it's the tension between us, between the abstract and the concrete, that injects life into the work."

Leah Venora, 'Talking Truth – A conversation with Dupin,' in *Rolling Stone*, March 1999.

A question: why Dupin and Pandolf? Why never Pandolf and Dupin? This alphabetical hierarchy of paired relationships is simply another male construct we should reject. Look at it from a phonetical point of view. There's a phonemic concordance which is ruptured if the relevant syllables are in too close a proximity. That double 'pan' in Dupin and Pandolf, the ear tells us it isn't right. There's an insidious merging, a slide towards 'DooPanDolf' which negates the separate identities, subsuming them into one entity, the being Doopandolf. And of course, given their personalities, what we know of them at least, the mask that Doopandolf inevitably assumes, is Dupin's, the male over-achiever. I don't want to get into that argument right now, but phonetically, there's no doubt it should be Pandolf and Dupin, where the first syllable is echoed in the last. What you have then is a totality that makes both linguistic and emotional sense. The ear tells us it's right and the final 'pan' sound gives us closure.

Camille Paglia, 'Da Doo Pan Pan,' *Salon.com*, April 4, 1999.

In the muted light, bizarre shadows twist and turn on the wall. A grating sound is heard but it soon settles into a labored rhythm. The camera pans slowly to the right and a previously unseen shadow looms into view. It suggests a figure standing over a surface on which something animate is laying. What might be an arm moves back and forth with a rhythmic noise. There is a gasp and the arm stops moving. A voice whispers 'Ssshhh'. The movement of the arm recommences and a minute later there is a thud as something hits the floor. There is a whimpering noise, continuing for eight seconds. The figure moves along the table and again there's a sharp intake of breath, followed by that grating noise and then the familiar, rhythmic sawing sound. The camera pans down towards the floor. It glides beneath a table, moving slowly, an image forming on the edge of the screen. Some dark liquid pooling, the sound of fresh drops falling from above. The image shifts, moves through a square of light, speeding up as it circles the room. There, seen once and only very briefly, on the floor beneath the table, a pale object, shaped like a foot.

Anonymous description of third film sequence forming part of the *Eye No* installation in module 7, *Work in Regress*.

It's impossible to talk about my reaction to the eighth module – I mean, after what I'd been put through to get there, after all those whisperings, those cries of suffering and torment in the sixth module and those appalling images in the seventh, Jesus Christ, who knows what I was expecting. You cannot arrive at that place without having formulated some idea about what awaits you, but expectations can sometimes be horribly ruptured. What should be borne in mind is the utter conviction you feel as you crawl into that cell. You're one hundred per cent sure you know what's there and seeing the cabinet in front of you only strengthens that certainty. This will be something totally unique, absolutely something you've never seen before but which you will, nonetheless, recognise the instant you set eyes on it. As I approach the cabinet I feel a sense of dread and fascination akin to that which must

Mike O'Driscoll

have been felt by the first visitors to the home of Dr Frederick Ruysch more than 300 years ago. The front face of this 'cabinet of curiosities' is shaped in the style of a proscenium arch, with two velvet curtains hanging over the interior space. My hands shake as I grip the curtains and in an effort to subvert the air of disquiet I force a laugh. It feels like I'm scraping sandpaper inside my throat. I steady myself, take a deep breath and pull the door open. What I see in there explodes any and every expectation I have brought along. For the first time ever in my life, staring into that cold emptiness, I see how alone each of us truly is.
    Karl Fraction, *Zone-Ex*, Fall, 1999, p.92.

Max Pandolf, accomplice to the artist Jerome Dupin, died last night of natural causes at his home on Nantucket. A spokesperson confirmed that Pandolf, who had been suffering from pancreatic cancer, had been deeply shocked at Dupin's disappearance a year ago. To date, no trace of Dupin has been found.
    Reuters News agency, May 16, 2000.

"It always bothered me that they only gave titles to three out of the eight installations. I mean Dupin was great with names – he had an instinct for the precise word or phrase to go with a particular image. You see it not just in *Work in Regress* but in all their previous works as well. The fact that he didn't name the first four modules, nor the eighth is significant. It tells us something. I don't know what it tells us, but knowing Dupin, it wasn't, as some have suggested, an oversight. I often find myself trying to second guess him, putting names to those pieces, perhaps The Anatomy Theatre and Footloose. They sound right at first, until you start to think about them and then, somehow, they just don't fit."
    Pierre Ozenfant, in conversation with Melvyn Bragg, March 2000.

Anybody who doubts the importance of *Work in Regress* should really examine their own motives. In less than two years it has achieved the kind of iconic status we reserve for such epochal works as Giotto's *The Mourning of Christ*, Michelangelo's *David*, Manet's *Olympia*, or Picasso's *Les Demoiselles d'Avignon*. Art can never again be simply an act of seeing. In truth it never was. It involves an interplay of all our

14

perceptional capabilities – it's not enough just to look or listen, we have to experience the totality of a work. What Dupin has shown us with his final masterpiece is that art is inextricably bound up with living and dying, that it is, in reality, life and death.

And let me emphasize that I do mean what Dupin – rather than Dupin and Pandolf – has shown us. The latter was clearly an important part of the organic chemistry but let's be brutally honest here, as Dupin himself never had the heart to be. Anyone who talked to them, who watched them at work or who took the time to study the works closely, will know that for all his undoubted craftsmanship, Max Pandolf had neither the wit nor imagination to originate a work such as *Work in Regress*.

Matthew Greenberg, *Modern Art Review*, June 2001, p.40.

– orrow it ends but I will not be erased. I conceived the whole thing, it is through my effort alone that the work has been completed. In doing so I have granted the liar's wish. I have unmade Jerome, transformed him from one state to another, into something that will last. It doesn't matter that he's there in his entirety, that he is, essentially, the work. It doesn't matter that I am to die, that I will be dead by the time you read this, for when word gets out, the world will recognise that in this achievement, as in all else, I was hi –

Recently discovered text in module 8 of *Work in Regress* for the exhibition's UK opening at Tate Modern, London, January 15, 2002. The text forms part of a faded collage on the rear wall of the cabinet's interior, and is alleged to be a fragment of Max Pandolf's suicide note.

Shadows

I've never had any illusions about what I do. I don't doubt that if you talk to some people in my line they'll try to convince you that they have, in some way too esoteric to explain, contributed to the greater good of humanity. These are the kind of people for whom money is a dirty word. They have plenty of it, for sure, but hey, that's not why they're in the business. In fact they try to kid themselves that what they're involved in has little to do with commerce, that what they *fabricate* – and I use that word because it's the right one – has some deeper level of meaning, like it's just one step removed from art. Yeah well, like I say, I don't see myself as any kind of artist – what I am is an ad man. Let me tell you, in this business you get an itch you scratch it, you tell yourself it's an allergy or something and then you refocus on finding the right form of words or images to shift the requisite number units to keep the client happy and the commissions rolling in. But the minute you think it's something more than an allergy, and you keep scratching away until, right there under your skin, you find a fucking aesthetic impulse, well, that's the day you need to consider some other line of work.

I get an itch, I scratch hard, then I remember who and what I am. You've seen my work – truth is, there's no way you could avoid it, not unless you're blind and deaf or maybe dead more than ten years. You remember *Where the Gas is always Greener*? I came up with that for Texaco. Or what about *The Mouse that Roared* – that was for an online stocks and shares business – or *Fill the Gap*, which helped an American teen fashion chain break into the UK. These words and images, they don't really mean anything – their real purpose is to serve as signifiers of need. And if you've seen or heard them, then it won't be that hard for you to imagine yourself in my shoes:

Nice house.

Nice wife.

Nice kids.

Nice job.

Two nice cars.

You know, the things that, when we're not lying to ourselves, we all aspire to. It is possible to do what I do and not feel bad about yourself. I think of myself as a decent man – I love my wife and kids, I get on well with most of my colleagues and tolerate those few I don't, I pay taxes and believe in free health care and state education, I give money to charities whose work I admire, I don't shit on those less fortunate than myself, I go to the cinema regularly and read books by contemporary writers who interest me, I like to loaf around at weekends and on occasion I drink a little too much, and sometimes at night, I lay awake in bed and think about those things I want but haven't got. Then, as I try and work out a strategy of attainment, my chest begins to tighten and I find it hard to breathe and I know, though I can't accept it, that some day I'm going to die and none of these things will save me.

We all have such thoughts but we rarely acknowledge them. Nobody wants to rock the boat. You allow me to play on your aspirations and you know the tools of my trade are lies. I'm as alert as you are to the contradiction between my self-perception as a good man and my job as a fabricator of dreams, but there's no irony in it. Irony implies that someone's getting shafted but the only lies I tell are the ones you want to hear.

So, there we were in the back of a cab on our way from Crouch End to *Fintan's* in Charlotte Street and I could have used a cigarette but I'd been off them nearly a week and didn't want to let Eleanor down. So I listened to her talking about Richard and Hayley, our kids, and what kind of day they'd all had and I tried to pay her the attention she deserved but for some reason my mind was distracted, flitting from one thing to another, mostly work related but a few other matters as well, none of which seemed at that precise moment, to have any bearing on my life.

Only when the cab pulled up outside the club and Eleanor play-punched me in the arm, did I remember where we were. Curtis Brown and Max Delany, the two senior partners in the agency, had organised a shindig, partly to celebrate landing the Glaxo contract, but also to let both the media and our competitors know that Delany Brown had arrived as a major player.

I paid the driver and followed Eleanor into the club. Lee Kurimoto met us just inside the lobby. "Hey, Closer," he said, "you know what time it is? Hi, Eleanor, you look gorgeous, but him, all that effort and for what?"

Eleanor did look beautiful, with her long, raven hair and brown eyes that seemed to radiate laughter and empathy in equal measure. She smiled and cracked a joke about how long it took me to get ready for anything. Lee kissed her on the cheek and then herded us towards a table at one side of the small stage, saying he wanted us to meet someone. Someone turned out to be his new girlfriend, Fiona, I think her name was, a tall, good-looking woman with an Irish accent, or maybe Welsh. This one was serious, he told me – after all he'd been seeing her for nearly a month.

After we'd circulated a while, we returned to the table, ate linguini in a pesto sauce, drank a couple of Mexican beers and some Italian wine. Lee got up on stage and made what appeared to be an impromptu speech – but which I knew he'd been working on for days – about Curtis and Max. It was witty and heartfelt and it caught the celebratory mood. Then Max and Curtis joined him to soak up the plaudits, making a show of embarrassment but underneath, you could tell they loved every minute of it.

I was mildly drunk when Eleanor asked me to call home to check in with the nanny. I went out to the men's room to escape the pounding dance music and made the call on my mobile. I was about to ask Joanna if the kids were okay when I realised that the answering machine had clicked in. I felt mildly irritated as I listened to my own voice telling me how neither Eleanor nor I could come to the phone right now, then I smiled at the thought that perhaps Joanna was upstairs checking on Richard and Hayley, or maybe she was using the toilet or –

My speculations were cut short as what I heard myself saying finally registered. I wasn't feeling well, the voice coming down the line was telling me. I was feeling bloody terrible and didn't think I'd be able to make the flight to Amsterdam on Monday. Hearing myself say these things, knowing that I'd left no such message on the machine, stunned me. I caught my reflection in the mirror on the wall and saw the disbelief clouding my eyes. What made it worse were the intolerable imaginings that suddenly filled my mind.

I hurried back to our table. Eleanor was talking to the girl who might have been Fiona and it was Lee who caught her attention, nodding towards me as I stood there, unable to speak for a moment. She glanced up at me, frowning, I guess at the panic that must have been fixed on my face. I told her we had to go. "What do you mean, Paul?" she said. "It's not even twelve. Joanna's not expecting us till after two."

I grabbed her arm and said, "Something's wrong at home. Joanna's not there."

"What?" She looked aghast. "You called her?"

Lee stood up, concerned. "Is everything okay?"

"No," I said, thinking about Monday and the meeting we had scheduled in Amsterdam. "I got the fucking answering machine."

"Oh Jesus," Eleanor said, as she followed me towards the exit. We stood on the pavement outside, me trying to flag down a cab and Eleanor tapping a number into her mobile. I was preoccupied and didn't notice that she was talking to someone on the phone. Talking to someone and looking at me as if to say, what kind of game are you playing?

"What?" I said. "What is it?"

She put the phone in my hand, saying nothing. I raised it and said, "Hello, who is this?"

"Is that Paul?" It was Joanna's voice. "What's going on? Eleanor said you called a few minutes ago, that you said I wasn't here."

"Where were you?"

"I was here, Paul. I've been here all evening."

"Why didn't you answer my call?"

"There haven't been any calls, not until now."

Eleanor managed to hail a cab. As it slid to a halt at the pavement, she took the phone from me, said something I didn't catch to Joanna, and hung up. Thirty minutes later we were home. I went upstairs to check on the kids. They were sleeping soundly. In the living room I poured a drink and tried to make sense of what had happened. Later, while Eleanor slept beside me, I tossed and turned, troubled by questions to which I had no answers. Some time before dawn I decided to check out the message on the answering machine, so I went downstairs to the front room and played it. "Hi," I heard myself say. "Sorry neither Paul nor Eleanor are here to take your call right now. Leave a message and we'll get back to you in a little while." That was it, nothing more.

I woke up hungover. The headache persisted throughout the day and by evening Eleanor was convinced it was something more. "I think you've been overdoing it," she said, placing a palm against my forehead. "You've been working too hard on this bloody Quasar project."

"Quasar could pay off our mortgage," I said.

"So you keep telling me. I think you should have an early night. Stay in bed tomorrow."

I did go to bed early but I slept fitfully and woke Sunday morning feeling worse. Eleanor wanted me to stay where I was but that was out of the question. "I've got to prepare for tomorrow," I told her. "The presentation needs fine-tuning."

She looked at me with a mixture of anger and resignation. "You're not seriously thinking of going to Amsterdam in your condition."

Lee and I were to meet senior executives from the Korean car firm at their European headquarters, to give a presentation on how we proposed to market the Quasar. "I don't have a choice. We've been working for six months solid on this. You know how much it means."

Eleanor sighed, knowing how stubborn I was. Besides, I told her, I couldn't let Lee down, and once the deal was done I'd take some time off and we'd all go away somewhere for a few days.

It didn't occur to me to tell her about the message on the answering machine, about hearing my own voice tell me I'd be too ill to make the flight. I couldn't afford to be sick right now, not when Lee and I were so close to clinching the contract. So I got out of bed and worked right through the day. When the alarm went off at six the next morning I felt terrible, as if all the blood had been siphoned from my veins and replaced with some hot, thin liquid. My temperature was up near forty and trying to move left me breathless and sweating.

Mike O'Driscoll

Eleanor wanted to call the doctor but I said no and took a couple of paracetamol. By the time they'd kicked in, I felt a little less feverish and believed I could make it through the day.

Downstairs, Eleanor said, "Jesus Christ, Paul, you're acting like a martyr. Call Lee, tell him you're ill."

I shook my head, determined not to let him down.

"If you don't," she said. "I will."

"Please, Eleanor," I told her. "I'll be fine. I'll be back tomorrow and I swear to you I'll spend a week in bed."

She stood by the kitchen table, looking down at me, on the verge of tears. "For Christ's sake," I said, wearily. "It's just a cold. Now why don't you call me a cab?"

"No," she said. "Call your own fucking cab if you want to kill yourself." She left the room.

I sat at the table for a while, too debilitated to move. My head was spinning and I wasn't thinking straight. Richard and Hayley came down for breakfast, but I ignored them until Hayley tried to climb into my lap. Then I seized her roughly and snapped at her. She ran from me, bawling, and I made no attempt to follow her. By the time I finally got round to calling a cab, I was running thirty minutes late.

The journey out to Heathrow seemed interminable. A grey drizzle slowed the traffic up more than normal and it was impossible to avoid glancing at my watch every couple of minutes. When I began cursing the traffic under my breath, I caught the driver looking at me oddly in the rear-view mirror. I fought an impulse to tell him put his fucking foot down and tried instead to conjure up a simulacrum of calm. It was no good – my mood fluctuated between anger and anxiety, preventing me from thinking straight. It was nine twenty when we reached the terminal. I hurried through to the KLM desk and handed my ticket to the receptionist. She glanced at it and smiled apologetically as she told me the flight had taken off ten minutes ago, as scheduled. She mentioned another flight at midday but I felt the last vestiges of strength drain from my body. I turned away and managed to stumble out to the taxi rank and hail another cab. As I settled down in the back seat I tried to convince myself that Lee would be able to close the deal alone. The rain was falling harder outside, blurring my vision of the world. I told myself that I didn't care, that there was nothing out there I wanted to see.

Eleanor was in the kitchen, crying, when I got home. She raised her head and made a choking noise when she saw me. Sick as I felt, her appearance unsettled me. She got up and put her arms around my neck. "Oh my God," she cried, "you weren't on it."

I didn't know what she meant and after I'd forced her to explain, I wished I hadn't. It had been on the radio, a newsflash less than twenty minutes ago. The flight I should have been on had come down somewhere in the North Sea. All seventy passengers and crew were feared dead.

*

Lee's girlfriend, Fiona, showed up for his funeral. I wanted to speak to her, tell her how sorry I was but I couldn't do it. I told myself it had to do with the irony of her being there while Lee, because his body hadn't been recovered from the sea, was missing his own funeral. But the truth was I was afraid to look her in the eye in case she'd see the guilt that was eating me from the inside. You didn't get on that plane, she'd say, because you knew. But afterwards, she slipped away without confronting me and I figured that after all, I wasn't to blame.

The meeting with the Quasar people was rescheduled, by which time I was back on my feet. I gave the presentation alone. Based on the blueprints Lee and I had put together, they bought the concept. I rang Eleanor before I called the agency, wanting her to be the first to know. It was for Lee, I told her. I owed him that much.

Back in London I was allowed to handpick my own team and Curtis hinted that another contract like Quasar would finally land me a partnership. I told him I wanted Lee's part in winning the contract to be acknowledged. "Don't you worry about that, Paul," he said, his arm around my shoulder. "We don't forget our people."

Only it never quite worked out that way, as I discovered when the adverts began screening some months later and the Quasar's sales began to soar. I was in a Soho bar with Marcus Owen, an ad man we'd headhunted from Bartle, Bogart, Hegarty. He'd been with us two months and had a brilliant head for startlingly surreal concepts. Give him any product and he'd come up with a juxtaposition of words and images that seemed crazy on paper but when you saw the finished advert, you just knew it worked. Remember the one with surfing horses advertising an Irish beer? That was Marcus. I was more than happy to have him aboard.

The Quasar commercial came up on the screen over the bar. "Any time I see it," I said, "I think about Lee."

Marcus said, "You ever think you might be overdoing the modesty thing?"

"What do you mean?"

"The way you keep on about how good Kurimoto was."

"You think I don't mean it?" I was annoyed at the implication.

He shrugged and tipped a bottle of Becks to his mouth.

"Is that what other people think?"

"Other people don't think about him at all. Only you. What does it matter how hard he worked? Everyone knows you put as much into it as he did."

"That's not the point."

Marcus laughed. "It's precisely the point. People don't want to be reminded of him. He died and that's a real pisser but you're still here and there's nothing wrong with you taking the fucking kudos. If I were in your shoes, I damn well would."

He was right of course. Thinking back over those first few weeks after Lee's death, it became apparent how quickly his contribution to the campaign had been forgotten. Worse than that, his colleagues seemed to have forgotten that he'd ever worked for Delany Brown, that he'd ever even existed. Maybe it was because people didn't like to be reminded of death, even when it was the death of someone they'd known and worked alongside. Perhaps they felt that in dying he'd robbed them of some small part of their own existence.

Some of the fault was mine, I guess. By constantly speculating on how he might have approached some new campaign, I'd kidded myself that I was keeping his memory alive when all I was really doing was attempting to ease my conscience. They all knew that and so did Marcus. The truth was although I regretted that Lee wasn't around to share in the Quasar success, I felt I deserved everything that had come my way. I finally understood their need for me to take the credit – it was simpler and cleaner that way.

*

I was managing a campaign for a new range of fruit drinks. If it proved a success, Curtis had assured me of a partnership in the agency. But translating the blueprints into something concrete was proving more difficult than I'd anticipated. I was working eleven, sometimes twelve hours a day and most weekends. Evenings I got home about eight or nine, took twenty minutes for dinner and worked another couple of hours into the night. Eleanor was concerned about my health but I told her I was thinking about her and the kids, that I was doing it for them.

"This time next year," I said, one night in bed. "We'll be relaxing on some beach in Bali."

"It's always next year with you," she said, laying on her back and staring at the ceiling. Earlier we had made love, after a fashion. I'd never thought it was possible that a guy would need to fake it – now I knew different.

"I know what you're saying, El, but it won't always be like this."

"Won't it?"

"You know it won't, honey. I'm thirty-three – another couple of years and I'll be able to pick and choose my projects."

"You just said it would be this time next year."

"A figure of speech," I told her, wishing she wouldn't take what I said so literally. "By the time I'm forty, I'll be able to pack it all in."

"If you're still alive," she said. She rolled over on to her side, her back towards me. I put a hand on her hip and felt her tense. If only I could make her see what I knew was coming.

Richard was having problems at school. Eleanor had noticed that he'd become morose and withdrawn. She was concerned that maybe he was being bullied. I told her I wanted to be there for him, but I was having problems of my own. At work, I said, not wanting to worry her with the slight chest pains I'd been experiencing. It was better she talk to Richard, he seemed to relate more easily to her than to me. Besides, I suggested, there was always the possibility that she was blowing it all out of proportion, that it was nothing serious, whereas the problems I was having with the fruit drink project were serious, though they seemed intangible and impossible to identify.

Over a drink with Marcus I tried to explain the difficulty. What looked good on paper or in a presentation, didn't always work on screen. I wasn't convinced that our approach would capture the public's imagination. "It doesn't bite," I said. "There's something missing."

"I've been thinking the same," he said. "So what do you want to do?"

I shook my head. "I don't know. It needs ... something else. Maybe I'm too close to see."

"I've got an idea I've been playing around with. I think maybe it could be adapted for the campaign."

I told him to work on it over the weekend. I'd try to come up with something and we'd compare notes on Monday.

Saturday, Eleanor came into my study and brought up Richard's problems at school. "I was right about the bullying," she said. "An older boy."

"That's good," I replied, continuing to stare at my Mac screen.

"I went to see his teacher. Are you listening to me?"

"Sure," I said, distracted.

"She promised to look into it, get to the bottom of things."

"Fine."

"It might help if you talked to him, Paul. I think he feels distanced from you."

"Right. I'll do that."

I talked to him later that afternoon, told him whenever he had any kind of problem I wanted him to come to me. But I think he sensed I was going through the motions – even at seven years old, he was a perceptive child. Serious too, way beyond his years. Even as I hugged him and kissed his cheek, he told me that I shouldn't worry. I think he knew my mind was on other things. Which it was. I was thinking about Marcus, wondering what he might come up with to get the campaign back on track. He called early that evening, said he thought he might have cracked it. I told him to come round the next day and run through it for me. I felt better after talking to him. I told Eleanor to cancel dinner, we were eating out. We even made love that night, and for the first time in many months it felt like it should have done, as if it meant something.

"When did you first notice these brown streaks in your phlegm?" Dr. Bloom said.

I buttoned up my shirt. "First time was yesterday," I lied, my mouth dry and gritty.

"And the shortness of breath?"

"Just recently."

He returned to his desk. "How are things at work?"

"Good."

He scribbled in my notes. "You're not overdoing it?"

I slid off the gurney and took a seat in front of his desk. "It's a busy time for me."

"There's more to life than work, you know, Paul."

"Don't start," I said, annoyed that he should unconsciously echo Eleanor's concerns. "Really, I'm fine."

"What about at home? Everything's okay?"

"Sure."

"You drinking much?"

I shook my head. "I don't have the time."

"Smoking?"

"I gave up a year ago."

He smiled lopsidedly. "That's good."

"Why do you ask?"

"I'd like to send you for some tests."

"What kind of tests?"

"Initially, some X-rays and a sputum test."

"What exactly are you saying?" Invisible fingers began tapping out a rhythm of fear along my spine.

"They're purely precautionary measures."

"Precautions against what?"

"At this stage, I can't say. Chances are you're fine. Maybe you could do with some time off, but the tests won't do any harm."

Easy for him to say, but I was the one who'd have to fret over results. Still, he was the doctor, he knew what he was doing and so I told him to arrange them. I decided not to tell Eleanor, at least until I knew for sure whether there was *something* to tell her. She already had enough on her plate, what with Richard and all. In the meantime, I had my chest x-rays and provided sputum samples for analysis. I wasn't a fool, I knew what Bloom suspected, but to even contemplate what it meant was more than I could do.

A couple of weeks later Bloom called. The tests were inconclusive.

Mike O'Driscoll

The x-rays showed a slight shadow on my lungs but that didn't prove anything.

"So, what does that mean?" I said.

"It means I want to run some more tests. Maybe arrange a biopsy."

"Biopsy. That's some kind of surgical procedure." I fought a wave of nausea.

"It's straightforward. It'll give a more accurate picture of what's really going on."

He scheduled the biopsy for the following week. I told Eleanor what Bloom had said and saw that she knew what he suspected, but thankfully she never spoke the words. I couldn't bring myself to tell Curtis or Max the truth, so I concocted a story about a persistent viral infection I had to have checked out. I'd need a week off work, I told them, maybe a little more. I reassured them that Marcus would be able to handle things while I was away.

As a child I'd been terrified by hospitals, somehow knowing that within those bright clean walls, and underneath that antiseptic smell, death was waiting to tell me all its secrets. When I went in for the biopsy, all that childhood terror came flooding back. I fought to hide it from Eleanor and Bloom, but they saw its mark on my face and told me I had nothing at all to fear. They presumed I was talking about the procedure when it was the knowledge it would reveal that made me want to get out of there. An intern administered a local anaesthetic before carrying out the biopsy. It felt uncomfortable, nothing more than that, until my temperature began to climb that night. The following day I had lost my appetite and become feverish. The look in Eleanor's eyes confirmed my fears. It was obvious the medics had confided something they were reluctant to tell me. Part of me wanted to know what it was, but not enough to ask. As long as I could avoid hearing those awful words spoken aloud, I believed I was still in with a chance.

They ran more tests and initiated a course of intravenous antibiotics. After five days my temperature began to fall. Bloom came to see me. "It's good news," he said, with his crooked grin. "You're on the mend."

"How? I mean, what about ..." I still couldn't bring myself to say it.

"It was pneumonia," he said. "Bacterial."

"Not cancer?" I felt my heart beating with new hope.

"You're on the mend, Paul. A couple of weeks rest and you'll be

28

right as rain."

Eleanor insisted I take another week off, so I worked two or three hours a day from home. My third night out of hospital I was dozing in front of a late news bulletin when the phone rang. I lifted the receiver and said hello. The caller hung up. I switched off the tv and went to bed, thinking nothing of it. A couple of days later I was alone in the house, scrutinising some copy Marcus had sent over. I looked up when I heard the phone. I waited for the answering machine to cut in, not wanting to lose my thread of concentration. I listened to myself telling the caller to leave a name and number. No one did. Curious I reached over and hit the last caller button. The electronic voice reeled off my office number and I hit call back.

"Scott," I said, when one of my team answered the phone. "Did you just call me here at home?"

"Not me, Paul."

"Anyone else trying to get in touch with me?"

"I'll check – hold on." He put me on hold for a moment. "Nope," he said, when he came back on the line. "Nobody called from here."

"Okay, my mistake." I hung up. Someone must have dialled my home number in error, I figured. No big deal. Except it happened again that afternoon. I didn't realise it at first because Eleanor had returned by then and took the call upstairs. A little later, I got up to make a coffee and automatically tapped in 1471 on my extension. I heard it recite my office number. I went through to the kitchen. Eleanor came down after me. She handed me a cup and said, "Finished for the day?"

"I might have to call into the office."

"Oh?"

"Pick up some files."

"Fine," she said, which wasn't like her at all. Not when I'd promised we'd take the kids for a walk on Hampstead Heath after school.

I returned to work the following week. Late one afternoon I was revising some copy Scott had written. Marcus was across the room, talking on the phone. He laughed quietly at something that was being said but when his gaze caught mine, he looked away quickly, as if he had something to hide.

Forty minutes later, he grabbed his coat and asked if I was up for a

Mike O'Driscoll

drink. "Not tonight," I said. "I'm beat."

"Fair enough. I'll catch you tomorrow."

When he had gone I went to his work station and hit the last number redial button on his phone. When Eleanor answered, I hung up.
I was looking for the original blueprints, the ones that had won us the fruit drink contract. I wanted to go over them again, see how they compared with what Marcus had put together. When he'd first outlined his idea he'd made it seem radically different, but since returning to work I'd begun to feel that his new concept was no more than a revision of my original proposals. A slight change in tone and emphasis, that was all it amounted to.

I figured that in the early stages of my illness, before I'd even realised I was sick, I mustn't have been thinking clearly. Maybe Marcus noticed something, but he'd bided his time. In my absence he'd gone to work, persuading people that he was the real creative mind behind the campaign. Having worked out what was going on I went to see Curtis and told him what I suspected. He expressed concern and asked to see my original blueprints so he could compare them with Marcus's proposals. Meantime, he said he'd talk to Max.

But for some reason the blueprints were no longer on my hard drive. No problem, I had them on a zip disk at home. Instinctively, I glanced across the room towards Marcus's work-station, but he wasn't there. Forty minutes later I was in my study waiting for my Mac to boot up. I'd found two discs in my desk and when the machine was ready, I slid the first one into the zip drive and looked for the file. It wasn't there. I swapped discs and waited with a growing sense of unease, already knowing I wouldn't find the blueprints. I ransacked my desk, but found no more discs, then raced upstairs and proceeded to waste time searching my bedroom. Finally, I went down to the kitchen and made a mug of fresh coffee, hoping it would clear my mind.

I stood by the sink and looked out the window at the toys scattered across the lawn. I thought of Richard and Hayley, imagined them playing out there and as I did so, I felt my mind beginning to slow down. I focused again on the disc, tried to think where else it might be. When it finally clicked, my sense of unease came back stronger than before. There was only one place it could be, I knew, the place I'd been avoiding.

I went and opened the door at the top of the stone stairwell that led down to the cellar. I hit the light switch but nothing happened. Damn bulb had blown. I found a torch in the kitchen and returned to the stairwell. My mouth was dry and my pulse had begun to race. For Christ's sake, I told myself, you're not a child. I switched on the torch, gripped the bannister and began to descend.

I counted each step as I went down, eighteen in all. It was cold down there in the darkness, cold and quieter than a winter cemetery. My short, rapid breaths made small clouds in the yellow light and my footsteps were muted on the damp flagstones. I moved the beam of light around the cellar, over an idle workbench and crates of old toys and clothes we'd never got round to taking to Oxfam. Dripmarked tins of paint stood on wall shelves, next to glass jars with hardened paint-brushes in them. A toolbox stood open on the floor, full of tools I'd rarely used.

The torchlight fell on the rear wall and in front of it an ancient desk piled high with a small mountain of discarded files and books and other accumulated junk. I hurried towards it, stumbled over something and lost my balance. I crashed head first against a steel filing cabinet and blacked out. It was only a few seconds, I figured, before I came to in the cloying dark. I pushed myself up on my knees and felt blindly about on the floor for the torch. A sound from close by made me pull my hands to my chest. I listened to the scurrying noise and tried not to think of rats. It's too quiet, I told myself, trying to reason the sound out of being. But however quiet it was, it was insistent, worming its way into my brain and prompting memories of childhood tales and their attendant fears. A scraping of nails against the walls, the crunch of tiny bones and there in the cave beneath the desk, the dim yellow eyes of creatures filthy with disease and cunning. I rocked back onto my haunches and hugged my knees, making myself as small as I could and squeezing my eyes shut as I did when I was kid, working on the logic that if I couldn't see them, then neither would they see me.

As the long minutes passed I withdrew further into myself, shutting out the noise and developing an immunity to fear and doubt. If I was not invisible, I was at least protected from whatever harm the darkness held. Soon it would crawl back into the pit of yesterday and the shadows would fall from my eyes. Whatever secrets this ritual might unwittingly yield, things could not be rushed. I stayed there a long time, breathing slow and deep, tuning out of the now and into the past where I could get a new take on the world and all its rubbish dreams. These new insights I gained were a comfort to me; they revealed the truth of who I was and why.

I never found the blueprints and without them I had nothing to back up the accusations I'd made against Marcus. Curtis called me in to his office and asked, in a neutral tone, if the pneumonia hadn't taken more out of me than I'd thought. I asked him what he meant.

"This business with Owen," he said, frowning. "I figured you of all people would see that this campaign of his is a winner."

"It's not his campaign," I said. "He ripped off my fucking concept."

"I don't understand you – you chose him for your team. Why make these accusations now?"

"Because they're true."

"I'm sorry, Paul," he said. "I think you're mistaken."

A month later we all gathered in a club on Brewer Street to watch the first broadcast of the ad. I sat alongside Owen and smiled through gritted teeth as we shared plaudits that were meant for him alone. In a futile attempt to nullify the sense of betrayal I felt, I began knocking back large measures of scotch and soda. Another mistake. When Curtis asked me to say a few words about the campaign, I knew before I opened my mouth that I was going to fuck up in big way. Marcus Owen, I told everyone, was a parasite. Conversations that had continued on after I'd begun to speak, stuttered into silence. He was a parasite, I went on, who lived off the creative energy of people far more talented than himself. He sucked up their creative juices and when they were spent, he passed off their ideas as his own. I knew this because that was exactly what the prick had done to me. Through the haze of alcohol I saw Curtis staring at me, horrified, and behind him, Marcus, wearing a mask of indignation. I raised my glass and shouted above the growing protests, "To Marcus Owen, a motherfucking charlatan."

I was grabbed from behind, ushered off the small stage, taken outside and sent home in a cab. Curtis rang the next morning and suggested I take a week off. When I returned to work, he said that everything was cool, that he and Max understood the pressure I'd been under. "It happens to the best of us," he assured me.

"What about Owen?" I said.

"What about him?"

"What will you do?"

"Jesus, Paul – face it, you made a mistake. So did I."

"What the Hell does that mean?" I said, seeing the regret in his eyes.

"The partnership," he said. "I'm putting it on hold. Just till you can show me you've got beyond this problem with Marcus."

Later that same day I found out they'd given him my partnership. It was a bitter pill to swallow, but not nearly as bitter as knowing he was fucking my wife.

I was certain of it, though I hadn't confronted either of them yet. I was working up to it, gathering evidence, waiting for the right moment, maybe even hoping to catch them in the act. I'd discovered his email, the message she'd forgot to delete from the inbox. I'd printed out a hard copy, item number one for the prosecution. *Baby*, it began. *I can hardly wait for Thursday. Thinking about what you did to me last time, the way you touched me, is driving me crazy. Don't be late.* Don't be late, the fucking prick – this was my wife he was talking to.

Preoccupied with their betrayal I found it hard to concentrate on work. Only when I was alone in the evenings, when there were no distractions, could I see the situation clearly. Remembering all those curtailed phone calls after I'd come out of hospital, I realised they'd been fucking each other all the time I'd been ill.

One night in a soulless pub on Stroud Green Road, fuelling my anger with scotch, I finally came to a decision. When the barman called last orders, I got up and left. A light rain fell and an empty bus hissed by without stopping. I began walking towards Crouch Hill, my brain no longer hurting now that I had made up my mind. It would end tonight. No more lies, no more betrayal. That was what I was thinking when I saw the four black kids standing beneath a streetlamp, caught in a pool of light. One of them held a boombox on his shoulder and they were all yakking away above the blaring hip-hop track. I hesitated for a moment, then continued on, telling myself this is not a problem. Be cool, chill the fuck out, okay? Yeah fine, except as I drew near, the guy switched off the music and his pals fell silent, their sullen, angry faces turned in my direction. It was too late to cross the street. To do so would be to give them cause to hassle me. Nothing for it but to keep moving, show them

I didn't see them as a threat, even if I didn't feel that way. I walked past them, fighting the urge to look back or to hurry on up the street.

I was halfway up the hill before I heard the hip-hop rhythm again and chanced a quick glance over my shoulder. They were talking animatedly, fingers jabbing and heads nodding, as if I had never existed for them at all. As I crested the rise, two guys stepped out of an alley and into my path. One of them reached for my briefcase but I pulled it out of his grasp and swung it at his head. He avoided it easily while the other guy laughed and said, "Fucking have-a-go-Johnny."

The first guy looked pissed off and I thought maybe I'd rattled him. He turned to glare at his buddy, then spun round and drove a fist hard into my stomach. I went down on my knees and he brought his boot up into my face, splitting my lips, cracking some teeth. I keeled over, stunned, hoping they'd take what they wanted and leave me to crawl the rest of the way home.

I felt a fist in my hair and my head was yanked up from the ground. A scarred hand waved a glittering blade in my face, but it was the tattoo of an eagle or some other bird of prey, ruffling its feathers on a forearm, that held my gaze. "You ever hear a fucking eyeball pop?"

"Please," I said, fumbling inside my jacket. "Take my wallet."

The other guy, the one who'd laughed, crouched down and took it off me. He slipped it into his own pocket then searched through my jacket. Finding nothing, he picked up my briefcase. "Not that," I said, spitting blood. "There's nothing in there you'd want." I was thinking of the email, the evidence.

The tattooed man slapped me hard across the face and pressed the point of his knife against my throat. "Shut the fuck up," he said.

His pal grinned down at me and said, "Yeah well, I'll be the judge of that."

"I need it," I said, stupidly.

"I believe you," he said, smiling as he leaned closer. I felt a twinge of hope before his forehead smashed against my nose. That's all I remember, the smile and the hope, nothing after that.

I sat waiting for Eleanor to say something, waiting to hear her defence, no matter how weak it was. I was owed that much. She stood across the room, gazing out the French doors to where Richard and Hayley were playing in the garden. She turned towards me, her eyes distant and preoccupied. "How did things get this way between us?"

"Things don't get to be any way just by themselves," I said, vindictively, wanting to hurt her. "They get the way they are because people cheat and lie."

"Yes." Her voice was full of emotions I didn't understand. "It's people who let each other down."

"What does that mean?"

She sat on the sofa and held my gaze. "I tried to tell you. I should have tried harder."

"Tell me what?"

"How I felt, how distant you became after Lee was killed. We were drifting apart and it seemed I was the only one trying to hold us together."

"You think that by fucking Marcus Owen you're holding us together?"

"That was later," she said. "And it's over. It never really began."

I wanted to damn her lies but her gaze never wavered. I wondered if it was possible she was telling the truth. "I'm not saying I'm not to blame," she said. "I knew what I was doing, but the truth is, I sleepwalked into it. I wanted you but you weren't there, not as I'd known you. You'd become someone else, someone I didn't know, a man I could hardly even see."

"You're not making any sense," I said, angry and confused because I recognised in her words a truth I couldn't face. "What do you mean, it's over?"

"With Marcus."

My anger faltered and I felt torn between the need to hurt her and the desire to take her in my arms. When I spoke, my words were splintered. "I ... was ... always here," I said. "You should ... have..."

She came and sat on the arm of my chair. Her hand was cool and reassuring against my cheek and her fractured smile was an echo of what I had almost lost. "I want us to try again," she said. "I want to believe you're back with us, the man you were before."

I held her hand in my own. "Yes," I said. "I want that too." I pulled her into my lap and we held each other in silence and after a while we kissed. Maybe I could be that man again, I thought, complete and unfragmented, once more in control of my life.

It takes time for certain wounds to heal, emotional wounds more than most and jealousy longer still. When Owen got my partnership, I realised I was finished at the agency. Curtis wrote me a reference and my track record meant I wasn't out of work for long. I was determined to make a go of it, show everyone that I still had what it took to make a good ad man. But I couldn't get Owen out of my mind – it ate into me, knowing what he'd done to me. On the outside I appeared calm and collected but inside I was seething. And the doubts never really went away. They were a scum on the surface of our marriage, present even when Eleanor and I made love. They made me wonder what she was thinking when she came, whose face she was seeing, whose cock it was she fantasised inside her, and they told me it wasn't mine.

My head was thumping as I stared at the blank screen in front of me. Wurhman was passing by my desk. He stopped and said, "Hey Closer, you all right?"

He was young, early twenties I guessed, and he reminded me somewhat of Lee Kurimoto. That's probably why I hated him. No more than I hated anyone else there, you understand, but this was a specific and focused hate. Wurhman, you see, was a reminder of everything that was slipping away.

"You want something?" I snapped, irritated at his good humour.

"You look tired," he said, grinning inanely. "Is there something I can help you with."

"Not a damn thing," I told him. "So why don't you piss off and leave me the fuck alone."

His grin crumbled and he hurried away. I turned off my screen, got up, grabbed my jacket and headed towards the exit.

"Mr Closer," my secretary called after me. "What about the copy for Poundsaver?"

I stopped at her desk. "Tell them," I said, slowly, deliberately. "Tell them their product is shit. Tell them the garbage they try to pass off as product isn't worth two fucking words out of my mouth."

I walked to a bar in Covent Garden and went to work on the hangover I already had. My hand shook as I raised the first glass of scotch to my lips but by the third I felt a little more in control. I started thinking rationally again. What I needed was to get out of advertising. That world was too artificial. I'd spent so long in it, I figured, I could hardly tell the difference between what was real and what was fake. Everyday I kept seeing people who reminded me of Lee or of Owen, people whose presence was like a slap in the face, saying, look how you fucked up. A change was called for, some new challenge. Things weren't so bad now that Eleanor had gone back to work. She was with a recruitment consultancy in the city. Ironic really, but that's how we'd met. She'd got me the job with Delany Brown. I was pleased for her. Her doing well meant I had a little leeway – I could take my time, decide what I wanted to do, not rush into the first thing that came along.

The more I thought about it, the more convinced I was that I was making the right decision. I would tell her this evening, let her know my plans. I knew she'd support me, that she'd be behind me every step of the way.

It was gone twelve when the cab pulled up outside our house. I noticed the police car parked across the street as I paid the cabbie, but it meant nothing. I staggered up the drive and stopped to piss over a flowering shrub. As I fumbled for my key the front door opened and there was a cop standing in the hall, looking at me awkwardly. "What you want?" I said, confused, wondering why Eleanor would have called him.

"Mr Closer?" he said. "We've been trying to contact you. You'd better come in and talk to your wife."

I stumbled past him into the living room. Eleanor sat there on the sofa, a policewoman beside her. Her eyes were red, as if she'd been crying and her lips trembled when she saw me.

"Jesus Christ," I managed to say. "What's going on?"

The policewoman told me I'd better sit down.

"For fuck's sake," I said, ignoring her. "What is all this?"

The cop had followed me into the room. He put a hand on my arm and said, "It's your son, Mr Closer. He's gone missing."

I turned to look at him, not sure that I'd heard him right. "What?"

"It's Rich," Eleanor said, tears streaming down her face. "Where were you, for Christ's sake?"

"What?" I repeated, refusing to recognise the fear that was biting

Mike O'Driscoll

into my heart. "What are you saying?"

"Your son went missing after school," the cop said. "Your wife says you were supposed to pick him up at three twenty. Evidently you didn't."

"Oh God," I said, cold and numb as stone. "Richard?"

Eleanor flew across the room and slapped me across the face. "You selfish fucking bastard," she screamed. "Don't you understand. He's only eight years old."

The policewoman pulled Eleanor off me while the male cop said, "I'm afraid he's been gone for more than nine hours. Do you have any idea where he might be?"

"No," I said, horrified at what the word meant, at how empty it made me feel.

"We have officers going door to door locally and in the vicinity of the school," he said. "It's too early yet to be thinking of ..."

But I wasn't listening anymore. My son was out in the night, lost and alone in the city. Or worse, perhaps he was with someone, someone who right at this moment would be – stop it, I told myself, stop thinking that way. I could only pray he was all right, if not for my own sake, then for Eleanor's. Keep him safe, I asked a God I didn't believe in. Let nothing happen to him. Send him back to us and I swear I'll do anything you ask. Just keep him safe.

We never saw Richard again. The days passed and then the weeks and we heard nothing. Nobody had seen him, nobody knew where he had gone. There are people who've never been through this, who've never experienced such nightmares – they call themselves psychologists or grief counsellors, and they believe they have some kind of special insight. How awful it must be, they say, not knowing what became of him. Better to know he was dead, they tell you, nodding empathically, to have a body so that you can begin the process of grieving. These people have no idea what they're talking about. If they really knew, they'd keep their fucking mouths shut.

Not knowing meant he could still be out there somewhere, not broken and brutalised, but alive and remembering us, missing us, and though this was hard to believe, it was better than seeing a body. This was the lie which sustained me.

38

But it didn't work for Eleanor. Not even for one week. I saw it etched in her face, the fear and the pain, the need for some kind of closure. Something I couldn't give her because I wouldn't accept that he was dead. Two months later she asked me to move out and soon afterwards, I was served with divorce papers.

I rented a flat off Holloway Road and went through the motions of looking for another job, still believing I had something to offer. My life wasn't over, I told myself. I still had ambitions and dreams, and as long as I clung to them I could still be Paul Closer.

But the process of unravelling had already begun – I just didn't know it.

The first inkling I had of the transition came when I put on my best suit and went down to the city, determined to start again. On the bottom rung if need be. In a recruitment consultancy on Bishopsgate, I sat for an hour with an application form and when I handed it to the consultant she looked at it for a few seconds and then asked why I hadn't filled in my career history.

"I don't need it," I told her. "I'm starting from scratch."

"I don't think we can help you, Mr Closer," she said. "Not if you haven't any relevant experience."

I went to another agency and met with the same lack of success. Walking across the piazza in Covent Garden, I passed by an Austrian cafe I once used to frequent. There were tables out front on the pavement where people sat drinking and talking. I recognised one face, even behind the aviator's sunglasses he wore like a disguise. I stopped a few feet away and looked right at Marcus Owen and felt no anger, no hate, no bitterness. Nothing at all. It was impossible for him not to see me, but he said nothing, gave no indication that he was even aware of my presence. I felt a momentary sense of displacement, no longer sure I was there, even if all the evidence said otherwise.

The following day in a Job Centre near Tufnel Park, I handed another form to a harassed looking young man behind a desk. I'd waited to talk to him for well over an hour, wanting to tell him my plans. He studied the form and said, "What'd you say your name was?"

"It's right there," I said.

He sighed, held the form out towards me and said, "Don't waste my time, pal."

Mike O'Driscoll

I took the form and stared at the blank spaces beside the words *name* and *address* and *date of birth*. Where my identity should have been, there was nothing at all. My whole life reduced to an empty page. I hurried outside, heart pounding as I tried to make sense of what was happening. I returned to my flat, turned on the TV and began flicking through countless channels, searching for some clue as to who I was. I couldn't figure out when or how it had started, but after two days staring at a succession of faces blurring into one another onscreen, I knew that the process of disintegration had gone too far, that I'd already lost my place in the world and there was no way back to who I'd been. The script had changed and someone else had got the lead role in my life.

I've asked myself what I did wrong but there's no big thing I can point to – no great sin or crime to satisfy my need for reasons. What would you have done in my shoes? What different course might you have taken? I made mistakes: I heard myself talking and didn't listen; I got ill and missed a flight; my best friend died and I didn't; I took a call not meant for me and made another I never should have done. I was right for a while, and then I was wrong. Do any of these things mean I deserve to be where I am now? Do they even sound like reasons? There are no reasons. All I did was take my eyes off the ball for just a second. Which was long enough. Now Paul Closer is gone and I have become a stranger to the world.

We don't accept this overnight. It takes time to come to terms with the stripping away of the things which make us real. When it's done, you don't see us anymore, not in the true sense of the word. Oh, you're aware of our presence all right, you know we walk beside you in your streets and parks, that we traipse your shopping centres and department stores, ride your buses and underground trains, but you never make the mistake of acknowledging us for fear that you might slip through those very same cracks. We are the depository of all your bad dreams, the shadows of your fears.

Maybe that explains why, after searching for you through every kind of season, when I finally found you and Hayley this morning in Queen's Wood, you had nothing to say to me. At first I thought you mustn't have seen me, that maybe your eyes were playing tricks. Eyes do that sometimes, when you least expect it, when the world seems exactly as it should – all it takes is a momentary lapse of concentration and you catch sight of something on the edge of your vision that says it isn't so. But I saw that flicker of anxiety cross your face, the look that told me you knew. Why else were you there, you and Hayley, a girl too old to be my daughter, carrying a picnic basket between you, re-enacting a scene in which I had taken part?

I drew closer, and even though the sky was clear, the sun was bright and there were no leaves at all on the trees, you still refused to acknowledge my presence. Then, you stopped and set the basket down on the dry, brittle leaves and in your hollow eyes I saw a pain I understood. You flipped open the basket, reached inside and pulled out the bones of some dead thing I didn't recognise as mine.

But I still hoped. I followed you through the naked trees, saying the things you once loved to hear. I walked in your steps to a house I didn't know and watched a stranger come out to meet you. He put an arm around the both of you and steered you through the door. You paused, just for a moment, whispered something to him, then turned and looked right through the spot where I stood. A second later you slammed the door in my face like I wasn't there. But I was and I'm not a ghost and I can't walk through walls.

This is the sound of loneliness – I call your name and you don't hear it. Even if you did, you wouldn't remember that it once meant something to you. I'm falling apart and even when I pull myself together, I find I've lost another piece of who I was. Any second now the shadows will quicken and run together. It's time to step out of the light.

In The Darkening Green

Everyone looks their best for the Carers, showing their potential. It is important to smile, to display white teeth and bright eyes. These kids know how to respond politely to questions and if encouraged, they ask questions of their own. Family Day is all about making an impression, and that is what they are all trying hard to do.

No one has asked Adu anything. She stares at her reflection in the window, readjusts her smile. The yard is empty but not because of the rain. On Family Day everyone congregates here in the hall. For two hours, sometimes less, they are on show. It's hard work but nobody complains. There are always half a dozen kids who get lucky. Three months ago Tassie was one. Now she is in Brampton, with her new Carers. Today it might be Adu.

A white woman stops in front of her, says something she doesn't catch. Adu tries to show interest. The woman asks her name and when Adu tells her, the woman sniffs, asks what kind of name that is.

She doesn't say it's African. She says, "It's my name."

"I see. Do you like it here?"

Adu is not sure what the woman wants to hear. She wants to say the right thing because that's how you get chosen. "I would like," she says, "to live by the sea."

"The sea?" Adu can tell by the woman's expression that she messed up. "You're not happy?"

Adu's smile is fragile. "I – I would like to be happy."

The woman stares, opens her mouth as if to speak again but doesn't say anything. She moves on down the line to talk to one of the other kids, Anna or Perry, someone who has learned to smile in the proper manner. The rain is falling hard outside. Rivulets run down the glass, washing away the last of Adu's smile. It doesn't take long. Tassie had a smile that lit up her face. It made people want to be close to her. She said that when she was chosen it would stop them altering her. That kind of smile would never fade.

Soon, the adults begin to leave. The couples go first, stopping briefly to talk with Mother. Sometimes they point to a particular child and when they do, Mother looks happy. She shakes their hands and when they have gone, she makes a note in her little book.

The ones who have come alone stay the longest. Like the woman who spoke to Adu. Their eyes move desperately from one kid to the next. Looking for something that Adu can't see. In another twenty minutes they have all gone and the kids file off to the rec centre. There is a buzz of excitement in the air as Adu hurries along the passage, a sense of anticipation. Later on Mother will call those who have been chosen to her office. Adu knows her name will not be called but even so, for these few hours she likes to believe in the possibility.

She finds Eric and a bunch of others gathered round a dreamsim. Perry is running up a high score. This doesn't mean his dreams are better than anyone else's, just that he has good hand/eye coordination. That's Eric's theory. Since Tassie left, Eric is the only real friend she has in *Happy Kidz*. She and Eric are the same age, twelve, though he's much shorter than her and skinny too. Maybe that's why he talks so much, just to make his presence known. She pulls him towards an empty machine. Inside the semi-dark cockpit, she says, "Will you run away with me, Eric?"

"What for, Addy?"

"If we stay, they'll alter us."

Eric claps his hands over his ears. "Not that again."

"Tassie said it's what they do. She said I wouldn't know who I was."

"Yeah, like she would know."

"Why would she lie?"

"She was always making stuff up." Eric shakes his head. "She was worse than you."

Adu is silent for a moment, thinking. "I miss her," she says, feeling an ache in her breast. "I wish she hadn't been chosen."

"Everyone gets chosen sooner or later." His voice softens. "I saw that lady talking to you today. That's a good sign."

"Is it?" Adu shrugs. "She didn't like my name."

"What did you say to her?"

Two faces are ghosted in the coloured screen, one white, one black. Not everything is there. It is hard to distinguish eyes and mouths. Adu traces their outline and says, "Do you always know what you're going to say?"

"Mostly," Eric says. "I think they want us as much as we want them."

"Do they want me the way I am?"

"I would."

She moves closer to him. "That's because you fancy me, Eric."

"No I don't." One face on the screen turns red. "I just – "

"It's okay," she says. "I won't tell anyone."

Later, she is summoned to Mother's room. Mother sits in an armchair watching TV. She does not seem young to Adu, but she's not old either. She wears the same light blue suit she wore for the Carers, but she has slipped her shoes off. "Adu," she says, as if the name is a burden to her. She has lovely chestnut coloured hair which falls in waves over her shoulders. Tassie called her elegant. Elegant is not beautiful. Her smile does not light up her face.

"Adu," she repeats. "What are we going to do with you, child?"

"Must something be done?" Adu asks.

"You have to learn to say the right things."

"I try."

"The past is still holding you back."

Adu watches the plasmascreen mounted on the wall. A beautiful actress whose face she recognises but whose name she can't remember. Which is more important – names or faces? Tassie has been gone three months but Adu knows she will still be beautiful, will still remember.

"There are lots of people out there who would have you," Mother is saying. "People who would care for you, give you a home and the nice things every child wants."

Nice things, people who care. Without these, life is empty. This is Mother's message, her warning. "I would like a home, Mother," Adu says. "Where I would have all the nice things."

Mike O'Driscoll

"Then we must help you to shine. But you have to want it, Adu. To want it with all your heart."

What Adu wants is not to forget. "Yes," she mutters.

"Good. I will see what I can do."

That night Adu has the same dream. The kids are playing in the field at the edge of the forest. They are playing a game whose rules are a secret they keep to themselves. Their voices roll across the grass and into the drowsing trees.

There is never a dull moment at the *Happy Kidz Child Nurturing and Development Facility*. Idleness is the source of evil, Mother says, which means the days are filled with learning and a wide range of interesting and useful activities. Eric and Adu are making a film. They have an old digicam but as yet they have not filmed anything. First, Eric says, you have to write a script, scout locations, raise money. Adu isn't sure he knows what all these things mean, but she admires his sense of purpose, his vision. Right now he is making a sketch, tongue sticking out in concentration. He calls this storyboarding.

"How old are we in the movie?" Adu asks.

"Grown up."

"How can I be grown-up?"

"You act."

"If I was altered, could I still act?"

"How do I know? You're the expert on that."

But she isn't. In fact she's worried it was just something Tassie made up, a way of making it easier to let go. Instead of admitting that a new life would cause her to forget, she'd come up with this stuff about alteration. Why couldn't she simply have told her the truth?

"Will you come back to see me, if you get chosen?" she says.

"I don't know," Eric says. "Would you?"

Adu is stumped. The truth is she wants nothing more than to leave, to have some kind of normal life before she's too old. It's not possible that she could be happy here at fourteen or sixteen. But she's afraid too, of changing, of forgetting. "Yes," she says, finally. "I would."

"How would you know me?" Eric doesn't look at her as he speaks. "If they make you forget?"

"Before they took her away, Tassie said she'd never let them make

46

her forget me."

Eric grits his teeth and starts drawing again.

Bored with the film, Adu thinks about the time Mother organised an excursion to the seaside. Eric wasn't at *Happy Kidz* that Summer. It took hours to get to the coast. Tassie said it was a hundred miles away. The sand underfoot was hot. Tassie and Adu stood in the shallows in their bathing costumes, letting the cool wavelets lap over their feet. They moved a little further out till they could feel the tug of the waves and the suck of the sand. Nanny White told them not to go too far out, but it was okay because they were used to the water by the time it splashed around their waists.

"I could swim the channel," Tassie said.

"What's the channel?" Adu said.

"They put grease on your body to stop you from sinking. You can swim all the way to France."

"Is it far?"

"No." The freckles were like grains of sand on Tassie's face. "It's beautiful and it's always Summer and they have ice cream and strawberries all year round."

They built a sandcastle. Two or three other kids helped, but Tassie and Adu were the architects. Adu wanted to call it Camelot, but Tassie insisted on Castle Adu. They decorated it with shells and gull's feathers. These were their emblems. When it was finished, everybody gathered to admire it. Mother took a picture and said that if there was a competition, then Castle Adu would win first prize.

The tide began to creep up the sand. They had dug a moat around the outer wall and Adu was thrilled as frothy water flowed into it and circled the castle. Soon, more waves were lapping at the walls, eating away at the foundations. They worked frantically to strengthen the castle's defences but each new wave cut a little deeper into the structure.

Tassie put down her spade and motioned Adu to move back from the castle. They watched as a wave finally breached the outer wall and the two towers at the front began to crumble, slowly at first, before collapsing in a liquid rush. One by one, the remaining six towers succumbed to the tide. The tall, strong keep was the last to fall. Adu felt something stir inside her. Tassie held her hand. "I wish I lived in Castle Adu," she said. Then she grinned, and ran off into the sea.

Eric's eyes burn with serious intent as he works, as he dreams. In France it is beautiful and they eat ice cream and strawberries all year round. Maybe Tassie is already there, building castles. Not in Brampton. She covered her body in grease and swam the channel. Now she eats ice cream every day and dreams in another language. Dreams of Adu.

Eric has been summoned to see Mother. Adu is focusing on what he has done wrong. This is a fact of life at *Happy Kidz* – do something wrong and you will be discovered and punished. Wrong things are called misdemeanours. Adu is familiar with misdemeanours and punishments. Mostly they are no big deal. The worst punishment is removal. Eric has never been removed – it will be difficult for him, first time. The loneliness. But Eric hasn't done anything wrong, nothing, at least, deserving of removal. It is something else, some other matter on which he has been summoned. But Adu doesn't think about that. Instead she concentrates on the faces of the couple who stopped in front of her today, who almost spoke. They looked like the kind of Carers who might have given her nice things. The sky outside was cloudy but it didn't rain. For a little while the sun came out and it was as if Summer had decided to linger on for a while longer. But the clouds returned, the sky turned grey. The Carers who'd come looking for kids to make their lives complete had left, full of hope or hopelessness. Depending on what you could see in their eyes.

Why do they need us to make them happy? Tassie, wherever she was now, would know the secret, but Adu will never learn. She will be here forever, making movies.

There is a movie playing on her screen. Diva Divine is singing about a boy who makes her heart beat fast. Tassie's favourite popvid star. Perfect voice and face, designed to make you happy. Adu doesn't feel happy. Diva understands. Whatever you might feel, she feels it too. Happy, sad, frightened, she knows the right buttons to press. Alone in her room waiting for Eric. Not thinking about Family Day. Not feeling. Diva Divine is ReallyReal, a construct. What does she know? What does she think about the things you're trying not to think about? You can always ask.

Instead, she pulls the sheet over her head. There's just too much stuff to not think about. What she has to do is concentrate on how to shine. If you want something not to happen, what you do is you put a massive effort into not thinking about it. What happens is, all the strength you put into denying it, stops it becoming real.

There is a knock at her door. Her heart is racing as she pulls the sheet from her face. Eric walks into the room. He sits at the monitor, not looking at her. She watches his face in profile, can see a struggle going on beneath his skin. He does not need to say anything. His face says it all, tells her that what she tried so hard not to think, has become real.

"I've been chosen, Addy."

She can't tell what that is in his voice – excitement, fear or sadness. Ask Diva. "There's still time," she says. "We can run away together."

Eric shakes his head, avoiding her gaze.

"You'll forget me."

"I won't, I promise."

Tassie had promised and yet Adu hasn't heard a thing in three months. No email, no call. "You won't have a choice," she says. "They'll make you different."

He sits on the bed and puts an arm round her back. "I'll be the same Eric."

Maybe he will but that doesn't matter. Once he is gone, she will be alone and stripped of another piece of her past.

They are at the Games Mall with Nanny White. Adu can't work up any enthusiasm for the holo-drives and simulators because she has other things on her mind. She is waiting for Eric to make a decision. He has only a week left at *Happy Kidz*, and then he will be gone. She should be spending all her time with him, imprinting herself so deeply on his memory that forgetting her will be impossible. But she's giving him room, time to think this through and see that she's right. But as she watches him riding a slamjet rig with Heather, she can tell by his stupid grin that the process of forgetting has already begun. As the programme ends and he climbs down from the rig, she tries to catch his eye. But Eric ignores her, says something to Heather. The girl laughs. Adu hates him then. Furious, she turns round and forces her way through the crowd, past the screaming and gunning machines. These things are designed to attract but today they merely oppress her.

The Mall is full of kids trailing the adults they belong to. Not all of them come from N&D facilities. Lots of kids are born already belonging to adults, though you can hardly tell which are which just by looking at them. Eric belonged to someone once. For eight years he had Carers. They were killed in an accident and he came to *Happy Kidz*. Other kids have had lives outside the facility, but most, like Adu, have always been there.

"Wait." It is Eric. His face is anxious, fearful. "You're not really going?"

"Yes," she says, still angry, but thrilled too, that he has decided to come.

"This is mad," he says. "Where will you go?"

His words slice into her heart. She tries to keep smiling, to hide her disappointment, her fear. "I have money," she says. "I'll find Tassie."

"Yeah? Like, how?"

"I – I don't know. I just will."

"Why?" Eric says, grabbing her arm. "She never looked for you."

"She wouldn't forget," Adu says, resenting Eric's doubt. Just because he has lived outside doesn't mean he knows everything there is to know about the world. He could still be wrong. "Why don't you admit you're scared."

"I'm scared for you."

"You're shitting yourself. Tassie had more guts."

"If she gives a toss, why hasn't she been in touch?" Eric says. "Because she's got a new life in Brampton, or wherever she is, and that means more to her than you do."

Adu yanks her arm free and lashes out with her hand, catching Eric across the cheek. He staggers back a couple of steps, his eyes watering. "Shit, Addy," he says, voice shaking. People are staring, kids and adults, their mouths hanging open. They are looking at Adu, seeing her for what she really is, a child who doesn't deserve to be chosen. There's hurt and fear in Eric's eyes, things she has put there. Horrified, she runs off through the crowd of onlookers.

She emerges into cold October sunlight and boards the first citybound tram that comes along. Her heart is racing and she can't make sense of all the thoughts that are tumbling through her mind. It is only when they have passed the third stop that the reality of her situation begins to dawn. She has done it, run away. But instead of the elation she expected, she feels frustration. It isn't fair that she should have to forget her past to make herself acceptable. There must be some other way for her to shine, to transform herself into the sort of girl who is wanted. She stares out at the unfamiliar streets, wondering how far she has come. At first the buildings seem strange to her, bigger and brighter than normal, then she sees they are just like those she has seen on TV. They have names that mean something to her – Sony and Phaze and Nintendo and ReallyReal.

She gets off at the next stop and walks into a Phaze store. They do clothes. Digital icons of Diva Divine strut their stuff atop glowpads. She wouldn't be seen dead in anything else. The aisles are full of kids and the people they belong to, all paying heed to Diva's message to spend spend spend if you wanna get Real. The kids all wear Phaze and winning smiles. It is not hard to see why they were chosen. She wonders if Tassie has been here with her new Carers. If they have bought her these clothes and made her life more ReallyReal.

Beneath the Golden Arches she eats fries and a milkshake and watches the hustle and bustle in the street below. There's so much going on, so many nice things on offer, it's easy to see how people can forget the promises they make. Maybe happiness depends on forgetting. Is that so bad?

After she has eaten, she wanders through other stores whose names have lodged in her head. *Happy Kidz* kids only dream about being here but she is living it for real. She feels envious of other children, resentful that she hasn't been chosen. Perhaps she was too hasty. Those boots. That jacket. This top. Who wouldn't want hair like that? All these nice things. She feels shame and regret. Poor Eric – she shouldn't have done what she did, or said those things.

She exits another store, her feet aching. There is a chill in the air as the day begins to fade. She walks aimlessly through the busy streets, anxious and uncertain about what she has done. Something has changed, something she can't put her finger on. She feels vulnerable, a little afraid. Her imagination is playing tricks on her, telling her that woman over there getting out of the car, telling her that's really a girl.

Out of the darkness a different city begins to emerge. The sound of traffic and the music spilling out of the stores is amplified by night. Light is pink and yellow and red and blue, never just light. Faces bleached of colour peer out of bar windows, mouthing words she can't hear. A group of girls her own age, maybe younger, are gathered beneath a neon sign that snaps and fizzes with promise. The promise of what? she wonders. She heads towards them, intending to ask them the way back to *Happy Kidz*, but as she gets a better look at their faces, their perfect faces, she backs off, heart thudding in her chest. She feels their eyes following her as she retreats along the pavement, trying and failing to make herself inconspicuous. She thinks of Eric, of what she said and did, and she is angry at herself. Is this the way she wants him to remember her?

She steps out into the road, dodging round the slow moving traffic. People are staring at her. Men are staring. There are no kids with them. Perhaps they're looking for a child to call their own. Maybe she is the one. She would smile if she had the strength, if she didn't feel so light-headed. The flickering lights dazzle her, like the fireworks she watched with Tassie on Bonfire night. Loud bangs and happy songs. She has not forgotten.

A man comes towards her. She should smile her winning smile. Tassie had one. She is falling. It doesn't hurt because the man catches her. He sweeps her up into the air, holding her tight and he is saying something that makes her laugh. The sound more than the words. He is warm and his arms are strong as he puts her into the back of the car. She lays down on the seat, dizzy, but no longer afraid. The man talks to someone else. The car begins to move. He is not driving because he is looking at her. His face is dark as old wood, like hers. Maybe he will care for her. He tells her everything is going to be fine. His voice is steady and strong. When the car stops, he carries her into the building. His companion comes too. He wears the same clothes, the same hat, though he is older and not as tall. She prefers the man who carries her, the one who tells her that she's safe now, that she has nothing more to fear.

Nanny White leads them to the surgery where Mother and the doctor are waiting. The man puts her on a gurney and talks to Mother while the doctor examines her, checks that she is okay. He listens to her heart and shines a light into her eyes. Afterwards, he speaks to Mother. He says she has a slight chill, nothing serious. Mother nods and everybody except the young policeman leaves the room.

He looks down at Adu with perfect, shining teeth. He reminds her of Eric, though he's more handsome and has a nicer smile. "You okay now?"

"I'm Adu," she says.

"I know that," he says. "Are you feeling any better?"

"Not so tired."

"That was a silly thing you did, running off like that. Promise me you won't do it again."

"Yes."

"You could get yourself into all kinds of scrapes."

"I was angry with Eric," she explains. "He's leaving."

The man nods. "I've spoken to Mother, asked her to go easy on you, okay?"

Adu manages a weak smile.

"You take care, Adu. Be a good girl."

She spends the night in the surgery and in the morning she showers and pulls on the clean clothes Nanny White has brought from her room. Nanny waits for her to dress, then says, "Okay, let's go."

"Where?" Adu has a bad feeling.

"You are to be removed," White says. "For a little while."

"But the man said Mother would go easy."

"Mother is in charge here," Nanny White says. "Not the policemen."

Frantic, Adu says, "But I have to see Eric."

White opens the door. "After removal."

"He'll be gone by then," Adu pleads. "I must see him now."

Nanny White catches hold of Adu's arm and pulls her along the hallway. She cannot believe this is happening – it isn't right. She came back. She was happy to come back. Mother has no right. She has to speak to Eric, tell him what she's seen, tell him why they forget. She struggles desperately as she is dragged through the Learning Block. Doors fly open and kids peer out into the corridor at the commotion. She calls Eric's name as White grapples with her. They fall to the floor, wrestling. White is bigger and stronger but Adu is driven by rage and love. And there he is, a face in a doorway, watching her along with all the others, but making no move to help her. Nanny White is screaming for assistance. People are hurrying towards them, strong arms clutching

Adu's limbs. She twists and turns till she catches sight of Eric again. "Please," she cries out. "I didn't mean what I said." He watches her, his expression a mix of fear and curiosity. Nothing else. No indication that he feels anything real. Adu screams as Eric turns away, as he abandons her.

Being removed from the daily life of *Happy Kidz* is never easy but Adu has always got through without any serious hurt. She has become accustomed to the isolation, to the lack of human contact. It is good for the soul, Mother says, because it gives the child an opportunity to reflect on her behaviour away from all distractions. She calls it a character forming process. Adu has never been sure exactly how this worked. Until now. It's been hard. The days have dragged, and despite electronic tutorials and other routine interruptions, she has had more time than she needs for reflection. Reflection, she sees, is a process that helps you to understand how the world really works. It shows you just how messed up everything is. What she has learned is that life is built on forgetting. You trade memory for nice things. Eric will have no choice but to forget her if he wants the nice things with which they will tempt him. They will purchase his life with treats, make him so completely their own, he will forget she even exists. All day long she reflects and is crushed by this terrible insight.

Sleep offers no escape from the craziness. She has the same dream every night, of herself, Eric, Tassie and other kids, playing together in a field near a forest. Only now the forest seems closer, hemming them in. Nobody seems to notice, or to hear the wind that keens through the leaves. They are too caught up in their game to feel the presence in there, the dull eyes peering out from the restless green. They are being listened to, their long-held secret overheard. When they fan out towards the trees, running off to hide in its dark places, leaving one girl alone to cover her eyes and count, she hears the sigh of shadows, sees the smile of night.

In the dream Adu finishes counting and goes off to search for the others, drawn to their hiding places by laughing whispers. Each night she returns with one less child until, by the end of the week, she is alone with only the eyes in the unfurled leaves to watch over her.

When she is brought back into the life of the facility, she goes immediately to Eric's room. The boy who greets her is not Eric, has never been Eric and does not know her at all. She knew this would be the case, but having his absence confirmed does not make it any easier. Eric is out there learning to forget. His past is being unravelled by the lure of nice things. He has so much past to lose, there will be nothing left of him. She returns to her own room, spends the day alone.

After dinner Mother comes to her room, finds her cutting things, notes, pages from her diary, pictures, storyboards. Adu wonders if this shredding of evidence will make it easier to forget. She doesn't believe so but she wants to put her memory to the test.

Mother gently takes the scissors from Adu. She scoops a fist of paper flakes from the bedspread, looks closely at them. Adu is glad she has cut them so small. "I'm sorry," Mother explains. "Eric was chosen. Your time will come soon."

"I don't want to go."

"Don't be silly. Every child wants someone to care for them."

"Not if it means being altered."

Mother turns her palm over, lets the confetti memories drift down onto the bed. "You are no longer a child, Adu," she says. "Not in the sense you understand. It's time to let these things go."

"Why can't I hang on to my memories?" Adu pleads. A powerful yearning builds inside her, threatening to break her in half. "What harm does it do?"

"It's not a question of harm – it's baggage, inappropriate baggage. When you're older, you'll understand. You'll be grateful that you don't have such things to hold you back."

"How can knowing who I am hold me back?"

Mother is silent, avoiding Adu's gaze. There is something unfamiliar in her voice when she finally does speak, a note of uncertainty. "Knowledge is the poison of innocence," she says. "It's innocence that will get you through, that will lead to nice things."

Adu slips away on the next excursion. It is not difficult. After all, she has been punished, she knows the consequences. It is assumed this knowledge will act as a deterrent. Certainly after a couple of hours, Nanny White's scrutiny is less intense. There are nine other kids competing for her attention and Adu has the demeanour of a child who has learned her lesson. She has learned better than Nanny White realises. This time her escape is not so dramatic, not a manoeuvre to draw attention. Merely a slipping away. One moment she is part of a small group of *Happy Kidz* out with their Nanny, the next she has melted away, become indistinguishable from any of a thousand other kids in the Mall.

It takes her thirty-six hours to find Tassie down in Brampton. It is a drab place just south of the city. No flash stores, no loud buildings, just lots of people she doesn't know. A black car pulls up outside the Pizza Parlour where Adu is picking at a thin and crispy. She is tired and dispirited, on the verge of giving up. Last night she slept on an empty bus. She watches a man get out of the car. He's white but he looks like the policeman who took her back to *Happy Kidz*. He catches her eye and smiles. Adu turns away, embarrassed. When she sneaks another look, he's nowhere to be seen but his car is still outside. There is a woman sitting in the front passenger seat, just a couple of metres away. It is only when she leans back in her seat that the woman, the girl, becomes recognisable as Tassie.

Adu gets up slowly, light-headed, afraid Tassie will disappear before her eyes. She makes her way to the door, steps out on to the street. She is hardly breathing, she's so intent on holding that face in her mind. She approaches the car, leans down, taps on the window. The face turns towards her. It is Tassie, there's no mistaking the spray of freckles or the shape of her mouth. But when she turns and lowers the window, Adu sees there's something odd about her – the lips are too full and red, the eyes older and emptier than they have a right to be. Even the winning smile seems out of place. "Can I help you?" she says. "You want something nice?"

"Tassie?" Adu whispers. "It's me, Adu."

The old young girl frowns, shifts in her seat. She is wearing a tiny pink skirt and strapless top. The kind of clothes Diva Divine wears. They don't look right on Tassie. "My name is Candy," she says.

Adu is confused and a horrible doubt is worming into her mind. Don't think it, she tells herself, and it won't be real. "You said you'd remember me, Tassie. You said you'd wait."

"What are you talking about?" Tassie says, the fraudulent winning smile beginning to break on her face. "Who the fuck are you?"

"Please, Tass, listen to me," Adu says, reaching through the open window.

The girl flinches, pulls away from her, tells her to fuck off. "I don't belong to you," she says, her voice angry, frightened. "Daddy will be mad if he sees you trying to touch."

"Daddy?"

"Hey, what's going on?"

At the sound of the voice Adu turns, sees two men approaching, one of them is the guy who'd been in the car with Tassie. "You want something, honey?" he says.

"She was trying to touch me, Daddy," the girl says, sliding out of the car and rushing into his arms. "She wouldn't wait."

The man looks at Adu as he strokes the top of Tassie's head. He smiles and Adu is stunned and suddenly afraid. She begins to back away. "Hey wait," the guy calls. "You want a lift?"

Adu keeps moving backwards slowly, watching as he says something to the other guy that makes him laugh. "Yeah," the second guy says. "I'll be your Daddy, little girl, if that's what you want."

Adu starts running hard as she can, not looking back, not even once. And as she runs she tells herself it wasn't Tassie. That girl was too old or too young, and all it was was her own wanting too much for it to be Tassie.

When she finds the policeman she almost cries with relief. But she contains herself, holds it all in until she's back at *Happy Kidz*, until Mother has shaken her head and spoken with that familiar sadness about how she's doing nothing to help herself. Only when Nanny White has escorted her off to removal, when she's alone and there's no one to see or hear, does she let herself cry.

The pretty black girl, tall for her age, sits on the high stool swinging her legs back and forth beneath the counter. Her hair is braided and she wears Phaze hot pants, t-shirt and skate shoes. She spoons strawberry ice cream from a tall glass onto her tongue and smiles at her reflection in the mirror behind the counter. Très sophisticated, très cool. The handsome man on the stool beside her, the guy with his hand on her knee, this is her Daddy. He really really cares for her. These are the nice things she has earned. The rewards of innocence.

Unbecoming

by Willard Grant

Two, maybe three minutes ago, I thought there was still time but now that I've read Newboy's words I understand how late it really is. I feel dissolute as my gaze drifts over the books scattered across the desk. In these pages is an explanation for what has happened but when I reach for it, my hands sink right through the words as if they were water. It doesn't matter – I know what's coming. All that's left is to try to tell everything about how and where I went wrong.

The nature of the mistake is hidden here in these dissolving words. They speak of some small slip, a momentary loss of focus, something I missed but which someone else noticed. A gap opened and somebody moved in to fill the space. Maybe if I had more time I'd find him, but like Newboy says, I'm already way too late.

*

Janine left a message on the answering machine. A quick hello to say she'd be back in Krebbling soon and was I missing her? I thought about that as I made fresh coffee, trying to work out how long she'd been away. Two months? Longer. The truth was, since I'd started writing again I hadn't given much thought to anything other than work. I replayed the message and was disappointed to discover the machine hadn't logged the time she rang. Somehow it made it harder to picture her making the call.

I retrieved my mail and browsed through it while nursing my coffee and the bowl of dry cereal I ate every morning for the good of my health. I tore the shrink-wrap cover from the magazine and began to skim through its pages. *Slipstream* didn't call itself a science fiction or horror magazine, but a 'journal of speculative fiction'. As if to confirm its seriousness there were no spaceships or monsters on the cover, but a bleak landscape with some kind of organic machine. No doubt surreal. Still, it paid seven cents a word for fiction and after four years of silence, I wasn't going to argue.

The story was called *Saint of Pain*. Nice accompanying graphic, vaguely Kurt Schwitters but darker, a collage that hinted at the tone of menace I'd tried to achieve. Reading the opening paragraph I felt something wasn't right. I glanced at the byline running down the left-hand side of the page in a shadow font. I turned the magazine sideways and felt cold, sharp needles pricking my flesh. I flipped to the end of the story and found the short biographical note. It was as I'd written it, except it described someone called Cole Trenton, a name I'd never heard. I shut my eyes for a few moments but when I looked again Trenton's name was still there, proud author of the story I'd written as Ernest Newboy.

I'd told nobody, not even Janine. As far as she or anyone else knew, I was still Les Steiner, a fantasy and science fiction author with two story collections and three novels under his belt. Not to mention a bad case of writer's block. What a shame, people said, for a guy with so much promise. Except that was only part of the story. For while Les Steiner remained unresolved about the kind of writer he wanted to be – the very thing which had caused the well of words to run dry – I'd created Ernest Newboy to provide a mouthpiece for the fictions of which Steiner – the attitudinizing prick – was still ashamed.

In less than a year the infant but worldly-wise Newboy had produced nearly a dozen stories and had started work on a novel. Steiner, on the other hand, was still plagued by doubt, unable to see merit in anything he'd written. He believed himself capable of great things, but he wasn't going to achieve it with works like *Ghost Dance* or *City of Dreams*. Yet he was pragmatic enough to see that although brooding silence might have been a fitting occupation for a man with literary aspirations, it didn't put food – not even dry cereal – on the table. Which was why it had been necessary to create Newboy, who had no literary aspirations other than to get the story written and published. Science fiction, horror, fantasy, erotica – it made no difference so long as it sold. They had, ten so far, and this was the first of Newboy's tales to see print.

Or it would have been, except for this aberration. I sipped my coffee but it was bitter and cold, offering no insight into Trenton's intent. I considered my options but they were limited. If Steiner had written *Saint of Pain* that might have meant something but Newboy was a nobody and that, for the time being at least, suited my purpose.

Using Newboy's account I emailed *Slipstream*'s editor, pointing out the attribution error and requesting payment which had been promised on publication. I wanted to do something more, but Steiner deemed it enough. A greater fuss meant risking exposure, and I didn't want that.

*

Two days later, *Weird Tales* arrived. Though it was ten years since I'd first appeared in its pages, I still recalled the excitement I'd felt, despite the fact it was no longer esteemed as highly as it had once been. It had history and to be part of that, to see my name where Lovecraft, Bloch and Bradbury's had once appeared was a real kick. But that was in the past and as I began flicking through the magazine, I wasn't sure what I was feeling.

Until I saw Trenton's name where Newboy's should have been, and recognised the cold dread gusting through my heart. It didn't seem possible but the taste of blood on my lips told me it was. I skipped to the accompanying biog. It was more or less the same, though the tone was subtly different, as if a gap had opened up between the writer it spoke of and the one I'd invented.

I resisted an impulse to lash out and tried to think through the implications of my predicament. It would be difficult for Steiner to claim the story as his own, given his prolonged silence and the care I'd taken to eradicate any connection between him and Newboy. Which meant Newboy himself would have to claim authorship of the story. But to all intent and purpose, he was a complete unknown while Trenton was a published author. It occurred to me that Trenton might have sold other stories, which would put him even further ahead. Caution still seemed the best option, so in the end I did what I had done last time, notified the editor of their mistake and requested a correction in their next issue.

The weakness of Newboy's response left me disinclined to work on my novel. I decided to take a break, figuring that a couple of days off hardly constituted a block, not for Ernest. I thought about the few friends I had in Krebbling and felt uninspired. Realising I hadn't heard from Janine in a couple of days, I drove over to her place on Main Street. The intercom remained stubbornly unanswered, so I left a note in her mailbox asking her to call. I drove up into the mountains, hoping to recapture some of the fascination with nature that had first brought me to the Colorado high country five years ago. After two hours hiking my enthusiasm was fading, and by day's end I was sick of rocks and trees, of the cold, thin air and the fingers of cloud that scratched at the bloodless sky. I ate dinner at *Neddy's Bar & Grill*, a twelve ounce steak washed down with a few beers. I returned to my apartment a little before ten and saw the light flashing on the answering machine.

I hit playback and felt a warm thrill when I recognised Janine's voice. "Hey honey," she said, then hesitated. "I'm sorry," she went on, faltering. "I – I guess I must have the wrong number."

My eyes began to hurt and something cold expanded inside my skull. I grabbed the phone and punched in her number. After a few seconds Janine's answer machine clicked in. "This is me you're not speaking to," she said. Her voice sounded distracted, far away. "Which means if you want to speak to me, I guess you'll leave a number so we can make it happen." Then a beep and an emptiness I tried to fill.

"Janine," I said. "It was me. Call back."

*

Trenton's life began to diverge from my own. This became clear when I read the note accompanying the fifth of Newboy's stories to see print. Whoever he was, it was no longer enough for him simply to pass my work off as his own; now he was trying to plagiarise my life. It was too much. He left me no choice but to fight back and the first thing to do was to find out who he really was.

Not that easy. I couldn't find a single mention of Trenton on the internet, despite the fact that he had five published stories to his name. So maybe it was a pseudonym for some no-talent fuck willing to go to any lengths to make a name for himself. Even stealing. Newboy was the ideal target – a man without material existence, blessed with narrative skills but unable to speak for himself. That he could get access to Newboy's stories suggested the impostor was known to me. Perhaps he worked for one of the magazines, an editor maybe, or an editorial assistant.

Whatever he was, I was on to him. I emailed every professional in my contact list, alerting them to Trenton's scam. Rather, Newboy did this – it was his livelihood that was threatened – but I was behind him all the way. He mentioned the stories that had been ripped off and asked that they be alert to any future attempts at plagiarism.

A week later the new *Interzone* arrived. I smiled as I noted the absence of Trenton's byline on the first page of *The Far Away Room*. But the smile slackened as I saw the name that had replaced Newboy's. 'Nicholas Sporlender.' On my lips it sounded like a lament.

I called my agent. It had been a while since we'd spoken, nearly three years. I guess my block wore out Racoona's patience. I couldn't blame her. I mean, why bother putting yourself out for a fifteen per cent cut of nothing? I hadn't told her about the Newboy thing – she wouldn't have approved. "I'm sorry," she said, when she came on the line. "Who is this?"

"It's Les Steiner. I know it's been a while, but can we talk?"

"Right – you're the author with a great future behind you."

"Okay, I'm sorry. I should have returned your calls."

"What do you want, Les? I'm real busy."

"I'm working on a novel." I hoped I didn't sound desperate.

A moment's silence, then, "You have something for me to look at?"

"Yes, but I need your help with something else first."

I heard the sigh. "This better be good."

I ran it all down for her, the whole Newboy business. I'll say this for Racoona, you never had to repeat things. Once was always enough for her to grasp the intricacies and implications of a situation before offering her considered judgement. "Forget it," she said.

"Forget it?"

"What do you want from me? It's a shame about the block Les, just when things were starting to happen. But this is not the answer. Short stories are an indulgence, a luxury you can't afford. If you still had the profile you had four years ago, then I might've sold them. But you come to me now, when nobody remembers you, when your profile is, like, non-existent."

"I'm not asking you to sell them."

"But better than that," she continued. "Just on the off chance there were some readers out there who might have been excited by the fact you were writing again, you come up with this pseudonym, which puts you on the same level as every other wannabe trying to make names for themselves. But somehow you manage to sell these stories without going through me, only for some other unknown to steal the credit for them. Like I said, Les, forget it."

"Is that it?"

"You mentioned a novel," she said, dismissing Newboy. "That's a start. Send me a few chapters, a synopsis. I'll look at it. A novel I can do something with, but please, no more pseudonyms. Newboy is nobody. Whatever you are now, Les Steiner was somebody once. We have that much at least to work with."

I spent the rest of the day brooding. The thought of giving up on my stories, of letting Trenton and Sporlender get away with it, was galling. But deep down, I knew she was right. It was a battle neither I nor Newboy could win. The important thing was that I'd rediscovered my voice and with it, an audience. That had been the intention all along, to take the pressure off Steiner by letting Newboy take the rap if the stories failed. In a way, it was only right that the wrong guy should have the credit, even if it wasn't my wrong guy.

So, when the remaining Newboy stories were published as by Leonie Hargrave, John Luther Novak, James Sheldon Jr. and Alex Blade, I bit the bullet and decided that the time had come to lay my alter ego to rest. Nothing mattered but the novel; nothing else could contain everything I had to say.

*

I determined to put everything behind me and give myself up to *Becoming* – my novel – hoping that Newboy and his problems would fade away. I established a routine over the next few weeks, writing twelve, sometimes fourteen hours a day. Janine called a few times, but I kept missing her. I wanted to talk, let her know what was happening, but to do so would have meant disrupting the routine. And I was in the zone by then, focused entirely on my characters, living and breathing their world, intent on resolving the turmoils and contradictions of their lives. Better to get it finished before trying to patch things up. After a month or so, I didn't notice if she was calling or not.

When the first three chapters were done I mailed them to Tiptree Associates along with a synopsis. They sent back a form letter acknowledging receipt of the manuscript which would, they said, 'be read with interest.' Racoona's idea of a joke. I didn't care because I knew that once she started reading, she'd be hooked. *Becoming* was like nothing I'd written before. It was the book I'd been working towards all my life, the novel that would establish my reputation beyond the insular, ghetto world of genre fiction. I emailed Racoona, telling her I saw the novel as a new beginning. Les Steiner was no more and the publication of *Becoming* would signal the arrival of K. Leslie Steiner on the scene.

It progressed quickly and I sent chapters to Racoona as soon as they were done. The agency emailed to confirm the safe arrival of the first eight or nine, and then, a prolonged silence. I wasn't bothered, not then. It was Racoona's way. She liked to take her time getting to know a work. It had been like that with my previous novels. So I tried not to get ahead of myself, to not get too excited. It was inevitable, I thought, that she would come through in the end.

*

It was done inside eight months, the last chapters mailed off and just the waiting to come. I tried calling Janine, wanting to explain and see if we could get back to the way we had been before. Her number had been disconnected. I drove round to her building, managed to get to see the Super, only to have him tell me Janine had never come back. He'd relet the apartment six months ago when she'd failed to renew her lease.

I went to *Neddy's* that night and got drunk, hoping it would ease the pain. Next morning it was still there. I bought a bottle of J&B, drank it, and repeated the process every day for a week. It took that long for the booze to do its stuff and let me rationalise that her absence shouldn't hurt because I was no longer the guy she'd belonged to. Better off to let her go. Besides, it meant I could catch up on all kinds of things I'd missed. A year's worth of movies and books. Getting my body back into shape. Maybe a visit to New York, touch base with some old acquaintances. Gradually, life began to settle into a kind of pattern, and as it did, the next book was starting to take shape in my head. But no word came from Racoona. Two months after I'd mailed the final chapters I called her on the phone. She wasn't available. If I left my name, some supercilious prick said, no doubt she'd get back to me.

I sat in front of my computer, needing a boost, some acknowledgement that what I'd done meant something. I typed my name into a search engine. Google came back with a whole load of nothing connected to me. I dug the heels of my palms into my eyes and tried to grind some clarity into them. I heard the walls creak and noticed a thick layer of dust on the windowpane, obscuring the outside world. The grain on the bookshelves seemed to have lost its uniformity, its flow interrupted by ugly, discoloured knots that protruded from the timber surface. I found an online database of SF writers, entered my name and pressed 'find'. No hits for either Steiner or Newboy.

Panicked, I tried different parameters, entering the title of my first novel, *City of Dreams*. The author came up as Sonny Powell. Time slowed until it seemed I was caught in a fugue. My fingers typed in the words *Ghost Dance* and I wondered how Lee Falconer could have written the same book. Fred Ewing, the author of my third novel, *Eye Teeth*, was as unfamiliar to me as Trenton or Sporlender. Which was almost a comfort.

I shut down the computer, wishing I could do the same to my head. There was too much strangeness in there, corroding my sense of self. I had to get out of the building, find someone to talk to, anyone, as long as they could confirm my existence. I walked the couple of blocks to what passed for downtown, stopping at a drugstore to buy a Snickers just to see if the woman behind the counter would take my money. She did. The guy I deliberately bumped into on the sidewalk acknowledged my apology with an untroubled 'forget it', while the barman at *Neddy's* put a J&B in front of me just as requested. He followed it with a couple more and I figured things maybe weren't so bad after all.

I left the bar and strolled across the street. Krebbling in Spring was a town in transition. The skiers had fled with the snow, while Summer's hikers and mountain bikers had still to arrive. The panic had left me and in the unhurried calm of downtown I found myself in front of *The Creeping Vine*, a fantasy bookstore. Janine had organised signing sessions there to promote my last two books. Maybe they carried my

Unbecoming

back catalogue. Inside, a skinny guy with a goatee sat at the counter reading a comic book. I pretended to browse while searching for my own books. There were none I could see.

I approached the counter and asked the guy if he had anything by Les Steiner.

He raised his head from the comic book and tapped the keyboard in front of him. After a couple of moments he shook his head. "We gotta negative on that one, Cap'n."

I asked him if he had a copy of *Eye Teeth*.

"Lemme see," he said, tapping the keyboard again "Yep, I think so."

"Can I see it?"

He nodded, came out from behind the counter and searched among a rack of shelves at the rear of the shop. Returning, he handed me a hardcover book with the title *Eye Teeth* emblazoned in a jagged white font across the cover, Fred Ewing's name underneath. "I changed my mind," I said, sounding steadier than I felt. "How about a collection called *No Eyes With Which to Speak?*"

He shrugged, checked the computer again and wandered off to find it. "This is a signed copy," he said, returning from the rear of the shop. "First edition."

I grabbed it without looking at the cover and flipped it open to the title page. Things seemed normal, date and place of publication, title of book, copyright details for each of the stories, name of publisher. Everything present and correct except that Cordwainer Bird had scrawled his signature beneath his own printed name.

I don't know what hour of the day or night I went home, but when I got inside I slumped into an armchair and laughed with sick relief. I was drunk yet it wasn't the booze that had caused me to expect some kind of change: a loathsome stench of doubt hanging in the air, things not where they should be, a small drop in temperature, a muted quality to the light. But everything was as it should be. Nothing was altered, all the detritus of my life was in its right and proper place.

I tried to work out what time it was in New York, found the task beyond me, but called Tiptree Associates anyway. A machine answered and I declined to acknowledge it. Still jittery, I went into the study and stood in front of the bookshelves. I pulled the limited edition hardcover of *Ghost Dance* from its place and read Lee Falconer's name below the title. Inside, she'd written *To Ernest, I'll save the last dance for you. Best Wishes, Lee Falconer.*

All the books I'd written had been signed to Newboy. I felt weak and my eyes hurt bad enough to bleed. I sat at the desk, breathing deeply, telling myself that it was okay. No matter what it said on the covers, I was the man who'd written these books, breathed life into their protagonists, determined the course of their events. I looked down at the book on my lap, saw the words that Sonny Powell had written there. *Once Upon a Time, All this was Yours.* Not any longer, he was telling me.

*

The morning was leeched of colour, the mountains as grey and stillborn as the sky. My head was clogged with ruined speculations about my predicament. I made coffee, drank three mugs to clear the fuzz and still couldn't think straight for more than a minute or two. Something had caused all this. It had to be there in my past, a minor detail just waiting to be recognised as the thing that had tripped me up.

In my study I confirmed what I'd seen last night, that I'd written none of my own books. I booted up the computer and opened the last email I'd received from Tiptree Associates, intending to force Racoona's hand on *Becoming*. As I was about to hit the reply button I noticed that it had been addressed to Newboy. The room was still, no sounds leaked in from the street. The world might have been empty. Nothing made sense anymore. Racoona had insisted that I drop the pseudonym. Why the change of mind? Unless she had some other plan, like wanting to keep my real identity hidden until we were close to publication. It was feasible but I needed further confirmation.

I dug out the original letter from Tiptree Associates acknowledging receipt of the opening chapters of *Becoming*. Like the email, it was addressed to Newboy. But what really cut me up was that the novel's title had been changed to *Unbecoming*.

Later, when I believed I could control myself again, I rang the agency and demanded to speak to Racoona. A guy said she no longer worked for Tiptree Associates, that she'd branched out on her own. I asked him who was responsible for my novel. He put me on hold for two minutes listening to some godawful muzak version of The Beatles. "I'm sorry sir," he said when he came back. "We don't have a record of receiving any such manuscript."

"I've got a fucking letter here acknowledging receipt," I said.

"Maybe you should take it up with Ms. James."

"Why don't you give me her number."

"Why don't you look it up," he said, before cutting me off.

I found a James Literary Agency on the web and called the listed number. The receptionist wanted to know the nature of my business and didn't respond well to my suggestion as to what she should do with herself. After three attempts to speak to Racoona, I emailed her withdrawing *Becoming* and terminating any agreement we might have had. I'd find a new agent or even market it myself. I knew people, after all, I still had contacts. That left one final thing. I went through all the files on my hard drive and trashed everything Newboy had produced. I should never have gone down that road. When it was done, I felt a weight lifted from my mind. Now I could go back to my own life, let people know who I really was.

*

I couldn't seem to get started on anything. I read back through all the notes, the synopses, the character descriptions I'd made for the follow up to *Becoming*, but the more I tried to get into it, the more hollowed out I felt. Half a dozen times I made a tentative start, getting a page or two written only to read through it with a growing sense of despair. The delete key took a hammering.

By the third day I could barely bring myself to sit in front of the computer without feeling it was conspiring against me. The email from the James Literary Agency was just another sign. They had no record of receiving a manuscript called *Becoming*, from a Les Steiner or anyone else, and therefore couldn't return what they didn't have. Maybe there was some logical explanation but I couldn't rid myself of the notion that I'd been screwed. If I lodged a copy of the manuscript with an attorney and sent the agency another copy, then they'd have to accept that I was its author. How else could it be in my possession before it was published? But I couldn't find the file on my computer. A thorough search of the hard drive revealed no trace of its existence. I turned the apartment upside down, sure I had printed a hard copy besides the one I'd mailed to Racoona. I didn't find it.

I rechecked the computer, then went through my files again, looking for notes I'd made, anything that would disprove the awful suspicion that was beginning to take hold. The feeling that I hadn't written it after all. That in desperation one of us, Newboy or myself, had merely imagined writing it, that in truth, *Becoming* had never really been.

*

Perhaps it would have been better for me if I had left it at that, if I hadn't discovered what I now know. I can't say when I first saw the way things really are. A week, maybe two. Or do I say that simply because time seems to have stopped and all experiences start and end at this precise moment? I can't figure it. I was walking down Main, near where Janine used to live, trying to flesh out the picture of her I still carried in my head. The image was corrupted, like a bad digital transmission, flickering and frozen into incoherence. Maybe I thought that if I could make her whole, then I could do the same to myself. Passing *Borders*, something about the storefront display caught my eye. I leaned forward and squinted through the glass. It shimmered and threw back fragments of my own face. Inside the store, I found the display and stared at the exploding, Futurist inspired image on the dustjacket of Ernest Newboy's *Unbecoming*. I picked up a copy, flipped it open to the last page and read there my final words of fiction.

These last few days I have re-read each of my books, looking for clues. Of course I accept that they are no longer mine, but even so, given time, I believe I can discover their secret truths. But the work expands and consumes me. Trenton and the others have been joined by Waldo Hunter, Wade Kaempfert, Charles Satterfield, Caleb Saunders, Laurence O'Donnell, Anson McDonald and Cassandra Knye. They feed off my words like they were their own. But I can't say that. I can't say much of anything now that I've read what he has to say.

It's right here in front of me, a website I stumbled across while searching for some mention of who I was. I never thought it would be him, even though I've followed his career from a distance. But here it is, in *Omniscient City*, the confirmation. In an attack on writers who seek to escape their genre roots, Ernest Newboy cites 'the late K. Leslie Steiner' as a typical example. I wish it was otherwise but the truth is I no longer have anything left to say.

Biographical note: Willard Grant is a musician. He spends a lot of time away from home and too much of his time in his own company. This has resulted in a short attention span which only playing music and reading short stories can resolve. This is his first story not to answer back.

The Hurting House

I must have missed that transitional half hour during which all the colour drains from the sky as day slides into night. My eyes were so tired of looking at tarmac it seemed like days, not hours, since I'd left London. By the time I'd reached my exit, I'd started to believe Swansea had somehow dragged itself further west along the M4. Now, with the heavens opening and a westerly gale sinking its teeth into the peninsula, I found myself lost on some Gower road I didn't know. Just the right time for hindsight, I thought, bitterly. I'd known all along that the reasons for staying away far outweighed those for coming here. But Richard Call and I had been friends once, and when he'd phoned me yesterday, I'd discovered, against all expectations, that I no longer hated him. He'd sounded broken and fearful, and his fragile attempt to reach out had been so unexpected, that I'd found myself agreeing to spend a few days with him. As I'd followed the motorway towards South Wales, passing towns and landscapes made insubstantial by rain, memories of the hurt he'd caused me began to override what dim recollections I had of what had bound us together.

By the time I'd reached Swansea, I was already regretting my impulsiveness and the foolish hope I couldn't yet recognise. Only when, unnerved by the hostility of the elements, I'd stopped the car to call Richard on my mobile and heard Maddy's voice on the answering machine, did I begin to understand. I left no message, not knowing whether he'd told her we'd talked. Things weren't good between them, he'd said. He needed to talk to someone who understood what he was going through. He'd understand if I refused, but he had no one else to turn to. I wondered how Maddy would react to seeing me. Would it be embarrassing or painful for her? Would she feel anything at all? After eight years of forgetting, I hoped I was strong enough to remain indifferent to her.

A couple of miles further on I ran out of road. The car hit a sheet of water and aquaplaned off to the right, finally coming to rest against a partially submerged rock. I hung on to the wheel, waiting for my heart to slow down. My flesh was cold and clammy as I rode out the panic. When it had passed, I reached for the Maglite I kept under the dash, lowered the window and shone the torch out over the expanse of wind-spited water. Swinging it to the right I saw a small lake had flooded out onto the road. The rock by my door was a marker stone, the words *Broad Pool* carved in a granite plaque. The water looked no more than a foot deep around the car. I turned the key and the engine caught. I eased forward till I felt the wheels find the edge of the submerged road, then drove up out of the water. The road climbed for another mile or two, then began to curve down towards the lights of a small village. Soon, I pulled up in front of an old hotel with half a dozen cars parked outside. Inside, I told the barman the name of the village I was looking for. He said I'd come too far out onto Gower. He drew a rough map on a beermat, showing the quickest route to Parkmill. I bought him a drink and a large scotch for myself. I sat in an alcove by the window, and called Richard's house again. This time I didn't even get the answering machine, just an endless, hollow ringing tone.

I sipped at the scotch, reluctant to go back outside. The bar was busy, the mood warm and cheerful. I thought about getting a room for the night, and wondered what had prompted Richard to call me out of the blue. It seemed odd that, after eight years, I was the one he would turn to for help. Did he assume that enough time had passed for me to have got over it, to adopt a philosophical attitude towards what he had done? Even if only partly true, his presumption pissed me off. Or maybe it was the journey that made me feel that way. Or maybe I was apprehensive about seeing Maddy, not knowing whether I could do so without feeling the old pain. The heat from the open fire in the bar began to seep into me as I watched raindrops race each other down the window. Beyond, the dark country seemed vast and empty, a cold, loveless world on which the sun rarely shone. The flames crackled and sparked and the jukebox played a song whose words I half-recognised. I caught sight of a woman sitting alone in the lounge. She was watching me, her gaze suggesting she knew who I was and why I was there. Her lips moved but there was too much noise in the bar for me to hear what she was saying. I waved, just as someone passed in front of me, blocking my view. By the time he'd passed, the woman was smiling and talking with someone else.

*

The house was set back off the main road, surrounded by wind-stripped trees on three sides. In the dim yellow light that leaked out from the front porch window, the stone building looked squat and ugly, scarred by time and inclement weather. I beeped my horn, cut the ignition and got out of the car. The front door opened and Richard Call appeared, different, diminished somehow, in a manner which had nothing to do with the passage of time. His coarsened features suggested a man abraded by something other than the normal stresses which hinder people's lives. He glanced over my shoulder, squinting, as if looking for something out in the night. For a few moments we stood there in awkward silence, then his features softened into recognition. He put a hand on my arm and welcomed me in a hesitant, nervous voice. In the porch he hung up my wet jacket and holdall. I had to stoop slightly beneath the low ceiling as I followed him through the hall to the living room, where a coal fire provided almost as much light as the single reading lamp that illuminated a few sheets of musical notation laying on a coffee table. A tape recorder sat next to the sheets of paper and an acoustic guitar rested against the side of an armchair.

Soon, I was sitting down with a glass of whiskey in my hand and Richard was shovelling coal on the dying fire. He was prevaricating, I thought, unsure how to begin telling me what he wanted to. Finally, after some unnecessary preamble about how neither of them had ever meant to hurt me, he told me that Maddy had gone. His eyes flitted restlessly around the room, as if trying to detect traces of her presence in the furniture, or in the books that lined the walls.

"She left you?" I said, not sure of the significance of the sudden quickening I felt in my heart.

His voice sounded crushed. "After a fight. I thought she just needed some space, that after a couple of days she'd come back. But it's been a week now."

He looked haunted. I felt sorry for him, but my pity rode on a more selfish emotion. "You should have called me sooner," I said. "I would have come."

"I was afraid you wouldn't. You had every right not to."

I told him to forget what had happened in the past, as if the choices we'd made back then were aberrations that had no bearing on who we'd become. What mattered, I said, was what was happening right now. Did he know where she was, I asked. Had she given some inkling? Had he seen this coming?

He slumped back in his chair and spoke hesitantly, as if trying to make sense of his feelings before articulating them. Staring blankly at the fire, his voice, initially, was little more than a murmur, but as he went on he became more animated, almost to the point of elation. I put it down to shock. Things had been tough between them for two, maybe three years. He wasn't great at reading signs. He'd been unable to distinguish between what he called 'the usual rows' that had always punctuated their relationship, and the more profound disagreements which had led, he supposed, to her gradual estrangement. She'd loved it, he said, when he'd first brought her here. The house, Gower, the university where, as undergraduates, Richard and I had first become friends. She'd got a grant to continue her thesis on American gothic literature, with the possibility of a lecturing position in the American studies department. He, meanwhile, was making a sporadic income writing jingles for TV ads, and had composed the music for a couple of daytime talkshows. He'd supplemented this through guitar tuition, while focusing the greater part of his efforts on writing the songs which he hoped would make his reputation.

Maddy had settled down quickly and made new friends. She'd completed her Phd and got the lecturing job. At the same time, Richard's career had stalled. Record companies, producers, promoters and music publishers seemed indifferent to his songs and even the ad jingle work began to dry up. He'd started playing in a band, doing cover versions of pop from the seventies and eighties, anything from Springsteen to Status Quo. The songs he played meant nothing to him.

He'd begun to feel programmed, a machine for churning out ersatz emotions. He worried about losing sight of his own aspirations. Trying to find some sense of direction in his life, he'd suggested they start a family. This was just over a year ago, he said. Maddy had seemed doubtful, said she didn't think it was the right time. Money was tight. She said it was a big commitment and she was worried about his state of mind. She thought he was depressed. Their rows became more frequent, but still, he hadn't thought they were serious. He'd be a good father, he'd told her. She wouldn't have to give up her job. He would cope. But nothing he'd said had changed her mind. I found it hard to reconcile the broken man who sat across from me with the one who, eight years ago, had stolen the woman I'd loved. For a long time I'd believed that he could never really love her, that the only person Richard Call could truly love was himself. And yet, listening to him talk in that dimly lit room, the fractured cadences of his voice as he spoke of her, I didn't doubt that he was hurting deeply.

"I made a mistake," he told me, the fire's red shadows dancing in his eyes. "I want her back."

"You heard from her at all since she went?" I tried to sound hopeful on his behalf.

He shook his head. "Nothing. She never gave any indication. Then she was gone."

"What about work – have you called them?"

He shook his head. "No," he said. "I mean, I called, but she's not there. She told them she needed to take some time off."

"Where would she go?" I imagined her sitting alone in some hotel, thinking about the past, what she had thrown away. Hurting, but still too proud to call me. Maybe she'd already tried.

Richard's voice brought me back to myself. "Where would she go?" he echoed, as if stunned by her absence. "This is her home."

After a minute or two of strained silence, in which the intermittent crack and hiss of the weakening fire became near intolerable, I asked him if he thought there had been anyone else.

He shook his head. "It doesn't happen that way to everyone. She'd never do that to me."

I asked him how he could be so sure.

He got up and beckoned me to the window. I stood a few feet behind

Mike O'Driscoll

him, watching him stare at his own face in the glass. "Out there," he said, gesturing into the empty night, "everything's unfocussed, out of control. In here, in this house, everything is certain. I know what to expect."

He fell silent, staring at his own reflection, or maybe it was my face just beyond his, the tension there, between the concern I was willing to show and something I didn't want him to see. Something I was unable or unwilling yet to acknowledge. "It's late," I said. "I'm done in."

"Yes, of course you are." Putting an arm around my shoulder he repeated how glad he was I had come. He led me upstairs to the spare room, apologising for its smallness and the junk which cluttered the floor. He pushed books, magazines and CDs off the bed, said he hoped the house wouldn't stir up old hurts, that I could find the kind of peace here that Maddy had found.

Alone, I wondered what kind of peace it had been that had driven her away. As I undressed, I tried to identify my emotions, troubled by the failure of my own indifference. Had Richard sensed what I was feeling? As I climbed into the bed I noticed a small framed picture on the bedside table. Curious, I turned it towards the light. It was a photograph of Maddy, one I'd taken about nine years ago, when she had been twenty, before Richard took her from me. Long black hair tumbled down her shoulders and her grey, restless eyes stared out of the frame to the right. She'd always felt she looked trapped in the picture, and though I'd never seen it that way before, now I understood what she'd meant. I wondered if even then she'd been looking for a way to escape. Maybe that was why she'd kept it, to remind her that she could do it.

The first year after she'd gone had been the hardest. Finding the discipline to retrain my thoughts, to bury the emotions which I associated with the memory of her crooked smile, the allure of her grey eyes, the honeyed promise of her voice. For seven years I had pushed those memories aside, and yet now I couldn't get her out of my head. As much as Richard had instigated my coming here, I realised my subsequent actions had, in part, been determined by the ghost of her memory. Last night I'd played the two Gram Parsons CDs she'd given me, two albums I hadn't listened to in years. His voice had sounded disconnected, tied to no place or time. Maybe that had been the point. At work today, twice I mistook people's voices on the phone for hers

78

and had been unable to speak. At Leigh Delamere Services off the motorway, I'd watched a woman crying at the next table, and for a brief moment I'd thought she was Maddy. It wasn't the way she looked or her tears, so much as the isolation she conveyed, like she'd arrived at some place she didn't want to be and didn't know how to leave.

In the darkness after I'd switched off the light, the wind moaning through the trees had kept me awake. Now and again a more powerful gust would cause the house to creak and groan and I'd imagine Maddy laying in the next room, listening to the same sounds and hearing in them an echo of her own discontent. Thinking of the picture, I wondered why she'd chosen Richard, and if, after all this time she'd realised her mistake. Later, I'd got out of bed, my head so full of her it seemed impossible she hadn't been there for so long. I flicked on the bedside lamp and went to the window. Outside, the storm had all but blown itself out. Ragged clouds pulled apart from each other, showing a half moon sailing over Cefn Bryn. There were CDs and books at my feet. I crouched, seeing Leidall's *Gulf of Darkness* next to a copy of Lance Canning's *Crazy Love*. I was sure I had read them once, though I could remember nothing other than their titles. I found a photo album among the books and looked through the first few pages. Here were Maddy and Richard laughing in some bar as they raised their glasses towards the camera. And here they were on a mountain, she standing in front of him, with his arms wrapped round her waist. Holidays, birthdays, Christmases, and always him in your place. You felt the hurt growing inside, a knot of anger and resentment that made you skip forward, not wanting to subject yourself to their happiness. And then other pictures slipped from the album. You picked them up intending to put them back, but the top one caught your eye, a picture of Maddy laying on a bed, the bed behind you, laying on her stomach in black underwear, propped up on her elbows so her pale, ripe breasts were half-exposed, her face staring directly at the camera, smiling an unfamiliar come-on smile. Despite yourself you looked at the remaining pictures, private images not meant for your gaze, but once you started you couldn't stop yourself.

Here she was in suspender and stockings, straddling a high back chair. In the next, she was gazing over her shoulder at the camera. Your mouth dried up and your breathing shallowed. Your cock hardened as

Mike O'Driscoll

you lingered over the images, seeing Maddy as you hadn't seen her in eight, nine years. As you'd never seen her, in fact, because she'd never displayed herself this way for you. You were appalled that she did this for Richard, and yet excited too, to discover this other side of her, this secret, unknown Maddy. Here, laying on her back, legs raised in the air, thumbs hitched into the waistband of her panties as if she was about to remove them; and here, on her side, head on the pillow, eyes closed, one arm draped across her stomach, as if asleep, one shadowed breast unconsciously revealed.

*

I laid in a pool of drowsy contentment, watching her as she stood by the window in the weak morning light. She seemed intent on something outside, her head turning slowly as if following some movement. Or maybe it was the whispering of the breeze through the naked trees that had caught her attention, some eagerness to discover their secrets. As her body turned, dustmotes danced in the shift she wore, seeming to slide through the flimsy garment, into her flesh. Sunlight streamed through her and as I watched she began to dissolve. A tender yearning immobilised me, stopped me from calling her name. In less than a minute, only the dustmotes filled the space where she had been.

Richard was strumming his guitar in the living room, eyes closed as he repeated the same sequence of minor chords. He'd made an effort to tidy himself up, but it had been superficial. Clean-shaven, he looked more gaunt, more afflicted by malaise than he had last night. He seemed oblivious to my presence, so caught up was he in the tune he was trying to put together. Every now and again he would start to sing, voice too soft for his words to be clearly heard. Then he'd stop, wait a moment or two, and start again, this time with some slight variation, as if trying out different combinations of words. All the time he kept strumming and I found myself caught in the music's spell, unable or unwilling to disrupt his magic. I lost track of how long I stood there listening, and it was only when he spoke that I became aware that he'd stopped playing.

"I can't get it right," he said. I told him the tune was beautiful but he seemed unconvinced. "It's the words – they don't make sense to me."

"Let me see."

He looked puzzled. "They're not written down. You have to hear

80

them." He began strumming again, but I interrupted him.

"Look, Richard," I said. "I know this must be hard for you, but don't you think you should trying to get in touch with Maddy?"

He put the guitar down and told me he had already tried. She wasn't with any of their friends, he said. He'd spoken to them all. He'd called her father in Manchester, but the old man hadn't heard from her in a while. "It's not why I asked you to come here," he said. "What I need is for you to understand. To be here and help me get through this. You did, after all. You know what it feels like. Just stay until I'm strong again, a couple of days, Jim, that's all I'm asking."

His anxiety was palpable, but I still wasn't sure what he expected me to do. Sit around the house waiting for a call that probably wouldn't come? The thought of it drove me crazy. "All right," I said, reluctantly. "But let's get out for a while. It will do you good."

He shrank back into his chair. "No, no. Not a good idea."

"Why not?"

"I'm not up to it. I don't have the strength." He picked up his guitar again, as if it gave him a valid reason for staying in the house. "What if she calls? You go. Go to the places she loved, see if you can find what drew her to them. I ... I never could."

I told him not to worry, that I'd find my own way. He nodded, then became absorbed in his guitar once again. I left him alone. The day was cold but clear, just a few grey clouds drifting out over the sea as I headed west. I needed to be away from the house for a few hours, give myself some space to think. Earlier, I had felt calm, in control, but now I was anxious, troubled by vague doubts that refused to coalesce into something concrete. I felt as if Richard's state of mind was affecting my own, his instability rubbing off on me. If he was like this all the time, it was no wonder she had left. I wondered if it was something more fundamental than her leaving that was troubling him. Some kind of identity crisis, a loss of confidence about what he was doing with his life. Maybe he had been falling apart long before she walked out on him.

I ran out of road at a village called Rhossili. I parked the car and walked along cliffs that loomed one hundred feet above the blue-grey sea, thinking about Maddy and the photographs I'd got all excited over last night. I had forgotten them, but now, as I pictured her in those poses, I felt a churning desire, a compulsive need to be with her. What if she had tried to call me? If he would do it, why not her? I tried calling my home but I couldn't get a signal. Seagulls trailed a small fishing boat out in the bay, their cries carrying across the water, reminders of a fleeting presence. Did Richard know about the album? Had he left it in the room? Not intentionally, I thought, though given how messed up he was, anything was possible. I found it strange that I hadn't remembered the pictures when I'd woke. I figured I'd dreamt the album up, the whole thing prompted by a sublimated desire for Maddy. I wanted to talk to her, find out if she still felt anything for me.

I stopped in a bar on the way back to the house. It seemed familiar, like some place I had been with Richard, though I couldn't swear to it. I sat at the counter and nursed a pint of Guinness, feeling restless, troubled by snatches of memory that seemed unconnected to my past. Reality had become less knowable, I thought. If I kept thinking this way I'd be right back where I was eight years ago. I couldn't go through that again, I told myself, but it felt more like a question.

It was dusk when I got back to the house. Richard was slumped in the same chair in the living room, his eyes frayed with exhaustion, the tips of his fingers bloody from chopping at the guitar strings. He barely moved when I entered, just muttered something that sounded like, 'Home is the hurt.'

"Are you okay?" I said. "You should try to get some sleep."

"Can't hear it then," he said, his voice a blistered sound.

I was half-drunk and tired of his self-indulgence. "You think a song will bring her back?"

He leaned forward, wiping his fingers on his jeans. "Maybe it will."

"Does she have a reason to?"

"No – she took everything, except, maybe some small sign."

"What kind of sign?"

"Could be anything," he said. "She'd want me to work for it. Hurt a little. But it'll be somewhere I can find it."

"How can you be sure you haven't already found it?"

He shrugged and a raw, hungry smile broke across his face. "Because I'm not hurting enough."

I went upstairs to shower. Afterwards, I knelt on the floor of my room, searching through all the junk for the photo album. Many of the books I recognised from the time Richard and I had been friends. We'd been compulsive readers, our tastes ranging from pulp to the esoteric, the more unfamiliar the writer the better. We used to swap old paperbacks, and though, over the years, I'd either lost or given away most of them, Richard, evidently, had hung on to his. I smiled at the tacky cover of Abendsen's *The Grasshopper Lies Heavy*, a ragged stars and stripes flying over the ruins of Berlin. Next to it was Rufus Griswold's only novel, *Julius Rodman*, which I'd read at Richard's insistence and about which I could remember nothing. I found the album under a guitar magazine. Nervously, I skimmed through it, seeing the same mundane snapshots of the two of them playing happy family. The last few pages were empty, their cellophane covers untouched. There hadn't been any more pictures. Confused, I worked my way back to the front of the album, making sure I hadn't missed anything. I felt disappointed, a little dirty and ashamed at having let my suppressed desires run riot in my head. I wondered why she'd left it here, if it wasn't in fact the sign that Richard was afraid to look for, the one that would hurt too much. I hid it under the mattress and went downstairs.

Over microwaved pizzas, I tried to sound Richard out about his plans but he seemed disinclined to discuss the future. He picked at his food, eating less than one slice. Afterwards, he poured a couple of glasses of J&B, and gradually seemed to overcome his anxiety enough to want to talk. He spoke about things we had done and people we had known as if they were the stuff of yesterday rather than ten or twelve years back. I felt disoriented, finding it hard to place myself in his recollections. Some of the incidents he described would sound familiar at first, then he'd wrongfoot me by resolving them in ways which didn't accord with my memories. I felt disconnected from my own past, as if the Jim James he remembered wasn't me at all. Despite his mental instability, it occured to me that these distortions might not be unconscious, that maybe they were deliberate, that they were meant to hurt.

Seeking more solid ground I dug around in my head for the truth. Richard and I had become friends here in Swansea and after we'd graduated, we'd shared a flat in London for two years. Things had got awkward when I'd started seeing Maddy. Almost from the start they were suspicious and even hostile to each other. She thought he was arrogant and controlling, and I guess he resented what he saw as her intrusion into our friendship. It got to the stage where she refused to spend the night at our flat so as to avoid having to meet him. A year after we started seeing each other, I'd found a one-bedroom flat in Wood Green. Richard was hurt, but did his best to hide it, even helping me move my stuff. When I took Maddy there the first time and asked her to move in with me, she'd refused. She wasn't ready to make that kind of commitment just yet. She swore she loved me, but she wanted her own space. Give it time, she'd said. Let the relationship grow. Fourteen months later, she moved to Swansea with Richard.

Richard was leaning forward in his chair, as if waiting for me to speak. Seeing that my mind had drifted, he repeated himself, asking if I'd suspected what was happening between them, before she'd told me she was leaving. My mind was dulled, my thoughts sluggish. Maybe it was the scotch or fatigue, but I found it impossible to say what I'd thought or felt back then, whether I'd had some inkling that I was losing her, or whether I'd remained in a state of blind, lovestruck ignorance.

"If you had known," Richard was saying, "what would you have done?"

"I don't know," I said. "What do you want me to say? That I would have tried to stop her? That I would have fought you for her? Some fucking romantic gesture like that? Isn't that why she lied to me for five months, to wear me down, make me too helpless to stop her."

"That was me," he said. "I was afraid you'd hurt her. I'm sorry. I know now how you felt."

Anger surged up inside me. How could he possibly know what it had felt like? How could he equate her leaving him with what they had done to me? He went on talking, making assumptions about my feelings and how I must have struggled to carry on with my life. I guess he was articulating his own fears, trying to chart a way through the ocean of emptiness that had opened up before him. I would have been happy then, to see him drown in it.

Soon afterwards, I left him and went to bed. He couldn't sleep anymore, hadn't slept at all since she'd disappeared, he told me. He was afraid he might miss something, a call, or maybe the sign she'd left for him. I laid awake, hearing him downstairs, strumming that same mournful tune, and through the chords, a stifled sobbing. His hurt gladdened me. Men like Richard don't expect pain in their lives. Their plans are rarely thwarted. Sorrow and regret remain strangers to them. Whatever bond we might have shared existed no longer, and I'd been a fool to think I could resurrect it. It wasn't for his sake at all that I had come here. Although he hadn't told me about Maddy on the phone, about her leaving him, somehow I had known. The minute I heard his voice on the phone, I'd sensed something had gone wrong. My head was clogged with thoughts of her, with memories that came crawling up from the hole I'd dug for them. I felt feverish, full of anticipation and desire. It was possible that I was deluding myself, but I doubted it. You knew, I told myself. Soon as you heard his voice, you knew she was gone. But what caused you to make that assumption? Her betrayal? Or was it something else, the possibility that she'd seen something in Richard which you'd only guessed at? Did that even matter now?

*

Sleep came reluctantly, and when it did it was fitful and brief. I woke in the early hours, mouth dry and raspy from scotch. I went to the bathroom, took a piss, and drank water from the tap. I could hear Richard downstairs, still playing his guitar, still struggling to articulate his hurt. I stood on the landing a while, listening, trying and failing to piece the words together. It didn't matter. The voice itself was one of surpassing beauty, one I could have listened to all night had it not ceased abruptly, as if suddenly aware of an unseen audience. Having no wish to speak to him then, I returned to my room. As I got back into bed, I felt something between the sheets. It was the photo album. I didn't recall taking it out from under the mattress earlier in the night. Confused, I opened it up and began leafing through the pages, the pictures made monotone in the silver moonlight. Maddy blowing out the candles on a cake. You counted twenty-five. Her and Richard in Trafalgar Square, feeding the pigeons, being tourists. Richard playing his guitar by a campfire, like some fucking gypsy troubadour. Her head on his shoulder, maybe passing on the sweet nothings you had whispered in her ear. These were the moments you could have had. You snapped the album shut, not wanting to see anymore. Everything passed you by. No holidays with Maddy, no Christmases together, no laughing at each other's funny little ways, no soulmates, no tender intimacy. An empty album.

Mike O'Driscoll

You opened it again, saw them with their new child. Maddy looking
exhausted but blissful after the experience of giving birth, Richard like
an overgrown kid with a new toy. The coming home pictures. The
baby's first Christmas, opening the presents, all the happiness that could
have been yours. Not the things you wanted to see. Not like those you
found at the back, pictures of her as you wanted her to be. Looking right
at you. The glint in her eyes that said she knew damn well you were
watching her, waiting for her to do things. So here she was sitting naked
on the edge of the bed, leaning back even as she reached one arm
towards you. Come to me, she's saying. And in the next one, laying
back, shoulders pressed into the mattress and her hips arched into the air
as she touched herself between the legs. And then fingers splaying her
labia, letting you see it all. Inviting. Opening herself up, telling you how
much she needed you. Saying do things. And so you did.

*

I was surprised to find myself alone in the house. Richard's absence
struck me as peculiar, but after last night I was grateful for it. I needed
to gather my thoughts, figure out how to find Maddy and tell her how I
felt. Even though he'd said he knew she wasn't coming back, I wasn't
convinced he really believed that. It had taken me a year to get over her
and, as I now realised, I'd been kidding myself. Richard would be
clinging to the same kind of stupid hope, and though he deserved
whatever pain was coming his way, it would be better for me if I could
help him come to terms with her leaving. These were the thoughts with
which I tried to justify my intentions. Phrases like 'it's for the best',
'you should think about moving on' and 'it gets easier in time,' echoed
uselessly in my head. I tried to drown them out with black coffee, but
nothing could disguise the fact that I was going to do to him what he had
done to me.

I tried to think of people I should call. The university, check to see
if she'd returned to work. Her dad. Her closest friend, Elizabeth, whose
surname I couldn't recall or if she still lived in London. What was
Maddy's father's name? Had I buried her so deeply that I'd lost all
memory of these things? For ten minutes I sat there, searching through
an empty past, trying to retrieve faces and identities. Mr and Mrs
Something Call. No. That was Richard's name. Maddy's maiden name

was...? My throat was dry, the skin on the back of my neck tingling. This was crazy. I was trying too hard. Maddy fucking what? Not James. Not Mrs Jim James. That had never happened. My body felt constrained, wrapped in some unyielding, suffocating fabric. I had to stop thinking about this for a while, get my thoughts focused on something else.

In the living room I browsed through the bookshelves, hoping that the sight of a familiar title might jog my memory. I recognised works by Ballard and Ellison and wondered what books had taken their place on my own shelves? I couldn't remember, couldn't name any book I had read in the last few years. It was as if my life had been put on hold, suspended while I drifted for a number of years in some in-between place, only half-existing. Perhaps it had been that way since Maddy had left me. Maybe this was why my life over the last eight years seemed so transient, so purposeless. It had no meaning without her. I glanced at a book of poems by Miles Coverdale and next to it the same copy of Barry Littlejohn's *The Worm of Midnight* I had given to Richard all those years ago. We used to compete with each other to discover obscure books, works on the Inquisition or witchcraft by men like Nicholas Eymeric and Henri Boguet, and I was surprised to find them still on his shelves. Some I could barely remember, works by Adeodato Lampustri, Ibn Schabao, Karswell and Roland Franklyn. I picked up an old paperback of Eric Keplard's *Maternal Intrusions*, its pages brittle and browning like dead leaves. We'd spent days talking about it and yet now all I remembered was its emptiness. I found my signature on the title page of Les Steiner's *Eye Teeth*, and beneath it a reminder to myself to check out more of his works. I never had. I was skimming through Frances Osgood's *The Fall and other Poems* when my restless gaze caught sight of something that prompted a frisson of unease. I reached up to the top shelf and pulled down a slim black volume by Poe, *Toady, and Other Tales*. The dust jacket was gone but I was pretty sure it was the same copy I'd found in the rank basement of a second-hand bookstore down in West Wales. Yellow fungus had colonised the walls, and some of the books down there all but disintegrated when I'd tried to pick them up. But the Poe had somehow resisted the damp and rot that had done for the other volumes with which it had shared a wooden crate. I hadn't read it since that first time, but I remembered the title story as an odd, disturbing tale of friendship and betrayal. Even though I was hazy on

Mike O'Driscoll

the details, the memory of its significance unsettled me. Was it possible that I'd perceived something of Richard and myself in the relationship of the two central characters? I dismissed the notion as the work of my agitated imagination.

Nevertheless, I couldn't resist turning to the title story and reading the first page or two. Something to help time crawl by a little faster. As I read my sense of unease grew deeper. The air seemed stale and thick with decay. My eyes were dry and irritable and the room appeared smaller, crammed with too much useless junk. The exterior wall was so thick that the daylight that fell on the two low-set windows seemed to have diminished by the time it touched the floor. I read another page, thinking vaguely about the people I had to call. The grey floorboards were mottled with knots that looked like bruises on worn skin. Richard's guitar had been infected, its front panel mildewed, the frets rusting. There were damp stains like lost continents on the ochre ceiling. They drew towards each other, pulling the ceiling in on itself. What use is another man's soul to anyone? I felt lightheaded and weak. I wished Maddy were here so I could start living again. I ground my fists into my eyes and gulped down a mouthful of musty, desolate air. I forced myself up from the armchair and staggered towards the kitchen. The room had shrunk, the floorspace barely wide enough for me to pass. I lurched through it somehow, reached the porch and barged out into the yard where I fell on the cold, hard ground.

It took a few minutes for my head to clear, and when it did I laid there, shivering and fearful with no concrete idea of what had scared me. The feeling lingered, an aftertaste of dread, even as I rationalised that it was a combination of my reaction to Richard's hysteria, and the surfacing of my repressed longing for Maddy. I sat staring at the house, seeing something poised in its old stone walls, a sense of waiting, of holding its breath. Then the moment passed and it was just an ordinary cottage again. I stood up and dusted myself down, determined to speak to someone who could tell me where Maddy was.

I searched for a contact book by the phone in the hall. Nothing. I checked the kitchen and the living room, then went upstairs and rummaged through the junk in my room. I hesitated outside Richard's bedroom, feeling I had no right to enter. Even as I opened the door I knew this had less to do with the possibility of finding a number, than

88

with a transgressive desire to see the place where Maddy slept. The curtains were open and sunlight spilled into the room. The bed was unmade but looked as if it hadn't been slept in for a while. There was a Toni Morrison book on a bedside table. I picked it up, saw that it was annotated halfway through in Maddy's handwriting. The remaining pages were pristine, unread. Why would she leave it here, I wondered, unfinished? A dressing table stood against the wall next to the window. It was cluttered with jars and small bottles. I sprayed perfume on my wrist, imagining it would draw me closer to her. Loneliness and regret fogged my brain. I opened the top drawer and removed a pair of her panties, feeling a stab of hurt deep in my gut. Among the other items of underwear was an opened pack of tampons. In the next drawer were her t-shirts, a swimming costume, two baseball hats. My eyes watered as I touched these things, held them to my face, smelled her on them. Six years without breathing her scent, without the taste of her skin, her lips, her tongue. This was a kind of compensation.

Her clothes still hung in the wardrobe, a mix of casual and more formal wear, and half a dozen pairs of shoes were neatly stacked on the bottom shelf. I lifted out a sleeveless black dress and tried to picture her in it, tried to imagine how it would have clung to her body. I thought too of the flesh beneath the skirt, the way she had revealed herself in those pictures, whether I had dreamed them or if they really existed. It seemed strange to me that her leaving had been so sudden. The Maddy I remembered had always been so deliberate, so focused on the details. Maybe it boded well for me that she had left him so abruptly. It indicated finality. She would need someone even so, a shoulder to cry on. Someone who understood that need.

I took the dress to the bed and sat down, feeling enervated, unable to think clearly. I needed to work out what I would tell Richard when I left. Maddy's smell was on the blankets and the pillow. I stretched out on the bed, wanting to sink into her residue. I grew aroused, thinking about her, imagining her thoughts, her drowsy desire, the way she touched herself, ran a hand over her breasts, squeezed one nipple. The other hand sliding down between her legs, through the tangle of pubic hair, one finger parting the gently swollen lips and slipping inside her own moist heat. Feeling what she was feeling, thinking what she was thinking. The sound of her voice, the texture of her thoughts in my head.

Mike O'Driscoll

*

Richard was there when I woke, seated in the cane armchair by the window. In my semiconscious state, I didn't really register his presence at first, not until he spoke, and then it was as if a sudden frost had iced my skin. "I cannot see," he said, "how my life has become so intolerable. This is not how it was meant to be."

"Jesus, Richard," I said, groggily. "What are you doing?"

"I paid attention. At least, as much as I could. But there are always demands, yes? Demands on time, spirit and flesh." He sounded as if he was struggling to comprehend something other than Maddy's leaving. "You understand how it is – meeting her needs. In time a routine develops and you both adhere to it. It means you can anticipate, plan ahead. Trouble is, you kid yourself you've thought everything through, and you let your guard down. And the second you do that, the second you look the other way, that's when she's gone."

His manner unsettled me. It seemed as if he was trying to account for something, something I couldn't bring myself to think about, not yet. "You were out," I said, awkwardly. "I was looking for a number."

"No matter." He stood up and left the room. I followed a few second later, wondering how long he had been watching me. What had been going through his head? Why had he lied about her taking her things?

Downstairs, I found him slumped in his armchair, whisky glass cradled on his lap. The only light in the room was the flickering glow from the fire in the grate. He looked up at me, a half-smile on his face. In a conspiratorial tone, he told me that over the last few months, he'd come to suspect she was seeing somebody else.

I saw Maddy in my head again, on the bed upstairs, alone and waiting. Someone else? That couldn't be, I thought. I'd dreamed them. Doubts assailed me. I felt weak, betrayed all over again. I tried to keep my voice impassive as I told Richard I didn't think Maddy would do that.

"No?" he said, satirically. "Wouldn't have it in her?"

A knot of tension tightened in my stomach. "I don't know."

"Sure you do."

"You're not thinking straight."

He drained his glass. "Is that what I should be doing? Would that

90

make things right?"

Shadows hung from the bookshelves like patient predators. The fire in the grate was all colour and no heat. The breath from my lips misted in front of my face. Richard was trying to tell me something I didn't want to hear. I felt powerless to stop him.

"Was it reason brought you here?" he said, a hard edge to his voice. "Did the rational man think she'd want to fuck him after eight years?"

"I came here to help you." The words tasted like ash in my mouth. "I came because you were my friend."

"I screwed you, Jim. Took Maddy from you. You didn't deserve that. Any reasonable man would say that was the case. But you know, I gave up on reason a long time ago." He got up out of his seat and stood in front of the fire. "You should know that Maddy finally came round to my way of thinking. I think in the end, it sustained her." He turned his back to me and crouched down.

He hasn't said it, I thought. As long as he didn't, then it wouldn't be so. I stepped towards him, still thinking I could reach him, make him understand. "I know what you're going through," I said, crouching beside him. "I've been there."

"Yes, you have." He picked up a log to put on the fire. "I can smell her on you," he said as he swung the piece of wood against my head.

*

Motion lulled me, kept me cocooned from all kinds of hurt. The sound of an engine was oddly reassuring, and even the voices I could hear didn't bother me. They were not my concern. I knew, in a disinterested way, that the cord binding my wrists together and the dull, throbbing pain in my head, should have worried me, but I knew that as long as they kept talking and I kept my eyes shut, everything would be fine. Gradually, I was able to differentiate between sounds, distinguish between two separate voices, both of them familiar. This is really hard for me, Richard, Maddy was saying. There is no easy way to say it. A click, followed by a pause, then I heard Richard's voice, clearer, more present somehow. "Well, you said it anyway. No matter how hard it was." Maddy was saying she had never wanted to hurt him. "But you did," Richard said. Maddy said she hoped he'd understand. Another click, and then, much sharper, Richard said, "I do." My eyes flickered, closed again, and slowly began to let the world in. Maddy was speaking again, an absence in her voice, like she was leaving a message on an answering machine. "You stopped speaking to me," Richard said. "You stopped before I could get it right in my head."

"Richard," I said, pushing myself up in the passenger seat. "What have you done?"

He reached over and brushed my face with the tips of his fingers. It felt like the caress of a phantom limb. He gestured at the road ahead. Through the windscreeen the night was featureless, the headlights illuminating only miles and miles of emptiness. And then they shone on something I recognised and all my transient invulnerability was swept away. Before I could say another word he braked hard and my head smacked into the dashboard. Maybe I passed out, I don't know. I was groaning and there was blood in my eyes. After a moment or two I felt him dabbing at my face with a piece of cloth, wiping the blood away. Thirty yards ahead and to his right, the headlights picked out the edge of the lake, dark water lapping at the side of the road.

"What's going on, Richard?" I said, barely able to speak. Pain crowded my head, muting everything but the fear.

"I discovered the sign." His voice was tense, as if he was trying to contain himself. "She came clean, told me everything."

"My hands." I held them towards him. "Take it off."

He shrugged, leaned close to me. "You know how to tell the difference between what people say and what they really mean? Listen to what they don't say. That's where the meaning is."

Blood trickled into my right eye. I tried to blink it away. "I don't understand," I said.

He nodded, turned the rear-view mirror towards me. "Don't tell me you can't see it staring back at you – that need for her. It *is* what you don't say."

"You're right," I said, forcing the words out. "I still feel something for her. But that doesn't matter. I'm saying you should let her make her own choice."

He looked puzzled for a moment, then he nodded, as if everything had fallen suddenly into place. "She already chose."

"Yes, but – "

"She spoke to me," he said, cutting me off. He dropped one hand to the gear stick, shifting it into first. "Took a while to understand what she was trying to say." The car began to move forward. "I couldn't get it right. I said to you, something wasn't right. But since you came, her words have become clearer."

"Richard," I said, glancing towards the lake. "What are you doing?"

"Words were always a problem," he went on. "The music was easy. The stronger the hurt, the easier it came. Beautiful, but not right. Lacking, you know? A discordant melody, she called it. And then you came and I began to hear them, the words tangled in the tune."

The car moved closer to the water. "Tell me what you did, Richard. Please."

He sighed, as if wearying of some tiresome business. "She called you here," he said. "She wanted you to hear the song too. She wanted you to listen to the echoes, to watch the shapes dance, to see the hurt coming. I didn't realise, not until near the end, when we kissed, and we laughed, and smiled no more."

The car lurched forward as he pressed down on the accelerator. I threw myself across him, trying to pull on the handbrake. But it was already too late. The car rolled into the lake, its momentum carrying it forward over the soft mud and out into the deeper water. We grappled each other, but it was only when the car was half full of icy water that I realised he wasn't struggling at all. I pulled away and saw his face, his eyes gazing out into the swirling blackness, as if searching for something. I raised my hands to my mouth and chewed at the cord binding them. It was no good, there wasn't enough time. The water was almost to my chin as the car sank towards the bottom of the lake. I reached for the door handle, trying to force it open. Water bubbled at my lips as I screamed at Richard to help but he just sat there, hands still on the wheel, peering intently out at where the headlights shone diffusely through the brown murk.

The water covered my head and as the car settled at the bottom of the lake I finally managed to open the door. I pulled myself out, then turned to help him. But he leaned across and pulled the door shut. He sat back and opened his arms, smiling, as if to embrace someone. I kicked against the bonnet and rose up to the surface. I half-swam, half-scrambled to the shallow water then dragged myself up out of the mud and onto the sodden bank. I laid there struggling to breathe. When I was

Mike O'Driscoll

able, I crawled further up the bank and sat there, staring at the lake. Beneath the still water I could make out the lights of the car. I tried not to think about Richard, down there, the significance of his smile, or his welcoming embrace. Then the light died in the water and I got up, wondering if the hurt was real enough to guide me home.

That Obscure Object of Desire

When you've been doing Léger for a while, people begin to assume a degree of plasticity. Like those amorphous creatures with Louise Brooks haircuts who blurred the distinction between art and reality as they floated through the Gallerie du Jardin. But I refused to let these minor hallucinations ruin the carefully structured ambience. Already five pieces had been sold. A bloated naked Barbie floated past, her puckered lips kissing the air. Or maybe it was the woman from *Supper II*, fallen from her place at the head of the table. A male doll in herringbone shook my hand fiercely. "You've done it this time, Haz," he said. I recognised him as the critic from the *Art de Morte*. "These are incredible, the best Léger's I've seen in years."

Before I could respond he'd moved on, leaving me stranded and wineless among the gathering of the real and imaginary. I simmered awhile in the brew of their approbation, osmotically touched by their impeccable taste. Lucy from the *Guardian* flashed me a smile and offered me a glass of fine white burgundy. "They have an oriental quality, Haz," she said, admiringly. "It's as if you've put something of yourself into the paint." I felt vindicated, almost holy.

"This stuff is shit." A voice harsh and cracked and old. It turned Lucy's smile to dust. An old man was cutting a swathe through the crowd, heading my way. I drained my glass and scanned the room for security, or at least for Allen, the gallery owner, but saw only Léger faces, round and white and vacant. I had to deal with this situation alone. The old man wore the signs of age – thin white hair, lines etched

Mike O'Driscoll

deep into his face, the smell of decay – like some badge of honour.

I set my mouth firmly and said, "Is there a problem?"

He jabbed a dirty-nailed finger against my chest. "You're bloody right there is." People fell away from him like an ebbing tide. "It's you, you and this whole stinking charade."

I smiled weakly, my insides churning. "I don't remember seeing your name on the guest list."

"You don't remember because you don't know who I am, none of you do."

"This is a private viewing," I said, feeling I was on firmer ground.

He poked me in the chest again so I tried to reason with him.

"You've obviously made a mistake. This is an art gallery."

"There's no art in here. Just crap and recycled crap at that."

I smiled as if he'd made some esoteric joke and lost the smile when I noticed people slipping out the door into Neal Street. Others were drifting towards the rear of the gallery, in search of escape. "Wait," I called out. "The exhibition's – "

"You wouldn't know a work of art if it crapped on you," he said. "None of these poseurs would. Léger's dead. Been dead nearly seventy years."

I stepped towards the old bastard and tried to grab him but he shook me off with his wiry arms, then crouched into a boxer's stance and hit me in the jaw. I laid on the floor and watched the gallery empty, knowing I was ruined.

Someone finally helped me stand. It was Allen. He muttered something about the old man.

"I don't understand, Allen. Why me?" I said. "What have I ever done to that old bastard?"

He shrugged and said, "I guess that's it for today."

I brushed myself down, hoping to shift the hurt and humiliation. It didn't work. It didn't work because I saw no 'sold' notices where they had previously been. "Allen," I said, pointing to their absence. "What does that mean?"

He looked embarrassed. "Someone spoke out, Haz."

"A lunatic," I said, my voice shrill.

"He made a value judgement," he said, offering me a pitying look. "What can I say? People take account of these things."

96

"Assholes," I said and left the gallery.

I went into the nearest bar and ordered a large vodka. On my fourth refill, I noticed the guy alongside me. He sat perfectly still, hands on the counter, eyes closed and a look of rapt concentration on his face. His shallow breathing was the only visible sign of life. I thought maybe he was having some kind of stroke and felt a sudden panic crawl up into my throat. I was about to call for help when he opened his eyes and smiled and I recognised the old man who'd ruined my show.

He spread his arms out over the counter and gestured at the space in front of him, which was filled with nothing at all. "What do you think?" he said.

"What do you want?" I said.

"Well?"

"*Well?* What do you mean *well?*"

He lit a cigarette and said, "Don't be so uptight."

"I don't understand – you just ruined four months of hard work."

"It wasn't personal, just you happened to be there."

"Nothing personal? Of course it was personal, you singled me out."

"You were the one calling yourself an artist."

I drained my glass, defeated. "Why? That's all I want to know."

"Tell me what you think of it first."

"Think of what?"

"My new piece."

"What are you talking about?"

"It's in here," he said, tapping the side of his head. "Not in a damn machine."

"Who are you?"

"I'm Eric Kemper. I'm an artist too, though not like you."

"Thank God for that."

"You shouldn't be doing Léger's," he said.

"What do you expect me to do? Scenes from the fucking Bhagavad-Gita?"

"I make art any time I feel like," he said and I saw a spark of fire in his eyes, which was strange because I never usually notice that sort of thing. Flames in eyes, clipper ship moons sailing across the night sky. It's a failing, I admit it. I bet I dream them though. But here I was, not dreaming at all, just drunk.

Mike O'Driscoll

"Sure you do." I figured humouring him was the best course until I could get away.

"Using a DADA machine isn't art. It's manufacturing."

I sighed, but kept my mouth shut.

"The only art that has real meaning is in here," he said, pointing to his head.

It was impossible. "You're talking crap," I told him. "You don't know the first thing about what art is."

He leaned in close, breathing smoke into my face. "Art is an act of creation that takes place in the imagination," he said, his voice low and intense. "Anything else, paint, canvas, words on a page, a performance, they're all extraneous, tools to pin art down. Just like DADA machines cage the art of the dead. Before any of that comes an act of imaginative creation. If you don't understand that, you have no right to call yourself an artist."

"That's ridiculous," I told him. "By your account any fool could be an artist."

"Jesus, an insight," he said, rising from his seat. "I made this today," he said, nodding at the counter where nothing was. "You have it. Hang it on your wall." When he was gone I stared at the empty space for ten minutes and the only insight I gained was of the absurdity of what he'd said.

*

The first DADA machines were developed when I was still at school and lumbered with outdated notions of what art was all about. I'd begun to outgrow those old ideas by sixteen, and halfway through art college I was fully tuned into the programme. The DADA machine – that's DADA for Device for the Assimilation of Dead Artists – grew out of the great glut of art in the world. There's a certain irony in that the problems of Art were solved by a machine whose acronym was derived from those like Arp and Picabia who were opposed to the very concept of Art. But we don't pay it too much attention.

Back then, it had gotten so that people couldn't even recognise art, let alone make value judgements about what was presented to them. The truth was they no longer trusted art – it had broken out of its cage and infested all walks of human life. People were suspicious and in searching for some essential truth, they turned back to the art of past generations.

The problem was they still wanted new works. Hence the DADA machine. It was developed out of VR technology and the idea was to take all the biographical and historical data that pertained to an artist's life, along with images of all their works, and download it into the DADA machine. The machine then assimilated this information and created a simulation of the artist which, when you slipped the machine over your head, used you as an instrument to create authentic new works. The technology was developed and patented by a bunch of Silicon Valley refugees who saw themselves as the Dadaists of VR tech. They did a deal with Apple to raise finance and started purchasing reproduction rights to lesser known artists.

By the time I was ready to graduate, art through DADA was the norm. It was just the initiative needed to rejuvenate public interest. Now people could acquire new pieces by all their old favourites. And it wasn't only young painters who were using DADA to produce new Picassos and Renoirs; writers and composers were using it to produce new Joyces and Mahlers. The way it worked was that on graduation you applied for a licence to practise as an artist, and on approval you purchased, with the aid of DADA Corporation loans, one, three, five or ten year franchises on the European, American or World rights for any non-living artist.

I'd hoped to get a Fauve DADA, not Matisse, I knew he was out of my range, but Derain or Vlaminck possibly. No chance, it turned out. I signed on with an agent, Mortimer, and he arranged the loan. Five million dollars – everything was dollars – got me a three year franchise on Jeanneret. It was a good move in terms of discipline – three years producing sterile still-lifes and architectural drawings that served as the basis for a moral and spiritual reconstruction were as good a way as any to rid yourself of pretensions to aesthetic experience. The hundred thousand I was left with after paying off the loan was some compensation.

After that, things turned sour. I got it into my head that I had a real talent for still-lifes so I had Mortimer seek out a franchise on a specialist. He got me a three year deal on Chardin and I threw myself into the work, producing a series of deeply symbolic *vanitas* still-lifes and domestic interiors. They sold poorly and looking back, I can see why. My Chardin's lacked some essential Chardiness, whatever it was that set him apart from the herd. I blame Mortimer. He should have known that the less biographical material the DADA machine had to go with, the less authentic the finished work. I mean, look at the poor ratings for the new Shakespeares.

Somehow I got through those years, largely due to the reputation of my Jeannerets. I sold enough to pay off the interest on the three million I'd borrowed for Chardin, but being taken seriously as a painter wasn't easy. Not when the colour of your skin prompts some dilettante to drool on about how he can see Jainistic and Mogul influences in your work.

So there I was at twenty-seven, less than a year into my Léger franchise and my first exhibition had gone down the pan on account of the ravings of some lunatic. It was a bad time for me. I was hurt and vulnerable and prone to self-doubt. Just the sort of situation that called for the kindness and comfort of someone close.

*

Within a week, Bebe had left me. All right, I was hurt and vulnerable and all the rest of it, but that was no reason to walk out. I needed her support and what did I get? A kick in the guts. Then Mortimer called to say that *Neptune's* in Glasgow had cancelled my show. "It's a shame, Haz, but we'll get through this."

I guess he was trying to encourage me but encouragement was no longer what I needed. I needed someone to blame. "How could you let that happen?" I said. It was bad form, I admit it. Totally shitty, but isn't that what agents are for?

"Your friend from the *Art de Morte* ran a piece on the Neal Street debacle," Mortimer explained. "You should never trust these people."

"It's not the money," I moaned. "It's my professional credibility I'm worried about."

Mortimer made a noise. "Did you just sigh?" I said. "I will not be fucking sighed at, not on any condition."

"Suit yourself," he said and hung up.

Fuck. I hadn't even told him what a bitch Bebe was. But that was okay, I had suffered before and would do again. It was good for the soul. Great art requires great pain. I read that somewhere. And alcohol, great amounts of it, amounts I'd never even dreamed it was possible to consume.

I lost a week or thereabouts. I know this because I remember watching the television while working my way through the first bottle of Stoli. I saw men land on the surface of some planet or other. Some guy speaking in Chinese, saying something about small steps and giant leaps, I suppose. And when I got back from wherever I'd been I saw us leave for home. "SEVEN HISTORIC DAYS," the commentator on the television said, just like that, in capital letters. "As they draw to a close let us reflect on what we have learned."

So what had I learned? That seven days drinking vodka fills you with emptiness and pain. I woke on the floor of my lounge and waited a long time for the world to set itself upright. I felt raw and wounded, as if my insides had been sandblasted. After a time, I crawled to the bathroom and found a couple of Diaphine tablets in the cabinet. I swallowed them, waited twenty minutes and stood up. I practised walking and had the hang of it within the hour. I made coffee and tried to recall what had happened. Nothing came to fill in the blanks. The emptiness was worrying.

I showered and put on clean clothes and caught a cab to the Tate. Maybe Léger could provide some clues as to what had gone on. I stood looking at *Le Grand Déjeuner*, hoping one of those women would impart some secret to me. They kept their lips buttoned and by the time I reached his country picnickers, the word had spread – watch out for the asshole posing as an artist.

Their vacant stares reflected what was in my head. But I was one up on Léger because I knew that before anyone studies an artist's life they've already decided that what he made was art, regardless of his intentions. Léger might have wanted these picnickers to say something meaningful but they don't say anything at all, yet they're still art. We say the work has value because it has certain aesthetic qualities or it shocks us in some way, not because of who painted it. Who are we kidding? That's exactly why we say a piece is good, because some famous dead guy made it. That's precisely the irony the DADA machine plays on – the artist's intention is irrelevant, but the only new stuff worth creating is by those whose intentions we respect. There was no aesthetic in the scam, I realised, but the insight gave me no relief.

Mike O'Driscoll

I stumbled on through the gallery, in a rush to leave. As I passed through to the lobby, something made me turn back. I hesitated and retraced my steps through five or six rooms, looking for whatever it was that had caught my eye. And then I saw it, the namecard on the wall next to a gaudy abstract about two metres square. Eric Kemper.

The painting was called *Canyon II* and beneath the title it said, *A late example of Kemper's work in which he continues to grapple with the problem of trying to represent the physicality of paint, the central concern of the 'Wall of Colour' school of artists, of which he was the prime mover.* Despite my jaded mood, I studied the painting closely, not sure what I was looking for, less certain that it was worth my attention. Nothing transcendent happened, nothing was revealed to me. Maybe that was the point of it – that there was nothing there. What was it the old bastard had said? That real art was in the head or something like that? He'd claimed to have made a work that day in the bar but I'd seen nothing there. I guess he wanted me to picture what he was just imagining. Crazy. No wonder he'd stopped painting.

I went home and tried to forget about Kemper. I thought that if I could just empty my head, not think of anything – not even Léger – for a while, I'd regain my equilibrium. But he wouldn't go away; the more I thought of nothing, the more I saw him lurking behind it, an endless iteration of Kempers. Finally, I succumbed to the itch. I turned on my computer and ran a search on 'Kemper, Eric – Artist.' Up came a link to an essay on late twentieth Century artists and scanning through it I found a footnote on the 'Wall of Colour' movement. It mentioned Kemper, saying he was the driving force behind the group and that he'd achieved a modicum of fame in the late nineties. A separate link brought up a half dozen or so colour reproductions, including the one from the Tate. Sort of Abstract Expressionism without the politics, Rothko without the spirituality, but not unpleasant to look at nonetheless. By the end of the millennium, his star was fading. No new work had appeared since 2007. I allowed myself a smile, feeling a little smug. Seems I wasn't the only one to fuck up, but while Eric was just a footnote, I was still active, still in with a chance to succeed.

*

A month passed and Léger continued not to sell. Mortimer flagged the idea that there were more opportunities in literature, saying he'd heard rumours that Bill Gibson was about to auction his own DADA programme to finance his cryogenic suspension. I told him to forget it, I was a painter of integrity.

"What about Schnabel?" he said. "A six month option just came up."

"Who's Schnabel?"

"The New Spirit guy," Mortimer said, "with the energized surfaces."

"Oh, him. Six months, how so?"

"Lucy Ogden had the franchise. She was killed last night when a Damien Hirst installation collapsed on top of her. Six months left to run."

"She was talented," I said, trying to remember who she was.

"It was tragic."

"How did you know she had the franchise?"

"I got it for her, a one year deal. She's made him hot, Haz, created a demand. We should flog the Léger and go with Schnabel. What do you say?"

I needed time to think about it, be sure in my own mind I was doing the right thing. He showed me Lucy's sales figures. I told him to set up the deal.

Mortimer had a show arranged inside six weeks, at *Simulacra's* in Cardiff. Okay, it wasn't London, but the gallery had a reputation for showing innovative work. Initially I didn't feel much of a connection to Schnabel, but after the first few canvases, his vigorous painting style asserted itself and I began to produce works full of optimism and romance. I felt they had a certain visionary quality that my previous paintings had lacked. I liked to think that it wasn't all down to Julian, but that some of my own soul was manifest in the paint.

The first day a fair number of knowledgeable collectors turned up to view the paintings. It was difficult to gauge their response, but Mortimer assured me it had gone well. The lying fuck. Next morning, most of the critics ignored the spirituality of the paintings and commented instead on Schnabel's old habits of cultural cannibalism and anti-intellectualism. I stormed into Mortimer's hotel suite, waving the papers at him. "It's a disaster," I said. "They hate me."

Mortimer took the papers and turned to the reviews. I watched as a smile spread across his face. "This is good, Haz, better than I expected."

His optimism made me suspicious. "How so?"

"These are the things they always said about Schnabel. This is a great sign."

"What are you saying?"

"It adds authenticity to the work and people like that. They want to know that when they part with their money for a Schnabel they're getting the real thing, not some third rate forgery."

The implication angered me. "Do they know how much of myself I put into those works?"

"Listen Haz, you're a genuine talent. You think I'd waste my time with you otherwise? By the end of the day, every painting on show will have sold."

He was right. All ten of the canvases I'd produced had exceeded their reserve price by close of business that day. After *Simulacra's* had taken their cut and Mortimer his, I was left with two hundred and fifty thousand dollars. But it wasn't the money that mattered, so much as the recognition from my peers. I felt as if I'd finally succeeded as an artist.

I bought a new car, even though I don't drive. It was Mercedes ZX convertible and I let Chrissie, my new girlfriend, drive it. I met her at a post-exhibition bash in Cardiff. She was beautiful and sophisticated and really knew about art. We'd discuss German Expressionists or French Purists just as easily as we did Schnabel or her particular favourite, Andy Warhol. She loved to quote the sayings of Andy, like 'I really do live for the future because, when I'm eating a box of candy, I can't wait to taste the last piece,' or 'Making money is art and working is art and good business is the best art.' She was always telling me I shouldn't settle for fifteen minutes of fame, but go the whole hog and grab an hour. It seemed a very Andy thing to say and I admired her for it. It inspired several new pieces, all of which sold. Chrissie was a tremendous source of strength and inspiration; she was just so giving and I knew that what we had was something special, a spiritual bond.

And before I knew it, the six months were up and the franchise ran out and so did Chrissie. I was devastated. I wasn't made to deal with that kind of hurt. My only option was to lose myself in work but Mortimer could only offer me deadbeats like Kandinsky or Whistler. I wanted more like Schnabel; I wanted Jeff Koons or Damien Hirst or Rachel Whitread; I wanted post-post-modern, post-nihilist, post-apocalypse. I wanted to be cutting edge.

So did every other loser out there. Not having any work to lose myself in, I pined for Chrissie. Then my Mercedes was repossessed and I pined for that too. When I received an eviction notice from my Highgate apartment, I remembered to pine for myself; I was owed that much, at least. But still I resisted Mortimer's offerings – having found my ouevre, there was no going back. Wasn't it Warhol who said 'To thine own self be true'? I had to find some modern painter whose rights had not yet been franchised for DADA, someone the art world had missed out on. That was when I remembered Kemper.

*

I found him in that same Covent Garden bar, swathed in a cloud of cigarette smoke, slightly more derelict than I recalled and a little more crazed. It had been over a year since he'd ruined my Léger show and I don't think he recognised me. I asked the barman what the old guy was drinking then paid for a vodka and a triple scotch and went over to his table. I put the drinks down, closed my eyes and stood still a while. When I opened my eyes again, Kemper was looking at me, a wry smile on his face. I gestured with my hands and said, "Well?"

"It's crap." He stubbed out a cigarette. "No redeeming features."

"Yeah, I rushed it."

"Do I know you?" he said, before picking up the drink I'd bought him and downing it in one gulp. I signalled the barman to bring another.

"You gave me one of your works, right here in this bar," I reminded him.

"The Léger man. So who are you now?"

"Nobody," I said.

"That's the best person to be." He lit another cigarette.

"Maybe, but I thought I might give you a try."

He turned the full force of his ancient gaze on me but I fought the urge to look away. The gaze finally softened. "You're serious, aren't you?"

"Assign the rights to me and I'll register them with the DADA Corporation. I'll raise the finance and you'll be comfortably off for the

Mike O'Driscoll

rest of your days."

"That's reassuring, but what makes you think I want to be Dadaized?"

"I'll develop the programme myself and you can have all the input you need. We'll make it the most authentic DADA programme ever devised."

"You don't get it, do you?" he said, shaking his head. "It doesn't work that way. Art isn't something you make with your hands – that's your first mistake. It's not a craft, it's something you feel, an emotion."

"Explain it to me," I said, wanting to grasp his secret. "How does it work?"

He sighed and spread his fingers as if holding something in the air. "If the work of art is an expression of emotion, then ..." he prompted me.

"Then ..." I tried but couldn't fill in the gap.

"Jesus," he said, disgustedly. "How did you ever get away with it? Look, if art is an expression of emotion, then you can't know what the work will be until you've experienced that particular emotion. Right?"

"I think so," I said, encouraging him to go on.

"You have to feel something and hold it in your mind, let it take shape, not force your will on it, not want it to be anything other than what it is." He paused to take the drink the barman had brought him. "What you do is, you express it through some act of imaginative creation, but this act isn't a means to an end; it exists as an end in itself."

"But how is that art? What about the objects, the things we look at?"

"Externalizations," he said, contemptuously. "We have this inability to see and it drives us to use paint or words or music to make art concrete. But these are just externalizations, not the art itself, because real art exists only in the mind."

"But don't we need the externalizations so that we can see what the artist was feeling?"

He took a sip from his scotch, then continued. "That was the thinking one time. But once the externalization becomes paramount, art becomes meaningless. There's no emotion to express. It's just a matter of commerce."

"So the only art of real worth is what we feel inside," I said, feeling I was treading on firm ground at last. "What's personal to us, in our heads."

Kemper nodded and drained his glass. "Nobody will take you seriously," he said.

"I'll make them."

"They won't see the work. They won't know how to."

"They'll see it," I reassured him, and I knew they would.

"All right," he said. "I'll think about it." He took out a pen and wrote something on his cigarette packet. "That's where I live," he said, tearing the packet and giving me the piece he'd written on. "Come tomorrow at six. I'll let you know."

"Great," I said, getting up to go. "You won't regret this." He wouldn't regret it because really Kemper was just like any other artist. Yes, he had integrity, but deep down, I knew he wanted the recognition too. It was only natural.

*

The next day I began searching the net for everything I could find on Kemper. I downloaded it all, then scanned in prints of all his extant works. After that I emailed the DADA Corporation and registered an interest in Kemper. They sent back the relevant documentation which I completed, notifying them of my intention, on Kemper's instruction, to draw up a DADA programme for him. I said I'd wire them proof of his assigning to me the universal rights to all his postmortem work.

At five I caught a cab to the Camberwell address Kemper had given me. His mock-Georgian apartment building overlooking Ruskin Park, was caught in a state of suspended gentrification. Kemper was on the third floor. I pressed his intercom and waited but no one answered. I pressed three more times to no avail. I started jabbing other buttons till I got a response and someone clicked the door open. Up on the third floor I found Kemper's door ajar. The other three doors on the landing were all firmly shut. Warily, I pushed open his door, calling his name softly, in case I disturbed him in the middle of some piece of work.

He was in the bedroom, an almost empty bottle of scotch on the dresser, an empty pill jar on the bed beside him. There was a handwritten sheet of paper on the floor and a note clutched in his hand. I picked up the sheet of paper and read it. It was the assignation of any future DADA rights to myself, signed and witnessed. I put it in my

Mike O'Driscoll

jacket then took the note from his cold fingers. It said, *Here it is, the work itself.* Just that and nothing more.

Later, after the police and ambulance had been and gone, I went home and tried to figure out what to do next. I felt bad initially, for having misjudged him, but I soon realised how to put things right. The new work, the new Kempers I would make, would gain him a greater reputation than he'd ever had. I downloaded the rough programme into my DADA machine then slipped it on for a trial run, just to get a feel for Kemper. Waves of colour emerged from nothingness, moving towards me, then receding slightly before coming on again. I imagined Rothko was something like this, shimmering reds on a field of intensely contrasting oranges and yellows. I switched off before it completely overwhelmed me.

The next day I paid a freelance operator to refine my crude programme and wired the assignation through to the DADA Corporation. Within a month I'd produced twenty canvases, ranging from a metre square to monumental pieces approaching four by ten metres. I gave them Kemperesque titles like *Immanence* and *Spector no. 3* and I had Mortimer commission an expensive catalogue to promote sales exhibitions in the Saatchi Gallery and *Neptune's* in Glasgow.

Everyone who was anyone came to the opening and Kemper got good press for the first time in twenty-five years. For a while I felt like I'd found my *raison d'etre* but it didn't last. The truth was, it never really got started. Oh, we sold a few pieces, the smaller canvases, but at way below estimated prices. Some young turks already had the rights to de Kooning and Rothko and were exploiting them to the full. I should have seen it coming; after all, who wants the DADA work of a third rate Rothko copyist when you could have the real thing?

I wallowed in self-pity for a month; it was my old familiar and it offered a modicum of comfort. When I got bored with it I tried on misanthropism for size, feeling that at twenty-eight and already washed up, it was the only new experience left to me. Occasionally, I'd run the Kemper programme in a vain effort to see where I'd gone wrong. I began to feel a strange empathy for him, for his rejection of the object and of the concept that there really was something there to see.

One night, fuelled by vodka, I began to piece it all together. I still believed that people wanted to see something when they looked at art, but the object wasn't it. Kemper was right – the object merely got in the way of real experience. How could you see what you really wanted to see when you had something else right there in front of you? How could anyone impose their vision on to someone else's? So what did they want to see? Nothing. Because with nothing there you were free to see whatever you wanted. Anything that could exist in the world or perhaps only in your head. The simplicity of it was beautiful.

I grabbed my DADA and wiped it clean. I put it on and pressed run. And caught nothingness, miles and miles of it, days on end of the stuff. Infinity, near as I could tell. But I stuck with it long enough so that my brain finally began to impose some shape and order on the dizzying chaos and I saw then that what I was making was my very own art.

*

The works never sold but, as Kemper saw, they were irrelevant. It was the experience itself that mattered. Of course I had to dissociate myself from Kemper's name, given our past failings, but I'm sure he'd have approved of the DadaDada, which gives people what they want, which is nothing at all. It's selling by the million as everyone goes in search of their personal aesthetic experience. Nobody sees how ironic it is that the very thing they used to kill off aesthetics, is what they're using to try and get it back. Or if they do, they're keeping quiet about it, same as me. I don't blame them – nobody wants to be seen as a Philistine; it's such a hurtful word. Much simpler just to congratulate each other on our new artworks. Mine is beautifuland yours is too; it's so much easier than trying to see what's really there. Think of the consequences of saying you don't see it at all?

Anyway, who wants to spend time looking when you can make your own art and not give a shit about what anyone says because they can never know its true worth? In this great future of ours, nobody will remember my name and really, why should they? In a world where critics are redundant and spectators no longer exist, why should one person be singled out for attention? See, we're all artists now.

Sounds Like

Holly is crying in her sleep again. For the third night running Larry Pearce listens from across the hall knowing that the right thing to do would be to go her, to soothe her nightmares away. But instead, he tries to ignore her cries, the way he did last night and the night before. Only this time the harder he strives for silence, the more the sound gets under his skin. Judith stirs beside him but doesn't wake. He wonders if she's somehow immune to the cadences of childhood fear. Maybe it's simpler than that, maybe she doesn't want to remember what it's like to be a child because of all the things that scared her back then. Larry wonders if Holly already has some kind of insight into fear and that her cries are an attempt to articulate that understanding.

After thirty minutes Holly's still crying and Judith hasn't moved. Larry slides out of bed, pulls on a pair of shorts and pads out to the hall. He hesitates at her open door, watching as a shaft of orange light from a streetlamp falls through a crack in the curtains and touches Holly's face. He moves closer and stands at the foot of the cot, listening to sounds too ancient to come from the mouth of a baby.

He's struck by her smallness, how alone she is, and despite not wanting to listen he wonders if it's this isolation she's trying to communicate. He realises that he's holding his breath, trying not to add to the noise she's making. Judith should be here. Not that she'd have any better understanding of Holly's intent, but her presence alone would confirm that he's not imagining any of this. These sounds are a language he doesn't understand. They might be saying help me or I'm scared or

111

make them go away. Something like that, but he's only guessing, really he has no idea.

He sits in a child's seat beside the cot even though he's way too big for it. His vision is a little blurred, but it's a few seconds before he realises there are tears in his eyes. He's not sure why. What he knows is that Holly is scared and that he should help her but he doesn't know how. He's scared too but in searching her face for some clue as to her meaning, all he sees is a smile, the kind that says 'sweet dreams in progress – do not disturb.'

Is that what he's hearing – the sound of her dreams? No, it's something more concrete, something he can almost touch. Her eyelids move but the little REM flickers reveal nothing of what's going on inside her head. She rolls over on to her stomach, but the sounds persist. He wonders if there's something wrong with her, if she has a medical condition, a syndrome or something he doesn't know the name of. He's not as clued up on childhood illnesses as he should be. It's too easy to leave such matters to Judith. Not that he doesn't care – after all, he's the one watching over her right now. But even so, he feels he's there under false pretences, because he's not able to give her what she needs. She wants someone to take her fear away, someone to tell her everything will be okay. Larry can't tell those lies. All he can tell her is to look for the silence inside herself, the one safe place.

As if to point her in the right direction, he reaches through the bars of the cot and touches her brow. His fingers tingle at the strange current flowing beneath her skin. He's surprised at the nature of the revelation. Don't say anything else, he whispers, keep it to yourself. Other parents might welcome such honesty but not Larry. Such openness in one so young worries him. He thinks about the future, when she's older and all the pain she'll have to face. He stands and withdraws from the room, but her sounds follow him back to his bed. Even when he crawls under the sheets and holds his hands against his ears, he can't retrieve the silence.

Larry's job is to listen. Ten hours a day, four days a week, sometimes five. He listens and occasionally, when the situation warrants, he makes an intervention. That doesn't happen often; mostly it's just listening, which means he's doing a good job. What Larry does is monitor calls –

eavesdrops, for want of a better word – on the conversations between his team and the public. It's called Quality Control. You have a problem with the service provided by his employers, you call the centre. A technical assistant takes your call, listens to your problem and tells you how to resolve it. Larry listens to the two of you talking. His unseen presence on the line ensures his team are prompt, polite and helpful, and most importantly, it ensures they don't take longer than ninety seconds to deal with your call, because by then there's another customer on the line with some new problem. Of course ninety seconds is not written in stone. Some queries can be dealt with in as little as thirty or forty seconds, but others can last much longer. Those kind of problems require more thought, maybe even a consult, before they can be resolved. But even then Larry expects his team to take no more than three or four minutes, five tops. These longer calls are balanced by the shorter ones so that, over the course of the day they average out at about ninety seconds each. You'd be surprised the amount of information that can be exchanged in ninety seconds, if both parties are on the ball.

Sometimes people call the centre because they have nothing better to do than waste Larry's time. It's this kind of call that usually prompts an intervention. They're not having technical problems, at least not with the service the company provides. They have other motives that don't concern you. They're pranksters, or they love the sound of their own voices, or they're lonely and want someone to talk to. Whatever. You're not the Samaritans and while they're using up your valuable time there are other people with real problems who can't get through. Too many calls like that, Larry stresses, can mess up the rhythm of your day.

Larry supervises a team of thirty technical assistants, each of them taking, on average, forty calls an hour. That's twelve thousand different conversations a day he's responsible for. Of course, he can't listen to them all and he wouldn't want to. What he does is, he switches between them, flitting from one conversation to another, staying just long enough to make sure your call is being dealt with in a proper and efficient manner, and if it's a new assistant, probably monitoring the length of time it takes to deal with the problem. He'll listen from his own workstation, or sometimes he'll move about among the team, motivating them even though, if they're really focused, they shouldn't notice his presence at all. Motivation is important because the vast majority of calls are pretty dull and repetitious. Doesn't matter what the problem is, they've heard it all before. Unless your problem is nothing to do with their service, in which case it isn't their problem and he'll make an intervention. He will cut you off.

That's about the only time in the day he gets to himself. Those four or five seconds of silence between cutting off a caller and deciding where to go next. Usually when he flits from one call to another, the transition is instantaneous. Well, maybe to a scientist there would be some measurable gap in time, a nanosecond or something, but to a layman, the transition would appear seamless. But when he's intervened, when he's taken a unilateral decision to terminate a call, Larry likes to take a few moments to reflect on what he's done, be sure in his own mind that it was the right decision. After all, he may be called upon to justify his actions. He calls these his moments of quiet. You'd be surprised at how few such moments there are in the day, all of which tells you he's good at his job.

This morning he cut a woman off for no reason at all. Then he took thirty seconds before moving on to another call. For the rest of the day he was expecting someone to point it out, to ask for an explanation, but nobody did. Not his boss, not anyone. Which means he got away with it.

When he gets home from work, after they've eaten, Judith wants to talk. It doesn't seem to matter what about and Larry understands that's because being alone with a child for twelve hours a day, she looks forward to adult conversation. It's no good telling her that he's listened in on four hundred or so adult conversations that day and that not one of them was in the least bit interesting. Irony doesn't cut it with Judith. Besides, he knows what she'd say. She'd say, 'It's all right for you, you get to interact with other people.' As if what he does is interact. Not by any stretch of the imagination does Larry think that listening to conversations between people who are unaware of his presence can be seen as interacting. The closest he gets is when he cuts them off. Still, he usually makes the effort, figuring that one more conversation won't make a great deal of difference in the scheme of things. Besides, he doesn't have to say much, the level of his participation being dictated by how much or how little she has to tell him. It's not that he doesn't have

an interest. He loves Judith and he wishes there was some way to make
her believe this without having to say it all the time. It matters to him
that Holly's started teething, or that she sleeps through the night. He
doesn't want to miss out on these important milestones. It's just that he
needs time to himself. Not because he's solitary by nature, but because
after listening to all those calls he looks forward to some quiet time, a
time when he can just switch off and listen to nothing but silence.

But tonight his heart isn't in it and when Judith tells him that Holly
took her first unassisted step today, he pretends he hasn't heard.

She throws a cushion at him, playfully. "Hey," she says. "Are you
listening?"

Larry says nothing. The news is on the TV but the sound is turned
right down.

"I said Holly walked on her own today."

He tunes into the quiet between her words.

"Larry," she says, and he recognises that note of irritation in her
voice. "Did you hear a word I said?"

He's trying not to, but he doesn't tell her that. It would only
encourage her and tonight, more than anything else, he needs the balm
of silence.

"What's the matter with you?" she persists. "Why are you being like
this?"

He wants to close his eyes but he's aware that would be the wrong
thing to do. It would exacerbate the situation. Instead he focuses on the
reflected light bulb on the TV screen, how it floats inside the head of the
woman reading the news. Every time she speaks, it's like she's having
a bright idea.

"For God's sake talk to me," Judith says. He wishes he could but it's
just not possible, not right now. How can he make her see that it doesn't
matter a damn what she's saying, or what the newsreader says about
poverty or the Middle East or that disaster in some place he's never
been. He doesn't need to hear their words to know what they're saying.
Their lips are moving but the sounds they make are the same as always.

Finally, Judith leaves Larry alone in front of the silent TV. One by
one he notes all the household sounds and filters them out of his
consciousness. The hum of the fridge, the rattling of pipes, the ticking
of a clock, the tired creaks and groans of the walls. As each sound

disappears he sinks a little deeper into the silence, where everything falls into place. He understands why people try so hard to keep the quiet at bay, why they need to make sense of everything that registers on the aural plane. It's because they're afraid of silence, because they see it as a second cousin to darkness, or maybe something closer.

Sometimes they speak to Larry as he drives home along the M4 towards Swansea. The hi-fi is switched off and he won't even be thinking about music. All he'll hear is the engine and the roar of overtaking vehicles, noises he can tolerate well enough. They come from outside, like the stink of sulphur pouring into the sky out of Port Talbot Steelworks. It wouldn't make sense to get pissed off about them. But then what happens is, it will start raining and he'll try to ignore it for a while, try to see through the blur but eventually it'll get so bad he won't be able to see a damn thing and he'll have to turn them on. Then it's, you know, that sound, swish, swish, and the drumming of the rain on the roof, and soon it just becomes too much and he finds himself reaching for the dial. He turns the music up loud to drown out those other noises. But Larry's not fooled – he knows it's a front, a fifth column of sound, behind which lurks the residue of the day's talking, and sometimes the whisper of conversations still to come. It wouldn't matter so much if they had something new to say but it's always the same. They're saying we are here, we are alive, we want you to know that. As if this is something he might have missed.

Larry is woken by Judith's screams. No – that's not strictly true. He's been awake a while, thinking about last night. He'd been immersed in a world of total silence in which his other senses were predominant. He was able to catch the scent of the city in all its subtle gradations; he saw tachyons penetrate the ceiling and pass through his body; he felt the cool slipstream of the turning world brush against his skin; even his thoughts were soundless, registering only as impulses somewhere in his brain. Until Holly started crying. He'd lain in the ruins of stillness, listening to sound bleed from her, understanding finally what it was she mourned, what she would so rarely retrieve. And as he'd listened, his heart breaking from the sound of her hurt, he told himself he would not let it happen, he would not let the world steal her silence.

And now it's Judith who feels compelled to announce her pain to the world. At first he doesn't know how to react. He's never heard her scream before, which may be why he's confused, why he's still laying in bed instead of rushing to see what the matter is. But even as he thinks this he moves into action. He jumps up and runs naked across the hall to where the sounds are coming from, to Holly's room. And there's Judith holding Holly in her arms and she's screaming and there are tears streaming down her face and though she's looking right at him, Larry believes she doesn't see him at all. That's when he notices how quiet Holly is, how quiet and still and pale. And he feels something horrible, a sharp, cold pain stabbing at his heart, and he tries to speak but the words get all jumbled up with fear and come out like the howl of a beaten dog, but it's a sound that says all there is to say.

His daughter is dead.

Later, an ambulance comes to take her body away, something Larry finds strange because he associates ambulances with rescue, salvation and repair. But Holly is beyond all that. He finds it strange that he's using the word 'body' instead of Holly or daughter or child. The police are very kind and considerate – they ask him hardly any questions and none at all of Judith.

The coroner's inquest returned a verdict of Sudden Infant Death Syndrome, which, Larry discovers, used to be called 'cot death'. Most such fatalities occurred between the ages of two and six months, whereas Holly was nearing her first birthday. Death was probably due, the coroner said, to a number of contributory factors, including the failure of the child to breathe because of reduced brain activity during sleep. Her death was more than likely peaceful, he said, as if that would make it easier for Larry and Judith to bear.

But Larry thinks he was wrong. Holly didn't suffer from reduced brain activity during sleep – on the contrary, she was far too active. How else to explain her sleeping sounds? The sounds that kept him awake so many nights? It does no good but he can't help thinking that he should have acted sooner to help her discover the quiet she craved. In truth he had so little of his own to give. Now she's gone and her absence is a sore that corrodes his heart. Despite his pain, Larry has to be strong for Judith's sake. If they're to get through this crisis, then he must give her all the support she needs. This is hard but not impossible – he loves his response is, they're tired or hungover, or they have a headache. Something small. But in this job, tone and inflection are everything, and if customers sense that their problems are not fully engaging your attention, or that there's something else you'd rather be doing, then they may cancel their subscriptions. At the very least, they'll probably call customer complaints. And of course, as is the nature of these things, complaints come back to Larry. He can't afford to carry people who let the team down and experience is telling him that David is one such person. In fact it's not so much telling him as screaming it in his ear as he listens to David telling someone to shut up a second. At this precise moment, Larry should intervene, remove David from the loop and pass the customer to another assistant. But he doesn't do that. He merely listens to David pouring scorn on the customer's lack of technical know-how, then tunes out and takes a minute to himself.

Of course, words are not the only sounds that signify. This morning he's heard coughing, sneezing and sighing, the tap-tapping of fingers on a keyboard, snatches of hummed melodies, the sound of someone eating or maybe just chewing the end of a pen, the strike of a flaring match and the loud inhalation of a cigarette, the countless variants of respiration, the blurring of background noises into a torrent of sounds that signify the machinery of life. It all seems banal to Larry – this compulsion to produce noise in order to remind yourself that you exist. The question people should be asking, he believes, is where does it all go?

After lunch he emails David, asking him to drop by his workstation. He's thinking about how to deal with him. Perhaps some kind of reprimand is in order, an official warning. Larry has to be seen to take action. But the truth is he's warmed to David, even has a sneaking admiration for what he's done. Which makes it all the more disappointing when he doesn't show up and Larry discovers that he's already quit.

Judith is upstairs, waiting for Larry to go and make a baby with her. He wants to, particularly as she's ovulating and all, but he can't. They tried last night and afterwards Judith was sure she'd conceived. But while she slept Larry became acutely aware of the sound of her breathing. He listened to the rise and fall of her respiration and it struck him just how much was going on inside her. Disturbed, he tried to block out the sounds. But the harder he tried, the more insistent they became. Unwittingly, he began to separate them from one another, codifying them according to frequency and duration in an attempt to reveal their meaning. He identified an occasional stutter in the otherwise smooth rhythm of her breathing, as if the inbreath had snagged on some obstacle of doubt. He catalogued stomach noises, lackadaisical groans, the almost silent hiss of a fart, the creak of her left knee, the one she broke years ago in a motorbike accident, the beating of her heart and the insistent tremor of her eyelids as she dreamed. But there was no sound from her womb. Nothing at all.

Larry watches *Seinfeld* on television. He used to enjoy this show. Now he watches it with the sound turned down because the characters' actions are too loud, as if they don't trust their tongues to say all they need to say. Their limbs flail and clack, their bodies howl in disgust and he's listening to these gestures trying to pretend he's forgotten about Judith, waiting upstairs. He doesn't want to disappoint her. Right now she's happy. At this precise moment she's laying there naked, or maybe she's wearing sexy underwear, baby-making underwear, perhaps imagining his sperm has already fused with an ovum but wanting to give it another shot just in case. But this kind of happiness is transient. In a couple of weeks, when her period comes on, she'll begin to fall apart.

He didn't ask for these insights; there is a perfectly good reason people's bodies are clothed in skin, and that's to protect them from the knowledge of what goes on inside. How can he explain? How can he tell her that he hears too much, that he can hear what's going on beneath her outer layer?

Larry's sitting there, pondering, trying to put off the inevitable, when he hears her calling. So he goes and he does his duty and says nothing about the noises he can hear, and those he can't, going on inside her.

Judith is talking names but Larry catches only half of what she's saying. He's listening to that guy over in the far corner of the restaurant, the fat man with a heart murmur who'll probably be dead inside a month. He feels an impulse to warn him, or at least tell him to make the most of what might be his last supper. But how can he tell a perfect stranger that he hears his irregular heartbeat from the other side of the room? Particularly when he's trying hard to concentrate on what Judith is saying.

"Elizabeth," she says, "if it's a girl."

Sparkling water fizzes down the throat of that young woman at the table by the door. It doesn't drown out the sound of her desire for the guy sitting opposite her. "Elizabeth is fine," Larry says, his attenuated voice lost in the blizzard of noise. The woman at the next table is menstruating heavily. She's a little self-conscious about the smell. Larry wants to lean across and tell her it's the noise, not the smell, she should be worried about, but he assumes she wouldn't appreciate the observation.

"Or maybe Candice?" Judith says, raising a glass of red wine to her lips. Larry flinches in anticipation and she asks him what's wrong.

"Nothing," he says.

"What did I just say?"

"Names, you were choosing names."

She frowns and he hears the dry scrape of her skin creasing. Be still, he wants to tell her, be perfectly still but before he can speak she says, "What's the matter?"

He can hear someone in the toilet, taking a piss. An elderly couple sitting at the window stare at him and Judith, smiling and whispering behind their liver-spotted hands. They're talking about love but Larry hears death whistling between their bones

"Larry, are you listening to me?"

He nods and watches as she licks a residue of wine from her lip. He doesn't want to spoil things for her tonight so he acts as if the sounds she's making are completely normal.

"Your face," she says, quite loudly. "You look so serious."

He forces a smile and even though he tries to keep it quiet, he's pretty sure she must have heard it. Still, it's not enough. She says, "What are you thinking about?"

He's thinking, how would it be for all of us here to live, if only for a while, in the silence? He says nothing in the hope of setting an example and for a brief moment he thinks maybe they understand. But Judith shatters his illusions by saying, "I'm not getting through to you, am I?"

Even as she speaks her words become distorted, amplified beyond meaning and he wants to explain why this is happening, how it's because of this need she has, they all have, to avoid the truth. But he keeps his mouth shut because he doesn't want to add to the volume. Already, the walls are vibrating beneath the immensity of sound; it pulverises their senses and everyone just sits there, pretending there's nothing going on.

Outside, the streetlamp hums orange. Nothing strange in that. Larry's sure he's heard it before – five years he's lived in this house overlooking the bay, so it stands to reason. What's different now is that he's aware of this particular sound, that it's impinging on his consciousness. He's considered the possibility that he's imagining it, but no, he really is hearing light. This isn't normal. Normal is, no matter where you live, co-existing with noise. After a while it gets so that unspecified, individual sounds merge into one constant thrum which blurs so far into other sensory input that people no longer register it as sound. But this illusion of quiet disturbs them, so they produce more sound to fill the void, as if this is the only way they can affirm their existence. And still there's so much they can't bear to hear and these sounds are filtered out into a shapeless background of unwanted information. But the more noise they shut out, the more that's produced to replace it, in an infinite regress. Larry's lost this ability – he can't stop himself from hearing. It's not just the obvious sounds like voices or television or telephones, like traffic and screaming, or the waves breaking out in the bay, but the more subtle ones, the sounds most people never hear.

Right now walls of sound are closing in and Judith doesn't even know it. How can she lay beside him and not care that each hiss of her breath, each beat of her heart is a reminder of what's slipping away? He leans across and tells her be still, but his words make no impression. He hates this intransigence, this selfishness which allows her to deflect the truth she doesn't want to hear. Having failed to make her see things from his point of view, he turns away and hears the radio-alarm whispering three-thirty even before he sees the LED display glowing red in the dark. He shuts his eyes not wanting to see the numbers when they change, but he hears it anyway, the sound of another minute gone.

What he doesn't want, what he's fighting against, is counting, because with Larry counting means counting down. He already knows where that will lead.

The bed creaks as Judith turns and drapes an arm over his stomach. He draws a sharp breath, fighting panic, lifts her arm and rolls out from underneath it. Sitting on the edge of the bed, he grabs the pillow and covers his ears. He breathes softly, not hearing anything. Beginning to relax, thinking he's found the silence, he becomes aware of a new sound. Except it's not really new. In fact it's all too familiar – the modulated sound of his own autonomic functions, those regulatory processes over which he has no control. Terrified by this heightened awareness of self, Larry sinks to the floor and pulls a sheet over his body to cloak himself in silence. But it's no good because these internal processes refuse to go quietly about their work. Yet there's something else more awful than hearing them, something he can't bring himself to acknowledge.

With an effort of will he climbs back up on to the bed, thinking perhaps Judith will know what to do. But she's just laying there, oblivious, like she bears no responsibility, sleeping through his fear, just as she did through Holly's crying. That's not right, Larry feels, a mother not hearing her child's night-time fears. Maybe Judith has infected him with her noise. Maybe it's not enough that she has to talk to him every evening after work, that she insists on filling his head with the emptiness of her days, but even while sleeping she deflects onto him the babble she's afraid to hear. Every night, this constant need to remind him of her presence. As if he could ever forget. He should talk to her about it, see if she's open to compromise. But there's already too much noise in the room, sounds which the darkness intensifies, lending them more power than they have in the light of day.

These are some of the things Larry hears: beads of sweat rolling down his chest; the dry crack of snapped twigs, which are the spasms of his facial muscles; his stuttering breath, like the hesitant query of a nervous child; a heart beating with the irregular rhythm of a broken piston. Even when, after an hour or so, he's managed to bring his body under control, he can still hear things it shouldn't be possible to hear: the creeping of insects in the walls, the scuttle of a spider across the ceiling, the babble of microscopic bedbugs in the sheets. All trying to tell him a truth he already knows.

When it was just Judith Larry could hear it wasn't so bad. On a good night it was still possible for him to withdraw into his own silence. That's all finished now. Even here at the far side of the room there's no getting away. The noise outside doesn't begin to compare with the noise that fills the room, the source of which he can't even see. He's trying real hard to think this through, trying to find some way to drown it out. Judith's there but she's no help at all. In her sleep she rolls on to her side, facing towards him. There's a smile on her face, prompted, he imagines, by some dream of contentment. He zeros in on her left eye which seems more animated than the other. He wonders if, in the same way that the light entering one eye is translated into a recognisable image by the opposite visual cortex, this movement of Judith's left eye signals a dream taking place on the right side of her brain. It's like she's having two dreams at once, with one somehow amplifying the effect of the other. Maybe that's how she does it, how she infects him. She dreams unwanted sounds into his head.

The logic of this is irrefutable, so Larry returns to the bed, grabs a pillow and presses it down on Judith's face. At first she doesn't react, so he presses down harder until she begins to resist. She reaches up and clutches at his arms, scratching, but he just brings more weight to bear, forcing the pillow tightly against her, doing his best to ignore her muffled protests, not even flinching when her nails draw blood from his arms, just concentrating, riding out the frantic thrashing of her legs against the mattress, refusing to be cowed by the tremendous noise she's making until, after a couple of minutes or so, she's still.

He lifts the pillow and stretches out beside her, breathing hard but that's okay because he knows something has changed. He stares up at the ceiling, at that strip of orange light and he's pleased at the way it just sits there, not moving, not making any sound. He takes this as a good sign, a sign that he's on the right track. His chest rises and falls and his heart pounds out a kind of triumphal message, which is understandable, but really he feels better now that things are quietening down.

When Larry wakes he feels renewed. He showers, eats some breakfast, goes to work. It turns out to be one of those days. Every second call is a major crisis, like sunspots are fucking up Earth's atmosphere or something. You can forget ninety second averages today if things continue on like this. After the fourth consult Larry turns down the volume and listens to dead air for an hour. That's a big improvement. It allows him to stay focused, helps him get through a difficult shift.

He leaves work a little early, intending to make up the hours tomorrow. He hurries home and makes a cold sandwich. The phone rings a couple of times but Larry ignores it, probably for Judith. He watches TV with the sound turned down, having no problems at all understanding what they're saying – the same as last night and the night before. Come midnight he goes upstairs and there's Judith, a little pale, waxy even, but perfectly silent. He gets into bed and finds her somewhat cold and unyielding when he tries to push her over to her own side, but that's okay, the main thing is the quiet.

Next morning, Larry finds himself thinking about David, even missing him. Rather, he misses what David's absence represents, which is silence. Without consulting Larry, the company has given him a replacement. This replacement is really on the ball though, you have to give her that. Not one call so far over ninety seconds. As she's new, Larry's been monitoring her calls and counting – ninety, eighty-nine, eighty-eight, eighty-seven, eighty ... so far he's only got down to twenty-two. She's cheerful and efficient and he wishes she worked someone else's shift and left quietness in her place. It proves to be a difficult ten hours, made tolerable only by the cumulative total of seventy-three minutes of dead air he listens to, dead air created out of the exceptional number of interventions he's forced to make.

On the way home he stops off to buy a Chinese takeaway – noodles, chicken and red peppers in a black bean sauce, some crackers. Picks up a mid-price Chardonnay at the off-licence next door and lays everything out on the kitchen table. But he just picks at the food, a taste here, a nibble there. He has no real hunger to satisfy. When the phone rings he disconnects it and throws it in the bin along with the leftovers. The TV is on but, feeling jaded, he decides to have an early night.

The following day is not so good. It starts off brightly when Larry wakes at dawn and the whole world seems perfectly silent, but it's just an illusion. Strangely enough, it's not the sound that alerts him but the smell. It's coming from Judith. Only after he's noticed that does he hear the noise. That feeling of almost joy he had just a moment ago has completely vanished and now he's confused. In fact his brain is hurting with the effort of trying to figure out his options. He makes a decision. He gets out of bed, walks across the hall to Holly's room, lowers the rail to her empty cot and climbs in. It's cramped, but the sheets are cool and it's quiet, which is what Larry needs right now. It doesn't matter if he sleeps late, he's not working today. What's important is to lose himself in the quiet. He's not sure why Judith has started making noises again, but at least he's put some distance between them. He's got a feeling that when she realises how little impression she's making, she'll fall silent again.

Larry manages to sleep for a while. At least he thinks it was sleep. He's not sure because he's finding it hard to tell the difference. He lacks the appropriate terms of reference at the moment. Despite his patience, Judith hasn't let up for one second. The irony of it is that she's louder dead than she ever was alive. The sound of her is filling the house top to bottom, like something's really bugging her. When he crosses the hall and looks through the open door at the ruin on the bed and sees the topographers of corruption crawling over her grey skin, he recognises the truth he's been trying to avoid. He hears it in the awful drone of the flies and the soft hiss of her putrefying organs, but more than that, it's revealed in the sounds of his own treacherous body. There it is in the dry rasp of his frown, and in the rush of air through nasal cavities, in the melody that flows through larynx and trachea and into his lungs. It's present in the strange harmony of spleen and gall bladder, the industry of pancreas and liver, the dance of his heart. But this is just scratching the surface – beneath these are a host of more complex sounds – the surge of blood through veins, its tides dictated by something other than the moon; the whine of stretched sinews and the grind of bone against bone; the whiplash of a blinking eyelid; the snowfall of flaking skin. Sounds like life ticking away, sounds he was never meant to hear.

Larry figures that he may have to resort to something a little more drastic if he's serious about getting things back to the way they were. He finds what he's looking for downstairs in the living room and sits a while, reading up on the subject. His research is no more than rudimentary, twenty minutes at most, but to do this properly would take more time than he has. In the kitchen he selects the most appropriate tool, then it's back upstairs. He sits in front of the dressing table and stares at his reflection in the mirror, feeling out of place. This is where Judith would sit to put on her make-up, disguising things she didn't want to see. We can choose not to see, Larry thinks, but once we hear truth talking, we have no choice but to hear it out. Unless ...

He picks up the carving knife, opens up the *Family Medical Advisor* and takes another close look at the anatomical drawings. Understanding what he has to do, Larry takes hold of the top of his left ear and hacks it off. Blood spurts and pours down his neck, sound falling out of him. Quickly, before fear overwhelms him, he slices off the other one. Looking in the mirror, he wonders if, at the end, Judith accepted the real meaning of sound. We are made of it and each sound heard is another piece stripped from our lives. He holds the knife out till the tip of the blade touches the glass. And he looks into his eyes and sees a true silence staring out, dark mouth moving in affirmation.

And of course it sounds like nothing he's ever heard before.

Rare Promise

Vincent lies face down in the sluggish water but he is not dead. He is slowing time the way Bear taught him to. "You lie still," Bear said, "like you're dead, then hold your breath and count as high as you can." One night, Vincent reached a hundred and seventy-five: the seconds slowed and coagulated, till it seemed he had dammed the flow of time. "A real dedicated practitioner," Bear said, "could add at least five years to his life." Having dreamt of immortality, Vincent felt cheated. The other thing about slowing time was the way it made the whole world sound different; you could hear things nobody else had ever heard, the susurrations that slip between sounds.

... Like whispers of the past, of days when the world seemed full of promise, when summer was a place of magic and secrets. Laragh Wood was such a place; a small, three acre gathering of ash and elm trees, bordered by a line of alders that ran beside the Graney. Here, he and Bear built a network of hidden dens where they acted out the rituals of adolescence unhindered by adult fears. It was a world in which they held no secrets from each other. Until, one fine spring morning, with the wood glistening in the after-rain sun, he asked his friend, "What do you really think of me?" Bear replied, "Think of you how?" Vincent laughed to hide his purpose: "As a friend." "Why're you asking?" Bear wanted to know. "I was wondering, when we're older if we'll still be pals." "I can't see the future, Vinnie, but me and you, we'll always be friends." "You promise, Bear?" "Course I do." But Vincent wasn't satisfied; already, at fourteen, he was beginning to sense all that might come between them. And though the wood remained a haven, he could never tell Bear the real fear, the real secret that ached inside him. There were some things, he began to realise, that you could never reveal, not in a place like Drumassan, not without cost.

... Like the brooding shadows that sometimes stalked his dreams, a hint of eyes, a murmuring, an earthen smell, the shape of a person he'd known long ago, the space that someone had filled. He'd wake suddenly, troubled by feelings of shame and a love, and a desperate need to please. He'd lie there, apart from the world, trying to focus on the remnants of his dreams. But when he'd get too close, it would disappear like those indecipherable shapes that linger on the edge of vision.

... Like the premonitions he'd had of Greta months before she came back to Drumassan. Alone one autumn evening sitting among the falling leaves, he felt the cold touch of rumours sifting through the jetsam of his past, creating unease about the future. It made listening to his father's plans for him seem more intolerable than ever. "You're still palling with that Sheehan fella," his father said. Sheehan was Bear: two years previously, at sixteen, he'd pronounced himself educated and promptly quit school. "He'll never be anything but a small farmer," Mr Fitzroy went on. "He hasn't got your potential at all. Can't you find some fellas you've something in common with?" Mrs Fitzroy added, "You'll never fulfil your promise mixing with the likes of him." They droned on, apprising him of all he had to live up to, unconscious it seemed, of the malice which seeded their thoughts. "You're looking at seven or eight honours next summer," his mother went on. "At least that if we're going for law." Now it was law; once, she'd harboured a wish that he take Holy Orders – like her elder brother, Dan, who'd died last winter of a stroke, and whom Vincent could hardly remember – but being an only child, she'd grown reluctant to give him up to God. Then, as if she'd only just recalled it, she said, "Your aunt and Greta are coming to live in Drumassan." The shock that drove him from the room was the shock of recognition. Greta, he was sure, was the one the voices had spoken of. That night, as he lay restless in bed, he fought the memory of those muted whispers, whispers that filled him with shame and at the same time, enticed him with the lure of something forbidden. So that by the time she returned to the village in the winter – red-haired, green-eyed and possessed of a strange allure, so different to the quiet, sullen girl he barely remembered from childhood – he had cultivated an immunity to her charm. Not so Bear; whatever exotic magic she possessed made him putty in her hands, and in no time at all, much to Vincent's disgust, Bear was doing a line with Greta, and he was out on a limb.

... And now, like the hollow moans that begin as subtle ripplings of the subterranean silence and become echoes of distant memories not necessarily his own. Not dead at all but floating, holding his breath, blocking out the world, catching single words and snatched phrases, the sighs and murmurs of the past ebbing and flowing against the shore of his mind; memories, absences, premonitions, resentments. Counting the minute long seconds and the hour long minutes. Yet a breath can only contain so much time, and when he clears the surface there is only the chittering of insects and a soft breeze rustling through the trees.

Which doesn't explain the sudden fear which makes him strain to hear what is no longer there. In a world made up of voids, those you have loved are signified only by their absence. Even memories can't be trusted. He grasps the reeds at the water's edge and lets his body stretch out in the gentle current. He wonders if he has imagined the voices. But did he imagine too, the tone of frightened pleading or of kindly, treacherous reassurance? And was it imagination that spoke of good and bad behaviour? Of how best behaviour got you sweets, like pear drops and blackjacks, and maybe a place in Heaven? And who had promised to never, ever say a word?

An awful scream tears the silence asunder, withering his heart, immobilising him in the water. He grips the reeds tightly to keep from going under, while the cry echoes horribly throughout the wood. It's not real, he tells himself but there's no escape in imagination: this happens now. And as the sound of hurt dies somewhere deep among the trees, a profound shame settles on him, a feeling of complicity in a sin he cannot recall. For one moment he wonders what a backwards step in time might reveal but a dark and irresistible dread has spiked his nerve. He hauls himself up on to the bank, pulls on his clothes and then, like a child with a guilty secret, he steals furtively from the wood.

*

This is what Vincent understands about power: when you love someone, you cede them the right to cause you pain. It's not even a matter of intention; a hurt caused in ignorance hurts nonetheless. So when Bear calls round after Mass on Sunday morning, he is entirely unaware of the pain that fills Vincent's heart. But Bear's troubles are written on his face and seeing them, Vincent melts.

This is power. Another example:

Once, in the teeth of his thirteenth winter, when snow settled in heavy drifts against the outhouses and in the ditches, Nancy Kelly took Vincent to her father's milking shed to show him something she had learned. There, in the cow-smelling gloom he stood in awkward silence watching his frosty breath commune with hers. She took his right hand and placed it inside her coat where he felt her small breasts through an Aran sweater. "D'you like 'em?" she asked, but he couldn't speak. Then her hands were at his trousers, unzipping, unbelting with silent purpose.

Afraid, Vincent's eyes beseeched the patient cattle, but they were content to yield their milk to the machines. He whispered, "What are you doing?"

But she just pulled down his trousers and underpants and said, "It's not very big, is it?" and took hold of his flaccid prick in her cold, pale hand. "I thought it'd be bigger."

"Jesus, would you let me go?" he cried, trying to pull away but she held on to him and, despite his fear, he felt it grow in her fist.

"Ah now," Nancy said. "Something's stirring." She pulled back the foreskin as if for inspection, said, "Hmmm," and began to masturbate him with quiet intensity.

"Christ," he said. "Go easy."

"It's like milking," she said, maintaining the rhythm of her stroke. "I saw me brother doing it once." Afterwards, she wiped her hand on a cow's back and said, "D'you love me now, Vincent?"

To which he had replied, "What for?"

Because back then he hadn't understood the subtleties of power or the implications of Nancy's unspoken contract. In rejecting her he drew her hatred; yet, the sense of rejection he feels now, is not enough to sustain a hatred for Bear.

"What do you want?" Vincent says, taking the proffered cigarette.

Bear says, "Still looking to be excommunicated?"

"Why change the habit of a lifetime?" It's three years since Vincent last attended Mass, the fact of which his parents are unaware.

"I'm ..." Bear begins, but falters. He takes a fierce drag on his cigarette, then mutters, "I want to explain, 'bout me and Greta."

"Forget it."

"She's different to other girls."

Vincent waves a hand, cutting him off. "I don't want to hear."

"I must talk to you about her."

"Talk to someone else."

Bear looks wounded; Vincent's moment of triumph is undermined by unsummoned compassion. "Sure, who else can I talk to?" Bear says.

Vincent sighs and gets into the blue Ford Anglia that Bear inherited on his father's death. They drive east through the village where thirsty worshippers congregate outside the twin temples of *O'Mahoney's* and *The Star*, one on either side of the road. Strange omens fill Vincent's mind while he waits for Bear to talk, and the even stranger certainty that he will have heard it all before. When Bear finally says, "I took Greta to the wood," he's unprepared for the feeling of betrayal that wells up inside. He gulps air as if it were in short supply and finally manages to ask just, "Why?"

"Jasus, why d'you think?"

But Vincent can hardly think at all, for he is remembering when all the world's secrets were hidden in the wood, and he and Bear were its custodians, sharing everything and keeping the world at bay. Now an inner voice prompts, *Everything?* Was the trust he'd shared with Bear any kind of trust at all? "She's a child," he barely whispers.

"She's sixteen, Vinnie, and we've been doing it for months. I know she's your cousin and everything, but don't think butter wouldn't fucking melt in her mouth. Sure, I wasn't the first she's been with."

"Why there?" Vincent asks, too numb to feel pain.

"Why not there? I knew you'd be contrary about this."

"It's the wood Bear, you know what that means."

"It's just a fucking wood, it's nothing special, it's just ..." Bear's voice tails off. He tries again: "Look, something happened up there."

Vincent feels the world quiver with fatal instability. "What?"

"She heard voices while we were going at it," Bear continues. "One minute everything's grand, the next she's lashing out, screaming so as you'd think I'd fucking raped her. But it wasn't like that."

"What was it like?" Vincent asks, catching faint whispers that seem to come from a time when the world was more solid and real.

"I heard nothing," Bear says, sullenly. "Nothing at all, only her going on about those voices, and some damn promise she made."

"What promise?"

"How the fuck do I know? She just lost her head, I swear to God. She knelt in the dirt, crying how sorry she was she broke her promise. I cracked then and, God forgive me, I ran. When I came to my senses and went back to find her, she was gone."

"This was when?" Vincent says, already knowing the answer.

"Yesterday afternoon."

There's no moisture in Vincent's mouth. He feels an unbidden and profound pity for Greta. "And you heard nothing?"

"Nothing at all," Bear insists. "I went to see her this morning before Mass but she wouldn't talk to me."

"Why're you telling me this?" Vincent feels his pity turn to anger, and then to something more.

"She's your cousin, I thought you might talk to her for me."

"Why would I do that?" Something livid and hateful inside him.

But when Bear says, "Because you're me friend," Vincent is forced to acknowledge that that takes precedence over his sense of betrayal, and over the inexplicable sense of shame that has seeped into the hollow spaces of his heart.

*

For once, Vincent feels little pleasure in the slowness of time; he waits for something to happen without knowing what that something might be. He tries to study Yeats as the hours congeal around him, devoid of promise and fulfilment. Even sleep is no escape, for his dreams too have descended into fretful darkness. He takes his final exams on Wednesday morning, and afterwards he finds that his vague, indefinite tensions have coalesced into an awful dread of what Greta might have to say. But he has promised Bear and such a thing is sacred. No matter that his friend has let him down, he cannot afford such moments of weakness.

He gets off the school bus outside *O'Mahoney's* and walks the half mile east to the cottage that his aunt rents from an impoverished farmer. Mrs Scanlon, a widow, is still a young woman in her mid-thirties, and unlike her sister – Vincent's mother – she has to go out and earn a living. She works as a receptionist in the Drumassan Co-op, a position Vincent's father helped her obtain.

He knocks loudly at the front door, assuming a confidence he doesn't feel. The door opens inwards and Greta appears before him, green-eyed and pale-cheeked, wearing a yellow cotton dress from which her arms hang like the limbs of a sapling. The fiery lustre seems to have burnt itself out of her auburn hair but she nonetheless manages an awkward, unsteady smile that reveals a vulnerability he had not known she possessed. She raises a hand to shield her eyes from the sun and says, "I knew you'd be coming."

Vincent is unnerved by her certainty. "How?"

She steps out into the bright sunlight. "I remembered," is all she offers by way of explanation, and then, "Will you walk with me?"

"Sure," Vincent says, and follows her to the boreen that runs behind the cottage and winds its way up the long, gentle slope of a hill. Apprehension fills the very cells of his being, preventing him from seeing clearly the child Greta in the Greta who walks beside him now. Has she changed that much, or is the change in him?

What he thinks are sly sideways glances become too obvious and Greta says, "Would you ever stop gawping." Then she climbs the ditch and runs off through a field of barley. Surprised, he follows her path till they come to a rocky outcrop that looms up out of the side of the hill. Greta skirts the base of the rock and picks out a path that leads them to the summit overlooking Drumassan lake.

She sits down, cross-legged, on the hard surface of the rock, "God, it's quiet around here," she says.

Despite himself, Vincent laughs and sits beside her. "Takes a bit of getting used to, I 'spose, after Dublin."

"It's like I remember, Vinnie."

"Ye should never have left."

Greta stares intently at him. "We had to, remember?"

Vincent has no idea what she's talking about. "It all seems a long time ago. Why did ye never come to visit?"

"Ma never said, but I understand now. Now it's safe."

Vincent shrugs his shoulders. "I wish I understood."

"You will, Vinnie, when you remember."

He feels that she's trying to read his mind and wonders if that would be so bad. Some animal swims through the ocean of barley below the rock, like a shark in search of prey. Calm settles on his mind.

"Have you a ciggie?" she says.

He lights one for her, then another for himself. "I forgot what you looked like."

She laughs. "You really know how to flatter a girl."

Neither mentions the wood, though the breath of cold murmurings clings to each of them. "I don't get much practice," Vincent says.

"Do you still have secrets, Vinnie?"

"Do you?"

"I useta have a crush on you," she says, her cheeks flushing red.

But there are holes in Vincent's memory, the deep darkness of which he cannot penetrate. Even peering over the edge requires a strength he doesn't have. Warily, he says, "I saw Bear the other day."

She stubs her cigarette out against the rock. Straggly curls fall across her face. He leans over and brushes them from her eyes and sees the sweat glistening on her forehead.

She says, "Why did you do that?"

"To see if I can see what he sees in you."

"And can you?"

"Tell me what happened, Greta."

Suddenly she leans over and kisses him on the lips. Her mouth is sweet and warm but he is shocked. He pulls away, confused.

"What's the matter?" she says. "Don't you fancy me?"

"Christ Greta, it isn't that, it's ..."

"Look at me, Goddamnit!" She undoes the buttons at the top of her dress, exposing her small, white breasts. "I'm no different to any other girl. No matter what they say. I'm as good as them."

"Cover yourself up. I didn't come here for that."

"Why? Is there something wrong with you?" Her bitterness stings, and so too does the accusation.

He stands up, feeling the situation slip beyond his control. She rises too, saying, "I'm sorry, I didn't mean anything by that."

"Look," Vincent says, "I'm doing him a favour, that's all. He asked me to talk to you, to apologise for not understanding."

"Do you understand?" she wants to know. "The things I hear?"

Doubt and confusion fill him like some foul potion. He doesn't want to say anything but the question can't be ignored. "I thought he might have hurt you."

"He didn't."

"He said you imagined some things."

"Not imagined," she whispers, her gaze turned towards him but her eyes focused on some point beyond his head. Her words are soft but sure. Things that were real."

It is as if she is speaking in a code no one has taught him how to decipher. "He said you were frightened."

"A secret forever," she continues, as if unaware of his presence. "Mine and yours and his, eternal and sacred and never to be shared with anyone at all."

"Dammit Greta," Vincent says, grabbing her arms. "What the fuck are you talking about?"

"You remember, don't you?" Her voice is like a child's.

But he can't remember, or maybe it's that he doesn't want to. A long forgotten fear undermines his few remaining certainties. He removes his hands from her and shouts, "There's nothing at all to remember, not a fucking thing."

"It isn't sacred after all," she says, ignoring his rage. "I understand that now. The promise was a lie."

"Shut up," he screams. "Leave me the Hell alone."

Before he can stop himself, he hits her across the face, knocking her down. "Don't talk to me anymore," he warns. "You're mad as fuck." He turns away and quickly descends from the rock.

She cries out above him, "I know you hear them."

He presses on through the barley, closing his mind to her words, shutting her out before the world he thought he knew falls apart.

*

Vincent gets a summer job as a builder's labourer, mixing mortar and shifting concrete block for forty pounds a week. At night, his limbs aching, he listens to the soft murmur of his parents' voices downstairs, as they plan a future to which he feels no connection. He hates them for failing to see the amorphous nature of his reality, for not warning him that the forces that shape him lay beyond his, or their, control.

A week passes before Bear calls by. Vincent lies to him, saying he hasn't talked to Greta. If Bear suspects the lie, he doesn't say. There's no word from her, but her presence hangs heavy over Vincent's dreams, informing and elaborating them with the tissue of her being. The sickness he feels in the pit of his stomach is the sickness of certainty that she is waiting for him to remember.

And it is this sickness which drives him to Tallamount, to the Church of Our Lady, on the first afternoon of the summer rain. It is safer than Drumassan, he tells himself as he climbs the steps to the porch, for no priest will know him here. In the musty shadows of the entrance he tries to recall how long it has been since the rituals of this place have had the power to frighten him.

He peers through the stained glass and sees a woman with flowers walking up the central aisle of the nave. She genuflects before the altar then begins to arrange her blooms on either side of the chancel. Warily, Vincent steps into the aisle and takes a pew at the rear. Two flies buzz around his head, their entomological sacrilege disturbing the hushed gloom. A low, musical sound pervades the warm, still air: the woman humming while she works. The scent of flowers is cloying, shrouding his thoughts. A door opens somewhere in the church and crisp footsteps sound on the mosaic floor. From the sacristy a priest appears behind the altar and greets the flower woman, then kneels to say a prayer. Vincent finds the nerve to proceed towards the altar. Something creaks in the almost silence, but he keeps on till he sees a dozen sinners waiting in the west transept. Solemn faces cast shameful glances in his direction, as if somehow he reminds them of their own sins. He takes his place among them as the priest, middle-aged and ruddy-cheeked, comes from the altar, and, nodding at the penitents, steps into the confessional. An old woman enters one side, a young boy the other. And as the recitation of sin begins, Vincent's mind slips back through time to bear witness to the nature of evil.

A gaunt priest stalked the classroom, a leather strap dangling from his long, thin fingers. "It isn't enough to simply turn a blind eye," he spoke softly. "A better man than me once said, 'ignorance is no excuse.'" He stared at the boys in turn, as if peering into their very souls. "What's needed is a willingness to confront sin wherever you find it." He stopped in front of Vincent and the strap whipped through the air, hitting the desk inches from the boy's hands. The priest's face broke into a bitter smile. "But sometimes, cowardice will get the better of you and you'll think you can hide the truth from the Lord. I know that there isn't one among you who hasn't got something festering on his conscience. Am I right?" Vincent wanted to argue the point, but some despotic glint in the priest's eyes made him hold back; some hint of potential violence ready to confront the slightest doubt. Vincent dropped his gaze and the priest moved on.

Even now, after three years, he still has an irrational dread of priests. As if in confirmation he feels the dead taste of guilt on his lips like ash. It is as if he has wandered from his own, familiar world into a place of blame and retribution, a place where all the hurt in the world is his. And now it is his turn to enter the box.

In the dark he whispers, "Bless me Father for I have sinned." He has come to find out what that sin might be. "It's a while since my last confession."

The scent of ripe, whiskey breath leaks through the curtain and he senses the bored irritation beyond it. Nervously, he recites a list of minor sins, some real, some invented. But when they are all used up he knows he is no nearer to discovering the truth. "I useta have a friend," he says. "Someone took him from me."

"And who was this friend?" The priest asks.

"The best friend anyone could have – but no longer."

"What do you mean, boy?"

"It's the truth."

"I doubt that."

Vincent detects a note of sullen brutality in the voice, and all the fear he's been holding back comes closing in. "There are things I can't remember," he says. "Bad things."

"Ah yes, bad thoughts," the priest suggests, as if on familiar ground. "Tell me about them."

"I can't."

"You touched yourself down there, yes?"

"I promised to never tell."

"We've no promises or secrets in here, so out with it."

"I tried to tell her the voices weren't real."

"*Her* now, is it?" Something lascivious in the words.

Vincent tries to express what he feels. "She took him from – "

"Him now again?" A movement beyond the curtain.

"I hate her for it."

"You're telling me you had impure thoughts about another boy? Is that it?" The priest's voice has risen noticeably. Vincent hears the almost imperceptible groan of a seat relieved of weight.

"You don't understand," Vincent says, "what he meant to me."

And a shadow passes from the curtain as the priest says, "By Jesus you're right I don't understand." But Vincent is already up and running down the aisle, even as the priest emerges and roars his pitiless rage.

*

"Promise me one thing," Bear says. "Just one thing."

But inside Vincent's head his dreams are putting substance to something that was lost; he presses harder on the accelerator as if it might be possible to outrun the truth. And Bear says, "Just tell me none of it was real, that it was just the wind in the trees, her mind playing tricks."

And Vincent wants to, he really does but right now he's hurtling forward through time, thinking he might just be able to escape the sense of unease that clots his days. This is not the first time he has driven Bear's car, but he has never driven so fast. Through the windscreen the world slips by in a blur; it's an epiphanic moment, one that reminds him of the first time he saw Bear naked, his lithe body striding out of the trees and diving into the cool water of the Graney. So unexpected a sight; so thrilling that Vincent had left his trunks in the towel and followed Bear into the stream. It was as if, at the age of eleven, he'd been shown a glimpse of a life he'd never imagined, one that erased the patterns encoded on his mind.

"I never hurt her, Vinnie," Bear says. "I'd never force her to do anything she didn't want. I love the girl."

Which is exactly what Vincent doesn't want to hear.

"I don't understand how things could change so suddenly," Bear continues. Vincent wonders how it would have been if he hadn't lied when Bear had once asked him, who, if he had the chance, he'd most like to fuck in the world. He's never forgotten that lie, not like his promise which – hidden for so long – is now coming home to roost.

"She saw a kid," Bear says, heeding neither the speed of the car nor Vincent's numb detachment. "But there was no one there."

Vincent understands this: empty spaces once filled by people he had loved and trusted, silhouettes whose faces he can't even recall.

"She wanted me to help the kid but what could I do?"

What did she tell? Vincent wonders. Her promise? Is that why light bleeds into the darkness, because of things she said that were better left unspoken? "I never heard them Bear?"

Bear is puzzled. "I never said you did."

"I'll look after you."

But Bear doesn't note the pledge, only callously reiterates his need for Greta. "I must help her, Vinnie, no matter what's happened, I want to be with her."

Vincent's hands grasp the wheel tightly, not letting it move, and he can feel Bear – the essence of Bear – extricating himself, cutting unseen bonds and wrenching himself out of his world into some other.

A sudden bend in the road causes Vincent to lose control of the car. It slams into the ditch and Vincent, unrestrained by a safety belt, whips forward, his face smashing into the steering wheel. Dazed, he's vaguely aware of the blood dripping onto his shirt, and is pleased at how unreal it all seems.

*

"You've got it in you, laddie, to be whatever you want," his father once said. It wasn't the wide vista of possibilities that most impressed Vincent then, but the realisation of how seldom his father called him by name. They should have christened him *Laddie*. A feeling that had long been latent in him crystallized then: the realisation that he was not who he had always thought he had been.

He remembers that now as he sits in a chair in the back garden, looking towards the sun with his fingers entwined over his eyes, allowing him to see the red beneath his skin that makes him real. Last night he dreamt he was a spirit returned to witness his own funeral, and like Tom Sawyer observing those who had wronged him, he felt both comforted and vindicated. Hearing a voice in the house behind him, he lowers his hands to his knees where they tremble visibly. Is it the way we see ourselves, he wonders, or the way we are perceived by others, that makes us real? Or is it the past alone that shapes us? And is that past immutable? If so, then when Greta comes out into the garden, she will say, "I came by to say I forgive you for hitting me. I had no right to go on at you like that."

And he will reply, "I was afraid of what you might say."

Laughing, she'll muss his hair and sing:

We made a promise, to keep silent and still,
So the past won't hurt us, and it never will.

It is a beautiful song but one she doesn't sing. She steps out into the garden and banishes the possibility of change. "Vinnie," she says. "I heard about your accident."

His heart begins to beat a little faster. He wonders how much of the world might be listening. "It was nothing," he says.

"Sure look at the state of you," she says, kneeling in front him. She touches his bruised face but such devices don't work with Vincent.

"I'm grand," he says. "I never felt a thing."

"And Bear? He's okay too?"

The name makes him feel cold. He can't speak it, not now. So many shadows in the world, dark, hollow spaces that echo with the sounds of torment and shame. Darkness flickering in her eyes; he wants her to close them but he's worried she might think him weak, that she might think he'd be the one to tell.

"I was right, you know," she continues. "What I said before; we have to tell someone."

"Please," Vincent says. "Don't talk about that."

But she persists. She speaks of pain and suffering and guilt, and though he recognises these feelings, he can't acknowledge that they were ever his own. She speaks of trust and lies, and of a promise that has sealed their tongues for years. On and on, relentless in her need to make him recall the time they both grew old.

"I can't do it on my own," she says. "I need you to help me."

"Jesus Christ," Vincent cries in anguish. "Would you just leave me be, Greta. You need to – "

"It needs to be both of us, together. No one will listen otherwise, no one will believe us."

"They won't believe you anyway – they don't want to know these sorts of things. They'll just fucking hate you for it."

"They'll believe the truth, Vinnie, someone has to."

Hot, bitter tears well up in Vincent's eyes. He has little strength to resist her will. "The truth? What is that? Fucking delusions, Greta, that's all. Yours, not mine. I don't see what you see, or hear what you hear. For all I know you've lost your mind."

Then she's on her feet, pouring all her anger on him in one final effort to make him understand. "You're lying, Vinnie. I know you, remember? It won't ever go away again, not for either of us."

"You need help, so you do."

"You're thinking you're a dirty little bastard and you can't bear to feel that way. But it's not our fault, for God's sake, we're not to blame. We trusted – "

Vincent claps his hands over his ears. "I'm not listening anymore," he screams. And at the core of his being, a dark revulsion has taken root. It taps into his mind and soul, offering glimpses, not of the past but of the future; he sees himself slinking through the village, past knots of people who whisper behind cupped hands and surreptitiously point him out to strangers; alone and friendless, shunned by all except the dark, insubstantial creatures who wait to gather him in their cold embrace. This is the world that Greta would have him accept. She would rob him of the power to choose whatever he wants to be, strip him of all his bright and shining futures.

He stands up, dazed, waiting to see which way the world will turn. But it's his own mind that starts to spin, furious and uncertain, fuelled by childhood demons, and dreams that once set the world to rights. The love and fear that bind him to the past tighten further around him while he spins faster and faster, with voices whispering inside his head: *You are ours, you always were*, taunting, warning, loving and pleading, burdening him with intolerable demands, getting the measure of him, sensing his weakness, sketching in the blanks, putting a face on the absence, warm and familiar, reassuring and safe, so that here and now he reaches out to make a connection, one that offers him a salvation, or at the very least, a return to the way that things once were.

A touch of light falls on him, illuminating his rare promise.

And Greta is there, standing before him shouting, "We can do it together, Vinnie, we can make him pay."

But that sort of power is beyond him. He turns and runs from the

Mike O'Driscoll

garden, out to the road. He speeds towards the place of secrets, her treacherous screams ringing in his ears, knowing that only the past can silence her lies.

*

A scent of rumour and complicity hangs heavy in the drowsy air, a tang of corruption rising up from generations of dead vegetation, imprinting its dizzying fragrance on bark and moss and flesh. The soft pink of twilight begins to fall through the watchful trees, stilling his troubled soul. He sits with his back against the rough bark of a broad-crowned ash, naked, a cigarette in one hand, his cock in the other. He tries to masturbate but it's a desultory attempt to capture a feeling that is gone; he is unable to give substance to the fantasy.

The reason he is here, he admits, isn't Bear; nor was it simply to escape Greta's insistence that he accept what she calls the truth. Truth hides in secret places, far from prying eyes. The strong secrets that bind lovers thrive in the dark spaces on the fringe of reality: the tight spaces beneath beds, under-stairs cupboards, cellars, dusty attics, the ruins of a stone cottage, a wood. You have to be in such places to understand what they mean. That's why he is here, letting cool shadows embrace him like an old friend.

A large, brown moth hovers in front of his face, then lands on his knee. He reaches slowly forward and catches one wing between his fingers. The other beats frenetically against his palm but it can't escape. He holds the cigarette in front of his face and blows on it till the pointy tip is burning red. He brings it down on the moth, incinerating its head, then tosses the dead thing away. He has come here to put flesh on the bones of a forgotten promise. He closes his eyes and starts to breath deep and slow. After an indeterminate time, a fragment of awareness slips loose from his consciousness. He takes one final huge breath and holds it, five seconds, ten, and he becomes aware of the gentle thrum of persuasion against his mind.

And in the trees, a murmuring begins...

... *Promise me now*, a voice like treacle implores above a muted weeping. *On the Bible, on Jesus's life. This is our secret, yours and hers and mine, nobody else's.*

I promise, a solemn-eyed boy weeps. *If Jesus says.*

Oh, he does, he does...

142

See the cold, shamefaced sun cast speckled shadows on fragile limbs where goosebumps rise but not with cold. And listen as the girl pleads, reluctantly, as if afraid to plead, *Please don't hurt me.*

A heavy groan, burdened by a tender, weighty love. *It's okay, my doughty, he won't hurt you at all...*

Vincent is trying his very best to pierce the veil of time but somewhere a skittish heart is racing, like the heart of some dumb beast snared in incoherent dread.

Up on her now, boy, that's the way. The watching man's words caught on the wind of his breath, urging him on. *She's a fine one, isn't she boy? A pure thoroughbred.*

The tremoring off the girl's body, the cold sweat on her flesh, the terror in her eyes. Seeing black garments being strewn on the ground. *Off her now.* A rhythm of brute need punctuates the words. *My turn, boy.*

Light falls among the shadows, pouring into the silhouettes, filling them with identity. See the arms and face and ruddy, quivering flesh of someone who was gone.

Bear witness, my boy, and never share this secret with another soul, lest the Devil come and carry you off to some bad place.

Please not there, the boy cries, plaintive notes rising and falling on a wind that sighs regret among the trees.

I'll save ye from the fire, the quickening voice assures. *Long as ye both shall tell no lies.*

No lies, one child promises. *No lies*, another echoes.

That part of Vincent which has slipped outside time fills with cold understanding: in this world of secrets, there is one more terrible than all the others, one that triggers a madness that threatens to disrupt the bonds between Vincent here and Vincent there. He siphons the air from his lungs and fills them anew till he feels the blood pounding in his head, and senses the backwards reach of time, coiling away from him, drawing him towards one who whispers...

Promise me...

And despite the fatigue that saps his strength he struggles to his feet, wanting to know, more than anything, who it was who had forced him on the girl, forced him to mimic what the man had done, and then made him watch as he did it to her again. And afterwards, the way he'd extracted a promise from them, as he'd extracted it so many times before. He stumbles forward in the failing light, groping towards the pain of understanding. And sees two children and the man, kneeling and praying together. *So ye must ask God to forgive ye for tempting me. Ye want his forgiveness, don't ye?*

Bless me Father, the children recite, while their Uncle begins the litany of absolution, words that ring hollowly down the years.

And Vincent flails through the spiteful vegetation that wraps him in tissues of unreality. Reaching out his fingers, he can almost grasp the truth; just a little further, beating a path through reassured undergrowth, ignoring the heart that threatens to burst inside him, driven on awful fear and numbing shame which in the end is not enough, never will suffice. He touches something, just for one moment, just long enough to feel the searing pain of truth. Then he falls among the musty leaves and the breath roars from his lungs like something foul.

And time snaps back...

Seconds slip by at their normal pace and in the here and now he sees a slight and graceful figure moving towards him through the trees, full of hope and reassurance. A soft voice calls out his name and for a moment, he thinks perhaps he is back in an earlier time, a time before secrets and promises, but when her eyes alight on his naked flesh, the memory of that earlier time fills him with shame. "I followed you here," she says, not seeming to notice his nakedness. "To tell you it's a promise not worth keeping."

Vincent nods for he finally comprehends the cruel lie of love that's been hidden for years. On his knees he waits to accept the balm of truth. Her arms enfold him and her breath roars in his ears, "It's okay, it's over now." And he knows how right she is as he feels the burden fall from his soul. She holds his face in her palms and kisses the tears from his cheeks, from his lips. "We'll tell the truth, Vinnie, they'll see we were innocent. Even Bear, even he'll love me again."

The words sink into his brain and with them, the knowledge of what he has lost. They hold each other tight, kneeling in the soft earth. He can't breathe because he is holding his breath, she, because he is holding her throat, holding tight and counting, reaching out, trying to recapture the ecstasy of forgetting.

*

The land slips away like a puzzled acquaintance, failing to understand the reasons for his leaving. It is not enough to say that Laragh Wood and the memories it contains belongs to the past, so he doesn't. He decides that what he feels is not loneliness, but anticipation. In fact, he feels very little at all. Ringaskiddy is soon left behind, swallowed up in the pale mists of morning and presently Vincent sees the tall, coloured buildings of Cobh sailing by the port side of the ferry.

He left home yesterday, hitching a ride to Cork and spending the night in the docks, not wanting to waste any of what little money he has. He reads the story in yesterday's paper one more time, thinking they might have used a more recent picture of his dead cousin. Bear was arrested the same day the body was discovered in the Graney. He's pleading his innocence, not understanding his own complicity in Greta's death, that he should never have taken her to the wood. In time they'll let him go and conclude suicide, or more probably a tragic accident, for you can't bury suicides in consecrated ground.

Years from now, when a general contentment settles again on the village, and parents recall her name only to warn children against hidden currents, no one will thank Vincent for sparing Drumassan the shadow cast by the monstrosities of childhood. For they will never know of his promise, and the manner in which it was extracted from him. They both were innocent, she'd said; their Uncle was to blame. But Vincent understands now that innocence, like truth, no longer has any meaning, not even for children.

And, accepting the shadow into his heart, he steps up to the rail and lets the newspaper fall over the side where it is snatched up by the wind and borne backwards and down into the engine-foaming sea.

The City Calls Her Home

co-written with Christopher Kenworthy

Euston station moved slow about Bernadette Coghlan, a few souls gliding by as if in some dream of home. She could wait here, unconnected, for days if she wanted to, if that was what it took for the dream to run it's course. An old boyfriend, a psychology student, had taught her self-hypnosis; this was that kind of peace, and she didn't want it to end. The stillness tranquillised her but a telephone ringing sliced through the narcosis and brought her back to the land of doubt. It was a public phone in a booth just off to her right. She left her case by the seat and went to answer it.

"Sammy?" said an irate voice that wasn't Gabriel's.

"I'm sorry," she said, quelling disappointment. "This is a public phone."

"You think I don't know where I'm calling?" the voice said, a man's voice. "He turn up yet? He shoulda been there by now."

"I'm waiting for someone too," Bernadette said, unsure if she should have volunteered this information. "But maybe he's been – "

"Get off the line," the man said. "Wasting my fucking time."

She slammed the receiver down and went back to her seat. She smiled, despite her anger. No point getting freaked over some obnoxious telephone jerk. Maybe it had been a mistake, she thought, following Gabriel. Impulsiveness was something new to her, a previously undiscovered facet that Gabriel had responded to. She'd decided to indulge herself. She was fed up being safe, dependable

Bernadette. *Only fair I get a crack at being the rebel.*

The station was busier, the noise having grown noticeably while she was on the phone. Her tranquil mood of a few moments ago had gone and she noticed how cold it had grown. Snow was falling outside. She pulled the hood of her ski jacket up over her red hair, hugged her body through the tracksuit. A shabby, overweight man pretended to read a newspaper a few yards from the phone booth, watching it, waiting. She wondered if he was Sammy.

She'd given up cigarettes last month, a mistake. Kill for one now. Earlier, she'd told herself, not believing it, that something must have happened to Gabriel. Now she was hoping that something had. It was easier to believe that, because the alternative, that he'd changed his mind and didn't want her in London, was too bloody awful to contemplate. Three hours she'd been waiting, called his number five times. Nothing. She'd have to make her own way to his flat, which meant the tube. The prospect daunted her. She'd used the DART in Dublin, but from what she'd heard there was no comparison. She was tired, hungry and pissed off. She got up and walked to a burger bar across the station.

She felt better after a cheeseburger and coffee, but the craving for a cigarette had grown worse. Don't think about it. She checked her purse. No cigarettes. Two hundred pounds in sterling, enough to get by for a few days, maybe a week. With no cigarettes. Next to the burger bar was a newsagents. She went in and bought twenty Silk Cut. The cigarette tasted good, even if it did make her cough.

Down in the Underground she tried for ten minutes to decipher the tube map while the crowds jostled past her, flowing in and out of the mainline station. Why did he have to do this to her? Put her through this bloody trauma? Still feeling rebellious, girl?

"Having trouble, lovey?" a middle-aged woman said beside her. She wore a white mac wrapped too tight around her plump body, and a red beret perched on auburn hair. "Where do you want to go?"

"Moray Road," Bernadette said. "Finsbury Park, wherever that is."

"That's wise, lovey, heading north. Here it is." The woman pointed it out on the map. "Straight up the Victoria line. I wouldn't stop there, though." She wandered off without another word.

Bernadette bought a ticket and found the platform she wanted. She boarded the first train that came along and sat next to an old man sleeping by the door. His legs stretched across the aisle, forcing passengers to climb over them. Okay, she told herself, you're on your way. Bastard forgot, that's it, no other explanation. She smiled at the woman opposite her, who merely frowned and averted her eyes. Anxiety was etched into the faces of the other passengers and no one talked. She looked at the sleeping man and thought, good for you, get no chat out of this miserable bunch.

They pulled into Kings Cross. Bernadette lit a cigarette and closed her eyes. On her third drag, she became aware of a mute but powerful hostility directed at her. Fighting her own awkward embarrassment, she opened her eyes.

"Can't you read, girl?" said a black man next to her. He pointed at the no smoking sign that she'd missed.

"I'm sorry," she said, hurriedly stubbing the cigarette out beneath her heel. "I didn't know."

"An' at Kings Cross an' all," she heard a woman say, under her breath.

How the hell was she to know? Why didn't someone say something when she took out the pack? Had they wanted her to make a fool of herself? What sort of place is this? She felt angry and humiliated.

She had to climb over the sleeping man's legs to get off at Finsbury Park. She thought, he hasn't moved. I've got a bad feeling about him. She glanced back once at the still form, then hurried off the train. Outside the station she saw two jets flying low through the heavily falling snow. She spent an anxious moment trying to get her bearings before she realised she'd never been there before. Then what the hell is this sense of *deja vu*? Some Dublin memory triggered by anticipation? Perhaps something Gabriel said.

Across the street from the station a sign above a shop said *Philippino Produce*. She dragged her suitcase into the shop and saw a young guy stacking fruit in trays. She asked him if he knew Moray Road. A sweet, faintly rotten scent, rose from the fruit. The young Philippino shrugged his shoulders. "It's Finsbury Park," he said. He looked past her and pointed across the street. Then he moved away to serve a customer. Bad manners, she wondered, or is it a cultural thing? She went out and found a minicab office a few doors up. Inside, she waited for the heavyset black man to finish on the radio, before asking for the street she wanted.

"Nuthin' at moment," he said. "An' we 'ave a dozen calls waitin'.'"

"No please," Bernadette tried to explain. "I just want to know where it is. If you tell me I can find my own way there."

"If ya come back after four," the man said, "mebbe I can get ya a ride outta here."

"I don't want to leave the city," Bernadette said, but he was speaking to someone on the radio. She left, walking on beneath a rail bridge, till she came to a set of lights at a junction. Across the road to her right was a pub. When the lights changed, she crossed.

She ordered a half of Fosters and found a table in a corner where she wedged her suitcase in next to the wall. She leaned back in her seat, closed her eyes and sipped her lager. Tension seeped from her body like the last vestiges of a bad dream. On the jukebox a man with a pained voice sang, *and to the voice that told her when and where to act, she said –*

"Can I sit here?" The voice startled her. It was a man, mid- twenties, she guessed, wearing small, round glasses, jeans and black overcoat. His blond hair was too short, but he looked interesting in a vague sort of way. London accent, not cockney, but what does he see? A naive, young Irish girl? Straight off the boat, they used to say. Suppose that's what he thinks I am? The thought amused her.

"There's plenty other seats around the place."

"Yeah, but this is where you are," he said. "Still, if you – "

"Ah, sit down, it's a free country." She could do with some company.

"So they tell me," he said, placing his drink on the table and sitting opposite her. "I'm Cook."

"Cook?" Cook the cocksure. "What's your first name?"

"Just Cook," smiling. "You?"

"Bernadette, just Bernadette."

She listened to his small talk for a while, then contributed some of her own. He seemed intelligent, maybe a little nervous. When he didn't try making a move on her in the first ten minutes, she thought he might help her. No harm in asking. She told him what had happened and he seemed concerned. He didn't know Moray Road, but figured it had to be reasonably close. He offered her a drink but she declined, not wanting to give him the wrong signal. She had to figure out how she was going to deal with Gabriel. Even if he had simply forgot, it didn't bode well for their relationship. It wasn't fair to take her anger out on Cook, but even so, she bought her own drink and they swapped cigarettes.

"Listen," he said, when she was midway through her second drink. "I got some business to take care of soon, it won't take long. Afterwards, if you want, I'll help you find this place."

She thought about the offer, about her suitcase and about Cook. He wasn't so bad and she could handle herself. When she'd lived in Dublin she'd completed a ten week self-defence course organised by a women's group at UCD. Never had the chance to put those skills into practice before. She figured she could cope if the need arose. She relented and Cook bought her another half.

"So you're thinking of staying here a while?" he said.

"You say that as if you don't think it's a good idea."

"Well, the way things've been going." He shrugged. "People here, we don't know how to communicate anymore."

"You're not doing too bad."

"I mean, there's no imagination."

She laughed. "That bad? You should see Dublin – it'd make you cry."

"Everything's shit," Cook said. She noticed for one brief moment a note of despair in his voice. Then he smiled and went on, "It's nothing, nothing anybody talks about anyway."

"Except you," Bernadette prompted, but Cook changed the subject and she didn't pursue it. She liked him better when he was laughing and joking. It was gone five when he left her, saying he'd be back in thirty minutes. She watched him disappear through a door at the rear of the bar. She lit another cigarette and considered telling Gabriel about Cook. That would shake him up. Who was she kidding? She loved Gabriel, right? Else why uproot herself from Dublin and pack in her job at the hotel? God, she hadn't even called her Mam and Dad yet. They'll have a fit. They don't even know Gabriel – he wasn't round long enough for her to take him down home. And even if she had done, she suspected her father would have disapproved.

Siren shrieks ripped through the evening calm. A young skinhead came running into the pub and threw a small package over the counter. Seconds later, five policemen stormed in after him. They began wading through the bar, nightsticks drawn, upending tables and chairs, smashing bottles and glasses, shoving people around. One guy said something and got smacked on the side of the head for his troubles. He went down like an old dead tree. It was pandemonium. The cops lashed out indiscriminately. She pulled her case from beneath the table and with one arm protecting her head, she made for the door. Something hard hit her in the ribs and a voice said, "where the fuck are you going?"

A cop loomed over her, his nightstick raised, ready to strike. Fear clogged her tongue. He said, "You can tell us about it down the nick." As he grabbed her, a glass hit him in the side of the face. His blood sprayed over her, but as he turned to look for his assailant he kept hold of her arm.

She screamed as she saw Cook jump on the policeman's back. "Run, fuck it," Cook shouted seconds before another nightstick smashed against the back of his head, sending his glasses flying past her.

Bernadette kicked the policeman in the groin, escaped his grip and dragged her suitcase outside. A hundred metres up the street she stopped and looked back towards the pub. Half a dozen police vehicles had pulled up, blocking the street. Cars, buses and trucks backed up the road as far as she could see. Across the road, naked trees glowing orange in the sick streetlight, lined a snow shrouded park.

She was afraid to go past the police, back to the cab office. She trudged wearily on through the slush, passing small hotels and shabby guesthouses on her right. She entered one that reminded her vaguely of the first digs she'd had in Dublin six years ago. An Arab woman took twenty pounds from her, gave her a key and said breakfast was served from six till eight-thirty, and to vacate her room by ten.

Her room was on the third floor. Opposite the guesthouse, the trees cast strange shadows on the snow in the park. Only the constant drone of traffic reminded her she was in the city. She was shaking, she realised, pulling off her ski-jacket. Must have been some drugs bust or something, though Cook didn't seem the type. There's a word for that – naiveté. Forget him – you were lucky to get away. Find Gabriel tomorrow. Not a small town culchie anymore. Dublin can be dangerous and I have survived it for four years. Live there, I can live here.

There was a television in the small, tidy room but she ignored it. She smelled under her arms, thought about a shower but was too tired to bother. She stripped down to her underwear and got into bed. She lit a cigarette and tried to recall the peace she had felt that morning, the stillness that had reminded her of home.

Moray Road was a street of run-down, red-brick terraces to the west of the park. The morning was cool and damp but she was warm beneath her ski jacket, sweatshirt and jeans. Every few minutes or so, jets arced across the gunmetal sky and people would watch them, nervously, the flesh pale and tight across their faces. They expect the worst, she told herself, though she didn't know what the worst might entail. It's human nature to look on the bright side, mine anyway. Why can't they be happy here? This ancient place, this adventure, it still had the capacity to excite her, to stir her imagination. First though, Gabriel. Her body tensed as she approached his building. The cold began to sink through her clothes. A burnt out van smouldered on the pavement opposite, its acrid stench making her wince. She rang the doorbell and waited, then rang twice more, before she heard a door open somewhere inside the house. A figure shuffled into view beyond the frosted glass of the front door.

The skinny guy who opened it looked about eighteen. Freckled and only wearing jeans, he looked as if he'd just woken up. He knuckled his eyes, yawned and then, as if only now feeling the cold, shivered.

"Jayzuz," he said, "it's bitter." He left his eyes alone and grinned. "You're not from the social are ya?" Dublin accent.

"Is Gabriel Casemont here?" she said.

"Sure, what's wrong with me?" the boy said, his grin growing wider even as his shivering became more violent.

"Just get him, will you." No time for this shit.

"C'mon now, don't be like that."

"If you don't tell him I'm here," Bernadette said, through clenched teeth, "I'll break your jaw." She felt she could do that, if she had to.

His mouth fell open in genuine shock. He stepped back a pace. "Ah bollix, I was only kidding. You'd better step in out of the cold."

She followed him inside and then through another door to a

Mike O'Driscoll

stairway.

"Friend of his are ya? Not from Dublin?"

She didn't answer as she followed him up two flights of stairs and into a small, cramped room with a microwave on a table by the window and a portable television beside it. Clothes and books were scattered on the floor. There was a single bed behind the door and a wooden stool under the table. He pulled this out and offered it to her. He sat on the bed and smiled again.

"Where's Gabriel?" she said. "Why didn't he come to Euston yesterday?"

"Was he 'sposed to?"

"What do you think?"

"Ah shite." He seemed embarrassed. "How well d'ya know him?"

"Is this his flat?"

"I'm Jimmy," he said, smile fracturing. "What's yer name?"

"Forget it. Just tell me where the hell he is."

He avoided her gaze. "This was his gaffe. He let me have it."

"What?" Panic touched her. "He let you have this place?"

"He left two days ago."

"Left?" she said. "He called me three nights back." Anger drained from her voice; fear seeped in. "Where's he gone?"

"You came over yesterday?"

"Just tell me where he is." Fear, and a little shame.

"Buggered off to the States," Jimmy's voice, small. "Went with his pal Conran. I woulda gone too, only, no fucken readies. He saw it coming."

"The States," she repeated, the words like ice on her tongue. "Did he mention that I was coming over?"

"The bollix never said nothing about ya. I mean, before he..."

"Did he say anything about..." she couldn't bring herself to ask. "It's not your fault," she said, getting to her feet.

"I was in a place on Holloway Road, but this gaffe was cheaper so he gimme the keys and said I was welcome to it," Jimmy went on, his words passing her by.

"I have to go now," dazed words, drifting towards the door.

"Wait," Jimmy said. "What's yer name?"

Numbed, she went down the stairs.

154

"Can I come with ya?" his voice trailed after her, but she knew that wasn't possible. She opened the front door and hurried towards Seven Sisters Road, trying not to think about why Gabriel had called and then hadn't waited for her to come.

She caught a tube. The carriage stank of sweat and disease. People refused to meet her gaze, as if afraid to share her pain. She got off at Palladin and dropped down to street level. She wandered aimlessly along Tottenham Court Road, in the shadow of the Avenue, the suitcase a dead weight in her hand. She sat in a cafe and after coffee and a roll, she slipped into a light trance, clearing her mind of confusion, focusing only on what to do next. Needed time to work something out. Couldn't just go back to Dublin with her tail between her legs. I don't give up that easily. I'm here now, have to adapt.

She went into Debenhams. There was a sale on. She spent forty pounds on a light grey suit that seemed to command respect. She hoped it would impress a prospective employer. She bought an evening paper and sat at a bus-stop, marking all the employment agencies listed. By six, she'd found a cheap hotel on a backstreet off Grays Inn Road. She showered and curled up on the sofa with a Samuel Delany paperback. She liked Delany, liked the baroque worlds he created and the way his characters tried on different identities like a new suit of clothes. Gabriel didn't rate him, but he didn't rate anyone who didn't write in Russian or Hungarian, or who was unfortunate to still be alive.

But tonight she couldn't lose herself in the book. It was impossible to get Gabriel out of her mind. She didn't believe he'd really gone to the States, not without telling her. He'd have waited, tried to persuade her to go with him. She mulled over their last conversation, searching for a clue as to his leaving. Did I read too much into what he said? She dozed a while and woke without having shaken off her fatigue. Loneliness had wormed it's way into her soul. She picked up the phone and asked for an outside line, then she dialled her parents' home in Bantry.

When her father's voice said, "Sam Coghlan speaking," she hung up. Hearing his voice, a surge of bitterness had welled up inside her. Why is it up to me to always make the first move? Why should I give in to his obstinacy? They'll know by now from Dymphna that I've left Dublin. Dymphna had been her flatmate. She was supposed to wait three days before calling Bernadette's parents, but she guessed

Dymphna wouldn't have been able to hold out that long. She could imagine them, panicking, wondering if it was an abortion. What could she tell them? That her boyfriend had missed her and wanted her to come live with him? That he'd buggered off to America and left her in the lurch? Imagine the look on Dada's face. The lecture he'd give me, as if I was still a little girl. And not, she reminded herself, a twenty-four year old woman who – seven years ago – had fled his petty tyranny, his smothering love.

Wait till she had a job and digs, then she'd call. Fuck Gabriel, the prick. I can get on. I'm not the ignorant culchie lass he took me for. She felt better. She could live here, she could take whatever obstacle the city put in her path. Having made her decision not to speak to her parents just yet, she lay back on the bed and, after a while, she slept.

Wearing her new suit, she waited half an hour for someone to see her at the employment agency she went to the next morning.

"Well Bernadette," said the female consultant, who had taken her details. "We'll call you if anything comes up."

"How can you? I haven't given you a number."

"Oh, well," the woman said. "Not to worry."

"Not to worry? What do you mean? What about your vacancies?"

"Vacancies?" the consultant's eyes were panic-stricken. "Vacancies?"

Bernadette rushed from the agency, frustration welling up inside her. At the next agency, someone saw her right away. Three consultants sat around listening to her relate her work experience. Two of them made notes and chewed the ends of their biros; the other one, who said her name was Julie, chewed her fingernails.

"Things are quiet right now," Julie said when Bernadette had finished telling them about her receptionist's job at the Sheraton Hotel.

"Look," Bernadette snapped, "if my qualifications aren't good enough, why don't you just tell me?" Her gaze seemed to make them uncomfortable. "You advertised in last night's paper."

Finally, Julie said, "Your experience is impeccable, Bernadette, and normally there'd be no problem recommending you for something."

"Anything," the other two agreed.

"But you have to understand," Julie went on, examining her fingernails, "it could be a while before things get back to normal."

"What is wrong?" Bernadette cried in frustration. "What's not normal?"

"What is?" Julie said.

"Look," one of the other consultants said, rushing towards the window. The other two followed her. Beyond them, Bernadette saw the column of beautiful fighter jets swooping low over Palladin Avenue.

She left, disturbed by their behaviour and curious about the jets. She'd have to watch tv tonight. She tried another two agencies without success. Dejected, she went into a pub off Soho Square, bought a lager and a sandwich and put money in the jukebox. She chose seven songs but the first one it played wasn't one of hers. Her mind wandered: instead of hearing the lyrics, other voices spoke to her, a million whispers, too quiet and plaintive for her to make out the words. She felt that, despite what had happened since she'd arrived here, it hadn't been a mistake to come. Although the city seemed huge to her, too big to understand and seething with strange currents of emotion, the truth was the mystery of it attracted her.

Up at the bar to get another drink, she saw last night's newspaper on the counter. She took it back to her seat. Last night she'd only looked at the jobs; reading the rest of the paper would take her mind off things. Catch up with what's going on in the world. *Government faces confidence vote*, the banner headline read. After two paragraphs, the story bored her. She wasn't interested in economics. At the bottom left of the page was a smaller headline: *Suspect dies in Police Custody*. Beneath that were two photographs. One showed the exterior of the pub where she'd met Cook, the other showed his face. Her stomach cartwheeled. She lurched from her seat and ran to the toilet where she threw up. She couldn't believe what had happened, that she was somehow involved in this nightmare.

She went back to the hotel off Grays Inn Road and paid for another night. At first she just tried to sleep and forget, but after an hour of tossing and turning on the bed she got up and switched on the television. She watched the news. There was nothing at all about the jets. She changed channels, searching for some explanation, anything at all. Screenlife went on, familiar and unchanged, portraying a constancy she no longer shared.

The city shut down for the weekend. She wandered the cold, empty streets by day and went back to the hotel in the evening. By Monday her money was running low. She dressed in her suit and after a cold breakfast, she checked out of the hotel. She caught a train from Libra Square to Marble Arch. The underground was quiet, nearly empty; subdued, almost as if the system had resigned itself to an unforeseen collapse. Outside, wet snowflakes floated lethargically to the ground. She shivered beneath her jacket and headed up Edgware Road, calling in to three more agencies. It was a waste of time.

She headed South again, into Hyde Park, resenting the burden of her case. But it was all she had that connected her to a life beyond the city, to the past. She saw two bums following her. Further on again, they were joined by three more, including a woman. She quickened her pace as she neared the frozen lake and followed the path to the right. Anxiety wormed into the marrow of her bones as she realised there was no one around she could call on for help. Empty rowboats trapped in the metallic ice were like huge, drowned insects with numbers painted on their gaudy, upturned shells, their brittle, timber limbs clutching at the sky. She moved on slowly, towards a bonfire at the north-west edge of the park. The group trailed a few paces behind her. Angrily, she turned to confront them.

"Well? What do you want?" she shouted.

They stood silent, watching her, waiting. One of them, an older man whose blue eyes gleamed at her, stretched out a hand.

"I can't," Bernadette said. "I've got nothing for you. Go hassle someone else." She saw how futile her words were. There was nobody else to hassle. The man moved closer. She lunged forward and hit him hard in the throat with her fist. He went down, croaking, and his companions backed away. Bernadette ran, dragging her case.

She rested in the shelter of a lodge and watched the bonfire blazing two hundred yards away. She focused on the silently falling snow and felt the tension leave her muscles. She closed her eyes, trying to still her mind. When she came to, her suitcase was gone. Her despair was tinged with relief. She had what she needed anyway – money, clothes, passport. She could still go home, if the worst came to the worst. She hurried out of the park and crossed the road to Lancaster Gate station. On the platform, a drunk stumbled into her, and swore. She pushed him away, but he caught her jacket.

He laughed raucously. "Fucking bitch," showering her with spittle. "Teach you a fucking lesson."

She escaped from his grasp and hurried up out of the station. The incident shook her, made her realise what the loss of her suitcase meant. She should ask someone where the nearest police station was, but the only people around were strays from Speakers Corner. She didn't need the hassle. She found a black man warming himself by the bonfire. He pointed across the park, to the south east.

Twenty minutes later she found the station. It was empty except for one desk Sergeant. "Get to you in a minute," he told her from behind the counter. "Got these papers to fill out." When he finally came and sat by her in the waiting area, he listened while she told him about the theft of her suitcase. He seemed distracted, a little anxious. "There's a lot of it about," he said when she fell silent. "Best just to forget it."

"What do you mean?" Bernadette said, appalled.

"Sorry," he said. "I'll write it down." He rose and disappeared into an office. Bernadette followed him and stood at the counter. He emerged from the office, pulling on an overcoat. He closed the incident book on the counter and left the building without another word. Outside, the vehicles were bumper to bumper and their headlights scorched the snow. The wind had picked up and the sergeant was nowhere to be seen.

She stood in the doorway of an electrical shop that had closed for the evening. Televisions lined the window, all tuned to different channels, none that she recognised. A weatherman mouthed silent words – expectations of a white Christmas. Dear Santa, show me the way to Gabriel. Another screen showed a tele-evangelist exhorting the faithful, while the one beside it broadcast pictures of tanks moving towards a ruined village.

Near Rosenkrantz station, a short, stocky man in an army jacket attacked her, punching her in the face. Stunned, she was dragged into an alleyway. He tore her ski jacket off and ripped her grey skirt. He started to slobber on her neck, his rancid breath roaring in her ears. She screamed at first, but nobody came to help. Then her mind became icy calm as she subdued the panic. She fell backwards, as she'd been taught,

Mike O'Driscoll

dragging him off balance. He fell with her, losing his grip. She hit the ground, then jabbed out with her fingers, catching him in the eyes. He howled, temporarily blinded. She struggled out from beneath him, and quite deliberately kicked him in the face. Grabbing her jacket from the ground, she fled the alley. On the street, people hurried by, pretending not to notice her.

"What's the matter with you?" she screamed at one passerby. "Someone tried to rape me." More people passed by, ignoring her. She examined herself; torn jacket and her snow-soaked skirt halfway down around her hips. Her cheek and lips were cut. She was a mess and it was nobody's fault, least of all hers. Why this damn shame then?

She found another police station in Wilde Grove. People milled around the reception desk, harassing a Sergeant. In the toilet she washed the blood and tears from her face, tidied her hair. Back in the waiting room, she sat next to a broken coffee machine and waited for someone to come and talk to her. She felt numbed with shock. She rocked back and forth on the bench and chain smoked her last few cigarettes.

She woke on the floor. The station was empty. No one had come to take her statement. No one gave a shit. The quietness frightened her. It meant something was wrong. She checked her money. Ten pounds. Gabriel would know what was going on. He'd know it was time to stop playing games. She should never have listened to that kid Jimmy.

The vending machines at the tube station weren't working. She jumped the barrier and ran down the dead escalator. The updraught moaned pitifully. The platform was empty, the light dim. An icy wind flowed out from the tunnel, but no train came behind it. Twice more the trainless wind came before she allowed herself to consider the possibility that the system had finally broken down. Abruptly, she heard a whistling in the tunnel and felt another draught speeding towards her. She stepped close to the platform's edge and saw two yellow pinpricks of light, speeding out of the dark. They were too close together, she realised, too small; not lights at all, but eyes, and behind them, metal hurtling through the dark, bearing down fast on her – no – on the bird, the huge grey owl that sped by her, fleeing the tunnel, screeching as it was swallowed up by the train.

Across the street from Gabriel's house a family were stacking

160

luggage into the back of a van. She went to ask if they knew Gabriel, but when the man saw her he ushered his wife and two kids into the car and slammed the doors. Bernadette rapped on the window. He ignored her and kept trying to start the car. He turned pale and his hands shook as he turned the key. The engine coughed into life and the car rolled off through the filthy slush.

The door to Gabriel's house stood open. She went inside, calling, "Gabriel?" and then, "Jimmy?" The ground floor rooms were deserted. She went upstairs to Jimmy's room. The door was unlocked. Inside, only the stench of stale cigarettes, dirty socks and spilt beer. She opened the window and smelled the coming blizzard.

There was a porn magazine on the bed, just pictures, no writing. *Maximum Screw* it was called. She supposed it was Jimmy's. There was a carton of yoghurt next to the tv. She peeled the top off, sniffed, then tasted it. Bitter, but edible. She ate it all. Afterwards, she sorted through the sprawl of clothes on the floor, wondering if any of them had belonged to Gabriel. She browsed through a pile of paperbacks – Turgenev, Dostoevsky, Kafka and the like – looking for clues as to Gabriel's existence. A photograph fell from one book, a picture of herself, taken three months ago on his last visit to Dublin. It showed her left profile, with strands of red hair falling across her face. Brown eyes were turned towards the camera, as if trying to catch one sly glimpse of Gabriel. She hadn't.

She smelled each item of clothing, flicked through each book, trying to detect some sign of his presence. But she couldn't recall his scent, the feel of him inside her, the taste of his sweat after they had made love, or the sound of his voice whispering how special she was. His absence left a hollow space in her heart. She put the picture back in a book and tried the tv – it didn't work. She found a couple of smokable butts in an ashtray. When she'd finished them, she lay on the bed, pulled the stale duvet over herself and dreamt of nothing, nothing at all.

In the morning she found Jimmy's body in a room on the top floor. He was naked under the mouldy blanket, his skin the colour of a candle. His eyes were closed, his freckles had almost disappeared, but he still had that stupid smile on his face. It puzzled her – you don't smile when you freeze to death. Poor bastard. Did Gabriel abandon you too? She pulled the blanket up over the body and went downstairs to the phone. She dialled 999 before she realised the connection was dead. She searched around for something to write with. She wanted to leave a note, explaining things to Gabriel, if he came back. She found nothing.

She left the house. What could she have said, anyway? Bastard didn't deserve explanations, he didn't even tell Jimmy I was coming. The roads were quiet this morning, the traffic intermittent. At Holloway Road a dozen people stood at a bus stop. She waited with them for an hour, but no buses came. She walked south towards Islington and found a small cafe open. An Asian couple sat at a table by the window, staring blankly out at the street. The woman held a sleeping child in her arms. Bernadette sat near the counter.

A woman wearing a brown apron came out and told her, "we got no bread, milk or eggs."

"Whatever," Bernadette said. "Everything."

The woman brought her a plate of bacon, sausages and beans, and a mug of steaming black coffee. After twenty minutes or so, the Asian couple got up and left. A few minutes later, Bernadette noticed the bundle on a chair by the table where they'd sat. She got up. Her knees felt weak, the pulse was pounding in her temple. She went and picked up the bundle. It was the baby the woman had held; the dead baby. She screamed. Later, when she'd calmed down, the woman told her how to get out of the city. She seemed to think that this was the wisest course, though she didn't say why and Bernadette didn't ask. She tried not to look at the still bundle as she left the cafe.

She headed South, towards the city, wondering what the woman would do with the child. It was worse than Jimmy. Why? Because she saw Jimmy as a loser? Saw his essential weakness, was that it?

In the West End she began to see more people. A few cars sped by overhead on Palladin Avenue and she welcomed this sign of normalcy. The snow had stopped and the sun shone brightly. The streets grew busier as she headed west. She saw the river, caught the scent of the sea from it and heard the screech of gulls from somewhere. It reminded her of home. There was music, a brass band, fading in the distance. She chased after it, trailing the music in and out of the Soho streets but never quite catching up. Still, it cheered her, made her smile and feel lightheaded.

On Shaftesbury Avenue she saw him, thirty yards away. Part of a group standing, listening to a white-haired preacher.

"Gabriel," she called out. "Gabriel."

She ran towards the group but he had moved on by the time she got there. She raced on towards the Square and caught a brief glimpse of him going into the Europa Centre. Inside, she fought her way through more people than she had seen in days. Piped music flooded the concourse; an invitation to spend. People poured out of the shops, pushing trolleys laden with clothes and electrical goods. She began to fear that she'd lost him, until, through a crowd of vacant faces, she saw him leaving a store with half a dozen cameras around his neck and a tripod under one arm.

She ran towards him, calling out his name. "Where were you?" she cried.

Something hit her in the stomach and she fell to the floor. Through her blurred vision she saw an arm reaching towards her and then pain exploded in her skull.

She came to in near darkness and dabbed at the blood congealed in her hair. She was cold and frightened. Staring through the gloom, she saw the wreckage that had been the Europa. It was carnage – goods, glass and blood everywhere. The only light came flickering from a tv set lying on it's side amidst a pile of videocassettes. She crawled towards it and watched the images, recognising the Houses of Parliament and the face of the Prime Minister. A newsreader came on screen and behind him, she made out the word 'CRISIS' in capital letters. There was no sound on the tv but it didn't matter. This world on it's side, at right angles to her own, could not be explained with simple words.

At Victoria Coach Station she found a phone booth that hadn't been smashed. She put a coin in the slot and dialled her parents number. An engaged tone. She tried three times. Then she called the operator and asked to make a reverse charge call. An electronic voice told her, "All International lines are busy. Please try again later."

She smashed the receiver against the side of the booth. It felt good. She crossed Westminster Bridge, heading for Waterloo station, thinking she'd get a train out of the city. Her jacket pulled tight across her chest, she tried in vain to hold back tears of frustration. Weak Bernadette, what use is that now? Dada won't help me anymore, not in this world. Do they wonder what goes on, over there in West Cork?

The street was quiet and badly lit. A car pulled sharply in to the kerb and a man leaned out of the open window. "I got a car, see?" he said, his hand caressing the door. "I'm going soon, tonight in fact. Wanna come?"

Warily, she approached the car and said, "what's the catch?"

"No catch," the man said. "I need company, that's all."

"All right," she said. He opened the passenger door and when she was inside, she said, "lay a hand on me and I'll bloody kill you."

He wiped sweat from his forehead. "No, I've no interest in that. Just someone to talk to, some company." His name was Harold. His wife had left him. Taken the two kids away a month back. No word of explanation, nothing. He'd been living in the car ever since. He'd been a cabbie, only there had been no fares since the weekend. In the morning, he would take her wherever she wanted to go. For free, he said.

Bernadette thought about it, thought about the place she would most like to be in all the world. Home. She would like to be home. Don't tell Harold though. Don't feel obliged to him. Let him do the talking. So she kept quiet and listened to Harold's story as the night and snow fell over the city.

The radio woke her, electric guitars and a morose voice singing about failed rituals. The engine was running but the car hadn't moved. She fought the powerful drowsiness which threatened to smother her and threw open the door. She fell on to the street, retching, puking up sour bile. Tears stung her eyes and her breath came and went in painful gasps. She lay there for ten minutes, letting the cold penetrate her clothes, not caring because if she could feel that, then she was still alive. Abruptly, the engine died behind her. Remembering Harold, she got up and went to the driver's door.

"Shit," she whispered. The plastic tube came up under the back seat from the exhaust. Harold was held in his seat by the safety belt, his tongue poking out between his teeth. One eye was closed, the other stared out at the city that had betrayed him.

At Waterloo the trains stood empty on the tracks, their buffet cars ransacked and looted, like the shops in the station concourse. Some men in suits were partying with magnums of champagne. A black girl approached and offered her a bottle. She took it.

Later, drunk, she headed north again. Some blocks were still lit, others were in total darkness. On a street beneath Palladin she found a van dispensing hot soup to a crowd of people. She held back a while, but after an hour of watching, hunger drove her to the two men who were ladling the soup from a churn into plastic mugs.

"Haven't seen your face before?" the younger man said. "Why did you come here?"

"Just give me soup," she said.

"Of course," he said, filling a mug and handing it to her.

She turned away before he could ask anything else. She walked thirty yards from the van and drank her soup in a few hot gulps.

An Asian woman came towards her from the van. "You're cold," she said. She wore a man's overcoat and what looked like half a dozen sweaters beneath it. "You come with me."

Bernadette's head was aching. She said, "I wish I was home."

"Not far," the woman said. "Nice'n warm." She moved away, Bernadette following, not knowing what else to do. They came to an alleyway crammed with debris. A warm draft wafted over them. They moved through the rubbish, the woman telling her to be careful where she trod. But exhaustion made her careless and she stepped on something, some creature of the debris. A mound of cardboard groaned and a head appeared out of a box, muttered a curse and disappeared again. "Ssshh now," the woman said. "Down here, nice'n warm." At the end of the alley, the woman cleared a place on the pavement, opened out a half dozen newspapers and told Bernadette to lie down. Then she lay beside her and pulled an old blanket over the two of them. She put an arm around Bernadette's waist and they slept.

In the morning the woman was gone. The day passed slowly and pangs of hunger gnawed continuously at Bernadette's stomach. She thought of the events that had reduced her to this state and tried to put them in sequence, to impose some order on them. After a while she gave it up, accepting that it no longer mattered. The city was evolving, the first stage of which was the breakdown of order and rationality. It was more than that though, but she lacked the details to complete the picture. It made no difference, everything was so quiet now, and there were no jets to shatter the still silence.

Days passed and she abandoned the idea of leaving the city. She slept in empty houses, moving to a new one each night. The others who had remained shunned her for this till she realised that like the city itself they were undergoing some sort of metamorphosis. As part of this new race she had to do the same. The last time she slept in a house, she woke, petrified in the awful dark. Listening to her heartbeat, she realised that the nightmare was not her own. She had taken on the dreams of those who had left. Their residual presence still clung to the crumbling bricks and mortar, but in time it too would vanish.

Some still talked about the old ways, but they were in a minority. Most, like Bernadette, accepted the imperative to adapt. In time, the buildings would fall and they would forget how they had made the transition from one world to the other. She never told the story of her old life, and chose not to listen to the stories of others. The funereal streets ushered in a silence, a peace she had unknowingly sought.

The city had called to her, using Gabriel, someone she didn't know. It did not matter why or how, only that she was here. She and the others would witness its passing and await whatever came next. She couldn't see it yet, had no hint, not even in dreams, but she had patience. This was her home now, the place to which she had been coming all her life.

If I Should Wake Before I Die

An hour before dawn, Lee dreamed alone in the car. Through the fogged windscreen he saw stars blinking in and out of the blue-black sky like faulty Christmas lights, and felt the cold tighten its grip on his bones. With an effort of will he wound down the window and sucked in a mouthful of freezing air. Moonlight shone on the frost-covered fields and the world seemed emptier than it had any right to be. He lit a cigarette, turned on the heating, then the radio, pre-tuned to a talk station. A man was complaining about East European prostitutes attracting unsavoury elements to his neighbourhood. Said he was embarrassed to walk his kids to school.

When the windscreen had demisted, Lee started the car and pulled out of the layby. He passed the lights of a Shell station and shortly after drove through the main street of a sleeping northern town. "They know nothing of our traditions," the man on the radio was saying. Lee saw himself staring out of the rear-view mirror, nodding. Talk-shows kept him informed about the important issues of the day. He saw no mystery in people wanting to talk to perfect strangers at five in the morning about the war or refugees or gay priests. Their voices offered as true a picture of the world as he wanted. Without them he might have remained unaware of the extent to which the country was being swamped by bogus Albanians.

The news came on. Lee flicked his cigarette out the window and wound it up. A terrorist bomb had killed twenty-eight people in a Marseilles marketplace. Interest rates were rising. A Russian oilman had been arrested. The government had failed in its promise to get tough on crime. Lee's head pulsed and his eyes kept drifting off the road. He reached into the holdall on the passenger seat and found he'd used up the last of his pro-plus. Should have stopped at the Shell station. Should have got a holdall with a logo on it, Nike for instance, or the name of a football team. He liked the idea of labels, the way they said things about you without anyone having to ask. When he was a kid he'd had a blue hoody with Quiksilver on it. Used to wonder what it felt like to surf. A woman's body had been found in a flat in Bedford. Police were treating her death as suspicious. House prices were continuing to fall in the south-east. A former Derby winner had died of MRSA. A teenage girl had killed herself live on the internet. Lee understood that people were affected by these things.

Lights appeared in the distance, coming towards him. He eased back on the accelerator, bringing the Astra's speed down to fifty. The lights grew brighter as they approached. He wondered if he closed his eyes, would he still drive in a straight line? Would the other driver guess that he couldn't see? He shut his eyes and began counting. At four, he felt something huge and powerful hurtling by on his right.

A woman was talking on the radio. Her voice faltered as she spoke. "They had no right," she was saying. "The things they said about me were lies." The talk-show host asked her what they had said and the woman started crying. There was no need. He pressed buttons, searching for another station. For a while he listened to a pop show and sang along with a song he recognised. He stopped when he realised that his words didn't correspond with the lyrics. He retuned to the talk-show and heard the same woman talking about all she had lost. As she listed each thing in turn, he repeated it aloud. In the mirror he saw himself nodding again.

Presently, Lee took a left onto a narrow, winding lane and followed it down into the valley. Pockets of mist settled on the fields and curled over the ditch into the lane. After quarter of a mile he pulled over on to a dirt track leading into a wood. He stopped the car, got out and stared into the fields. Amorphous shapes drowsed in the mist, dreaming animal dreams. Feeling nothing. The eastern hills were edged with pink light, though it would be a while yet before it swept down into the valley. Back in the car he wondered if the woman had said her name. Unable to recall, he edged the vehicle slowly into the trees until the low, spindly branches of hawthorn and mountain ash crowded too tight around him. Insects were caught in the glare of his headlights while larger creatures flew back and forth across his field of vision. He tried to follow their flightpaths but the bats were too quick for him. The woman was having difficulty composing herself. "I feel wretched," she said.

The talk-show host said he understood.

"They never said goodbye," the woman said. "They didn't know."

Abruptly, the man went to another call. Lee wondered if the woman was aware she'd been cut off, or if her voice still carried on, speaking in dead air. He lowered the window and changed stations. A hip-hop song blared out of the speakers and something hit the windscreen. He stared through the glass and saw that it was moving. Curious, he turned off the ignition and got out of the car. The creature made feeble, squeaking noises as it tried to rise from the bonnet. One of its wings appeared to be broken. He picked it up and held it a few inches from his face. When it squirmed and tried to flap its good wing, he gripped it a little tighter. Its heart raced, a thousand beats a minute. As if trying to cram a whole lifetime into a few seconds. Opening his fist, he saw that he had crushed its lower body. Its hairless skin seemed translucent, and he wondered if the air passed right through. Years ago he had bought a bird for a girl who kept it in a cage. He'd forgotten the bird but now he remembered how it had groomed itself, smoothing its green and yellow feathers. The way it had perched fearlessly on his finger as he'd removed it from the cage.

More bats flitted through the air around him, as if sensing their brother's desire to fly one last time. A desire that drained it of life. After a few seconds it was still and he laid it carefully on the ground.

He got the holdall from the car. The leaves crunched beneath his feet as he trudged deeper into the wood, the dank smell of dead vegetation filling his nostrils. He couldn't remember the bird's name. Dry leaves cracked up ahead as something walked over them. Its footsteps matched his own. Not a fox or a badger. They made piglike noises, rooting around in dirt. This was different, more deliberate. It made his palms sweat. When he stopped to try and identify the sounds, he couldn't hear them at all. He moved on, clambering over fallen trees or ducking under low, ground-scraping branches, making noises to drown out those he

169

Mike O'Driscoll

hadn't made.

After five minutes he leaned against a maple tree and lit a cigarette. Sweat cooled on his face as he listened, hearing nothing. The absence of sound eased his tension. Close by, a dry leaf moved. Peering intently, he saw a mouse busying itself with a piece of debris. He squatted, drew on the cigarette and saw the tiny creature more clearly in the orange glow. It seemed unperturbed by his presence. An almost human sigh drifted through the undergrowth. Like sleep-talking. When he was younger and had lived in the residential unit, some of the kids had talked in their sleep. He used to lie awake at night and listen to them. They made more sense in the dark.

The mouse was standing up on its hindfeet, looking right at him.

What does it feel like?

He turned his head slowly, looking to see where the voice had come from. He'd imagined it; his sudden unease was a trick of the wind. Except, there was no wind. He stared at the mouse, trying to fathom its purpose. Nothing was clear except his own foolishness. He took a long pull on the cigarette till its tip was glowing hot and bright, then he lowered it towards the creature's head. The mouse scuttled away before he could burn it.

Overhead, the night was losing its depth and a pale, watery light was beginning to filter into the trees. He felt a quickening sensation in his stomach as he set off again, a strange hunger that unnerved him. A sheep began bleating from one of the nearby fields. It wasn't saying anything real, but even so he wished it would shut up. Just as he wished whatever was moving through the trees to his right would be still. Something else came behind it, making a whistling noise. His skin tingled and he fought the urge to look over his shoulder. It was a disappointment to discover that the numbness that gripped his heart worked less effectively on his brain. More bleating sounds came, closer now, inside the wood. Broken voices answered them, like voices from a badly tuned radio. They had nothing to say, no new insights to offer the world.

He pressed on through the trees until he came to a drystone wall and the garden stretching beyond. The lawn was coated with frost and half a dozen frozen dog turds glistened there like oversize jewels. At the far end of the garden stood the house with its pale walls and dark windows, solemn as a judge's stare. He leaned against the wall, wondering if it was the same dog. How old would it have been? One human year was seven for a dog, which meant it would have been over a hundred.

It was immaterial. He wasn't even sure how old Frank and Carol were now. He'd never thought much about it when he had lived with them. They were just grown-ups, people he'd lived with for a while. In the ten years he'd been away, he'd hardly given them a thought.

He unzipped the holdall. The dog's name was Buster. Some kind of terrier, white with patches of brown on his back. He took out a small package and put it inside his leather coat, then touched the other items in turn without removing them from the bag. The hammer made him think about a Christmas present Frank had given him when he was ten. A carpenter's belt complete with its own tools – screwdriver, clawhammer, a tenon saw – and pouches for nails and screws. Now you've got your own, Frank had said, maybe you'll stop messing with mine. Once, he'd used them to build a den in the woods, but that had been about the only thing he'd ever made. Mostly, he took things apart.

As dawn crawled down the valley slopes, Lee leaned against the wall, feeling enervated, like something was leeching off his numbness. Fragmented memories buzzed round his head, none of them welcome. He tried to focus on the things that really mattered, the fundamentals. Money, security, health. They were what people talked about on the radio. Everything else was gloss. Losing sight of that was the road to hurt. If he ever had kids, that's the first thing he would tell them. Like Frank and Carol should have told him.

Ten days since he had slept in his own bed. Hard to imagine it now, the other side cold and empty. He lit a cigarette and smoked it hurriedly, afraid the nicotine would choke that train of thought. His intentions were still inchoate but he sensed that time was slipping away from him. Soon, he would have to flesh them out, not only for himself but so that they too would understand.

For a while he sat and stared into the trees, aware of the quiet. He felt weightless, and imagined himself made of mist, drifting up above the world. Voices were like that, which made them easier to relate to than the people whose mouths they escaped from.

A dog barked suddenly. A light had come on upstairs. A minute later, the kitchen light came on and the backdoor opened. A dog ran out into the garden and Frank appeared in the doorway, in shorts and a t-shirt.

He yawned and stretched while the dog squatted and pissed on the lawn. Not Buster, but some German Shepherd he didn't recognise. People replaced things too easily. He'd never thought much about what might have happened after he'd left, but now he couldn't stop. He imagined another kid moving into the house, sleeping in his bed. The thought festered, reminding him why he had learned not to feel. After Frank and Carol, if somebody hurt him, he always said it was all right.

The dog was running towards the wood. Lee grabbed the holdall and scrambled a little further back into the trees. He heard her sniffing at the other side of the wall and then she growled. He took the hammer out and put his hand around the cold steel head, trying to draw its hardness into himself. Frank's footsteps sounded noisily on the lawn and a low snarl came from deeper in the wood. The German Shepherd yelped and retreated. Lee rose slowly, peered over the wall. Frank was halfway down the garden, the dog at his side. He patted her head and made soothing noises as he gazed into the trees, frowning.

Lee felt a stab of anger. For some reason he'd imagined Frank would be little changed, but although he was clearly recognisable as the same man, he was also different. As if something had been altered inside him, some small but essential thing that had defined him as Frank. It didn't matter. It changed nothing.

Frank turned and walked back to the house, the dog following him. An impostor. Grabbing the holdall, Lee moved through the trees to the eastern corner of the garden. He climbed over the stone wall and made for a small shed about thirty yards up from the trees. Its creosoted walls were dusted with frost which cooled his cheek as he pressed against it. The sudden crunching of grass startled him, and before he could squeeze into the space between the wall and the shed, a sheep ran past towards the wood, with something brown and white snapping at its heels. The sheep scrambled up and over the wall. As the dog clambered up after it, a young boy raced into view, waving a stick and urging the dog on. Lee felt a sudden burst of excitement in his chest and made to follow them, but before he had taken half a dozen steps, all three had vanished into the woods. He stopped in the middle of the lawn, confused.

Feelings belonged to memory and the less time you spent thinking about the past, the less chance there was of old pains rising to the

If I Should Wake Before I Die

surface. The boy reminded him of his friend, Robert. Most evenings after school they had played in the woods but it was one time he was remembering now, almost their last time together. He had felt that someone had seen them coming out of the wood, had known somehow, what they had done. The sheep had gone in there of its own accord. They'd just stumbled across it, tangled in thick undergrowth. It was an opportunity, he'd told Robert. Robert's face had been uncomprehending as he'd explained about the test. How to find out what an animal was capable of feeling, if what they felt was different from people. Robert, reluctantly helping him hold the sheep as Buster barked with excitement, wincing as Lee had smashed the hammer against its head. The sound of splintering bone and having to force Robert to take the hammer, to finish the job. Insisting that their friendship depended on it. It had taken three more blows for him to do it, and afterwards he'd stood there slack-jawed and silent. It meant they were brothers, Lee said. It meant they would never let each other down.

Except he'd seen the shock written all over Robert's face, and he'd known that the woman who'd seen them come out on the far side of the wood, away from Frank's house, had seen it too. Already he'd understood the extent to which your feelings could betray the things you'd done, and though he'd been able to still his own emotions, Robert's haunted face had signalled their guilt to her.

He trudged back to the shed and crouched there, shivering. Crows were cawing in the woods, a harsh noise that grated on his nerves. He wrapped his arms round his body, more to hold himself together than to keep out the cold. It had been inside him ever since those long, lonely nights of laying awake so as not to have to dream. If you thought about the things that scared you instead of dreaming them, they became less real. Not darkness or demons, not ghosts or vampires, but people. Their absence. Not being where you expected them to be. After endless hours of sleeplessness, birds would signal the dawn and he'd go quietly to their room and sit on the edge of their bed while they slept. The radio-alarm was his cue to start talking, trying to explain about vanishing people. Ssshhh, Frank would say, making a space for him to lay down. Listen to what they're saying. He would do that, and though he didn't understand, it was the sound of the voices that had held him, the inflections of emotion, the intimations of how life might turn out, all

173

heard in a warm half-light, the kind of dream he wanted to have.

He took the package from his coat, opened it and pulled out a set of photographs. It wasn't the first time he'd looked at the pictures, but no matter how often he'd studied them, he still couldn't understand what they were trying to tell him. They seemed unrelated, a series of random snapshots rather than the cohesive narrative he had anticipated.

Pillars of mist rose up from the trees, making it seem as if the woods were on fire. Two gulls soared overhead, riding on the sun's first rays. A voice told Lee he was not asleep, that he was not empty. Light sparkled off the strands of a web strung between the wall and the shed. Thoughts oscillated inside his brain, making it hard to stay focused. A spider hung there. He wondered how it perceived him. The pictures made him angry. It wasn't real anger, just the memory of being angry. He didn't understand why he was remembering feeling. The spider crawled towards the top of the web. He put the pictures back inside his coat and leaned closer till his face was just inches from the strands of silk.

It was the photographs talking to him, making him feel. He straightened a forefinger and touched the web, letting the spider crawl onto his hand. Waking you to pain. He turned it palm upwards and the spider moved boldly into the creased flesh. He couldn't describe it. Some kind of sadness. He closed his fist on the spider and realised that he had been holding his breath. He let it out slowly, through his mouth, surprised at how long it took to empty his lungs. Indefinable anxieties sapped his will. He was no longer sure why he had come here, felt uncertain about what he was supposed to do next.

He unwound his fingers and the spider descended from his hand like a parachutist. It landed on the bottom plank of the shed and crawled underneath. Did it see itself as alone? Did it hurt when its legs were pulled off? A weight had settled on his brain, crowding the grand emptiness with useless thoughts. There were things he would have changed, but how, he couldn't say. Maybe he would have come back here earlier. Start with Frank and Carol, not have to go any further. Not have to feel what the woman on the radio felt.

The thoughts belonged to someone else. He rubbed his eyes and squinted at something laying on the lawn. Fingers of ice scratched at his back, driving the cold deep inside him. He tried to move but his limbs did not respond. The body of a young boy. Buster appeared, moving hesitantly towards the motionless form. The dog sniffed the boy's face and licked the too white flesh. It was Robert, he saw, feeling a wave of strange emotions crash over him.

Buster raised his head and looked at Lee. You killed him.

Lee shook his head. It wasn't true.

He couldn't stand it. What you made him do.

Lee thought about the sheep and the woman who had seen them coming out of the woods. What was her name? Shouldn't have made him do it. Tell by his face he didn't want to. But it was a test, a test to prove he had the guts. The sheep was as good as dead anyway.

Music distracted him and with it, Frank's voice singing along. Prince? Michael Jackson? He could never remember whose song it was. Only that Frank would always join in despite the fact that he couldn't sing for shit. Robert was scared when Lee told him to keep his mouth shut. It was just a dumb animal, while the test was a bond between them. The woman had asked questions, wanting to know what they got up to in the woods. She needed a warning, Lee explained, something to make her understand to keep her questions to herself. He'd told Robert about her cat, explained that it could be a test of loyalty.

You made him do it, the dog said. He did this for you.

No, not for me. To shut her up.

Buster laid his head on the dead boy's chest.

Here boy, Lee called. Good dog. Buster ignored him and closed its eyes. Lee felt he was on the verge of disintegrating. He picked up the holdall and set off in the shadow of the wall. As he neared the house, the music faded and he caught snatches of a news programme from the kitchen. He crouched beneath the window and tried to focus on the voice as a way of shutting out what he was feeling. The government was to face a confidence vote. A famous actor had committed suicide following the diagnosis of a rare skin disease. Police were linking the death of a woman in Bedford to the murder of Grace Lehane whose body had been discovered eight days ago in Bristol. A new type of star had been discovered at the edge of the Milky Way. A religious leader said it marked the beginning of the end of the world.

Lee wondered how anyone could tell. It made sense to think that for everything new that appeared in the sky, something had disappeared from somewhere else. His fingers losing their sense of touch meant some other part of him was feeling too acutely. He cradled one fist in the other and blew into them. He worried about frostbite and wondered if he was becoming irrational, letting emotions get the better of him. He listened to the radio, yearning for the comfort of other tragedies.

A shadow moved across the splintered light at the edge of the wood, something swaying in the November breeze. Small tremors ran through Lee's body as he tried to deny what he was seeing. Buster hanging from the branch of a hawthorn tree, his tongue lolling out between his teeth, longer than it had been when he was alive. He didn't do it. If he said it often enough it would be true. He could believe that. Like he believed Lizzie's death was nothing to do with him. Except for the bird. He'd bought it for her when they'd lived in the residential unit. She was his girlfriend. A budgie. What was its name? Cost ten pounds, and the cage was extra. He'd gone to the unit after he'd left Frank and Carol. Lizzie came later, when they were both fourteen. They were in love and had sex all the time. Fucked like rabbits until she'd dumped him for some older boy. Watching the bird preen in its cage. Whistling to it, knowing that it trusted him. A test. He remembered coaxing it out of the cage. Squeezing the life out of it. Leaving its broken body on Lizzie's bed.

How old had Buster been? Seven dog years to one human. He'd fought hard and Lee had cried. Only time in his life. Lizzie's new boyfriend had attacked him the next day but Lee had a knife. Stabbed the fucker in the thigh. Lizzie's shrill screams reminded him of the bird. It was good to be able to translate, to render things abstract. Lizzie's fright was a bird. Not the first time, but two nights ago. The first time it was the boyfriend who was altered, his blood becoming the sky at dusk. They sent him to a young offenders' institute and that became home. No different really to Frank and Carol's place.

What appeared to be one thing was quite often something else entirely. When you made things abstract it meant they couldn't hurt you. He could look at the photographs and not feel anything because they were just representations. As long as he didn't walk into the house, the voices he was hearing might just as well have come from the radio as out of the mouths of Frank or Carol. It was no trouble turning off a radio.

He peered over the sill and saw them sitting at the table. Carol looked older, in her red towelling robe and moccasins. Maybe it was because she hadn't yet brushed the randomness of sleep out of her dark hair or maybe the dreams etched into her face were not those she would have chosen. The same sense of disappointment seemed to have touched Frank, painting lines of grey in his sideburns and stealing the spark from his eyes. Lee tried to remember them the way they had been, and what they had meant to him. He felt weak, as if his resolve were dissipating in the November chill. After three years, why had they sent him away? If they had loved him, why hadn't they stuck by him, instead of packing him off like faulty goods? If they hadn't done that Buster might still be alive instead of hanging from a tree at the bottom of their garden. The hurt was theirs. He'd told them it was okay, he was all right. It meant nothing.

Carol smiled across the table. The kind of smile that didn't go anywhere. Frank was nodding in time to a song on the radio, something old that Lee half recognised. Dexy's Midnight something? He gave a piece of toast to the dog sitting at his side.

Carol frowned. You always do that, she said. No matter how many times I say.

Does no harm, Frank said.

She shook her head. It encourages bad habits.

You can't encourage something unless its already there.

They used to say the same things about Buster. Frank petted the dog and Carol watched him. Lee wondered if they ever thought about Buster. Her gaze drifted slightly and focused on Lee. Her eyes seemed to come to life through the glass, and she smiled again. Lee felt a muted ache in his chest. It was only when you let people get close to you that you felt this way. In pain. You thought being close to someone was about trusting them but in reality it was about them discovering your weaknesses, finding out how to make you hurt. First, they make you love them, then they tear you apart. Do they even remember who you were?

He squatted, his back against the wall. The sun had edged up over the trees, making his eyes water. Unfamiliar emotions had filled the emptiness inside him. It had been a mistake to return. He took out the photographs again and looked through them, hoping they would make sense to him now. The duct tape over Lizzie's mouth, hiding lips that would never kiss again. The stillness in her eyes which signalled the realisation that his face was the last she would ever see. In Bedford, everything had been much clearer, what he had to do, his reasons for doing it. Afterwards, when he had taken the pictures, he'd felt no doubts. He'd understood that it had been wrong to kill the bird. But she had betrayed him, just as Frank and Carol had done ten years ago. He'd done Buster because it was the only way he'd known how to make them feel what he was feeling.

If Grace hadn't walked out on him ten days ago he might never have woken up to the truth. How love was simply the abstract of pain. The thought of it sickened him. Laying himself bare so she could stab him in the heart and then the excuses – that he didn't know how to trust, that he had too much anger inside him, that he was afraid to let people get close. If that were true, if he'd stopped her getting close, then how was it she'd caused him so much pain? He'd tried to make her see the necessity of distance; all along he had believed himself capable of maintaining it. Before it happened, if someone had said to him that she would walk away, he would have felt indifferent, unaffected, able to carry on. But it had cut deep into him, exposing his weakness, his self-delusion.

Calm settled on him as he looked through the pictures, finding a kind of peace in their stillness. The purple bruises around Grace's throat, the trickle of blood on her chin from where she had bit her tongue. Even before he had tracked her to Bristol, he had known what he had to do to kill the pain. If she had had a dog or a cat or a bird, he would have left it unharmed. Now, staring at her dead eyes, eyes that could no longer betray him, he felt he could finally trust her.

There was a purity in his feelings towards both women, an acceptance of what they were, what they had represented. He thought about Frank and Carol, tried to imagine feeling the same towards them and realised how much he wanted it to be. He laid six photographs on the path. Another two he rested on the sill above his head. His body felt lighter, as if the burden of feeling had been lifted. He crept towards the kitchen door and placed another eight pictures on the step, arranging them in two neat rows.

People were talking on the radio inside the house. He heard Frank and Carol's voices, as if they too were speaking on the radio, offering their opinions on the war, on refugees, on the dispossessed. He imagined that they were speaking for his benefit, that they were no longer abstract but knew that he was still somewhere out in the world, listening to what they had to say. Perhaps they sensed how close he was.

He took the hammer and duct tape from the holdall, and started to rise. The sense of weightlessness empowered him, made him aware of how little he felt. As he reached for the door handle, someone called his name. Turning, he caught a glimpse of movement at the bottom of the garden. He shielded his eyes against the sunlight, saw strands of vapour rising from the grass, and through them, a young boy standing at the edge of the wood. His heart lurched, then began beating faster as he recognised the clothes, the blue, hooded sweatshirt with the Quiksilver logo, the baggy jeans, the Adidas trainers. Buster waited at the boy's side, anticipating some new adventure.

The boy beckoned. Lee felt a tremor of excitement and then a slow crumbling of emptiness. He put down the hammer and tape and searched through the remaining pictures, shaking, aware of a growing sense of urgency. In the one he wanted, Grace smiled out of the frame, the sunlight seeming to set her straw-coloured hair ablaze. Her eyes seemed to hold the key to some unrevealed secret. He stood beside her in the picture, one tentative arm around her waist, half-smiling, as if caught between the desire to know and the comfort of unknowing. He wished he had had the guts to ask her what the secret was. How it really felt.

He slid the picture under the door, left the others on the step and turned back towards the wood. The grass sparkled and crunched beneath his feet as he made his way down the garden. His heart thumped painfully, as if trying to beat its way out of his chest. The boy's fingers were cold as the earth as he took hold of Lee's hand. A sudden fear touched him, yet he went with the boy, as if compelled to follow his body in consummating a union he didn't yet comprehend.

It's all right, the boy said. It's okay.

Diffuse sunlight brushed the low spindly branches and was swallowed in pools of darkness. Something scraped against Lee's face and drew blood across his cheek. Thin shadows chased each other back and forth across their path. He tripped on a root and sprawled in dank leaves, biting his tongue to silence his fear. As he tried to get up his hands sank into a wet, yielding warmth. He scrabbled back from the animal remains, not wanting to see what it had been. He stifled a sob as he tried to wipe the blood and slime from his arms against a tree trunk, but the stink of decay burned in his nostrils. He hugged the tree to steady himself, pressing his face against the rough bark. Sweat stung his eyes but failed to wash away the memories of things he had done to stop himself from feeling. Denying reality. Saying it was all right whenever he was hurting. The bark softened a little against his face and grazed his skin. He pulled back instinctively and saw a small tongue withdrawing into rough puckered lips, a drop of blood from his cheek glistening on it.

I felt this way, the boy said, crouching beside him. He looked older than he did just a few moments ago. His blank expression was a reminder of Lee's lost emptiness. If he had killed them, what would be different now? If Grace or Lizzie were alive, would his pain be any more real? He wondered if it was possible to feel anything other than fear.

The boy yanked on his arm. Come on, he said, pulling him deeper into the wood where soft noises oozed from the earth like dead creatures' prayers. He tried to imagine what they were feeling. It wasn't at all like he thought it would be, the sharp tang of dread and the quick, intense moment of pain, uncomplicated by any kind of anger or hate. They detached themselves from the trees and stepped out of the shadows. He caught glimpses of his own face, sometimes feathered, sometimes furred. He thought about what he had been and what he was becoming, surprised at the strength of his fear. Even so, he wanted to feel more.

Lizzie stepped out from the hollow of a tree and he felt a stabbing sensation in his heart. She was fourteen again, but the silver tape over her mouth was much more recent. I'm sorry, he said. What I did to you.

She nodded, reached up and pulled the tape away. Opening her mouth, she stuck her fingers inside and pulled out a bird. She put it on his head, and as it gripped him he felt all the terror and pain she had felt in her last moments. His flesh coarsened and split as the past crawled out of him. Memories and their attendant emotions flowed through his mind and, seeing her smile, he accepted that she had the right to do this.

She urged him on, past everything he had tested. They were whole again and no longer afraid. Robert too, welcomed him into the wood, handing him the cat they had killed. Its touch burned him but he held onto it, feeling its heart begin to beat and seeing the livid rope marks fade from Robert's neck. There were a dozen or more kids walking beside him through the trees, mostly boys, and though he could hardly bring himself to look, he knew they all carried a piece of his hurt. He thought he knew what was coming and tried to ready himself for it, but even so, seeing Grace laid in a shallow grave still shocked him. Her body was pale and bruised, her tongue swollen and protruding from between her blackened lips.

Touch her, the boy said. Feel what you made her feel.

He didn't think he could but as he stared at her unmoving form, he was overwhelmed with pity and remorse. She was beautiful still, in spite of what he had done to her. He knelt and raised her head in his hands. I'm so sorry, he said. I'm so fucking sorry. It didn't seem enough but he didn't know what else to say. He was appalled at the tears that filled his eyes but had no power to stop them. Grace moved beneath him and he shuddered as her cold fingers touched his cheek, transmitting her feelings to him. Don't, he said, before she gave him back the fragments of a humanness that allowed him to see what he had lost when he had driven her away. How much she'd loved him, and how crazy he'd been to fear what he'd felt for her.

I take it all back, he told her. Grace smiled but there was no life in her eyes. Its absence mirrored his own awful emptiness. He'd finally gotten what he'd always striven for, he realised, but it wasn't what he wanted anymore.

He turned back to the others. It was difficult to move, even harder to speak. The tear that strayed onto his cheek was a tiny glacier. I'm afraid, he said in a brittle voice.

Grace put her arms around him, the coldness of her embrace penetrating deep into his flesh, freezing his still beating heart. In a moment she let him go and started to move away.

He called her name as she drifted towards a part of the woods he didn't know. She turned and glanced back at him, a soundless question on her lips.

Loud enough for her to hear, he said, I'm not all right.

Grace said, You will be, and left him alone with himself.

Hello Darkness

I feel the life slipping from her like shedded skin. She is still now, all her protests ended. I'm envious of her absence of emotion, and curious as to what she sees in the place where she now exists. But she is almost beyond speaking, and the silence itself seems enough to bring us closer.

When she does make a sound I prop myself up on one elbow and study her porcelain face. Her eyes are empty, and she has a rare smile on her face that touches me deeply. She seems grateful when I wipe saliva from her lips, not like before, all those demands she made. "That wasn't really you, Hopi," I tell her. "This is who you were meant to be."

Dolores sits in the corner by the window, touched by neon, waiting for Hopi to join her in plastic aloofness. She is our silent witness, her permanent smile hinting at qualities to which I can only aspire.

Hopi's lips move so I lean closer but can't decipher her words. I kiss her gently, and notice a tear in the corner of one eye. This evidence of lingering emotion unnerves me and quickly I wipe it away. "No more need for that."

The desert of her being arouses me. I pull back the sheets to reveal her pallid, naked body, then touch the taut flesh that clothes her ribcage. Beads of sweat shine there, jewels embedded in skin. I lick her nipples, tasting the unreality of her being, wanting to share it. But I'm still wary of the dark place, and of the dreadful emotions that lurk there. Even though I have become adept at not feeling, I know that if I come too close I risk ceding her the power to hurt me. Gently, I guide my hand through the tangle of her pubic hair, down to her cunt where I part the

Mike O'Driscoll

labia and insert two fingers into her dryness. I pull them out and wet them on my tongue, then part her flesh again, easing them inside her, tenderly greasing her working parts. I whisper her name, afraid to say it aloud in case I bring her back. "What can you see, Hopi?" I ask, as I move on top of her. Her flesh is touched by frost and as I slide into her I feel it melt beneath me. Now that she's almost gone, I feel so connected to her that I want to extend the moment. Her eyes have fallen closed so I open them, and feel her self-absorption enveloping me, sucking me into the cold and empty expanse of her new world. I move inside her like a voyager on a sea of darkness, and as I navigate the small moments of her dying, feeling the bond between us tighten, I try to outrun the pale light of dawn that I know will wipe out our beautiful intimacy.

In the light I reach for her and find nothing there, not even an imprint in the place where she had lain. I search the room and find nothing of hers, no clothes or jewels or other signs of her existence. I sit on the edge of the bed, dazed, not understanding what has happened. Hopi was dead, I was sure of that. All that tequila and nembutal. In the corner Dolores leans against the wall, haughty and impassive. I carry her to the bed and lay her down in Hopi's place. I found her in New Orleans, legs sticking out of a dumpster in an alley, like some corpse. Her right arm from the elbow down is missing and she has no hair, but she has other charms that more than compensate: she never condemns.

There are two pills on the bedside cabinet. I wash them down with tequila, hoping they'll do something to my punch-drunk brain to make it work. My racing heart begins to slow and Hopi skips out of my mind. I turn on the television and flick through the channels till I come across an episode of *Santa Barbara*. Ronald Reagan lives there, I think, along with all these charming, beautiful people, whose unblemished bodies radiate an unreality that I once possessed.

It's past midnight and Hopi hasn't returned. Maybe she's had enough of Albuquerque. I try to manufacture some hostility toward her but it doesn't come off – the truth is I feel nothing at all, just a raw emptiness in the place I thought she filled.

I pull on my cleanest dirty clothes and check my wallet. A grand or more in cash. The Hopi I knew would have taken it for drugs. I step

184

outside the room and hurry along the walkway to the office where Xabier is watching a porno movie behind the check-in desk. He's unshaven again, which I don't like, and he pretends not to notice me, which I do.

"Hopi?" I ask him. "You seen her today?"

A shake of the head, nothing more.

"This morning," I persist. "You saw her go out?"

"Ain't seen her, man," Xabier says, without looking at me. He leans forward and turns up the volume, allowing the fake sexual moans to preempt anything else I might have to say.

I stand in the doorway, hesitant, afraid of what the outside contains. The old Thunderbird I bought in Abilene three months ago, just before I met Hopi, sits outside in the parking lot. I might be safe in there. Taking a deep breath I stumble toward it, not exhaling till I'm in the driver's seat. I try not to look at the stars as their sheer number tends to overwhelm me. I picture Hopi instead, sitting in the corner of that truckers' bar, a stoned Barbie-doll whose glazed eyes scanned every corner like closed circuit cameras. I asked the bartender about her. Said she'd showed up about two weeks before with some biker. He'd hung around a day or two then had run out on her. She came to the bar most days, shot a little pool, drank a little beer. He figured she was in some sort of transitional phase.

I watched her for awhile, fascinated by her stoned indifference, the way she seemed to exist almost in another world, one that seemed a step or two beyond my own. When I got talking to her, her detachment, her emotionlessness, was immediately apparent, which made her all the more attractive. When I asked if she wanted to head west with me, she came along as if she really had no other option. In time, she became my conduit to reality, sparing me unnecessary contact with the outside. It isn't exactly agoraphobia, it isn't the open spaces that scare me; it's more an uncertainty about who occupies those spaces. Her indifference to the world gave her a natural immunity to its horrors. She could connect without risk, getting whatever it was we needed to survive. Except, of course, that they did finally get to her.

I clasp the wheel firmly as I turn on to the road, trying to subdue it to my will. I head downtown with no clear notion of where I'm headed. Normally, I'm a nervous driver, but not tonight. The city is washed clean of life and the pools of light spilling from the department stores act like candle flames, drawing me into their spheres of influence. I stop in one such pool, caught by the disdainful gaze of three timeless women. Sitting in lighted windows in exotic lingerie, they remind me of Amsterdam's red light hookers. Except I'm certain these three have a clearer understanding of where I want to be.

I wait, allowing them to attune their rhythms to my own. When I'm ready I reverse out into the centre of the road, turn towards the plate glass window and hit the accelerator. I crash through into another world, but before I can join them the cops have arrived, and drag me back to where I don't want to be.

"Well, Cicero, I useta watch *High School Blues*, but you don't look like Casey," the cop says, and I guess he's checked out my story. He's young, about my age, and has a small blond moustache that blights his otherwise good looks.

"It was fifteen years ago," I remind him.

"Ran three seasons, right?"

"Four."

He nods. "You know, you're the first ex-child star I ever busted."

"I did other stuff after *Blues*," I tell him, defensively, even though I don't feel any real connection to that Cecil Cicero. "I did *Frighteners* for three years."

"Yeah, I remember the show. Can't place you though."

"I did guest slots."

"So what happened – the offers dried up?"

I point at his notes. "I guess it says right there what happened."

"Well, you wouldn't be the first young actor to get a habit. How'd you get out of the jam?"

"I had a good lawyer."

"Well, I guess your old man has done it again. Got a hot shot Albuquerque lawyer waiting outside for you. Your father was your agent, right?"

"He wires me money to stay away. I guess that's what an agent does."

"Tough break. One minute you're king, next thing your new pilot show is shit."

"You a critic?"

"I guess that's L.A. So much bullshit and people promising you the world, by the time you're sixteen or seventeen, you're in some detox clinic along with the old pros."

He's beginning to piss me off so I ask him if we're done.

"You're positive for barbiturates and booze."

"I was depressed. My girlfriend walked out on me."

"Where is she?"

"Just gone."

"And the store, what were you after?"

"Nothing man, I was just out of it."

The cop grins, despite his play at toughness. "Whatever you say. I'll get your lawyer."

"No. I don't want to see him."

"That's up to you. You're out of here for now."

The car is a little beat up but it gets me back to the Lorlodge on Central Avenue. I throw my things into a suitcase, carry Dolores out to the car and head east on Central till I hit the freeway where I double back on myself and check into an shithole off Lomas that rents rooms by the hour. When I show the guy behind the check-in desk a hundred dollar bill, he grins and says I can have a room for three days. His teeth are yellowing and rat-like and I wonder how such a man can be real. "Number seventeen," he says. "You want anything, just ask. Name's Lennie, okay?"

"Food?"

"We got cable and fuck films. You want food, nearest place is a Taco Bell down the road. Oh, and the ice machine's fucked."

When I was eleven my father and three friends of his took me out on the ocean in a launch to show me what being a man was all about. I had just finished the first series of *High School Blues* and it was about to go nationwide on NBC. We were going after marlin, my father said, worthy opponents. He scared me, even then, but I hadn't yet grown to hate him. Truth was, I was excited about the trip. The men drank beer and offered me a bottle. Father frowned, but when the others joshed him, he told me to go ahead. I drank it and afterwards felt lightheaded and a little sick. But I didn't want to let my father down, so I bit my lip and held on tight to my guts. Finally, my father hooked something and after a tremendous battle he hauled a dolphin alongside the boat. It thrashed frenziedly in the crimson-foaming water. I'd seen on television that dolphins weren't fish at all, but mammals, like humans. They were intelligent and felt things the same way we did. Things like pain and terror. I screamed at them to cut it loose but they laughed and told me not to act like a kid. Finally, my old man drove a metal spike into the creature's brain and cut the line. Appalled, I stood by the rail, watching its dead eyes stare at me, as it sank below the swell.

Tonight it's not a dolphin we hook but a mermaid. The men drag her up on to the deck where she pleads with them in a language they don't understand. They have clubs with which they begin beating her, the way I've seen Canadian hunters battering seal cubs on television. But she has no fur, only scales that cover her long, graceful tail which thrashes about on the deck, spattering blood everywhere. When she is still, the men open their trousers and piss on her. But all the time her eyes are focused on me, as if she recognises the fact that I am no part of this at all.

I wake with horror's fists at my throat, my screams lost in the darkness. I flail wildly till I grab the cord above the bed and drown the dream in light. The breath rasps in and out of my lungs and I almost hate Hopi for abandoning me. I put my arms around immutable Dolores, hoping she'll keep the darkness at bay.

I play a porn video I've rented from Lennie. It's a cheap, grainy piece of work, filmed with a jerky hand-held camera. The soundtrack is indecipherable but the actors fuck and suck each other as if they really mean it. The performance is disconcerting, made more vivid by the total lack of artifice. I don't recall it ever being like that. I kneel in front of the television, curious, but can feel no connection to the actors whatsoever. "I'm not like you," I whisper. "I don't feel what you feel." But they simply go on fucking and pay me no heed. I retreat to the bed and watch them out of the corner of one eye. What makes them this way? What triggers these terrible needs? They demand the right to participate in this and experience that, to indulge themselves in so many different ways I can't see how they can appreciate any of it. Though I have no recollection of ever being like them, I think that I must once have been.

And then I see the girl in the background, her quiescent body sprawled across a sofa. The camera zooms in on her face which is animated by nothing stronger than profound disinterest as a skinny kid ejaculates over her face, her breasts. She neither smiles nor frowns nor gives any indication that she is even aware of his presence. She is a ghost on the screen, her white face framed by black, bobbed hair, somewhat less than real. I watch the clip again and again, unable to take my eyes from her, until, some time round dawn, exhaustion does it for me.

It's the ferocious New Mexico heat which finally brings me round, that and the failure of the A/C machine. I crawl into the shower and share it with a huge cockroach. He fights a losing battle to climb the lip of the tray but I give him ten for effort. I shave and leave him to it. I pull on jeans and a t-shirt, grab the videocassette and wander down to Lennie's office. I'm still thinking about that girl, thinking how much she reminds me of Hopi back when Hopi was dead.

Lennie asks if I dug the movie and I tell him no, just one girl.

"That right? His eyes light up like he thinks we're on the same wavelength. "Which one is that?"

"You know them?"

"Could be I know a guy who does."

"I want to talk to him."

Lennie hisses, exposing his rat-teeth, signifying a memory lapse. I put a twenty on the counter which prompts total recall. "There's a place across town. Guy there distributes these movies."

"They made local?"

"Out on Montano towards Almeda, place called *Triple X*. Ask for Newton and tell him I sent ya."

It's in a one-storey adobe building with a painted sign above the entrance, three neon X's and a naked woman. Discreet. Inside there's a few johns checking out the videos and sex toys, while a Mexican kid slouches behind the counter. There's a corridor to the left of the counter above which is a sign saying *Video Booths & Live Girls*. I push through the hanging drapes into the darkened space and step into the first available booth, close the door behind me and slip a couple of quarters into a slot in the wall. There's a control panel set below the screen. I press the first button and the screen comes to life, showing two women, licking each other on a bed while a guy stands over them, jerking off. I press the next button and the screen changes; this time it's a young girl being fucked by two guys, one in the mouth and one in the ass. The third channel has more of the same. I see her in the fourth sequence, her bobbed hair half-obscuring her profile as she's getting fucked from behind by some heavily muscled ape. A brief glimpse of her lifeless face reveals that she's not really there.

I leave the booth and head further down the corridor till I'm stopped by a tall, bearded guy in leather who puts a hand on my chest. "Sorry bud, no babes till eight."

I step back, recoiling from his touch. "I'm looking for Newton."

"Why?" He walks towards me, so I keep moving backwards. I bump into someone and flinch. Turning, I see it's the Mexican kid with a bucket and mop.

"Lennie sent me."

The bearded guy stops and says, "Who the fuck is Lennie?" He lets the Mexican kid step past. "That's Miguel," he says. "Best workers in the world. Who else is gonna wipe the come off the floor for less than a dollar an hour." He laughs, but all I can manage is a weak smile.

"Runs a motel out on Lomas. Gets movies from here."

"I sell videos all over the place."

"You're Newton?"

"Yeah."

"There's a girl in one of them," I explain, trying to stay cool, but knowing he sees right through me. People can do that, since I became less real. "I'd like to meet her."

"Let's talk in my office," he says and he beckons me to follow him along the corridor to a cramped room behind the counter. He sits in a chair at a desk, waves me to a plastic packing crate. "So, who we talking about?"

"Pale girl with the Louise Brooks hair."

"Lulu, huh. You think she's gonna open Pandora's box for you?"

"No, I just – "

"Forget it. All I'm saying is, she's special. She don't talk much, but I guess you already know that. She's more expensive too."

"That doesn't matter."

"Okay, come back about ten," he says, scratching his beard. "But fella, just one thing – if she does say anything, don't go believing it."

I don't know what he means but I say, "Sure," and leave before he sees that I don't really fit in.

High School Blues was a top rated sitcom for three years, before audiences slumped in its fourth and final year. *Frighteners* ran for three seasons before the revamped *Twilight Zone* killed us off. In one episode I played a kid who has wild fantasies about an unobtainable prom queen. She gets killed in a car wreck that was somehow my character's fault. But he kept fantasizing about her until, one night, she came to him in the form of a succubus and sucked the life out of him. It was a good show, ahead of its time.

I sit in the car outside the *Triple X*, waiting for it to be ten o'clock, thinking about that episode because it reminds me of Dolores, the first Dolores, who was the first flesh girl I ever really loved. When I was fifteen, with *High School Blues* already in my past, my mother employed a seventeen-year-old Mexican maid as an accoutrement to our Hollywood lives.

After the sitcom had ended my father lined up auditions and screen tests but, apart from three television movies, it was to little avail. He took it out on me, accusing me of a lack of commitment. He couldn't see hate's scar tissue hardening on my heart. To escape his bullying I took to spending as much time away from our Bel Air home as I could. I hung with a pack of other rich kids and we spent our time doing booze and coke and dope and, just occasionally, making out. One night, my head full of vodka and barbiturates, I found myself staggering alone in our grounds off Stone Canyon. I crawled as far as the pool before passing out. When I came to I was on a sofa in the house, a blanket thrown over me and Dolores urging me to drink coffee. My parents were away, she said. She smiled and I saw genuine concern in her eyes. I guess it was the first time I'd really noticed her, and doing so, I saw how beautiful she was.

She stayed with me, talking, for half the night. When she finally got up to go, I grabbed her arm and pulled her close. She resisted at first, then let herself be drawn into the kiss. What I felt then, and what I knew she had the potential to make me feel, put all my adolescent gropings into perspective. We made love that night, and afterwards, the more time we spent together, the more permanent and unbreakable it seemed, was

Mike O'Driscoll

the connection between us.

How little I knew of the workings of reality. How stupid I was not to see that its rules were not the same as those of my onscreen world.

It ended one evening when Dolores failed to meet me after finishing her shift. She avoided me for the next two days until finally I cornered her in the kitchen. Tears welled in her eyes as she told me it was over. I told her she wasn't thinking straight but she insisted it had been a mistake. I pleaded with her, begged her not to abandon me, but when I saw the traces of terror etched in her face, I knew my father had discovered our relationship.

I confronted him that night. "What have you said to Dolores?"

He looked up from his paper, stubbed his cigarette out in the ashtray and frowned. He was a cold, cruel man, the virus of whose ambition had never really taken root in me. Finally, he spoke. "I can't let you jeopardise your future, Cecil. The business with the whore has to stop."

Rage boiled up inside me and I lunged at him. He swatted me aside like the child I was.

"You just don't think for yourself," he went on, standing over me. "If the trades got hold of it, it would ruin your career."

"But I love her," I cried. "She's special."

"Love?" he sneered. "No, Cecil, she's using you. It's her nature, just like any other illegal spic bitch." He smiled in that superior way he had and touched my face like I was some errant child. "I'll take care of it, the way I always do."

Two days later, I saw what he wanted me to see. In his bedroom, the door open, Dolores on her knees in front of him, sucking his cock, his face a mask of boredom and disgust, showing me that what I had thought was mine was really his.

She left us shortly after, but it was only when I had started work on the first series of *Frighteners* that I heard she'd been deported. Slowly I came to see how fatal the touch of emotion really was, saw how it fuels betrayal and pain, and came to recognise that it was only through withdrawal and disconnection that I could safely navigate a path through existence.

The store is busy with hungry men whose realities intrude on my own. I rush past them to the cubicles that look in on the live show. Most are occupied but the eighth one is free. I feed money into the slot that causes a small panel to slide back in the wall. I'm looking into a room where recessed lamps in the ceiling give off a subdued red light. On a podium in the centre of the room, a naked girl lays motionless on her back. She has black hair, but her face is turned away from me. A thin beam of light moves across her opalescent flesh, like a laser, exposing hidden parts, leaving a trail of thin vapour to curl into the air. For one horrible moment I imagine the internal organs, broiling beneath her skin, and I feel a small yearning inside the mechanism of my heart.

A leather-clad man steps out of the shadows and looms over her. He bends to suck each nipple in turn, then pulls a nightstick from his trousers. I shudder, recalling an ancient dream, but he doesn't beat her, just caresses her with it, running it down her body to her crotch where it nestles in her pubic hair. Then he retreats and fades back into the shadows. She hasn't moved at all. Presently, a trolley laden with strange machinery appears, a masked man in surgical robes wheeling it up to the podium. He flicks buttons on a machine and an electronic hum fills the room. He picks up a gleaming metal implement and prods at the girl. Satisfied, he attaches two cables to her nipples, stands away and throws a switch. There's no sound but her body convulses. The man leans forward to examine her again, then removes the cables and lifts up his robe. Beneath it he's naked. He crawls on to the podium and loops his hands beneath her buttocks, raising them, then plunges his cock into her. He fucks her for ten minutes till he comes, then he wheels his trolley back into the darkness. And still the girl has neither moved nor made a sound of her own volition. Blood pounds in my temples and I'm filled with concern, though I don't yet recognise her as unreal.

After a minute, the first guy returns and stands over her. He unzips his jeans, pulls out his cock and strokes it till it's hard. Then he takes her unresisting head, cradles it and forces her mouth open with his thumbs. He proceeds to fuck her in the mouth, occasionally muttering the single word, "feed." He withdraws from her before he comes, to let his hidden audience verify the authenticity of his performance. In the gloom, the semen drips into her mouth like blood.

When she stirs, I rock back in my seat, stunned. I lean forward again, in time to catch her face, a Lulu who is even more perfect than onscreen, as she rises from the podium and moves around the room, head bobbing like a mechanical doll, acknowledging her silent voyeurs

Mike O'Driscoll

without condemnation. Then the red light fades and darkness swallows our dreams.

In the store, Newton is waiting. I give him three hundred dollars. For that she will stay with me the night.

I'm sitting in the Thunderbird as she shuffles across the parking lot in stilettos and stockings, a black microskirt and black denim jacket. Her lips are smeared with red and her eyes are dark and empty. She sits in beside me without a word of greeting. I thrill to the silence that swamps us both, making verbal communication unnecessary.

When we arrive at the motel she follows me unsteadily to my room, seats herself on the bed and uses the remote to switch on the television. I turn the sound down, which she doesn't seem to mind, and pour two drinks. She takes hers like a machine performing a task, running on autopilot. When I see she's noticed Dolores by the window, I lead her across the room and place her hand on Dolores' face. She keeps it there, stroking the plastic, then lays her own face where her hand had been. I feel good about their closeness, and sense the approach of some revelation. Something strange and wild, a place of darkness reaching out towards me.

Lulu returns to the bed and says, "She sees things differently."

"You like her?"

She begins to undress and, giggling, she says, "She's like me."

But I already know this, and, noticing the track marks in her arms for the first time, I know what it takes for her to be this way. I carry Dolores across the room and place her at the bottom of the bed, so she can share our secrets. Lulu waits, laying on the bed, her eyes turned to the television, as if to emphasise the completeness of her disconnection from the world. I strip off and lay atop her brutalized flesh, searching her eyes, trying to find the courage to follow her into the darkness.

"What are you doing?" I ask, waking to find her going through my things.

Naked, she turns toward me, hesitantly. She seems agitated. "I feel like ... I, this doesn't mean anything." Grey morning light streams through the blinds, mottling her flesh.

"No," I agree. "It means nothing."

She shakes her head and wipes a hand across her face. "But you

194

want it to," she says. "You just act out the emptiness instead of making it real."

Her words unsettle me, make me consider my motives. "You think this is an act with me?"

"Isn't that usually the case?" she says. Her junkie eyes are restless, moving ceaselessly round the room. This new animation concerns me. "You look at me and you think you understand how it feels. You have no fucking conception."

"You don't want to feel anything, right?"

"You think it's the junk? You're dead wrong," she sneers. "It's just a tool."

I get out of bed and grab her arms. "I can help you, Lulu. Stay here, I'll get whatever you need."

"Lulu? She isn't me," She pulls free of my grip and begins to get dressed. "She belongs to Newton."

"But you want to be her. All the time."

She shrugs, slipping on her shoes. "I can make that happen," I tell her, trying to hide an unfamiliar anxiety.

"Sure," she says, moving towards the door. "I heard that so many times."

"Wait," I cry, frantic for her to stay with me.

She hesitates, smiling with anticipation as I dig some notes from my jacket. I fight down an impulse to tell her to go. "Good," she says, holding out her hand. I place two fifties in it and try not to look in her eyes because the need in them seems too real.

"Newton won't let you be in that place," I tell her. "He wants to keep you real. Remember who I am, Cecil, and remember I want to be there too."

"It's a fucking act, don't you see?" she says, turning her back on unreality.

For two days I try to convince myself that she was wrong. I watch soaps and game shows and Oprah but don't feel the old connection. It's like the horrors have infected them all. Even when I try and picture Hopi, she's wearing Lulu's face. But I'm certain she belongs more in my world than in theirs. Finally I make a decision. I shave till my face looks smooth in the mirror and if I try real hard, I can see only emptiness in my eyes. Not as good as Dolores, but getting there. I get a take-out from Taco Bell, my first meal in three days, and leave it behind on the bathroom floor. Time is altering almost imperceptibly, becoming slower. When I reach the *Triple X* my watch says mid-afternoon but it could be yesterday. The sweat that glues the shirt to my back serves as a reminder of dreadful reality.

In the store, I hide among the racks of fuck-books. Just the kid at the counter, no sign of Newton. I slip into the corridor and make my way to a door at the far end. It opens and I step into some kind of changing room; there's mirrors on the walls and costumes hung over the backs of chairs. I can feel something of Lulu here, the scent of her machine oil. I pick up items of leather underwear off the dressing table and sniff them, wondering which is hers.

"Cecil," says a voice behind me. "Kinda fucking name is that?"

I turn and see Newton blocking the doorway, a baseball bat hanging from a meaty fist. He smiles but it is cold and hard, mirroring his diamond eyes.

"I want Lulu," I tell him.

"I told you she's special."

"She needs my help."

"Only thing she needs is me. Playing dead ain't easy. I got a lotta time and money invested in that cunt. And you want to steal her away?"

"You don't understand, it isn't just an act."

"You got a jones for her," Newton laughs. "That's too bad."

"Why not just let her – " I don't get to finish what I'm saying because he hits me in the stomach, driving the air from my body. I go down on my knees like a dead man praying. The bat explodes repeatedly against my head. For some time I exist only in a world of pain. Then there's nothing. Later, it comes back but different, somehow. I'm laying in a darkened alley, between the wall and a dumpster. It's a while before I can move even a finger, longer before I can stand. I try to puke up some internal organs but only blood comes. Finally, I manage to stagger round to the parking lot where the Thunderbird waits. It takes a night and more for the car to slip through the gleaming city, as I look for the place where the dark used to be.

This scar tissue signifies my readiness to cross over; it says I'm almost

196

unreal. As if to confirm this, I don't feel much, which is good, and certainly I don't feel any pain. When Lennie asks me what happened I tell him that I had a bust up with a redneck at a bar. He shakes his head and makes sympathetic noises but I know he's secretly pleased. He sees me as capable of feeling pain; like all real people he takes pleasure in the suffering of others. He smiles knowingly when I ask him about a piece. I put a twenty on the counter and he says he'll make a call and get back to me. About two, he calls my room and gives me the address of a bar in the Old Town and says there'll be a black dude there who can get me what I need.

I pack all my stuff and put some clothes on Dolores and a baseball cap on her head, and sit her in the backseat of the car. They only serve to emphasize her unreality, which pleases me greatly.

I stop at a bank and withdraw two thousand dollars, then call into a liquor store. I'm at *Kennedy's Irish Bar* in the Old Town by five and find Lennie's friend waiting for me. I know it's him because he's the only black guy in the place. He doesn't ask my name so I don't offer it. Out in his car he shows me a Saturday night special. Nothing fancy he says, but get close enough and it will do the job. Two hundred dollars and he'll throw in some extra rounds.

Afterwards I head north to the *Triple X* and park across the street. I take a pull on a bottle, imagining the tequila lubricating my working parts, fine-tuning a precision machine. I practice stillness, which comes easier now I'm on slow time.

He comes out of the store just before midnight, climbs into his Chevrolet Jeep and heads downtown. I follow him to a hotel on the Eastside. It's a fuckshack called *The Palace*. I wait a few seconds then follow him into the lobby. There's a worn-out looking guy at the reception desk and I nod to him like I'm a regular. No elevator, only a stairwell off to the left. I take it, afraid I might lose Newton. When I hear him on the third floor, one flight above me, I remember to breathe. He leaves the stairwell and when I stick my head round the wall, I see him fumbling with a key outside the second door on the left. I take the gun out now, to give it time to get where it needs to be, then step into the corridor and call his name. He turns, reaching inside his jacket.

"Don't," I tell him.

Seeing the gun, he drops his hand and asks me what I want.

Mike O'Driscoll

"I want Lulu."

He opens the door and I follow him in. Lulu in her underwear, is strapped to the bed, her mouth gagged. Her body seems to hum with tension and the need to escape this awful reality. "What have you done to her?"

"Stopped her hurting herself, asshole."

"Set her loose," I tell him.

"You picked the wrong guy to fuck with," he assures me.

"Just do it." He moves to the bed and starts untying her hands and legs, making a meal of it. I wave him out the way and finish the job. With the gag removed, Lulu whimpers like a sick animal. Sweat burns on her face and the need in her dark eyes fills me with uncertainty. I back away from her, telling her to get dressed. As if sensing my unease, Newton makes his move. But the round I fired minutes ago catches him in the arm. As he falls, the second one explodes in his guts. He screams but doesn't die. I lean over and remove the gun from his jacket, then help Lulu dress. As we're leaving, Newton spits and fumes, forcing himself up on an elbow. "I won't forget this," he says. "I'll fucking find you, you cocksucker." I don't have anything to say to him so I pull the trigger again. When it finally connects, I see I've done for him, because there's a lot of blood and no more screaming. Lulu sobs at this brutal reality. As I grab the keys from Newton's pocket, we lock eyes and I feel the strength of his hatred and realise the extent to which the world feeds on our collective pain. I half drag, half carry Lulu downstairs out to the street and put her in his Chevrolet. She's shivering violently and keeps biting her lips. "Not anymore," she says, "please, no more," repeating it, like some kind of mantra.

"No more what?" I ask her.

"No more anything," she screams, lashing out at me with her skinny hands.

"Listen, Lulu," I say, holding her wrists. "I'll make you what you want to be."

She sinks back into her seat, her suspicion fading. "You're the man," she giggles, slyly. "I told Newton, said you're gonna make it all go away."

"That's right, no more Newton."

"Seh-sill?" she says and I think maybe she does understand.

198

"Stay quiet now," I tell her. When she nods her head and closes her bleary eyes, I start the car and pretty soon we're heading south on I-25. An hour out of Albuquerque, I leave the freeway and join route 54, heading towards El Paso.

We run into the border patrol just south of Alamogordo and my heart slows to a clockwork beat while we wait in line behind a truck. But the cop who leans in my window is bored. "Where ya headed?" he says, disinterestedly.

"Las Cruces," I say.

He yawns and says, "Well, pal, you're on the wrong road." Pissed off.

"Must've gone wrong back in Alamogordo."

He gives me a look that says I'm a moron. "You want route 70," he says, finally waving us on.

We reach El Paso a little after four and abandon the jeep in an underground parking lot. I get a cab to take us over the border into Juarez. It takes a while to find a hotel, a while longer to buy the heroin.

The blinds lay slats of shadow across Lulu's cold, unyielding flesh. Outside, Juarez has come to life while in here we're winding down. She's been out since we made love, after I had prepared her fix. Like sex with Hopi the last time, I had almost experienced the moment of revelation but something unseen had deterred me from entering the darkness. Something more than feeling, when all I want is no feeling at all. I watch her sleeping, wishing Dolores were here to help me take that last step.

About midday, Lulu wakes. We don't talk at all – there's no need. She watches as I prepare the fix, and sighs with pleasure as I slip the needle into a vein in her throat. "I'll be coming soon," I say, painfully aware of my own fear of letting go. She slumps back into her stupor, leaving me alone to find the courage to accept the dark's embrace.

Hours pass while I practice my stillness, shallowing my breath to the faintest murmur. Shadows lengthen as darkness crawls across the floor. A shimmer of tension spoils my mechanical poise. I get up and prepare the last of the heroin. It's a massive dose which I draw up into two syringes. I slide into the bed and, placing my head against her waist, I listen to the noises that come from inside her, no longer organic but mechanical. I kiss her navel, her ribs, her breasts, reviving her one last time. As if by instinct she reaches for me but I tell her no, not quite yet. I show her one hypodermic and she nods. "So quiet in here," she says, and I know she's almost there.

She shudders and a small gasp escapes her lips as the smack enters her bloodstream. I extend the moment, savouring it for as long as I can. When it's all gone, I smother her ghostly face with kisses. "Wait for me," I say. I put an ear against her mouth, feel the faintest murmur of breath and hear "Cecil," though it is hardly a sound. And then something that might be, "I'm waiting," and then nothing at all. I pull back her eyelids, searching for meaning, but find nothing there.

I lean close to her lips but feel no whisper of breath. This confirmation of her having moved on thrills me to the very core. I feel no fear as I reach for the second hypodermic and stick it in my arm. Nothing counters the rush that fills my brain. I raise myself over Lulu, stunned by the pale moonlight that glistens on her glacial breasts. I reach between her legs, feeling the chill that has taken root inside her, while my tongue savours the hardness of her erect nipples. As my cock stiffens and I sink into the hollow space of her being, I feel my skin toughening, becoming hard and pristine, like steel, as our bodies mesh like machines working in perfect unison.

And even as I welcome the embrace of darkness, sensing the strange climax gather inside me, drawing me ever closer to a state of absolute unreality, even then, I can hear the screech of tyres outside, car doors slamming and angry commands. But I'm not afraid because those footsteps rattling along the corridors, those guns being prepped for action, those people coming for me, won't find me here at all, nor in any world they know.

Evelyn Is Not Real

Ray was in movies. Or he used to be. Low budget, independent, left-field, cultish – these were the words he used to describe them to strangers. When you got to know him, when he felt you were on his side, he dismissed them as movies nobody saw.

I got to know Ray a year after my husband Nick was killed. Nick was driving across an intersection in Daly City when a man in a blue Explorer ran a red light and ploughed into him. Ten minutes earlier, the man had robbed a drugstore in San Bruno. The night before we had spent two hours talking about our trip to Europe. It was to be our two year delayed honeymoon. We would go to all the places we had read about in books, seen in movies, or already walked through in our dreams. We would hire a car and spend four months on the road, driving wherever fancy took us. Amsterdam, Innsbruck, Sarajevo, Venice, Barcelona, Lisbon. The names tripped off our tongues like potent mysteries. We might camp out under Tyrolean skies or check into a small, family run pension where the owners would speak not a word of English and Nick and I no word of whatever tongue it happened to be. But fancy had other plans which saw Nick's life bleeding away before the fire crew could cut him free from the mangled wreck of his Toyota.

Ray had been in twenty movies or so. The 'or so' was an addendum to cover the four of five from which, he suspected, his part had been cut. Suspected because, in those cases, he had never seen the finished product. When he said he'd appeared in movies nobody saw, I hadn't thought he meant himself. Ray's proud boast was that he'd seen the work of all the greats but not worked a scene with any of them. I'd never met anyone like him, and yet, he was the only man apart from Nick who could take me outside of myself.

After Nick was killed I sort of fell apart, but only for a short while. After a week I pulled myself together and decided to get on with my life. Despite the protestations of well-meaning friends to let it out, to process the hurt, I could see no benefit in it, either to Nick or to myself. To wallow in hurt and misery? Surely the man I'd loved deserved something more. So I threw myself into my job, zeroing the space into which any hurt might be born. I managed the downtown branch of a medical recruitment agency, and in the six months following Nick's death, my commissions rose by thirty per cent. And then I sold the bungalow we had bought in Pacifica, took out a loan on a one bed apartment on Sunset about a mile from Ocean Beach, quit my job and flew to Paris.

I bought a second-hand Peugeot, a small convertible, and for three months I drove to one fabled city after another, trying to find traces of the life Nick and I had dreamed. I imagined myself chasing after some intangible essence, trying to relive an emotional transaction whose worth I'd never quite grasped. Without Nick, the places through which I moved seemed populated only by ghosts. By the time I hit Athens I felt as if the world was receding from me. In an effort to draw closer to it, I took a job in an Irish bar, began to take account of people, started to put names to faces. And then, when I felt the first stirrings of what I thought was hurt, I inoculated myself against further pain by falling, briefly, in love with the owner of the bar. He was an Athenian who, ten years before, had married and been abandoned by an Irish girl after she had ran off with his best friend. We drank a lot together, told each other jokes and had sex. Our relationship was built on a mutual desire for forgetting. Yet, neither of us had the will to get all the way there and so, after five months away, I returned to San Francisco and found that all the hurt I had been running from was waiting right there for me.

We were eating shrimp with mango at *Firecrackers* on Valencia the first time Ray spoke about Evelyn. We had been to see David Lynch's new movie, a remake of Von Sternberg's *The Scarlet Empress*. Ray always wanted to eat Chinese after a movie, as if celluloid provoked an appetite that only noodles and the like could satisfy. I didn't get Lynch, nor most of the films Ray liked to watch. My tastes were what he called mainstream. It didn't matter to me who directed a movie, though I knew names like Hitchcock, Ford and Hawks. These were the guys whose movies Nick used to watch. He had turned me on to Hawks, particularly the films he'd made with Cary Grant. I watched them all the time, except for *Only Angels Have Wings*, which I couldn't bring myself to look at since his death. Not that Ray was a snob about movies. He liked Hawks too, and I think the fact that he'd acted in a few stinkers kept him grounded.

He was talking about the film we'd just seen, telling me, in between mouthfuls of shrimp and Mexican beer, how Lynch had failed to out-perverse Von Sternberg. He stopped suddenly, chopsticks held a few inches above his plate, his gaze fixed intently on my face.

"What is it?" I said.

He continued to stare at me, as if at a stranger he thought he should know.

"Ray – what's the matter?"

He seemed to see me then, for real. He scrunched his eyes and pinched the bridge of his nose. "Nothing," he said. He looked down at the last few shrimps on his plate but left them there.

"Tell me."

"Sometimes you remind me of someone I used to know."

"Should I be flattered?"

He shrugged, then laughed. "I don't know. Evelyn was, ah, somebody I worked with once."

"She was an actress?"

He nodded. "We made a film together."

"How do I remind you of her?"

"I'm not sure – maybe I glimpsed it before in you, but never clearly until now."

"Glimpsed what?"

"This is going to sound stupid, but it's a kind of serenity."

"Serenity, huh?" I sipped my wine to stop from guffawing. "You think I'm serene?"

"You have a certain stillness. Evelyn had it too."

The way he spoke about her suggested a deeper connection than

Mike O'Driscoll

professional respect. I felt something odd then, something vaguely familiar which I didn't want to feel. Ray and I had been seeing each other for four months and one of the things I liked about him was that he never quizzed me about the past nor offered to fill in the details of his own previous affairs. From the first he had seemed to realise how much I was hurting, and that it was delayed but necessary hurt, one that I could no longer run from. He didn't try to tell me it was time to move on, or that the grieving process was a healing one. He offered no homilies, just listened when I wanted to talk, and made me laugh when that was what I needed. "I never thought of myself as having 'stillness'," I said. "I can't really imagine myself that way."

"Forget it. I don't know why I brought it up."

"You and Evelyn – you were together?"

"For a while," he said, distantly.

I guessed that he didn't want to talk about it. If it had ended badly between them, I could understand the desire to escape the past. And yet, I was already intrigued and no matter what hurt it might bring, I let my curiosity get the better of me. "Tell me about her," I said.

Ray reached across the table and took my hand. "There's nothing really to tell. It was short, intense, and then it was over."

Before I could stop myself, I was asking him how long ago it had been. Ray stood up, leaned across the table and kissed me on the lips. "Forget it, Grace. You're nothing like her."

Outside, as we walked west along Jackson Street, Ray started speaking about *The Scarlet Empress* again, comparing it unfavourably to Lynch's earlier films. A young couple walked by us, engrossed in their own conversation. A cable car rattled south along Powell, a peculiar beast at odds with the stillness of the hour. Ray's voice drifted in and out of my head and as we walked I felt the presence of someone else nearby, watching us. I looked back over my shoulder but the street was empty. Ray seemed oblivious to the unnatural quiet, and to the sudden quickening of my heart. I wanted to ask Ray how I wasn't like Evelyn but the moment passed and did not come again until much later.

It felt like I had been away a lot longer than five months. The city seemed different, and not just because of the winter rain. I had sold most of the furniture from Pacifica, keeping only what I needed to occupy the

204

emptiness of the apartment on Judah. It wasn't much and what there was I no longer recognised as belonging to me. I got a job with a medical temp agency at two thirds the salary I had been earning before I went away. Christmas came and went and I told myself I didn't mind spending it alone. Being with friends would have made it harder. I wasn't ready yet for all their best intentions, their reassurances, their talk of how well I was doing. In the new year a few people began to call, asking how I was. How had Europe been? Had I settled into my new apartment? Not a word about Nick. As if they were afraid the mention of his name would be intolerable to me. Only after I had spent time again in the company of those we had called our friends did I realise that it was themselves for whom the memory of Nick had become intolerable. By getting killed, Nick had transgressed the rules. And, as I began to understand by the silent, coded signals that passed between them, my presence was an unwanted reminder of the frailties they refused to recognise in themselves.

I met Ray for the first time in a DVD rental store on Sutter a block from my office. I was browsing through the new releases, looking for something to numb the pain for a couple of hours. Nothing grabbed me and so I graduated towards the back of the store where the older films were being offered at a 'rent two for the price of one' deal. I picked up a copy of *Bringing Up Baby* and smiled at the picture of Cary Grant and Katherine Hepburn on the cover. Nick used to do a perfect imitation of Grant as David Huxley taking delivery of the intercostal clavicle.

"A match made in heaven."

A man in a black leather sports jacket was standing at my shoulder. Before I could say anything, he gestured at the DVD I held and said, "Nobody ever died of sadness watching Grant and Hepburn."

"I can choose my own film," I cut him off and replaced the DVD on the shelf.

"It's true. I know from experience."

He had an accent, British, I thought. He had brown eyes and light brown hair that hung almost to his shoulders. "Excuse me," I said, moving away from him.

"And with the two for one deal you should take this too."

I glanced back at him. He was holding *His Girl Friday* towards me. Despite myself I smiled. "How do you know what I should watch?" I asked him.

"I was in movies," he said. "I have an instinct for these things."

"Are you serious? You're an actor?"

His smile seemed awkward somehow, even a little embarrassed. "Not sure if I still am."

"What do you mean?"

"Haven't worked on a movie in a while. It's like, if you're dead, can you still call yourself human?"

The absurdity of the question made me laugh. "See, you haven't even watched it yet and it's already working."

"I've seen them before," I said. "All of them."

He nodded, turned away and moved off to another part of the store. Puzzled, I stared after him for a moment than returned to browsing. A minute later he came back. "Try this," he said, handing me a DVD called *My Back Yard*.

I looked at the cover and recognised a younger version of the man standing in front of me. In the picture he was standing on the porch of a ramshackle house, looking out over a weed-strewn yard.

"It's you."

He shrugged. "It makes people forget their woes."

He couldn't have been more than twenty-five, twenty-six, when the film was made, I thought.

"That was fifteen years ago. Second picture I made in America."

"I never heard of it."

"Yes, well. It wasn't exactly a hit." He looked forlorn for a moment, then smiled. "But please, I think it will make you laugh."

"All right." I looked at the cast list. "Raymond Dunbar, I'll give it a try."

"It's Ray now, just Ray."

"And if it doesn't make me laugh?"

"Then you won't see me again. But if you do laugh, then I'll be waiting here this time tomorrow evening." With that he turned and left the store.

I rented the movie and *His Girl Friday*, just in case. At six the following evening he was waiting for me at the store.

I have a brother who plays in a band. They almost made it big five years back. Got some kind of recording deal, made a couple of albums, toured the West Coast. I took Nick to see them play support to Jim White downstairs at *Johnny Foley's*. My brother had grown his hair long and a thick beard covered his cherubic features. Maybe that's why he grew it. His voice though, was still as sweet as an angel's. He called me after Nick was killed, from a hotel room somewhere in Amsterdam. The band was touring northern Europe to promote their new CD. He sounded despondent. I thought it was because he had really liked Nick and was going to miss him. But instead he was afraid the band were going to break up. He felt things weren't working out for them the way he'd hoped. He was thinking of going back home to Kentucky. He wanted me to tell him not to lose sight.

In *My Back Yard,* Ray played a young man who returns to the family home in northern California after an absence of ten years. He finds the place abandoned and run down, full of ghosts and memories. The story takes place over the course of a twenty-four hour period, with Ray's character connecting with all kinds of people and memories from the past. It could have been depressing, but the truth was, it was funny as hell. He was pleased when I told him that, said he was glad he was able to make me forget myself for a little while. I wondered how he'd known that that was what I wanted to do but I didn't ask. I was too busy agreeing to let him take me to dinner.

Sixteen years ago Ray had left England after appearing in three highly rated TV shows and half a dozen low budget movies, a couple of which had played the city's art houses. One night, after we'd been seeing each other for a month, we caught one of these early films on cable. It was an odd, kind of surreal gangster thriller called *Lester Bows Out*, and halfway through I realised I'd seen it before. It felt weird, I told him, seeing a movie I'd forgotten I'd seen, while lying naked next to the man who played the lead role.

His hand stroked my belly. "Some of the shit I appeared in I wish I could forget."

"That bad, huh?"

"Hey, you're supposed to defend my thespian skills."

I rolled onto my side and kissed him on the mouth. "Raymondo," I said, reaching down between his legs. "I could never fault your performance."

Earlier that evening, when he'd called into my office downtown, Ray had picked up the framed photograph of Nick I had on my desk. He stared at it intently for nearly a minute while I watched him, curious and a little apprehensive about what he would say. "Losing someone you love," he said. "It's beyond belief."

I hadn't known how to respond to that. Before I was even aware of it, my eyes were full of tears. Ray came and knelt next to my seat, put his hands on my cheeks and told me Nick was the luckiest ghost alive. I don't think I'd ever heard anything so corny, but it brought a smile to my lips and diminished a little of the lingering pain.

Ray did commercials now, mostly voiceovers, with the occasional front of camera job. I tried to encourage him to get back into serious acting but he laughed and said commercials were more honest than anything else he'd done. They told it straight, he said, no bullshit.

I began watching out for his movies on TV. Whenever one was broadcast on some obscure cable channel in the graveyard slot, I'd get him to come over and watch it with me. They weren't what you'd call mainstream. Apart from his first three American pictures, all the others were made by small independents and had either got a limited release or gone straight to video or DVD. We sat through two or three together, including one in which he starred as an ex-child actor with a doll fetish. He didn't seem interested in them. He'd make the odd comment, criticising his own performance, or that of the other actors; he'd pick holes in the script or laugh at some directorial ineptitude he hadn't spotted before. Mostly he seemed listless, irritated by the films, as if they reminded him of part of his life he would have preferred to forget.

On Saturday I was cycling in the Haight district, stopping to browse in the book and music stores. In a thrift store on Lower Haight I saw a rack of second hand DVDs and on impulse I asked the lanky kid behind the counter if they had any Ray Dunbar films in stock.

He shook his head and gestured at the shelves. "Just what's there."

I started to look through the films. "He was in *My Back Yard*, and another movie called *Joey Elegant*. You know those films?"

The kid had come out from behind the counter and was rummaging through a crate of junk by the shopfront. "What'd you say that guy's name was?"

"Raymond Dunbar."

"Gus hasn't catalogued this stuff yet. Only came in yesterday." He reached down into the crate and pulled out a slim, plastic case. "But maybe this is something."

I walked to the crate and he handed me a DVD case with a sheet of lined paper inside the sleeve. Handwritten across the front were the words 'The Last Time, with Raymond Dunbar.'

I opened the case. There was a handwritten label stuck to the disc. "You know this movie?"

"Naw. I just seen that name on the cover this morning."

"Is it kosher?"

"Five bucks and it's yours."

I gave him the money. Outside the store I called Ray on my cellphone. "Ray, when you come over tonight, bring wine and a Chinese."

"I thought we were going out to catch a movie."

"We'll catch one in. One of yours."

I heard him groan. "Must we?"

He arrived just after eight, and once we'd eaten I showed him the disc.

"Jesus – where'd you get that?" He seemed surprised.

"Store on Haight. It is one of yours, right?"

He took the case from me and hurried through to the living room. By the time I had followed him there, he already had the disc in the DVD player and was sitting on the edge of the sofa. He seemed excited and edgy as he waited for the film to load.

"What's up, Ray? I usually have to bribe or bully you to make you watch your own films."

He dragged his eyes from the screen. "Come and sit down," he said, eagerly. "It's the one I told you about before. The one I made with Evelyn."

I can't say I was much taken with *The Last Time*. It was too dark, too obviously indebted to Lynch in its weirdness, but at the same time it seemed oddly lifeless, as if the characters were somehow aware of their own unreality, conscious of themselves only as 'characters'. Sometimes the actors spoke dialogue that seemed unrelated to their respective storylines. The protagonist, played by Ray, was some kind of

Mike O'Driscoll

cop or detective, though I couldn't figure out exactly what he was working on. There was a blonde woman, very beautiful, a femme fatale, with whom the PI became enthralled. I figured this was Evelyn. It was never clear whether she was helping or hindering Ray's character solve the mystery that lay at the heart of the film. At the end she disappeared, at which point the plot seemed to feed back into itself, as the cop began to investigate the fate of a missing woman.

The film unsettled me. Thankfully, Ray didn't seem in the mood to discuss it. I could tell it meant something to him, more than any of the other films we'd watched together. I guessed it was because of Evelyn. While watching it, he'd made none of his usual jokes or sarcastic comments about the script or the performances. Instead, he'd remained silent, intent on the convoluted story as if searching for the key to its mystery. Maybe it had more to do with what had happened between him and Evelyn than with the storyline. I wondered how it had ended between them.

Afterwards, Ray sat staring into space, as if transfixed by a film that was still playing in his head. I watched him for a while, puzzled at the effect it had had on him. Was it not how he had remembered? Or had it dragged some painful memories to the surface? I made coffee, brought it back to the living room. I would have asked him what he was thinking but I wasn't sure I really wanted to know. Instead, I cuddled up next to him and laid my head on his chest

He put an arm round me and raised my head with his other hand. There was an intensity in his gaze that startled me, but before I could ask him what the matter was he pressed his mouth hard against mine. In the few months we had been seeing each other Ray had always been a tender lover, but now he seemed hungry, almost ruthless as he pressed himself on me. I though about Nick for one moment, pictured his handsome face before it morphed into the image of a broken body on a morgue slab. I shuddered and responded to Ray, clamping my mouth against his. I tore at his shirt and pushed him down on the sofa, feeling something primitive and savage come awake inside me.

Josh and Lynsey were talking movies one morning when I arrived at the office. Both had worked for Meditech for over a year. I think they were sleeping together, but I wasn't sure. I poured myself a coffee and made

210

small talk with them. Josh seemed to be something of a movie freak so I asked him if he'd ever seen *The Last Time*.

"Who was the director?"

I shrugged. "No idea. I'm not big on directors."

"You know who wrote it?"

"No," I confessed.

"You missed the big question, Josh," Lynsey chipped in. "Who're the stars?"

"Actually," Josh said, disdainfully, "I was going to ask the year of production."

"British actor called Ray Dunbar played the lead role," I said.

Lynsey had never heard of him.

"Dunbar?" Josh frowned and tapped the edge of Lynsey's desk "Raymond Dunbar. Starred in *My Back Yard, Joey Elegant, The Daemon Next Door*. Made a couple of decent thrillers in England before taking the Hollywood buck."

"I'm impressed," I said. "What about *The Last Time*?"

"Is it one of his Brit movies?"

"No, American. Not Hollywood though. Independent, low budget."

"So, anytime in the last fifteen years?"

"More recent, say five or six years ago."

"What's it about?"

"It's kind of a weird, noir type of thing. Confusing, amateurish in parts, but compelling too." I racked my brain trying to give Josh something more specific but the storyline was hazy and all I could really remember were one or two striking images. "Near the end," I tried to explain. "There's a scene where the protagonist, a cop, opens a door in a motel room, expecting to find the woman he's looking for. He knows she's there. He's seen her go in just a couple of minutes before. He opens the door and steps inside. She's not there. The room is empty. There's no other way out."

Josh shook his head. "Sounds familiar, but there's maybe a hundred movies with similar scenes."

"You really don't know it?"

"No," he said, sounding disgusted with himself.

Ray got a contract to do a series of scotch whiskey commercials down in LA. Said he'd be away a week, maybe longer. I didn't want him to go. I guess that meant I was falling in love with him.

One morning while he was away, I was riding the BART downtown to work when I was struck by the oddest sensation. I felt sure that someone was watching me. It only lasted a moment, but it was enough to raise the hairs on the back of my neck. The next morning I felt the same thing, only stronger. There were a dozen or so people in the carriage. I stole glances at each of them, but saw nothing to indicate that any of them were watching me. All the way downtown I couldn't shake off the tension, and though it had gone by the time I reached the office, it left me feeling on edge through most of the day.

That evening as I walked south from Sutter towards Market Street Station, I kept a close watch on the faces of the people I passed, furtively scanning them for someone I recognised. I called Ray that night, wanting to tell him about it. He would have had some explanation, I knew, something about how maybe I was feeling guilty at getting over Nick and this was my subconscious getting its own back. But instead, Ray talked about the commercial, how much he was missing me and what he'd do to me when he got back. He said we should get out of the city for a weekend, maybe spend a couple of nights in Sausalito.

Next morning, after another fraught journey to work, I asked Lynsey if anyone had been trying to get hold of me. She reeled off a list of clients and the names of three people I had scheduled to interview. "Anybody sound ... wrong?"

"Wrong?"

"I don't know. Like they were pissed off or something."

"Sure Grace. Every last one of them."

Lynsey's flippancy did nothing to ease my fears. Every time the phone rang I'd hesitate before taking the call, half-afraid of what I might hear. I kept an eye on my colleagues, wondering if one of them was responsible, if he or she was playing some sick joke at my expense. I was aware too, of a strange allure in letting my guard slip, in suspending myself in a kind of disbelief, as if this would somehow weaken my sense of dread.

Ray was away six days. When he got back, we hired a car, drove out to

Sausalito and checked into a quaint old seafront hotel. He'd bought me a present, a blue Hermes scarf from a boutique on Rodeo Drive. He insisted I wear them out to dinner. We ate lobster and fries and got half drunk on white wine. We made love by moonlight on the beach and talked afterwards about where we went from here. He asked me if I thought we were moving too fast. I thought maybe we were but I didn't tell him that. Despite my doubts, being with him felt so right. I didn't tell him either, about what had been happening to me. The paranoia, if that's what it really was. It felt distant, as if it was something that I had heard about, but which hadn't really happened to me.

Back in the city, the sensation of being watched, of being the object of someone's close scrutiny, returned. It wasn't there all the time. Just certain moments when I'd be talking on the phone or typing something into my computer I'd feel the weight of an unknown gaze creep over me. I'd stop what I was doing and scan the faces of my colleagues, the passers-by out in the street, trying to hide my own anxiety. Then, just as quickly, the sensation would fade and I'd feel foolish and self-conscious as I became aware that my colleagues really were looking at me, wondering what the hell Grace was so jumpy about.

Tuesday morning walking down Sutter on my way to the office, I bumped into Josh. The ride in on the BART had been uneventful. I'd felt nothing untoward. I was okay, a little edgy, but nothing I couldn't cope with. Josh fell in beside me and we started talking, the usual office gossip. Right then I felt it. Someone following me, watching my every move. I froze in the street, heart racing. I was afraid to turn round.

"Grace?" Josh cried. "What's wrong?"

I tried to say something but I couldn't. Josh took hold of my arms and tried to reassure me. "It's okay Grace. It's okay."

I forced myself to respond. Slowly, I looked back over my shoulder, terrified of what I might see. There were just people I didn't know, moving past, oblivious to my fear. And just as suddenly as it had come on me, the feeling disappeared.

I told Ray about it that night. We were at an Italian restaurant on Noriega. "I know I sound paranoid, Ray, but I think somebody really is following me."

"You think of any reason someone would do that?"

"No – but crazy people don't need reasons."

Ray grinned. "I'm sorry," he said, seeing how pissed off I was. "Look, I'm not laughing. I'm trying to understand, Grace, really I am." He did his best to reassure me, saying that if I really believed someone was following me he'd go with me to the police tomorrow and report it. I could tell he didn't really believe me, but his concern was genuine and the last thing I wanted was for him to think I was neurotic.

We went back to his place in Ingleside. He had something to show me. He poured me a glass of chilled Pinot Grigio and disappeared into his bedroom. He came out a few moments later carrying a Neiman Marcus bag. "Close your eyes," he said.

I did as he asked, and when he told me to open them I saw a black skirt and jacket draped over the back of the sofa. I looked at Ray. "You don't have to get – "

"I wanted to. I like buying you things. I want you to look beautiful."

I shrugged, feeling a little light-headed.

"Do you like them?"

I picked up the jacket and pulled it on, then held the skirt to my waist. "Yes," I said. "It's a beautiful suit." And it was.

That night, I dreamed about Evelyn.

The next morning I felt feverish and weak. I got out of bed but didn't have the strength to get dressed. I called work and told them I was ill. Ray said I had a cold coming on and told me to go back to bed. He brought me a cup of tea and some aspirin. After swallowing the tablets and drinking half the tea, I managed to doze off.

When I woke again, it was after midday. The fever had abated somewhat but I still felt weak. Ray had gone. He'd left a note saying he'd be back around six. I put fresh coffee on to brew and took a shower. The Neiman Marcus outfit was still draped over the back of the sofa. After I'd dried myself I put it on, then went back through to the bathroom and wiped the steam from the mirrored wall. The suit looked good on me. It made me feel sexy, alluring. There was something right about it, I thought, something familiar. Maybe Ray had an instinct for clothes. The mirror began to steam over again. I moved closer to it, looking at my face. What did Ray see when he looked in my eyes, I wondered? Did some vestige of pain still linger there? Or was it the absence of grief, the emptiness inside me that attracted him? It seemed a strange notion but I couldn't shake it off. I puckered my lips and pulled the hair back tightly behind my head. What would he think if I dyed my hair blonde?

After eating a bowl of cereal my head began to ache again. I took another couple of aspirin and curled up on the sofa. I closed my eyes but the pain grew sharper when I lowered my head. I sat up and gazed round the apartment, surprised at how sparsely furnished it was. There were no pictures on the walls, no nick-nacks or books on the shelves behind the TV, none of the accumulated junk we use to make statements about ourselves. I slid off the sofa and crawled across the floor to where the widescreen stood on its metal stand. A few DVDs lay on the metal shelf between the DVD player and the TV. I recognised the covers of *My Back Yard, Lester Bows Out* and *Joey Elegant.* The fourth film was *The Last Time,* still in its handwritten cover. I opened the case, took out the disc and put it in the DVD player.

I sat on the floor a few feet in front of the screen. Like a child, I told myself, feeling an odd but not unpleasant sense of detachment. As the opening credits rolled I mouthed the words 'the last time', trying to recall what had happened in the film. Evelyn was more beautiful than I remembered. She had an air of profound mystery and sadness about her, as if she knew in advance that some terrible fate awaited her. The story was told in flashback, with Ray's character investigating her disappearance. As he got closer to the truth he became obsessed with Evelyn, determined to save her from her inescapable fate. I felt myself being drawn deeper into the twists and turns of the narrative, yet I still struggled to make sense of everything that was going on.

The ending was different. I was sure of it. The first time, Evelyn had vanished. It was that event, I remembered, which had triggered the circular narrative. I realised now that she had been trying to get away from the cop whose obsession had begun to destroy her. This time she was still with him at the end. The camera froze on Evelyn standing at a window. I noticed the blue scarf tied around her pale throat. Her eyes seemed haunted as she stared out from the final frame, searching for someone or something beyond the camera.

When it was over I slumped on my side, feeling empty and drained. It was an impossible love, I thought. I could never hunger for somebody that way. Such feelings would consume me. I remembered the intensity, the excitement in Ray's eyes the night we had watched the film together. Was he still in love with Evelyn? I wondered. Was that why he had showed me the film? So I would understand?

*

I took a taxi to Bowley Street off Lincoln, and headed north through the picnic area, and on over the dunes that bordered Baker Beach. There were dozens of nude sunbathers along the northern shore, most of them male. They didn't pay me much attention and I had no interest in them. I had wanted to get out of the apartment for a few hours, think about me and Ray, where we were going. I had only been to Baker Beach once before, with Nick, when he'd brought me to see what he said was the best view of the Golden Gate Bridge from anywhere in the city. Maybe that's why I hadn't been back since he was killed. Still hiding from the pain.

I wanted to ask Ray about Evelyn, but at the same time I didn't want to open any old wounds. I thought about the space he had given me to come to terms with losing Nick, and felt guilty for doubting him. Yet, I was sure that if I did ask, he'd be more than willing to tell me. So why my hesitation?

I got up, packed away the few things I had brought with me, and slung the backpack over my shoulder. I wandered south along the shore, till I had to clamber back over the dunes and follow the path as it rose towards the cliffs. As I climbed up higher the tension ebbed from me and I began to feel exhilarated. I could hear the sea pounding into the rocks below, and the gulls screeching as they sped over the surf. I was sweating and breathing hard as I reached the highest point. I threw my backpack on the ground and sat down. I let my eyes take in the vast sweep of the ocean, the rocky coast to the west, the mile long stretch of Baker Beach to the north, the bridge, and the Marin headland beyond. I'd never walked those cliffs before, and yet everything about them was familiar to me. I knew that a little way off to the west, the coast would fall steeply to China Beach. I could picture myself swimming there in the ice cold ocean some years ago, but when I tried to flesh out the memory it slipped from my grasp like a morning dream.

Up there on the cliffs I was alone, cut off from the world. I was no longer even sure why I was there or what it was I had hoped to find.

There were gaps in my memory, empty spaces where important parts of my life had been. Get a hold of yourself, girl, I told myself. You're fretting too much. Overanalysing. Letting old fear and doubts bring you down. It was because of Ray, I knew. I was in love with him, and that scared me. Was I ready to put myself through this? To risk losing him? I wondered what or who it was that I might lose him to, but deep down, I knew.

The bad feelings began to recede, and I no longer worried about someone watching me. Ray said it was because I had moved on, come to terms with the past. He was right. Once I had acknowledged my fears, it became easier. Not having to deny the way I felt about him seemed to make everything clearer. He was so good to me, really, I couldn't have been happier. He bought me clothes and jewellery, showered me with all kinds of things. He said he wanted to make me beautiful. I wondered if I had ever been beautiful before. In a sense, Ray said, I had recreated myself. I took him at his word and dyed my hair blonde.

We were in a bar on Geary one night, when I recognised a song by my brother's band. Jim sang about the sound of a beating heart being the only proof anyone would ever need. Proof of what? I wondered, unable to hear the words clearly above the talk and laughter. "You hear that, Ray?" I asked him. "You know what that means?"

Ray smiled and squeezed my leg beneath the table. "What is it Evelyn? What's bothering you?"

"Nothing," I said. "I'm fine." Had I heard him right? Or had I just imagined him saying what I wanted to hear?

"You want to go?"

I nodded. Ray called a cab. It took us west out of the city, all the way to the ocean. A great bank of fog rolled up along the shore from the south as we stumbled down on to the beach and kicked off our shoes. The sand was cold beneath our feet. I pressed my body against Ray. He pulled me down to the ground where we tore off each other's clothes and had quick, frantic sex. It was not the first time we had done this. I asked him if he had ever brought Evelyn here. If he had ever fucked her on this stretch of beach.

He didn't say anything for a while. The fog was cold and tight about us. We pulled on our clothes and sat listening to the invisible surf.

Mike O'Driscoll

"Would it matter if I had?" he said, finally.

"I guess that depends," I said. "On what you really want from me."

"What does that mean?"

"Do you still want her? Do you still love her?"

"Evelyn is dead." The words were brittle on his tongue. "She died shortly after the film finished shooting."

"I'm sorry, Ray. I didn't know."

"How could you have?" he said, bitterly. "She was never anyone."

I put my arms around him and held him tight. I squeezed all the love I could into him and told him it was all right. I was here. Nothing else mattered.

Of course other things mattered, but what mattered most was not feeling any pain. For me that meant not losing Ray. I understood now, that hunger I had seen in his eyes when he had looked at Evelyn. I felt I had cured him of her, that the feelings that remained were all for me.

Ray moved into my apartment. The plan was to buy a place outside the city the following Spring. Somewhere north of the bay. He made the future seem real, brought snatches of it alive in the here and now. We were always making plans, for tomorrow, next week, or next year. We'd get married. We'd move out of the city. I'd quit my job and we'd have babies together. All of this would happen, he said. Soon.

I kept my job, waiting for the day. After a while I noticed that Ray was always home before me. He began to look tired and dishevelled. He no longer shaved every day, the way he used to do. There were some days I was sure he never left the apartment. I'd managed to track down most of his films on DVD. I felt he needed them to remind him that he had once been someone. But he rarely looked at any of them, apart from that one pirated copy of *The Last Time*. I never had been able to find an original. He kept asking me to watch it with him but I couldn't. I was afraid it would have changed again.

I came home one evening and found the place in darkness. I turned on the lights and saw timber boards nailed over the window frames. Ray was lying on the floor, drunk.

"Goddamit Ray," I said, stunned. "What have you done? What's happening to you?"

He mumbled something indecipherable.

218

"Say it Ray, tell me what this is."

His eyes flickered open and he looked up at me. "Evelyn? Where you been?"

"No Ray," I said, infuriated. "It's not fucking Evelyn. It's Grace."

"Grace?" He looked confused. He crawled to an armchair and I helped him up onto it. He grabbed my arm and pulled me close. "Tell me," he whispered.

"Tell you what?"

"Tell me it isn't true."

"No Ray. It is true. She's dead. You told me yourself, remember. She's gone." I tried to pull myself free but he held on to my wrist.

"Lying bitch."

"Listen to me, Ray, you're not yourself."

"No, Evelyn," he said, grinning drunkenly. "You're wrong."

I couldn't stand it anymore. I lashed out as hard as I could, catching him in the mouth. He fell back in the chair, unconscious. I stood over him, my anger dissipating. What had I done? There was blood on his lips and his breathing was shallow. For a moment I thought about calling an ambulance, then realised that all he needed was rest. Someone real to take care of him, draw him out of his obsession.

I grabbed his arms and pulled him forward off the chair. I dragged him by the hands to the bedroom, where, after a couple of attempts, I got him up onto the bed. I took off his clothes and pulled the sheet over him. Goddamn you, I thought. For letting me down. For being so weak. I couldn't go through that pain again. I had promised myself. In the morning, I would leave. Walk out the door and not come back.

I went through to the kitchen and stuck a pasta dish in the microwave. Forced myself to eat half of it. Nothing seemed right anymore. Everything was crumbling. This was not how it was supposed to be. I wondered if I'd said the same thing when Nick was killed. Thinking about him I began to cry. Hot, angry tears, full of self-loathing. How little pain I had allowed myself to feel for him. How afraid to accept that such hurt was part of the deal. Was I really such a coward? Could I abandon Ray the way I had Nick?

I returned to the bedroom. Ray lay on his back, his head turned to one side. His chest rose and fell, almost imperceptibly. I undressed and got in beside him. He felt hot and clammy, and the undersheet was damp

Mike O'Driscoll

with his sweat. "Ray," I whispered, holding him. "I'll make it right, I promise."

Ray didn't stir. I tossed and turned for more than an hour before getting out of bed, sticky with his perspiration. I showered, pulled on a clean t-shirt and knickers and went through to the living room. I stood in front of the television, hesitating. Maybe the answer lay in the film. Could I bring myself to watch it again? Would I learn something new? All I was sure of was that something would have changed.

This time at the end it wasn't Evelyn trapped in the final frame, but Ray. He had found her in the motel. She'd looked out the window, her eyes drawing him in. Like a fool he'd gone to her. The final shot was of the detective standing in the doorway, hands writhing, mouthing silent oaths. Caught in an impossible desire.

In the morning I left Ray sleeping and went in to work as usual. I kept telling myself I was not going through the motions, that I would do whatever it took to cure Ray of the past. He was mine now, not some dead woman's.

At midday I found some time to myself and logged on to a movie website Josh had told me about. I typed in Ray's name and after a second a small picture appeared on screen next to a brief biog. He didn't look much different to the way he looked now. His hair was shorter and he had a goatee in the photograph, which suited him. Including his British films, there were twenty movies listed in which he had appeared, dating back to 1986. His TV credits were also listed but there was nothing at all for *The Last Time*. I scrolled back up through the list and typed in the name of the movie. Three titles came up, two recent shorts and a Michael Keaton movie which was in post-production. I must have got something wrong, I thought. I tried different permutations of the film's title, Last Time, The; Last Time; Time Last. None of them gave me anything.

I leaned back in my chair, trying to figure out another approach. I started to enter Evelyn's name before realising I didn't know her surname. I typed it in anyway but when I hit search, the database came back with over six hundred matches. I tried to cast my mind back to the opening credits. I could remember Ray's name being listed, but no Evelyn. I wondered if that was her real name or if she had used another name professionally.

I hurried home from work that evening, half-expecting to find Ray still in bed, or watching his damn movie again. He wasn't there. He'd left no message to say where he'd gone or what time he'd be back. I felt angry with him, finding it hard to believe he could treat me this way.

The windows were still boarded up, small cracks of evening light bleeding through the gaps. I turned on the television and pressed play. I watched the opening credits, knowing I wouldn't see her name. I skipped forward to her first appearance then slowed the disc to normal play. It was there, what I was too stupid to hear all along. Evelyn wasn't the name of the actress, but the character. I was about to skip ahead to the end credits when something familiar caught my attention. It was a view of the Golden Gate Bridge from the cliffs above China Beach. Sweat trickled down my back. Evelyn was there, searching for someone. She wore a black jacket and skirt. I recognised other places in the movie, places I had been to, alone or with Ray. At Ocean Beach. In the bar on Geary, my brother's forlorn voice singing about a woman he'd lost. As the story unfurled I realised that Ray wasn't trying to find Evelyn. He was trying to get away from her. I could see how it would end, the whole twisted plot curling in on itself. I didn't want to watch any more of it but I didn't have the strength to turn away. Even before they appeared I knew what the end credits would reveal. The woman who played Evelyn Elms was Grace James.

Appalled, I backed away from the TV screen. It was impossible. I would not accept it. I turned towards the door and saw Ray standing there, frail and dark-eyed, a desperate smile on his face. "It's okay, Evelyn," he said. "We found each other."

The Silence of the Falling Stars

Nothing is infinite. In a lifetime a man's heart will notch up somewhere in the region of 2500 million beats, a woman's, maybe 500 million more. These are big numbers but not infinite. There is an end in sight, no matter how far off it seems. People don't think about that. They talk instead about the sublime beauty of nature, about the insignificance of human life compared to the time it's taken to shape these rocks and mountains. Funny how time can weigh heavier on the soul than all these billions of tons of dolomite and dirt. A few years back a ranger found something squatting against the base of a mesquite tree at the mouth of Hanaupah Canyon. It was something dead, he saw, and the shape of it suggested a man. Curious, the ranger crouched down and touched it. The body, or whatever it was, had been so dessicated by heat and wind that it started to crumble and when the desert breeze caught it, the whole thing fell away to dust. No way to tell what it had really been, or if it was heat alone or time that caused its naturalisation.

Fifty year highs for July average 116 degrees. Anyone caught out here in that kind of heat without water has a couple of options. You can try to find shade, which, if you get lucky, will cut your rate of dehydration by about fifteen per cent. Or, you can just rest instead of walking, which will save you something like forty per cent. But the ground temperature out here is half again higher than the air. Ideally what you want is a shaded spot elevated above the ground. If you're lucky enough to find such a place, and if you're smart enough to keep your clothes on, which will cut your dehydration by another twenty per

223

cent, then you might last two days at 120 degrees max without water. If you're out of luck, then just keeping still, you'll sweat two pints in an hour. If you don't take in the equivalent amount of water, you'll begin to dehydrate. At five per cent loss of body weight you'll start to feel nauseous. Round about ten per cent, your arms and legs will begin tingling and you'll find it hard to breathe. The water loss will thicken your blood and your heart will struggle to pump it out to your extremities. Somewhere between fifteen and twenty per cent dehydration, you'll die.

Which goes to show there is, after all, one thing that is infinite, the length of time you stay dead. There is no real correlation between what I'm thinking and the SUV that heads slowly south along the dirt road. Even when it pulls over and stops beside the dry lake running along the valley floor, I can't say for sure what will happen. I'm unwilling to speculate. Even when nothing happens I don't feel any kind of surprise.

I scan the oval playa with my binoculars. Indians are supposed to have raced horses across it, which is why it's called the Racetrack. There's an outcrop of rock at the north end which they call the Grandstand but I don't see any spectators up there. Never have. Below the ridge from where I watch, there are clumps of creosote bush and the odd Joshua tree. Further north, there are stands of beavertail and above them, on the high slopes of the Last Chance Range, are forests of juniper and pinyon pine. A glint of sunlight catches my eye and I glance towards the vehicle. But nothing has moved down there. I shift my gaze back out on to the playa, trying to pretend I don't feel the cold chill that settles on my bones. I look away at the last moment and wipe the sweat from my face. Thirst cracks my lips and dust coats the inside of my mouth. There's plenty of water in my Expedition, parked a half mile further south along the road, but I make no move to return to the vehicle. Whatever is happening here I have no choice but to see how it plays out.

A shadow moves on the playa. When I search for it all I can see are the rocks scattered across the honey-combed surface of the dry lake. I scan them closely, looking for a lizard or rodent, even though nothing lives out there. The air is still and quiet, no breeze at all to rustle through the mesquites. Then something catches my eye and the hairs on the back of my neck stand up. A movement so painfully slow I doubt it happened at all. Until it rolls forward another inch. From this distance, I estimate its weight at eighty to a hundred pounds. I glance at the rocks nearest to it but none of them have moved. Only this one, its shadow seeming to melt in the harsh sunlight as it heaves forward again. There's no wind, nothing to explain its motion. All the stories I've heard about the rocks have some rational explanation but there's no reason at all to what I'm seeing here.

Except maybe that SUV and whatever's inside it. I look back to where it was but it's not there. I scan the dirt road to north and south and still don't see it. I search the playa in case the vehicle drove out on the mud but there are only scattered rocks. The sun is at its highest now, yet I'm not overheating. I don't feel nauseous and my heart isn't struggling. Maybe it's because I'm barely breathing. I stare along the dirt road for an age, looking for something I might have missed. But there's no trail of dust, or anything else to signal they were ever here.

*

The guy wore jeans and a loose fit shirt, the woman had on shorts, t-shirt and a baseball cap. He was leaning over beneath the open hood of the Japanese SUV. A rusting stove lay on its back beside the road and beyond it two lines of rubble were all that marked a building which had long since gone.

The woman's face creased in a smile as I pulled up in front of the Toyota Rav4. I got out of my vehicle. "You need a hand here?"

"I think we've overheated," she said. I didn't recognise her accent.

The guy stood up and wiped his face on his shirt. "Bloody air conditioning," he said. "I guess I was running it too hard. We're not used to this kind of heat."

I nodded. "How long you been stuck here?"

Before the woman could answer, a young girl stuck her head out the back window. "Henry Woods," she said, reading my name tag. "Are you a policeman?"

"No, I'm a park ranger."

The woman leaned over and tousled the girl's hair. "Ranger Woods, meet Cath. I'm Sophie Delauney, this is my husband, Paul."

I shook hands with both of them and asked Delauney if there was anything they needed. He frowned, then laughed and said he doubted it. "I suppose you'll tell me I should have hired an American car."

Mike O'Driscoll

"No. You just had bad luck, is all." I leaned in over the engine, saw there was nothing I could do. "Could happen to anyone."

"Yeah well, it happened to us."

I got some bottles of water from the cooler in the Expedition and handed them around. Delauney went back to fiddling with the plugs and points, unwilling, I figured, to accept that all he could do was wait for the engine to cool.

"How'd you find us?" Sophie Delauney said.

"We have a plane patrols the Valley. Must have seen you here and called it in. I was up at Zabriskie Point, twenty miles north of here."

"I didn't see it," she said, shielding her eyes as she looked up at the cloudless sky.

"I saw it," the girl said.

"Did you baby? You never said."

"I did. You weren't listening."

"Where you folks from?" I asked.

"England," she said. "We live outside London."

The girl frowned and shook her head. "No we don't – we live in Elstree."

"I know dear, but Mr Woods might not have heard of Elstree."

"I always wanted to see England," I said. "Just never seem to find the time."

"You should."

Delauney finally saw that merely willing it wasn't going to get the engine to cool any faster and came to join us. "Where you headed?" I asked him.

"Not far, by the look of things. Can you recommend anywhere close by?"

"About an hour's drive will get you to the resort village at Stovepipe Wells." I don't know why I didn't mention the Inn at Furnace Creek, which was closer.

The girl piped up. "Do they have a swimming pool?"

I nodded. "Sure do."

Sophie drank some water. She wiped her hand across her mouth and said, "Do you ever get used to this heat?"

"Breathe lightly," I said. "It won't hurt so much."

After quarter of an hour I told Delauney to try it again. The engine turned over and cut out. He tried again and this time it caught. "There you go," I said. "You should be okay now – just keep an eye on the temp gauge."

"Thanks for your help, Officer Woods," Sophie said. "It's much appreciated."

"It's what I'm here for."

They got in the vehicle. "Thanks again," Sophie said. I watched as they drove off, the girl hanging out the window, her mother too, staring back at me. Alone in the ruins of Greenwater, I tried to imagine what she saw, wondering if she had seen something in my eyes I didn't know was there.

*

I paid rent to the government for the bungalow I occupied near Stovepipe Wells. It was small but even after six years, I didn't seem to have accumulated enough belongings to fill the available space. Rae Hannafin said it looked unlived in, said if I hated it that much I should ask to be rehoused. She thought I was stuck in a rut, that I had been in the Valley too long and that I should apply for a transfer. But I didn't hate Death Valley or even the bungalow. Though I used to imagine that one day I would move on, over the years I've come to realise that I had reached the place I'd always been heading towards. It's not just the solitariness – it's the Valley itself which gets under your skin.

I sat in Arcan's Bar drinking Mexican beer. It was quiet, a dozen or so people, mostly couples, a few regulars shooting pool, half a dozen familiar faces perched on stools at the counter. Kenny Rogers, someone like that, on the jukebox. The young hispanic behind the counter made small talk with a couple of girls. I caught his eye, he fetched another beer, set it down in front of me, gave me a scowl and went back to work his charm on the señoritas. Jaime had been working there nearly two years and still complained about the customers treating him like shit. Just because he was Mexican, he told me one time. No, I said, it's because you're an outsider.

"That 'sposed to make me feel better, man?" he asked.

"Yes," I said. "Because we're all outsiders here."

That was about the most I'd ever talked to him at one time. I'm not good at small talk. As a rule I only talk when I have something to say.

This is probably a failing on my part. Hannafin says that talk is a social lubricant, that it's part of what makes us human, even when it doesn't mean anything. I'm not convinced. Everything we say means something, even if it's not what we intended. But I had to admit that it worked for her. She seemed to be able to get through to people, make them understand her meaning without spelling it out. Maybe that was what made her such a good ranger, why she would maybe one day make Assistant Chief.

I took a pull on my beer and stared in the mirror behind the counter, looking for something to take me out of myself. It was getting to be a habit. I'd watch other people and imagine their conversations or what they were feeling, see if that made me feel any more human. Sometimes I'd see other men just like me, that same soft hunger in their eyes as they searched for someone or something to help them discover meaning in their lives.

"Hey ranger."

I came out of my reverie and stared at the guy who'd spoken.

"I was right." It was the guy whose SUV had overheated. "I said to Sophie it was you."

I saw her sitting at a table by the window with her daughter. The kid waved. "You're staying in the motel?"

"You recommended it," Delauney said. "Look, ah, let me buy you a drink."

I was about to decline when I looked at Sophie Delauney again and saw her smile. "Sure," I said. "I'll have another beer."

While he ordered drinks I walked over to the table. "Ranger Woods, what a surprise," Sophie said, and asked me to take a seat. "You live in the resort?"

"Bout a mile away."

"Where's your hat?" the girl said.

"That's for keeping the sun off my head, not the stars."

"You look different but I knew it was you. Daddy thought you were someone else."

"You must have what we call the eagle eye."

"What is that?"

"It means you see too much," Sophie said, as she stroked the girl's hair. I wondered what she meant, what were the things the kid saw that she shouldn't have seen. "Since you're off duty, is it okay if we call you Henry?"

I told her it was fine. Delauney came over with two bottles of Dos Equis, a glass of red wine and a juice for the kid. I still felt a little awkward but something about Sophie made it easy to be in her company. She steered the conversation so that I didn't have to say too much, mostly listened as they talked about their own lives back in England. She taught history in high school, Delauney was an architect. They'd made their first trip to America nine years ago, when they got married and spent a week in New York. Now, with their daughter, they'd come to see the West. They'd flown to LA, spent four days down there, doing the 'Disneyland thing' and the 'Hollywood thing', which was the way Delauney put it, rolling his eyes. They'd driven up to Las Vegas, had two nights there, before rolling into the Valley this afternoon along highway 178. The Greenwater detour seemed like a good idea at the time. Sophie's charm made me feel something like a normal human being. Sometimes I lost sight of that, and I was grateful to her for reminding me who I was.

I got another round of drinks and when I returned, Delauney asked me about the Valley.

"What are the best places to see?"

"How much time you got?"

"A day."

"Don't try to squeeze in too much."

"He won't listen," Sophie said. "Paul has to turn everything into a major expedition."

He laughed. "Okay, tell me what I can't afford to miss."

I thought about it a while. "When you start to look closely," I said, "you'll notice all the things that aren't there." I wondered if Sophie understood, if she was capable of seeing what was missing.

She started to say something but Delauney talked across her. "I'll stick with what is here. Like Badwater, and maybe a ghost town."

I nodded. "Chloride City's an old silver mining town about a half hour north-east of here. Not a whole lot left up there but there's a cliff above the town will give you some great views of the Valley."

The girl said, "Ask about the rocks."

"The rocks."

Mike O'Driscoll

"Daddy said they move."

Delauney seemed a little embarrassed. "Guide book said that rocks get blown by high winds across the surface of a dry lake." He sounded sceptical but also willing to be persuaded. "Said they leave trails across the surface."

I took a sip of my beer. "I've heard that, too."

"Have you seen them move?" the girl asked.

"Never have."

"I still want to see them anyway," she said.

"Maybe," Delauney said. "But tomorrow it's the ghost town, okay?"

"You won't be disappointed," I said.

Sophie was looking at me. She seemed unconscious of the intensity of her gaze or that I might be aware of it. I wondered what she saw in my face, whether there was something there that revealed more than I wanted her to see. There was a spray of freckles splashed beneath her eyes and across the bridge of her nose. She was beautiful. I wanted desperately to know what was inside her head at that moment, but Delauney leaned close and whispered something to her. Something I didn't catch. She laughed and her face flushed red and I didn't know what that meant. It was Cath's bedtime, she said. I smiled to let her know it was okay, but I could see she was bothered. She told Delauney to stay a while if he wanted. But I felt troubled suddenly, angry that she was going. I wished he'd kept his mouth shut.

"I gotta go, too," I said, standing up. "Early start in the morning."

"No problem, Henry," Delauney said. "Thanks for all your help."

I turned to Sophie. "It was good to meet you," I said, shaking her hand, using formality just to feel the touch of her skin. There was no harm in it. "Enjoy your stay. You too Cath, keep that eagle eye on your folks."

Sophie frowned, as if puzzled at something I'd said. I left the bar and set off out into the quiet darkness. It was less than a mile back to the empty bungalow but it seemed like the longest walk I ever took.

*

Before I came to the Valley I lived out on the coast. I was a deputy in the San Luis Obispo's Sheriff Department. I was good at the job and had ambitions to make Sheriff one day. There was a woman I'd been seeing

230

and I'd begun to think maybe she was the one. But things didn't turn out the way I planned. Something happened I hadn't counted on, one of those situations nobody could foresee. There was no time to think and what I did I did instinctively. IAD ruled that it had been self-defence but I knew as well as anyone the kid never had a gun. After the investigation things began to fall apart at work and my girlfriend began to cool on me. A week after she left I quit the department and spent eighteen months drifting round the mid-west, feeling sorry for myself and listening to songs about regret. Living in Death Valley cured me of that. Like Robert Frost said, whatever road you're on is the one you chose and the one you didn't take is no longer an option. I came here, worked as a volunteer, then, after six months, got a ranger's post and, in time, I saw there was no going back.

Some people find that hard to accept. This morning I got a call to check out a vehicle parked up at Quackenbush Mine. There was a dog in the back seat of the truck, a German Shepherd. Her tongue lolled out her open mouth and she managed a feeble wag of her tail against the seat when she saw me. The window was cracked open a half inch but even so it must have been over 130 degrees inside. It took me twenty minutes to find the driver, coming down from Goldbelt Spring. He was a heavy-set guy, in shorts and vest, a 49ers cap hiding his close-cropped skull. Had a woman and two kids with him, boy and a girl about ten or eleven.

"Is that your truck down there at the mine, sir?" I asked him.

"The Cherokee, yeah."

"Your dog is dying in there."

"Aw shit," he groaned, lurching down the slope. "I knew this would fucking happen."

They always say they knew what would happen. Which, instead of justifying what they did, only compounds the situation. He bleated on about how he didn't want to keep the dog on a leash and how his wife kept on about you had to because that was the rule and so, in truth it wasn't his fault, he was just thinking about the dog. I led him back down to his vehicle, got him to open it up and lift the dog out on to the ground. Her eyes were glazed, her body still.

"She's still alive," the guy said. "I can feel her heart."

"Step back out of the way," I told him. I unholstered my gun, stuck the barrel against the dog's chest and squeezed the trigger.

The woman screamed. The open-mouthed kids stared at the dog, then at my gun.

"Jesus Christ," the guy said. "Jesus fucking Christ – you killed her."

"No," I said. "You did that." I stood up and checked the vehicle over to see if there was anything else I could cite the son of a bitch for apart from animal cruelty. I gave him the ticket and drove off, leaving him to bury the dog in the dirt.

Heading south on the Saline Valley Road, I heard Rydell's voice crackling over the Motorola, requesting assistance at an incident in Hidden Valley. I responded and told him where I was.

"It's a vehicle come off the road, two people injured," he said. "Quick as you can, Henry. Hannafin's already on her way down from Grapevine."

I spun the Expedition around, throwing up a cloud of dust as I accelerated north along the dirt road. My heart was racing like it knew what I was going to find but the truth was I had no real idea what to expect up there.

When I saw the truck turned on its side ten yards off the road, the feeling of anticipation disappeared, leaving me vaguely disappointed. Five kids were seated in a semi-circle a few yards away from the vehicle. One of them, a fair-haired kid about eighteen, got up and came over to me. "I think Shelley broke a leg," he said, nodding towards the others. "And Karl's maybe busted an arm."

"You the driver?"

He hesitated before nodding.

"You been drinking? Smoking some weed?"

"No way, man, nothing like that. Just took the bend too fast, I guess."

All of them were cut and bruised but only the two he'd named were badly injured. Shelley looked like she was in a lot of pain. I was splinting her leg when Hannafin arrived and went to work on the others. When we had them patched up, we put Karl and Shelley in Hannafin's vehicle and two others in mine. The driver made to get in front beside me but I shook my head. "Take this," I said, handing him a two litre bottle of water.

"What for?" He looked bewildered. "Oh man, you saying I have to wait here?"

"There's a wrecker on its way from Furnace Creek. Should be here in three hours."

The journey to Grapevine took the best part of an hour. The two in the back remained silent for most of that time, either too dazed to talk or wary of saying something that would incriminate their buddy. Or maybe they sensed my own unease, a feeling of disquiet that had been bothering me all day. I'd been expecting some kind of revelation but all I had was the feeling that I'd been asking myself the wrong questions.

There was an ambulance waiting at Grapevine Station to take the two injured kids to the Emergency Room in Amargosa Valley. The other two said they'd wait at Grapevine for the tow truck to show up with their vehicle and driver. In the station office, Hannafin made fresh coffee while I stared out the window towards the mountains bordering Ubehebe Crater. She said something I didn't catch and I didn't ask her what it was.

"Is it any different today," she said, "from how it was last week?"

"They're the same," I said, though I knew she wasn't talking about the mountains.

She handed me a mug of steaming coffee. "You been keeping to yourself, lately."

I felt weary and disinclined to have the conversation she wanted.

"What's bothering you, Henry?"

I sipped the coffee, trying to put my thoughts in some kind of order.

"It's good to see you've lost none of your charm and conversational skills."

I forced a smile. "I'm sorry, Rae," I said. "Got things on my mind, is all."

"Anything I can help with?"

I liked Rae, liked her a lot, but that's all it was. I wasn't looking for any kind of relationship. I was never much good at explaining such things, feelings, or their absence. "Just some stuff I have to deal with," I said. "Nothing that matters too much."

"A problem shared is a problem halved."

"There is no problem."

"I forgot," she said. "You don't have problems, ever." She bit her lower lip, I guess to stop from saying anything else. I didn't know what she might have wanted to say and I didn't care. I felt empty inside, empty and lifeless as the salt flats.

I drained my coffee and set the mug down. "None I lose sleep over."

"I think you should talk to someone."

"I talk to people all the time."

"No you don't, Henry. If you did you wouldn't be losing touch."

"I'll be seeing you, Rae," I said, leaving the office. Hannafin was my friend but that didn't mean she knew all there was to know about me. It was never that simple.

*

At first I saw nothing on the road. I drove past the Grandstand on my left and headed south another mile before pulling over, somewhat confused. I picked up the radio, intending to give HQ a piece of my mind. But before anyone could respond, I'd got out of the vehicle and was watching the small dust cloud that had appeared away to the south. I grabbed the binoculars from the dash. Between my position and the cloud a vehicle was stopped in the middle of the dirt road. The dust cloud seemed to be moving further south, as if marking the trail of some other vehicle, one I hadn't seen. Dry heat rippled across the exposed skin of my arms, sucked all the moisture from my mouth. As I stared at the dust cloud it was pulled apart by a wind I didn't feel.

Nothing moved around the SUV. I scrambled up the slope to my right, moving south-west towards a patch of creosote bush. From there I looked down at the road, first at my own vehicle, then at the other, half a mile, maybe less, from where I stood. I squatted down in the scrub, removed the Sig Sauer 9mm from my holster and laid it on the ground. The sun was falling slowly towards the mountain behind me, but its heat seemed to have intensified. A sudden movement caught my eye. I watched through the binoculars as a man got out of the SUV and walked to the edge of the dirt road. He just stood there gazing out at the playa like it was a picture of beauty rather than heat and desolation. Two other people joined him, standing either side. I tried to see what they were looking at but nothing moved out there, not even the goddamn rocks. The mountain's shadow bruised the edge of the Racetrack.

A fourth person had arrived. I watched his lips moving as he pointed across the dry lake. Sound travels a fair distance in this stillness, but I didn't hear a word. There was something unsettling about the way he held himself, thumb looped into the belt at his waist, that made me feel numb and disconnected. After a few moments the first three set out walking heading east across the playa. The last guy stood there a while, till they were two or three hundred yards out, then he followed them, taking his time, keeping his distance. A redtail circled above him and when he stopped to glance at it, the bird flew off to the north. A line of thin ragged clouds chased each other away across the valley, as if anxious not to intrude. Beads of sweat dribbled from beneath the straw hat and down my face as I worked to fill the silence with the imagined sound of their footsteps crunching across the Racetrack.

Nothing made sense.

Long, thin shadows followed them, clawing the dry mud like the fingers of a man dying of thirst. The figures grew smaller as they receded into the distance. I clambered down the slope to the Expedition and drove south until I reached their vehicle. I thought about calling Rydell but wasn't sure what to tell him. All I'd seen was some folks set out across the Racetrack on foot, same as countless visitors had done before them. But if there was no mystery, then why was my heart racing so fast? Why couldn't I shake off the feeling that this was all wrong?

I stood by the side of the road, no longer able to see any of them, accepting that I had no choice but to follow. Strange, disorienting sensations flowed through my body, setting flares off behind my eyes and thrumming in my ears. I began to walk. The ground was hard and bone dry, but even so I found a trail of footprints. They were quite distinct but what disturbed me was that there was only one pair, not four. I tried to ignore this and figured how long it would take me to catch up with the group. After thirty minutes I should have been able to see them, but nothing moved out there. I quickened my pace. The mountains to the north and west punctured the sky, opening wounds that bled over the horizon and down onto the playa. Ten minutes later I stopped and listened. Nothing, no birds, no wind, no voices. I unholstered the 9mm again, held it up and fired two shots. And was appalled when I heard nothing. My hand shook as I stared at the pistol. I'd felt the recoil and the smell of cordite on the breezeless air contradicted the silence. I checked the magazine, saw that two rounds had been discharged. It was just the sound that had been lost, a realisation that made my isolation more complete. If sound couldn't exist here, then what could? When I stared at the mountains enclosing both sides of the valley, I knew that even memories were not real in this place. I felt more alone than anyone had ever been, without even the company of the dead. With the light fading, I took a bearing on a western peak and set off towards Racetrack Road.

It took me the best part of an hour to find my vehicle and by then night had settled on the valley. I stared up, overwhelmed by the immense darkness. There was no moon, and the night seemed blacker than usual, as if half the stars were missing from the sky. It seemed the only way to account for the intensity of the night. I sat in the cab, radio in hand. I wanted to speak to someone, hear some familiar voice but I was stopped by a doubt I couldn't explain. The feeling of wrongness persisted, had grown stronger in my head. It didn't make sense at first, not until I'd grabbed a bottle of water from the cooler, turned the key in the ignition and flicked on my headlights. The road in front of me was empty and I was alone with the fallen stars.

*

I sat in the Expedition in the parking lot, feeling a deep weariness in my bones, the sort that can hold you for hours on end. My hand was on the door but I couldn't move. I watched cars come and go, people walking by, like this was normal, like nothing at all had changed. I even saw Sophie Delauney walking across the parking lot, hand in hand with her daughter. She stopped halfway across the lot, turned, smiled and waved at me. She seemed unaware of the people around her and I felt my mind melting, my sense of being fading away in her presence. I thought maybe there were things she wanted to say, words she'd left unspoken. I felt the wrongness of letting her go without talking to her again, at least one more time.

But before I could go to her, Delauney himself walked past, though he appeared not to see me. He carried two large suitcases which he stowed in the back of the Rav4. A vein began to throb in my temple. Drops of sweat stood out on my brow though the sun was low in the sky and the air con was blowing. He got in the driver's seat and started the Toyota. Sophie stood by the passenger door and glanced my way again. She looked right at me but I knew she wasn't seeing me at all. Whatever look she had on her face, it didn't mean anything. By the time I got out of the Expedition, she'd climbed in beside Delauney and they were pulling out of the lot.

Later, I sat in Arcan's nursing a beer. Troubled by what I'd seen, I tried to cloak the strangeness in reason but I couldn't make it fit. The feeling that I was thinking about someone else had taken root in my brain. That I had no control of my own life nor any clear idea where I was heading. Maybe I'd spent too long in the Valley. Maybe it was time to leave. Only I wasn't sure I could.

Old Arcan himself came in the bar and made one of his regular attempts at playing the host. He claimed to be a direct descendant of one of the first men to cross Death Valley, but nobody believed it. His ex-wife told someone he'd been born plain Bill Judd. I watched him move from one guest to another, carefully selecting those on whom he wished to bestow his hospitality. Thankfully, I wasn't among them.

I found myself thinking about Sophie Delauney. They were the kind of thoughts I had no business thinking, that caused pleasure and pain in equal measure, but I thought them anyway. Some lives were full of certainties but mine seemed to be made up only of 'what ifs' and 'maybes'. It should have been no surprise that it had become less real to me.

I ordered another drink and stared into the mirror behind the counter. The people in there seemed to have purpose in their lives, to know what they were doing, where they were going. If I watched long enough, paid attention to the details, maybe I'd discover how to make my life more real. Arcan was holding forth to the group of Japs sitting round a table across the bar. Jaime was working his routine on a blonde girl at the end of the counter. She looked bored, and I guessed the only reason she was tolerating his bullshit was the lack of any other diversion. I wondered if the real Jaime was having any better luck than the one in the mirror. And here was Sophie Delauney, standing just a few feet behind me and watching my reflection watch her, or maybe it was her reflection watching us. Do mirrors take in sound the way they do light? I don't think so. I couldn't hear anything, no music, no talk, not even the clink of glasses. It was a long time before I remembered myself and thought to say hello. But a second before I did, she beat me to it. She climbed up onto the bar stool beside me and caught Jaime's eye.

He was there in a shot. She pointed to my half-empty bottle of Dos Equis, told him to bring one of those and a glass of Merlot. I said I hadn't expected to see her again. She shrugged and told me they'd had a long day. Drove down to Badwater where Delauney had decided to hike out on the salt flats. Went half a mile before the heat got to him and he returned to the car. Later, they went to Chloride City. She wasn't looking at me as she talked, but at the guy in the mirror, the fellow who looked just like me but whose thoughts were not the same as mine. The ache in her voice seemed to hint at some inner turmoil. I wanted to offer words of comfort and reassurance, tell her everything would be okay. But thinking the words was easier than saying them.

I asked if she'd seen any ghosts up there. She shook her head and smiled. No ghosts, just dust, heat and silence. I understood about the silence but with all those ghosts up there she'd expected something more. Why hadn't the inhabitants from Chloride City's second boom period learned anything from the first? I told her there were more fools in the world than she might have imagined. Gold wasn't the only illusion that drew people to the Valley.

Did I mean that literally? I wasn't sure. I wondered if Delauney had seen anything out on the salt flats beyond Badwater, if his mind had been troubled by visions he couldn't explain. But I saw no sign of his existence in the mirror and didn't think to ask. Sophie wanted to know about my life and I told her some things that seemed important, others that kept a smile on her face. She told me Paul wanted her to have another child. She wasn't sure what to do. The dreams and ambitions she'd once had were largely unfulfilled, there were things she hadn't yet grasped. I understood her to mean that this was something she'd never told Delauney.

And then he was there, clapping me on the back and giving Sophie a proprietary kiss on the cheek. She fell quiet then, seemed to retreat into herself. I tried to maintain the connection to her but his voice kept intruding on my thoughts. There was nothing to distinguish his words from the other noises in the bar, a wavering chorus of sounds whose real purpose was little more than to fill the silence. A feeling of despair grew inside me as I watched Sophie close herself off. Her smile was gone and the lines around her eyes signalled the dreams she could no longer give voice to.

Delauney was asking me if it was possible to go to the Racetrack and join route 190 heading west without coming back on himself. I told him it would add sixty or seventy miles to his journey, most of it on poor dirt roads. He nodded and said they might make the detour on their way out of the Valley tomorrow. I asked him what he hoped to see up there. Same as anyone, he said, he wanted to see the moving rocks for himself, or at the very least, the trails they left in their wake.

I told him he wouldn't, no one ever did. He believed me, he said, but seeing beat believing any day of the week.

*

I watch the shadows compose themselves. The way they move across mountains or desert dunes reveals how fluid identity really is. What we think of as solid, has no more real substance than a whisper or a lie. It's just light and shadow which make the unknown recognisable, which sculpt unfamiliar surfaces into configurations we think we know. We stare a while at these faces or shapes, glad they mean something to us even if we can't name them, and then we blink and when we look again the face has changed to something we can't recognise. We try to retrieve the familiar face, needing to see it one more time to confirm that it was who we thought it was but the new image persists, erasing the old. It's like trying to see the two leading faces of a line drawing of a transparent cube at the same time – it can't be done. One face is always behind the other. We close our eyes again and when we look one more time there isn't even a face to see, just a shadow moving over rock, sliding into all its dark places. It was the kind of illusion that made me feel less certain about my place in the world.

I woke up this morning no longer sure I am who I thought I was. I showered, dressed and ate breakfast, feeling like an intruder in my own home. I sat in the Expedition, spoke to Rydell on the radio and drove up towards Hunter Mountain, feeling I was watching another man try out my life. I had hoped to find some certainties up there, something to which I could anchor myself but all I found was that everything flows. I didn't need to see it to know it was happening. Even the forests of pinyon pine and juniper were further down the mountain slopes than they were the day before.

Mike O'Driscoll

wife, loves her so much that the thought of being without her causes him anguish.

In the first months after Holly's death, Judith retreats into herself. She becomes quieter, more contemplative and Larry takes this as a good sign. Some evenings they sit together over a Chinese takeaway and eat without talking. He watches her as she eats, looking for signs that might indicate she's turned a corner. He finds himself hoping that this apparent numbness, this absence of feeling, is something more – a genuine silence.

One evening he asks her if she'd like to have another child. When she looks at him he sees the conflicting emotions in her eyes. For a moment he wonders if this was the wrong thing to say, then she puts a hand on his shoulder and says, "It's not that simple, Larry."

She's right in this observation, he believes, but when she tells him it's not just a matter of getting another child from the baby factory because the first one, the one that didn't work, was still under guarantee, he's not sure she really comprehends. It's not that Holly didn't work, but that she worked too well. He doesn't say this; instead he says, "I'm not saying we should have another child to replace Holly – no one can take her place. But if she were still alive we'd have been talking about another child anyway. All I'm suggesting is we bring it forward."

"I ... I don't know if I'm ready," she says, her hand falling to her side. She begins to turn away but he reaches out and pulls her close.

"Please, Judith, I need this as much as you."

She says nothing but there are tears in her eyes, big, fat, luminous tears that well up and roll down her cheeks. She's crying but she makes no noise and for a moment he thinks she understands. But as he watches the tears fall, he sees himself reflected in them, his own face, huge and round and screaming, and he knows her silence is only skin deep.

Larry can tell that David isn't going to work out. Technical assistants hardly ever lose their cool, but he's noticed that odd inflection in David's voice that signifies irritation. If Larry's picking up on it, then you can bet the customer is too. Already this morning, he's detected that tone four times in David's conversations. Four times is the limit. You hear it more than four times in one day, you take the assistant aside and have a quiet word, try to find out what the problem is. The usual

240

The Silence of the Falling Stars

In the Spring, after heavy Winter rainfalls, wildflowers turn certain parts of the Valley into a blaze of purple, red and orange. It wasn't possible to reconcile such beauty with that scorched and barren hell. If such a vastness could be transformed in what, in geological terms, was less than the blink of an eye, how could any of us hope to ever stay the same?

All those voices I heard on the radio – how could I be sure that they were speaking to me? If I couldn't be certain who I was, then how could they know I was the one they wanted to talk to? So when Rydell's voice came out of the radio, I had no way of knowing if it was really him. Short of driving down to Furnace Creek and standing right in front of him. And even then, there was no guarantee.

I heard Hannafin – or someone who sounded like her – asking where I was. I wanted to answer her but when I tried to talk I realised I had nothing to say. I already knew where I was and where I was going. There was nothing Hannafin, or the voice that might have been hers, could do for me that I couldn't do for myself.

This person I had become had no more illusions. He was capable of seeing things as they really were. As he drove past the talc mines, across Ulida Flat and north into Hidden Valley, he was aware the land was watching him. He heard the creak of Joshua trees, the distant groans of the mountain ranges and the listless sigh of an unfelt breeze. And in those sounds he heard himself also, speaking in his usual voice, his tone neutral, the words precise, as he told them all they needed to know, the way he always did. Only it wasn't him talking.

*

The SUV is pulled off the dirt road on to the edge of the playa. The front passenger's door stands open. I glance up towards Ubehebe Peak, see no movement among the stands of mesquite. Approaching the vehicle, I move round the back and peer through the windscreen. There are two large suitcases behind the rear seat. I continue on round the Toyota till I come back to the open door. I reach inside and grab the carryall on the rear seat. Inside is a money belt with close to four hundred dollars in cash, plus a book of travellers cheques. There's also a Nike fanny pack in there with three passports, a driver's licence and car hire documentation. I look at the photographs, just for a moment, then put

Mike O'Driscoll

everything back in the holdall. On the floor by the front passenger's seat, there's a video camera. It's a Sony Hi 8 and the tape is about three-quarters of the way through. I sit on the running board, my feet resting on the ground, trying to decide what to do. The last thing I want to do right now is play the tape but I know that if I don't I'll never find the answers I need. Flipping open the viewfinder, I touch the play button and get nothing but blue. I press and hold the rewind, listening to the machine whirr as the world runs back to where it has already been. I watch shadows grow westwards from the Cottonwood Range and a strip of broken cloud which pulls itself together as it scrolls back across the sky. After a minute I release the button and the tape rolls forward.

Sophie Delauney and her daughter walk out of their apartment at Stovepipe Wells, holding hands. They stop halfway across the parking lot and Sophie turns, smiles and waves toward the camera before continuing on to the Rav4. The scene changes to a view of Ubehebe Crater from the north rim, stretching a half mile across and five hundred feet deep. The girl skips into the shot from the right, Delauney from the left. Something blurs the picture for a second or two, but I can't tell what it is – a hand or part of a face in extreme close-up. Delauney talks about how the crater was formed, sounding vaguely authoritative. The kid complains about the heat. Next I see Sophie and the girl standing in front of the sign at Teakettle Junction. Delauney enters the frame from the left. The girl has a stick and she starts tapping out a rhythm on the kettles and pots hanging from the arms of the wooden cross. Sophie and Delauney start dancing round her, whooping like a couple of movie Indians. They look foolish but the girl laughs. No one seems to notice the single shadow which slips down the mountain behind them.

The scene changes abruptly, showing the three of them sitting in their vehicle, smiling and waving. After a second or two, I realise there's no soundtrack. They get out of the Toyota and start walking directly towards the camera, their faces growing in the frame. The jump cut I'm expecting doesn't happen. Instead, as Delauney draws close, the scene shifts slightly to the left and catches his face in profile as he walks past the spot where the camera had been. It catches the other two as they walk by then turns and tracks them to the side of the road. Their smiles have disappeared and they avoid looking at the camera until something prompts Sophie to glance up and say a single word which might have

242

been *please*. Moments later, she takes the girl by the hand and walks out onto the playa. After a second or two, Delauney wipes his face and follows them. The camera pans left and zooms in on the Grandstand to the north, holding the outcrop in the frame for what seems like an eternity. Nothing moves onscreen, even when I hold down the fast forward button. When I release it, the camera moves upwards to capture a clear and cloudless sky. The tape has played almost to the end. The final shot is of Sophie, Delauney and the kid, three hundred yards out on the playa, growing smaller as they walk on without looking back. And then the screen turns blue.

My head has started aching and the heat is almost intolerable. I put the camera on the seat, understanding what I have to do. At my vehicle I grab the radio, press the call button and speak my name. Instead of voices all that comes out is feedback and white noise. I try once more but whatever I hear, it isn't human. I lack the will to do this, but there's no one else. I load half a dozen bottles of water into a backpack, grab my binoculars and head out onto the playa.

There are no tracks in the honeycombed surface. I walk five hundred yards due east, a little further than I had seen them go before the tape had stopped. I figure they must have been looking for the rocks, or at least one of their trails. I look north to where the slanting sunlight blurs the edges of the Grandstand. Shielding my eyes, I turn my gaze southwards and pick out a few rocks of varying sizes scattered across the dry mud. There's little else to see out here, no signs of life. I head south and try not to think about the tape and the expressions on their faces as they had trudged past the camera. Almost twenty minutes pass before I am walking among the silent, unmoving rocks. Though I don't want to admit it, their watchful stillness bothers me. I don't want to think about what they've seen. Instinctively, I lay a hand on the Sig Sauer at my hip, drawing some comfort from the touch of the gun. There's a picture forming in my head. It's the haunted look in Sophie's eyes as she stared at the camera for the last time, just before she took the child's hand in her own and started walking. I'd like to think she looked back one last time but I really can't be sure.

I search among the lifeless rocks for an hour. The ground is flat and the rocks are neither plentiful nor large enough to provide cover for anything much bigger than a gecko. Finally, as the sun falls towards

243

Mike O'Driscoll

Ubehebe Peak, I sit down on a rock, feeling dizzy and nauseous. I drink about half a litre of tepid water and pour the rest over my head. I raise the binoculars and see the vehicles where I left them, two dusty sentinels watching over the playa. As I shift my gaze northwards I'm startled by a flash of light from the mountains above Racetrack Road. I turn back to the cars, then search the slopes above them, looking for something up there in the creosote. I lower the binoculars and feel a tightness across my chest. I breath slowly, head hanging between my knees and that's when I see it for the first time, the faint trail cut like a groove in the dried mud. It ends at the rock between my feet. It wasn't there when I sat down, I think, but I'm not certain. I'm spooked a little by it, even more when I notice more trails terminating at the other rocks laying nearby. I try to picture a rain-softened surface and a hundred mile an hour wind pushing them along but it's all in vain.

The flesh crawls on my back and for some reason the air feels cooler. The silence is weird and when I hear the two shots ring out, I need no further prompting to leave the rocks behind. I pick up the backpack, unholster my pistol and set off at a slow trot north towards the sound of the gunfire. I don't think about what has happened, about the mess Delauney has got them into. Instead I concentrate on getting there, on locating their position even though there are no further sounds to guide me towards them.

I pass the vehicles on the road, a half mile or so to my left, without having seen anything I don't recognise. But I keep on, another mile, until I realise I'm heading right towards the Grandstand. I don't turn back. There's no point, even though I won't find anything there. Nothing alive. Yet I have to see.

There's nobody at the Grandstand. I drink another bottle of water to quiet my despair. Shadows stretch out across the playa towards the outcrop, painting the surface the colour of blood. For a while I stare at the rocks, losing track of time. There are a dozen or so, scattered in a wide circle round the outcrop. Had these shapes seen Sophie? I grind the dust and dirt from my faithless eyes and when I open them again I see that the rocks have drawn closer. The last rays of sunlight pick out their newly laid trails. My heart is racing and the band across my chest tightens even more. At first I think I'm having a heart attack, that I'm really dying, but after two minutes I realise that isn't possible. I focus

244

on the nearest rock. It's eighteen inches high, a little more than that from back to front, weighing I guess, about 300 pounds. The ground is bone dry, not even a whisper of wind. Even though I haven't seen it, I accept that the rock has moved. It's too late to matter a damn. I don't feel anything as I set off towards the road

The sky is almost dark by the time I reach the two vehicles. The Rav4 stands empty like a ruin. I sit in my own vehicle and try to call HQ to report the missing people. But once again I get no proper signal, no voices other than my own to trouble the darkness. I keep trying but nobody responds. After a while, I return to the Toyota. The camera is still on the seat where I left it, the tape stopped in exactly the same place. I press play and watch the blue screen, trying to see beyond it to what's on the other side. I let it run for a minute but it's a waste of time. Just as I'm about to stop it, the blue turns to white, which slowly reconfigures into a honeycombed pattern which moves back and forth across the frame. In quick succession three shots ring out on the tape, the first sounds since Teakettle Junction. I am calm, I don't feel any fear, not until another minute has passed and a fourth blast sounds out and the screen fades to black.

Outside, I peer into the dark and see the more intense darkness of the Grandstand looming up out of the Racetrack. It's no closer than it was before, I tell myself, though I no longer feel any inclination to trust my perceptions. An hour has passed when I climb back into the Expedition. Nobody has come. This time, when I call HQ, I do finally get something, a voice reporting an abandoned SUV out at the Racetrack. I shut the power off quickly, drink more water and try not to imagine the rocks gathering out on the playa. I think about the voice I heard and what it was saying. Speaking only to myself I respond, "You won't find anything out there."

And after a minute's silence, I add, "They're gone."

Hearing something, I get out of the car. I walk to the side of the road, feeling the weight of the night as it falls on the Valley. I can't see anything but I look anyway, knowing the rocks are edging their way up from the south. I tell myself someone must have heard them, that someone will come. These are the certainties which sustain me. I can't stop myself from listening so when they stop it comes as a shock. Then, before I can register it, they start moving again, heading west, towards the road. I have no strength left. I sit down in the dirt to wait for someone to arrive even though I already know that nobody is coming here, that no one else belongs. The truth is I have as much right to be here as the dark. It's reason that's out of place here, that doesn't belong. Reason can't explain the rocks that roll, the moans of night or the flakes of sky that drift quietly down to Earth, which, given time, I probably could.

More quality fiction from Elastic Press

☐ The Virtual Menagerie	Andrew Hook	SOLD OUT
☐ Open The Box	Andrew Humphrey	£3.00
☐ Second Contact	Gary Couzens	£5.00
☐ Sleepwalkers	Marion Arnott	SOLD OUT
☐ Milo & I	Antony Mann	SOLD OUT
☐ The Alsiso Project	Edited by Andrew Hook	SOLD OUT
☐ Jung's People	Kay Green	SOLD OUT
☐ The Sound of White Ants	Brian Howell	£5.00
☐ Somnambulists	Allen Ashley	SOLD OUT
☐ Angel Road	Steven Savile	SOLD OUT
☐ Visits to the Flea Circus	Nick Jackson	£5.00
☐ The Elastic Book of Numbers	Edited by Allen Ashley	£6.00
☐ The Life To Come	Tim Lees	£5.00
☐ Trailer Park Fairy Tales	Matt Dinniman	£5.00
☐ The English Soil Society	Tim Nickels	£5.99
☐ The Last Days of Johnny North	David Swann	£6.99
☐ The Ephemera	Neil Williamson	£5.99
☐ Unbecoming	Mike O'Driscoll	£6.99

All these books are available at your local bookshop or can be ordered direct from the publisher. Indicate the number of copies required and fill in the form below.

Name_____
(Block letters please)

Address_____

Send to Elastic Press, 85 Gertrude Road, Norwich, Norfolk, NR3 4SG.
Please enclose remittance to the value of the cover price plus: £1.50 for the first book plus 50p per copy for each additional book ordered to cover postage and packing. Applicable in the UK only.

While every effort is made to keep prices low, it is sometimes necessary to increase prices at short notice. Elastic Press reserve the right to show on covers and charge new retail prices which may differ from those advertised in the text or elsewhere.

Want to be kept informed? Keep up to date with Elastic Press titles by writing to the above address, or by visiting www.elasticpress.com and adding your email details to our online mailing list.

Elastic Press: Winner of the British Fantasy Society Best Small Press award 2005

Coming Soon From Elastic Press

Extended Play:
The Elastic Book of Music

What does music do for you? Is it an art form, mood enhancer, or just something to jump around to? From the orchestra pit to the mosh pit music inspires our lives, is universal and personal, futuristic yet primordial. As the soundtrack trigger to a thousand memories it can be seductive yet soulful, energetic and prophetic. But the immediacy of music has rarely been exploited within literature. Until now...

In these ten stories writers use music as a springboard for their fiction, their characters lives entwined with the metaphorical music of the spheres as well as that played upon the stage. Like the mid-length EP, Extended Play showcases work of longer length than the average story, allowing greater characterisation, depth of theme, and complexity of plot, whilst still benefiting from the conciseness of the short. This anthology brings new meaning to the phrase one hit wonders.

Accompanying the fiction, songwriters comment on how fiction has influenced their music, with contributions from JJ Burnel, Gary Lightbody and others

www.elasticpress.com

Previously from Elastic Press

The Ephemera by Neil Williamson

Neil Williamson's collection of bittersweet tales features fourteen stories of impermanence: from the ends of love affairs and the brief sanity of wartime convalescence, to the fading away of old languages and the dying of humanity itself.

Emotionally complex and displaying a keen eye for detail, the stories in Neil Williamson's collection The Ephemera are a rich and rewarding read from a stylish new Scottish talent – Jeff Vandermeer

Forthcoming from Elastic Press

Photocopies of Heaven by Maurice Suckling

In Maurice Suckling's debut collection slices of life react and interact against a consumerist background where expectations of what we are and where we should be going are frequently in conflict with reality. Combining traditional storytelling, vignettes, emails, text messages, and a cartoon, Suckling reinvents the short form for a society that has replaced its gods with technology, yet still prefers the permanency of love over a quick cyber fix.

A collection of succinctly observed events, characters and phenomena which takes a fresh look at the world and our collisions with it – Dirk Maggs (director of the Hitchhikers Guide to the Galaxy Radio Series)

For further information visit:
www.elasticpress.com